TAKE ADVENTURE INTO YOUR OWN HANDS
WITH BOOKS BY BILL DOYLE!

Escape This Book!

Titanic

Tombs of Egypt

Race to the Moon

The Fifth Hero

The Race to Erase

Escape Plastic Island

THE FIFTH HERO

ESCAPE PLASTIC ISLAND

BILL DOYLE

RANDOM HOUSE 🏠 NEW YORK

Text copyright © 2024 by Bill Doyle
Cover art copyright © 2024 by Aubrie Moyer

All rights reserved. Published in the United States by Random House Children's Books, a division of Penguin Random House LLC, New York.

Random House and the colophon are registered trademarks of Penguin Random House LLC.

Visit us on the Web! rhcbooks.com

Educators and librarians, for a variety of teaching tools, visit us at RHTeachersLibrarians.com

Library of Congress Cataloging-in-Publication Data
Name: Doyle, Bill H., author.
Title: Escape plastic island / Bill Doyle.
Description: First edition. | New York: Random House, 2024. | Series: The fifth hero; #2 |
Audience: Ages 8–12 | Summary: Five climate hero kids with special powers try to save animals left out in the cold by the evil Calamity Corporation—and readers must make a choice in scenarios that change the course of the adventure.
Identifiers: LCCN 2023035464 (print) | LCCN 2023035465 (ebook) |
ISBN 978-0-593-48641-2 (hardcover) | ISBN 978-0-593-48643-6 (ebook)
Subjects: CYAC: Plot-your-own stories. | Superheroes—Fiction. | LCGFT: Superhero fiction. |
Action and adventure fiction. | Choose-your-own stories.
Classification: LCC PZ7.D7725 Es 2024 (print) | LCC PZ7.D7725 (ebook) | DDC [Fic]—dc23

The text of this book is set in 12.25-point Adobe Garamond Pro.
Interior design by Megan Shortt
Logo hand-lettering by Jacey

Printed in the United States of America
10 9 8 7 6 5 4 3 2 1
First Edition

For L.L. and J.R.
Thanks for getting the ball rolling.

CHAPTER ONE

"**Y**ou've got five seconds until Earth melts . . . LIKE HOT CHEESE!"

The shout echoed in the school gym, and the forty students jumped in their seats. Up on the gym's stage, a skinny boy stood on a chair. Wearing a mask with a hot dog emoji drawn on the front, he towered over a small girl who crouched beneath him. She wore a mask too, but this one had a drawing of a muscle arm.

The girl gasped. "You can't turn Earth into *melted cheese* during the Race to Erase. That's too weird!"

"Watch me, Muscle Arm!" Hot Dog bellowed. "I'm starting the five-second countdown now. Five . . . four . . ."

"Hot Dog!" the girl whined, stomping her feet like a toddler having a tantrum. "Melting cheese is not *fair*!"

"Of course it's fair," the boy fired back. "I'm Hot Dog of Climate Club, and fair is my life. Now let's return to the countdown. Three . . . two . . . !"

Before he could get to *one,* Muscle Arm shrieked, "Wait! I'm in Climate Club too, and I'll save the animals and the bats before you melt everything!" She extended her arm, showing a circle drawn above her wrist, and cried, "Zap!"

Hot Dog halted his countdown. "Zap? You can't just say *zap* during a battle!" Now *he* sounded on the edge of a tantrum. "What does *zap* even mean?"

"I created a potato chip tornado!" Muscle Arm yelled triumphantly. "And it's blowing you away!" When Hot Dog didn't move, the girl pouted. "Come on, Hot Dog. You've got to be blown away."

"Fine," Hot Dog sighed. "Don't be such a crybaby." Reluctantly, he waved his arms and fell limply off the chair. But there was nothing limp about his landing. When his feet hit the floor, Hot Dog held up his palm and aimed it at Muscle Arm. "Zap zappity zap!" he cried. "I command all the chocolate chip cookies to shake the ground! So you've got to shake!"

"Okay, okay." Muscle Arm took a deep breath and cried, "Oh no! I'm shaking and all off-balance!" She staggered around and slid in slow motion off the edge of the stage. Once on the gym floor, she bounced off a cafeteria table . . .

. . . and that was the table where Jarrett and Malik sat with their friends Agnes and Freya. The fifth graders were sharing a box of doughnuts.

"Whoa there, Muscle Arm!" Malik laughed and slid the doughnuts to safety before the masked girl accidentally jabbed the box with her elbow.

Everyone at the table—except Freya, who was writing furiously in a notebook—had been watching the pair of first graders play a game called Climate Club. Jarrett couldn't look away. After all, while no one else knew it, the game was based on him and his three friends. Agnes appeared the most enchanted. She had draped her long black curly hair over her shoulder and was absentmindedly braiding it as she focused her attention on the game.

Malik leaned close to Jarrett's ear and whispered, "Holy moly, Hot Dog and Muscle Arm need acting lessons, am I right?" Malik's breath smelled like the chocolate-frosted and raspberry-filled doughnuts he had mashed together to make one "raspolate" doughnut. But Jarrett didn't mind.

"True," Jarrett whispered back. Then again, he thought, they weren't at a movie. It was morning recess inside the gym. They never played *outside* anymore—the pollution and natural disasters had made that too dangerous. Or at least, Jarrett thought, that's what the Calamity Corporation wanted the world to think so everyone would move to the company's space colonies orbiting Earth.

By now, the Climate Club game had spun out of control. Hot Dog leapt off the stage, and he and Muscle Arm dashed between tables and rolled on the floor, screaming "Zap! Zap! Zap!" and pointing their palms at each other.

Finally, Hot Dog announced dramatically, "I didn't want it to come to this, but you've given me no choice, Muscle Arm! I've combined the power of all four palm spheres into One sphere, and I will now use the One to—"

"STOP!"

Everyone froze, including Muscle Arm and Hot Dog. Jarrett wasn't surprised to see that the scary command had exploded from his classmate Lina Limwick. As Lina stormed furiously toward the stage from across the gym, her shaved head and black plastic jumpsuit reflected the overhead fluorescent lights.

Lina stepped between the two first graders and extended her arms, making herself into a T, then shouted, "SCOOT!"

"Ahhh!" the smaller kids screamed in terror, as if a real villain had suddenly appeared in their game. Tearing off their masks, they darted away to join the rest of their class.

"Oh, don't be such babies!" Lina called after them. Then, noticing other students at nearby tables watching, she seemed to rethink her frightening tone. "Juice boxes on me later!" she chirped in a fake cheery voice, and blew air kisses to the two fleeing kids. "Love you, mean it!"

With that done, Lina spun around. As she slammed her hands down on the table where Jarrett and his friends sat, she nearly flattened the doughnuts for a second time that morning. Everyone jumped, except for Freya, who was still lost in thought while writing in her notebook.

Lina unleashed a full-on glare at them. All signs of cheeriness, fake or otherwise, were gone. "Ahhh!" Jarrett said, imitating the kids who had run off.

This got an eye roll from Lina, but no other reaction. He guessed she was too furious.

"Why are those little kids still playing that stupid Climate Club game?" she hissed at them. "It's been part of recess for weeks!"

"Oh, I think it's cool we inspired a game," Agnes said. Then she seemed to regret it, as if knowing she was baiting Lina. "Come on, Lina. What's the big deal? It's just a game about the last Race to Erase."

"Exactly!" Lina cried. "How do they know about what happened at the end of the race and about . . . *other things*?"

Clearly the "other things" were what had Lina so furious, Jarrett thought. She had started shouting when that first grader used the word *One*. Was that it? But Lina kept talking before Jarrett could ask. "You four are the only people—other than me, of course—who know the truth about that day. That means someone here has been talking. Which of you is it?"

Jarrett bit his lip. He *hadn't* blabbed. Why would he want to even think about the Race to Erase? Lina's parents and their powerful company, the Calamity Corporation, had almost wiped out all life on Earth with their races to erase what they called "pests"—and had nearly killed Jarrett and his three friends in the process! The only things that saved the four were the high-tech orbs that accidentally embedded in their hands, giving them superpowers and the ability to work with the mysterious Fifth Hero. Jarrett rubbed his thumb over the bump in his palm and kept silent.

When no one responded to her question, Lina snatched the notebook from Freya's hands, snapping her out of her fog.

"Unacceptable!" Freya protested. "Return that to me immediately." Her long legs were stuck under the table for a moment, but she managed to get to her feet and reach for the notebook.

Lina danced away a few steps. "Ugh, Freya, we're all eleven, not eighty. Can you please learn to speak kid?" Lina flipped through the notebook's pages, scanning here and there. "Blah, blah, blah. Nothing juicy here anyway. Just more words. Poems about space elevators? Really? And who even writes with a pen anymore? Boring."

"Lina!" Jarrett objected.

Lina lifted her hands, as if she understood she'd gone too far. "Your writing is *super* pretty, Freya," she said more gently. "But you've got to admit it's boring. No? Can't admit it? Fine."

Tossing the notebook to Freya, Lina turned to face Malik. "What about you, Malik? Have you been blabbing your head off about the last Race to Erase?"

Clutching the briefcase in his lap, Malik shook his head rapidly. "Me? No! But I do want to *blab* to you about my parents' new elevator—"

Lina cut him off by whipping her head toward Agnes.

"Not me either!" Agnes spluttered. "I wouldn't do anything to mess with you, Lina. You scare me too much!"

Speaking of fear, Jarrett decided to nip things in the bud before Lina turned her anger on him. "I swear, I haven't said a word," he blurted, waving his palm in front of her face. "We all still have the fake skin you gave us to hide the Ponies!"

"Don't say the P-word . . . *ever*!" Lina hissed, glancing around to make sure the other kids hadn't overheard. "What's wrong with you?"

"Lina . . . easy there." Jarrett felt like he was dealing with an angry bear in the woods (again).

But Lina wasn't listening. "Did you—the four heroes!—forget everything?" she demanded, hitting the word *heroes* with a heavy dose of mockery. "Let me remind you. You *barely* escaped getting captured at the Race to Erase! I had to give you a ride back from Arizona with you hiding in the trunk of my FuelFlighter. And that trunk still smells like exploding space robot, thanks to you!"

"Hold on!" Jarrett said. "Why'd you send us that message demanding that we meet here now, Lina? To show us how scary you can be? Because we already know that."

Lina cocked an eyebrow at him. "No, smart guy. I called this emergency meeting of the Climate Club for a very different reason. But before we start, I guess I need to remind you of our deal," she said. "You don't use the superpowers you got from the . . ." She mouthed the word *Ponies*. "And you do *not* talk to anyone about anything that happened a month ago at the Race to Erase. If you manage those two very simple things, I will keep your secret and cover for you. I won't tell my family you stole the P-word. I wouldn't want that. And you wouldn't want that either, would you?"

No, no, I would not, Jarrett decided with a shiver. In a quest to retrieve the trillion-dollar Ponies, Lina's brother, Tommy, had launched two asteroid-eating robots on a cross-country mission of total destruction. The Climate Club had barely escaped the robots, Slicer and Dicer, with their lives, and Tommy and the Calamity Corporation had plenty of other tricks in their arsenal. Nothing would stop them if they knew the Ponies were buried in the kids' palms.

"Everybody in the audience at the Race to Erase had phones," Malik said. "Anyone in the crowd could have shot a video of us freeing those doomed bats and put it online."

Lina shook her head. "Those videos have been scrubbed off the internet. The Calamity Corporation made sure of it. After all, you made my parents look awful, didn't you?"

"Even if all the videos were destroyed, the people who were there can still talk," Agnes argued. "Besides, you saw the way those first graders were playing. They don't even know what kinds of powers we have or what we look like."

"Good point, Aggie!" Jarrett chimed in. "I mean, I can talk to animals, not potato chips or cookies. Malik's thing is all about water, not melting cheese. And, Agnes, you're what? Like, earthquakes or something?"

"Earthquakes for sure," Agnes said, and then turned to Freya. "I remember what you are, Freya. You're air, right?"

Freya glanced up from her notebook and nodded absentmindedly. Then she returned to writing.

Their denials finally calmed Lina. With a sigh, she plopped down on the bench next to Jarrett. "Here's the thing. We need to make sure our real Climate Club—and our message that Earth is the worst—is way different from that dumb Climate

Club game. The game is spreading around the world. Before long, millions of little kids will want to save Earth, and we all know it's way too late for that, don't we?"

Jarrett wasn't so certain anymore. He doubted nearly everything the Calamity Corporation wanted them to think.

Without warning, Lina switched gears and jumped to her feet. "Okay, people, let's go," she ordered.

"Um, what?" Malik asked, echoing Jarrett's confusion. "Where are we going?"

Another eye roll from Lina. "If you bothered to listen to the club announcements on *The Lina Show,* you'd know," Lina snapped. "We're going to New Plastic Island."

This got Freya's attention. "Oh, is that today?" She put down her pen for the first time all morning. "I had that in my calendar for next week."

Jarrett remembered now too, or sort of. Hadn't Lina planned a field trip for the Climate Club? She'd yelled about it on her daily livecast, *The Lina Show,* which Jarrett only watched with the sound off—Lina shouted *a lot.* Still, he'd managed to pick up bits of information. The plan was to fly out to an enormous island made of plastic about a hundred and fifty miles offshore.

"You want to go *today*?" Agnes protested, gazing at the first graders like she wanted to see more of their game. "But we have school."

"This is way more important than school," Lina corrected her. "My parents called your parents, and it's set. They're all excited. Especially yours, Malik. They started crying with joy. Gross."

Embarrassed, Malik clutched the briefcase in his lap tightly, and his face went splotchy.

"My point is," Lina continued, "everyone understands that the Climate Club is more important than algebra or whatever else goes on here. So, I repeat: let's go!"

With that, she spun on her heel and stormed toward the exit, sending first graders scattering before her in fear.

CHAPTER TWO

The four friends left at the table shrugged at each other.

When Lina got like this, there was nothing they could do but go along with her plans, as weird as they might be. Honestly, though, Jarrett wasn't sad about the surprise field trip—he had a quiz in life science that afternoon and he'd be glad to miss it.

Jarrett said, "What do you think, Malik? Should we—?"

Malik cut him off by leaping to his feet and rushing after Lina.

"What's his hurry?" Agnes asked, eyebrows raised.

Jarrett had an idea, but he hoped he was wrong. He merely shrugged again, grabbed his backpack, and hustled out of the gym with the girls in tow. By the time they caught up to Malik, Lina had already disappeared down the hallway. Jarrett knew where she was headed, though. Lina had a spot in the faculty parking lot for her FuelFlighter, her gas-guzzling flying ship.

Every other kid had to wait till they were at least sixteen to get a license to fly a FuelFlighter, but not Lina. Rules, as she was happy to tell anyone with ears, did not apply to her. After all, her family's company made the FFs, so she figured that gave her special rights.

A corridor led outside to the parking lot; it was covered, of course, to protect everyone from the sun's harmful rays and the air pollution. There! Ahead three rows, dirty exhaust was already billowing from Lina's twelve-seater FF. The hatch was open, so Jarrett and the others piled inside.

The door closed behind them, like a trap snapping shut. Lina stood at the controls in the center of the ship, her hands gliding over the blinking panels.

"Prepare for takeoff!" Lina said. But she didn't wait for anyone to prepare anything. Instead she slammed three fingers onto a panel. With a thundering jolt, the FF's front rose and the ship shot into the air with explosions of more filthy exhaust. Luckily, Jarrett and the others had found seats on the couches that lined the windowed wall and the glass floor. The boys sat next to each other, with Agnes and Freya across the way.

Jarrett felt chills. This was the first time he'd been in Lina's FF since that terrifying trip to New Mexico with her brother, Tommy, chasing them. Picking up on Jarrett's nerves, Malik tapped his arm. "You okay? The glass floor getting to you?"

Shaking his head, Jarrett said, "Kind of, but it's more than that." He kept his voice low, almost a whisper, so only Malik could hear him. "Why are you in such a rush to follow Lina's plan today? And why are you still trying to sell ideas to her family?"

When Malik didn't answer, Jarrett pushed gently. "Tell me what's going on."

"Okay, okay," Malik finally said. "I wasn't sure how to tell you, but maybe it'll be easier from up here." He gestured toward the glass floor. "Look down," he instructed.

The view of Earth hundreds of feet below sent Jarrett's stomach lurching. But he kept control, and after a moment, he recognized Malik's neighborhood. Then, with a bit more scanning, he spotted Malik's house. Jarrett had only been there once. That was when Malik's mom said the two friends were spending too much time together.

"There's your house," Jarrett said. "Is that what you want me to see?"

"It's my house . . . for now," Malik responded. "But maybe not for long."

Jarrett's stomach heaved again. This time much worse. "What does that mean?"

"If my parents don't sell their space elevators to Lina's parents and the Calamity Corporation," Malik answered, "they say we'll be in big trouble. Without that money, we're going to have to move. It's too expensive here. We'll go to the West Coast and live with my CG."

Jarrett remembered Malik talking about his CG; it stood for Cranky Grandma. "But she has a one-bedroom condo, doesn't she? And there are five of you, right?"

Chuckling in a sad way, Malik said, "Yep, it's a tiny one-bedroom. But worse than that, my grandma's house is hundreds of miles away. I'd have to switch schools and everything. I didn't tell you because I didn't want to upset you for no reason. It may not even happen."

"What can we do to make sure it doesn't?" Jarrett asked eagerly.

"Well, Freya's already helping," Malik said. "She's been busy writing a song that will help my parents sell the elevators."

Jarrett looked across the ship to where Freya sat. Her lips were forming the words of some rhyme. She smiled, gave him a shy but supportive wave, and returned to her notebook.

Jarrett started to say he'd help too. That he'd do anything

to keep Malik from moving away. But it sounded too obvious. He knew Malik understood. So instead he took Malik's hand and held it. It was safe to do, even with the Ponies embedded in their palms. An explosion and recharging of the spheres only happened if all four kids touched when their Ponies were completely drained. And they had promised Lina and one another not to use their powers, to keep their Ponies at full power and the Calamity Corporation from noticing any strange activity. Jarrett's face flushed. . . . That was one promise he had not kept.

That was another reason Jarrett kept quiet and held Malik's hand. He was worried he'd blurt out a confession he wasn't ready to give yet. So instead, to distract himself, Jarrett listened to Agnes and Lina talking. Agnes had joined her on the other side of the control panel.

"Why did the first graders' game freak you out so much?" Agnes asked Lina. "Is it because they said 'One sphere'? But why? That's something they made up, right?"

Lina pursed her lips as if the questions were something sour. "What about you, *Aggie*? You had the opposite reaction. Why'd you love watching their game? You couldn't get enough of it."

"Fine, if you won't answer my questions, I'll answer yours," Agnes said, and then laughed at how silly that sounded. "Their game reminded me of using our Ponies.

It's just us, Lina. I can say *Ponies*. I like—I mean, I *liked*—having a superpower."

Lina smiled tightly. "Well, I'm glad you got to enjoy it. Because that's over."

"But why?" Agnes almost whined. "You don't know how it was. I felt mighty. Are you going to tell Superman he can't fly? Or Wonder Woman that she can't use her lasso?"

"No," Lina said, her smile disappearing. "I'm telling the thief that she cannot use what she stole. You are not superheroes. You're criminals. You stole the Ponies. You don't get to turn this situation around and say that it isn't all your fault."

"That's . . . ," Agnes spluttered. "That's . . . that's . . ."

When Agnes couldn't seem to find the words, Jarrett jumped in to help his best friend. "That's as bonkers as bat bubble gum!" He went to the control panel, Malik trailing behind him. "Lina, you were on the pink FuelFlighter when we grabbed the Pon—"

"Everyone stop saying the P-word!" Lina pounced. "And besides, that's not true!"

"You were there!" Jarrett fired back. "Those spheres *that will not be named* were going to fall on Earth and destroy everything!"

"Not everything," Lina grumbled.

"Really?" Jarrett asked. "One was created to destroy the

air we breathe, another for the animals, a third for Earth itself, and the last for water! We didn't have a choice. We had to grab them to stop them, and now they're stuck in our hands!"

Continuing to jab furiously at the control panel, Lina kept her head down. "There is always a choice. Ask the Fifth Hero you guys keep jabbering about. That ridiculous person apparently makes choices all the time—most of them really weird!"

Jarrett thought she sounded a little jealous. Freya must have too, because from her spot on the couch, she said, "You could be the Fifth Hero, Lina."

As always, Lina didn't seem to know how to react when faced with kindness.

"Oh, please, why would I want that?" Lina snapped. "A fifth of nothing is still nothing. Besides, I wouldn't dream of taking that job away from whatever imaginary goofball you think is out there waiting to answer questions about choices, probably wondering why they haven't gotten to make a choice yet in this latest adventure!"

Goofball? Ouch. Jarrett hoped that somehow the Fifth Hero, whoever that person might be, wasn't listening right now. "Um, Lina, you okay?" he asked.

As an answer, Lina slammed a hand down onto the control panel. In a flash, the FF tilted into an almost-vertical nosedive and rocketed toward the ground. Lina was braced against the panel, but the others tumbled toward the front of the craft.

"Oops, sorry," Lina said in a fake, flat voice. "I meant to say, please prepare for landing. Thank you for flying Lina Air."

With his face pressed to the glass floor, Jarrett watched in growing panic as the world below shot toward them. The frightening view showed a warehouse on a bay that led out to the ocean, and a landing pad on the end of a dock. They were coming in way too fast! Then, at the last second, Lina leveled out the FF. She brought it to a gentle rest on the pad, like a feather drifting onto a pillow. Jarrett had to hand it to her: she was the best pilot he knew.

Still in a huff, Lina flicked off the FF and opened the hatchway. The smell of dead fish wafted into the ship. Without glancing over her shoulder at her sprawled-out friends, she led the way onto the dock. "Let's go. We need to get inside the warehouse."

"Um, this isn't New Plastic Island, is it?" Jarrett asked as Malik helped him to his feet and they both caught up with Lina.

"I'm aware, thanks," Lina said with an eye roll. "There might not be a landing spot on the island. I'll take a boat from here."

"Don't you mean *we*?" Agnes said, brushing herself off as she and Freya took up the rear of the group. "We could surf everyone across the water . . . if you let us use our Ponies."

This idea clearly made Lina even more annoyed. "You know, Agnes, I've been thinking," she said. "You sure sound like a person who can't resist using the trillion-dollar item she stole. Let me see your hand. I want to see if the sphere's power has been drained."

In shock, Agnes said, "I can't peel off the fake skin you gave us. None of us can!" As if to prove it, she raised her hand, but not close enough for Lina to really see it. Jarrett wondered: was Agnes trying to hide something?

"Stop waving it around!" Lina demanded.

Jarrett held his breath. If Lina had told *him* to peel away the fake skin on his palm, she would have seen something that would have really upset her. All of them would.

With squinting eyes, Lina appeared more suspicious than ever. Jarrett needed to put a stop to her investigation. He opened his mouth to say something—

"WHAAAAGGG!"

A jagged scream sliced through the air and froze their feet in place. Jarrett smacked his hand over his lips as if he had made that horrible sound. But no, it wasn't him. It had come from inside the warehouse. His friends—even Lina—looked shocked. Before anyone could move, the scream came again.

"Someone needs help!" Malik said, and started toward the warehouse.

But Lina grabbed his arm. "Quit being heroes!" she ordered.

"WHAAAAGGG!" Another scream, this one even more desperate . . . *and* scary. Freya and Agnes looked frantic to help and were already moving toward the warehouse.

"Fine," Lina said with a sigh. "That's where we're headed anyway. But don't burst in with your palms blazing."

With the other kids pushing her to go faster, Lina led them through a rusty steel door into the warehouse, then down a dirty hallway into a room. Inside was a lone figure.

Dressed in a black plastic jumpsuit like Lena, the teenager perched on a cheap folding chair. With wires running around his feet, he faced a large screen monitor that slanted haphazardly on a tripod. The wall behind him was cloaked in dark shadow.

Jarrett almost couldn't believe his eyes. Was that who he thought it was? No, it couldn't be! And then Lina confirmed his darkest fear by saying to the figure, "I've brought them to you. They're all yours, Tommy."

Tommy. Lina's brother.

Now Jarrett was the one who felt like screaming.

CHAPTER THREE

To keep from crying out, Jarrett clenched his jaw so hard he thought he might crack a tooth.

This was a trap! Lina had led them straight to Tommy!

Instinctively, Jarrett reached for Malik's, Agnes's, and Freya's hands so they could use their Ponies. But Lina stepped between them before they could connect. "Now, now, no need for that," Lina said under her breath. "The looks on your faces are priceless." Then, more loudly, so Tommy could hear them: "Like I was saying. I've brought you helpers."

Tommy still hadn't so much as glanced at them. Wires ran here and there along the floor, and he wore gaming glasses on his head. On the screen, fish were fleeing from whatever character he was playing. The word *LEVIATHAN* floated at the top of the screen. Was that the name of the video game?

Lina cleared her throat impatiently. With a deep sigh, Tommy finally shoved his gaming glasses up on his forehead so he could see the Climate Club. Jarrett waited for him to shout "Thieves!" or "Grab them!" Instead, Tommy asked, "Who are they, Lina?"

Jarrett felt his jaw unclench. Obviously, Tommy didn't recognize them as the kids he'd chased during the Race to Erase. Jarrett mentally thanked those goofy emoji masks they'd worn to hide their identities.

"Oh, these are your *friends* you keep going on and on about," he said, not very nicely, eyeing them up and down. "Looks about right."

"Rude!" Agnes said quietly, and Jarrett nodded in agreement.

Tommy went back to his screen. "I don't want people, Lina," he snapped. "You know what I want. The *One* thing I want." The way Tommy said *One,* it was clearly capitalized.

"Mom and Dad said you can't have that, Tommy," Lina replied. "Not until you get this job sorted."

"Fine." Tommy waved a hand in the air. "Tell your *friends* to get to work."

Jarrett glanced around the room as if "work" would present itself if he looked hard enough. This place was so different from Tommy's lair in their family's mansion. That sleek space was the size of a basketball court, complete with blinking lights and a multi-screen command center.

This new lair stank like dead sea creatures that floated on top of the filthy bay. Overhead, dimly flickering fluorescent lights created a creepy strobe effect on the dirty walls, where old paint was peeling off in sheets. The trash-strewn floor felt sticky with grime under Jarrett's white-and-lime-green sneakers.

"Tommy, come on, they don't know what to do," Lina said, and flicked a nearby light switch. Powerful lights burst to life overhead, and Jarrett gasped in horror. The wall that had been concealed in shadow was suddenly moving. More like squirming!

Stacks of at least sixty animal cages lined the wall from floor to ceiling—some as small as a shoebox, others the size of an oven. The bright lights startled the creatures inside. Most cowered at the backs of the cages and were hard to see except for the dim reflections of their large, frightened eyes. Between the bars of other cages, noses—some wet and snuffling with mucus, many covered in spiky, twitching whiskers—poked out and sniffed the air. Probably searching for a meal made of fifth graders, Jarrett thought queasily.

He felt dizzy and stumbled a little. Was he having a nightmare? Must be. Being this close to all these wild animals was his greatest fear. Malik took his arm to steady him. "It's okay," Malik said soothingly. "They can't get out, and I think they're way more scared than you are."

Jarrett doubted that.

Meanwhile, Agnes was squinting to get a closer look at the furry prisoners. "The screams we heard must have been coming from one of these," she said. "Are they more weird Calamity Corporation inventions?"

Tommy appeared insulted. "My family's company didn't invent these oddballs! The animals we'd make would be attractive and amazing." Then he added with disgust, "These *things* are all natural-born Earth creatures."

Grabbing a plastic bag of carrots off his desk, Tommy walked over to the bottom row of cages. He waved a carrot in front of one. Whatever was inside started whining. It was a beady-eyed little monster with a pointy snout and sparse patches of hair over its gray skin. But the creepiest thing about it was the one long finger on each hand that ended in a yellow claw. As he always did with animals, Jarrett calculated how much flesh its sharp little teeth could tear off in one bite.

"That's an aye-aye!" Freya said.

Tommy squinted at Freya. "You're right. How did you know that?"

"She knows about animals," Agnes said, obviously proud of her friend.

"That's a star-nosed mole," Freya continued as she gestured from one cage to another. "That's a baby proboscis monkey, and that's a tiny warthog."

Agnes took a step closer, peering into the warthog's cage. "What are we supposed to do?"

"Get to work!" Tommy shouted. When the other kids continued to stand there dumbfounded, Tommy rubbed a hand over his eyes. "Okay, I'll start at the beginning," he grumbled. "My parents put me in charge of finding four stolen spheres. They're worth billions. When I couldn't track them down, my parents punished me by giving me this job. While I'm waiting for the One to be delivered, I'm supposed to stay out of trouble."

There was that word *One* again, Jarrett noticed.

When the others didn't respond, Tommy continued peevishly. "It's really a promotion if you think about it," he said, waving the carrot toward the animal. It kept hissing and backing away. "I think this one's broken. It's not eating. Fix it." Without warning, Tommy tossed a carrot at Jarrett, who snatched it out of the air instinctively.

"Fix it?" Jarrett asked, gazing at the vegetable.

"No, not the carrot," Tommy snapped. "Fix that!" He pointed to one of the animal cages. "Fix that, make it eat, and then it can go!"

"Go where . . . ?" Agnes asked.

"Duh, where do you think?" Tommy fired back. "To space. My job is very important. I choose which Earth animals are too weird to take to the Calamity Corporation's new space communities. We have the chance to start fresh, with only fancy frills. . . . Why would we want to bring creepy critters along?"

Freya frowned. "What will happen to the animals that you don't choose to go?"

Even Tommy could hear the concern in her voice. "They'll be fine. We'll freeze them and launch them into space, where they'll float around in orbit."

With wide, freaked-out eyes, Freya asked, "For how long?"

"Forever, I guess," Tommy answered. "You never know when one of these fur-trocities will come in handy. So we'll keep them floating around. Though how this bug-eyed odd-ball could ever be helpful is beyond me." He gestured at the aye-aye's cage and then at the warthog's. "Or this one. Besides, being up in space by yourself forever is still better than being stuck on Earth, right?"

Jarrett was having a tough time keeping up. Tommy was the person who decided which animals got to join the new human space colonies? From what Jarrett knew about Tommy, he didn't think Lina's brother was the person to handle that job.

"How do you decide?" Freya asked Tommy.

27

"I use eeny-meeny-miny-moe," Tommy continued. When the others, especially Freya, appeared too shocked to respond, he asked testily, "What's wrong with that?"

Everything! Jarrett wanted to shout. But Malik said, "Nothing. That sounds super scientific. You know, when you're deciding the fate of an entire species, why not eeny-meeny-miny-moe?"

Tommy glared at Malik to see if he was being sarcastic. Malik flashed him a smile, and that soothed Tommy, who got back to giving instructions.

"Your job is to turn these animals into those frozen blocks, like Han Solo in *The Empire Strikes Back*." He indicated the strange cubes stacked in the corner. "Just slide the animals through the freeze machine and they'll come out as slabs of ice. That way we don't have to feed them or anything in space."

Jarrett's ears were starting to hurt from how bonkers this sounded. "Is this a joke?" he asked Lina in a low voice.

But Lina didn't respond. Tommy went on. "Once you're done with that, take each ice animal to hangar six. Put it in the FF waiting there and return here for more frozen furballs. Each of you needs to pick one animal to freeze, one that won't be allowed in the new colonies." When the kid remained frozen, Tommy tapped Malik's chest. "You first."

Nodding, Malik said, "Happy to help the Limwicks."

Ugh, Jarrett thought. Malik was still kissing up.

Taking a step closer to a particular animal cage, Malik eyed the creature inside. "Um, speaking of picking, this guy's picking its nose. And . . . wait for it . . . he's eating it."

"See what I mean?" Tommy said. "You really want these disgusting fur weirdos living with us in space? The Calamity Corporation's idea is so much better!"

Lina clapped her hands. At first Jarrett thought she was applauding, but he was wrong. "Okay, great. I'll leave the Climate Club with you, Tommy," Lina said. "I need to get out to New Plastic Island. Mom and Dad said I can take the Glass Submarine. Where is it?"

"Do I have to do everything?" Tommy grumbled, tapping a screen to access the information. "This is so not fair, Lina. Mom and Dad give you the Glass Sub, and I get a bunch of weird animals and your strange *friends*."

"Nice manners," Agnes muttered under her breath.

Tommy waved his hand at the screen. "The Glass Sub will be ready at pier six in ten minutes," he said grumpily, and then added, "You're welcome, Your Royal Highness."

"Okay, bye," Lina chirped. "Have fun!" With that she spun on her heel and rushed out of the room.

Wait, what? Jarrett shared a startled expression with Agnes, and then he raced after Lina.

"Whoa, whoa," Jarrett called. "Lina, wait!" She whipped around, put her hands on her hips, and tapped one foot impatiently. Jarrett spoke fast, before she could run away again. "What is happening? You want us to shoot frozen animals into space with Tommy?"

Lina glanced at her watch. "Yes. That's exactly what I want."

Flabbergasted, Jarrett asked, "You don't think that's a tad bit ridiculous?"

"Nope," Lina replied instantly. "I've thought this whole plan through. Tommy is going to be here with you. And I'm going to be on Plastic Island with your—" Suddenly she clamped her mouth shut.

"On the island with who?" Jarrett demanded. "Does this all have something to do with the One, whatever that is? Why are you lying?"

Frustrated, Lina threw her hands in the air. "Fine, yes! I'm lying!" she admitted tersely. "About almost everything. But it doesn't matter. You have to trust me. I need to get going. Now." She pushed past him down the corridor. "And, until I return, do what Tommy says, and remember, don't be—"

"Yeah, yeah, don't be heroes." Jarrett finished her sentence as the door to the outside slammed shut behind her. He listened to Lina stomping off down the dock for a second. Then, with nowhere else to go, he turned to rejoin the others in Tommy's lair.

When Jarrett walked into the room, the freezing contraption was chugging away in the corner, releasing nasty puffs of black smoke. But Freya, Malik, and Agnes were gone, as were a few animal crates, including the aye-aye's. Only Tommy remained, and he was back in his wobbly chair playing his Leviathan video game.

"Um, Tommy?" Jarrett said quietly. When this failed to get Tommy's attention, he raised his voice. "Where are my friends? And the aye-aye?"

Tommy didn't stop playing the game, but did grumble, "You weren't here to choose an animal, so I did it for you. That aye-aye monster is next in line to be transformed into a block of ice."

For a minute, Jarrett panicked. *Next?* Had Tommy frozen his friends and launched them into space too? He'd only been gone a minute! "My friends . . . ?" he gasped in shock.

"Can't you see I'm busy here?" Tommy said. "Those other helper kids are already bringing their frozen animals to the FF."

Oh, that sounded a little better, Jarrett thought as the horrible, smoke-belching machine finally went silent.

"Now it's your turn—get to work!" Tommy commanded, waving a hand toward the machine. "Take the frozen aye-aye to hangar six. And then come back here for more fur monstrosities. I've decided to freeze all of them. They'll all float around forever. So much easier that way, and I can get back to what's important." Tommy returned his full attention to his game.

Not sure what else to do, Jarrett shuffled to the far end of the machine, where an ice block the size of a shoebox waited. The freezer had embedded the block with a plastic handle so Jarrett could easily pick it up. With a grunt, he hefted the ice with both hands and carried it past the distracted Tommy and out of the lair. Once he was in the hallway, the brighter overhead lights provided Jarrett with a better chance to examine the ice block. What he saw made him gasp—and he almost released his grip.

Inside the ice, Jarrett could see the aye-aye's wide-open eyes and its one long, bony finger was pointing up past its small head. Suddenly, Jarrett felt a wave of sadness. He imagined this little monster floating around in space forever with his long, bony finger grasping at nothing. Maybe Jarrett could still help the aye-aye?

Jarrett scanned the garbage strewn about the hallway floor. He quickly found a plastic bag that had red letters printed on one side: *I'M A PLASTIC BAG! RECYCLE ME INTO A NEW PLASTIC ISLAND. HOW? SIMPLY PUT ME OUT TO SEA AND LET ME BE WITH THE BAGS THAT ARE FREE!*

Free? Jarrett liked the sound of that. He slid the frozen aye-aye into the bag and lifted it. Much easier to carry, and the block was hidden from view. Now he needed to walk past Tommy's lair to reach the outside door. Should be easy, right? After all, Tommy was focused on his game.

Nope. As Jarrett eased his way down the hall, Tommy happened to be gazing out the lair doorway, and his eyes met Jarrett's.

Oh no.

"Where do you think you're going?" Tommy demanded. "You're supposed to be working!"

"I, um . . ." Jarrett didn't know what to say. "I, um, need some air outside."

Ugh, that was the wrong thing to say. And Tommy pounced. "Outside? The air outside will make you sick. Everyone knows that. What's in that bag?"

Maybe the worst person at lying, Jarrett tried for something that was close to the truth. "It's a giant Popsicle."

Tommy's distrustful gaze transformed into hungry curiosity. "I like Popsicles, you know. What flavor do you have?"

Hmm. What would an aye-aye taste like? Jarrett made a wild guess. "It's a pickle-juice Popsicle."

Tommy cringed. "Gross. Why do all you guys eat such disgusting Popsicles?" he mumbled, losing himself in his game again.

All you guys? What'd that mean? Jarrett wondered. Not the time to ask. His feet carried him quickly out of the building. As the glaring sunlight hit his face, questions exploded in his head, like: What if the sun melted the aye-aye and it woke up? Did aye-ayes bite? And most importantly, what was he supposed to do now?

The answer came when a voice said his name. "Hey, JarJar."

He turned to see Agnes waving at him. He shouldn't have been surprised to find his three friends all standing just outside the door with their own iced-filled plastic bags. They must have been waiting for him.

"I couldn't do it," Agnes said sheepishly, jiggling the bag in her hand. "I've got the baby warthog."

"I got all the way to the hangar," Malik said, "and I couldn't do it. Star-nosed mole here."

"Me either," Freya said, and held up her bag. "Tiny proboscis monkey."

"What are you talking about? Couldn't do what?" Jarrett asked innocently. "I don't know about you guys, but I don't have an aye-aye. I have a Popsicle in here."

"So do I," the other three said at exactly the same time, and they all smiled. Even Freya had a giant grin.

"Okay, now what?" Malik said. "We've got frozen ugly animals. How do we get them back to our houses?"

"Malik!" Jarrett groaned. Even after all they had been through in the Race to Erase, Malik still had the habit of thinking he could snag any wild animal or plant out of its environment and bring it home. And that he wouldn't have to lift a finger for it to survive.

"Right, right," Malik said, picking up on Jarrett's tone. "These animals need to be outside, even if it's supposed to be deadly for us to be out here too long. But where and how can we get them somewhere safe?"

"Scarier question," Agnes said with a shudder. "What will Tommy do to us once he figures out there are no animals on the FFs?"

"Or Lina?" Malik added, and then his eyes lit up. "That's it! She's the solution!"

"Um, how?" Jarrett asked. "I think you mean she's the problem."

Malik shook his head. "She's going to New Plastic Island, and that place could be perfect for these guys!" he said. "Hold on, Jarrett, before you give me that look. Think about it. There's all that island in the ocean that no one's using right now. Sure, Lina's family is going to sell it to people to build homes on before we all go to space. But that's even better! The animals will have humans around to help them for a bit. This is a great plan!"

"Love it," Agnes said. "We'll take our frozen friends there. They'll adjust, because that's what animals do, and they can make their new homes. We need to get on that boat."

Jarrett glanced at Freya. She was sometimes a little flaky, but he had come to rely on her calm, easygoing attitude during tricky times. What did she think of this bonkers plan?

35

Clearly guessing what he was wondering, she gave him a small smile that seemed to say, *It's better than doing nothing.*

That would have to be good enough for Jarrett. "Okay," he agreed. "We take them to Lina's boat. Didn't Tommy say her boat was leaving in ten minutes from pier six?"

"Correct," Freya said, and the four turned to look at the signpost directly behind them. A cluster of electronic arrows pointed the way to piers 1 through 10. And the sign that read PIER 6 was blinking.

"Lina's ship must be leaving now," Jarrett said. "We need to run if we want to catch it!"

Easier said than done. Running with blocks of frozen animals took some skill, especially for Malik, who had his briefcase in one hand and a plastic bag in the other. To keep his own bag from dragging on the ground, Jarrett slung it over his shoulder, where it slammed against his backpack with each stride.

The harbor complex stretched on for what seemed like miles. As they followed the arrows on the signs toward the correct pier, the number 6 started blinking faster . . . as if signaling an imminent departure.

Tommy's voice came over the loudspeakers that were stationed every hundred feet or so. "The ugly animal Fuel-Flighter will launch in thirty seconds," he said, and his voice had a menacing quality. "All my underlings, stop eating Popsicles and return to my lair now."

Jarrett brought the bag around to the front. He could actually run faster this way, but now the frozen aye-aye banged against his leg. He was about to say they might have to go back when—

"There! Do you hear that?" Freya asked.

"Hear what?" Agnes asked.

For a few seconds Jarrett couldn't hear anything other than his own heavy breathing and pounding feet. Then he heard it too. The sound of singing.

They turned one last corner, and finally! They reached pier 6. A sixty-foot silver seacraft bobbed gently in the dirty water of the bay as it motored away from the dock. But it wasn't the ship that captured Jarrett's attention. Shockingly, standing on the deck was their teacher Mrs. Cook, along with the rest of their fifth-grade classmates—including Lina! And everyone except Lina was singing.

We love the Climate Club
The real one, that is
Not the one that's a flub.
And we're off to the Island of Plastic
If you don't believe us
Why did you ask it?

"That is the song I wrote!" Freya said. "Lina said she hated it!"

The boat continued pulling away from the high dock. Freya started singing along. As always, Jarrett was surprised that a girl who often had a tough time expressing herself while speaking could sing so gorgeously. And for someone who spoke so stiffly, her lyrics were funny and flowed smoothly.

Meanwhile, Lina had hustled to a doorway in the center of the deck. She opened it—

Jarrett and Malik shouted to get her attention, but maybe she couldn't hear them over all the singing, because she kept moving. Agnes could shout louder than any of them, and she didn't hold back as she roared, "LINA! STOP RIGHT NOW!"

That did it. Lina turned to look at them, shaking her head like she couldn't believe they could be such knuckle-heads. Then she went inside the tower, closing the door.

Now the ship started sinking very slowly, an inch at a time.

"The boat's going down!" Malik said.

Their classmates were still on top of the boat and sing-ing happily. They didn't seem to notice the water rising all around them. And they were too far to make the leap to the dock. Why was Lina doing this?

Putting down their plastic bags, the four friends rushed to the end of the dock and continued shouting warnings to their classmates and Mrs. Cook. But nothing. The group kept singing away as if the water weren't rising all around them. . . . Soon it covered their feet.

"We have to save them!" Jarrett said. "Malik, you're the water guy. Do something!"

With a shake of his head, Malik said simply, "I can't."

Jarrett was baffled. "Are you worried we don't have our masks? They'll see us, but we don't have any choice."

"You don't understand. I *can't*." With that, Malik peeled off the fake skin from his palm. His sphere was dark. That meant only one thing.

"You've been using your powers!" Jarrett was shocked. "We all agreed not to!"

Malik said, "How do you think I got an A on my seawater science project after staying up all night playing video games?"

Shocked, Jarrett turned to Agnes. "What about you, Aggie?"

She too peeled away the fake skin from her hand. A dark sphere sat in the center of her palm. "Did you really think I made that life-sized sculpture of you out of granite to cheer you up without using this?" she asked.

Jarrett's gaze landed on Freya. "And even you?"

Looking him in the eye, she tore off the skin and showed him her dark sphere. "I wanted to give birds some wind to play in," she explained. "And I got a little carried away. Remember that surprise tornado two months ago? Well . . ." She shrugged.

"You can yell at us all you want later, Jarrett," Agnes said. "But right now you're the only one with power in their Pony."

"She's right," Malik said. "Reach into the water and ask the fish or an octopus or something to save them. Quick!"

But the dock was too high above the water. Jarrett couldn't reach down to the surface, even if he wanted to . . . which he most definitely did not.

The others were moving so fast that Jarrett didn't have time to explain why this plan was a terrible mistake. Before he knew it, Malik had hooked one arm around a piling and grabbed Agnes's hand, who in turn grabbed Freya's. They had formed a three-person chain that could stabilize Jarrett so he could reach down to the water without falling in.

But Jarrett was stepping away from them, his hands in the air. "You have to listen to me!"

"No time!" Agnes shouted urgently. "Freya, take his hand!"

"No! Wait!" Jarrett shouted. "There's something I need to tell—"

Too late. Freya snatched his hand—

BAM!

An explosion of bright white light tossed all four kids into the air.

HURRY! TURN TO PAGE 108!

CHAPTER NINE

Silence. Even as they floated deep below the surface of the ocean, Jarrett thought the silence was odd—even stranger than the plastic bags that kept swirling around his legs.

"Um," Agnes said, sounding confused. "That was weird."

"Weirder than normal, that's for sure," Malik agreed, batting away a plastic bag from in front of his mask.

"At least our Ponies are recharged," Freya said. "But why didn't the Ponies' talk start and end with the word *YOU*? That's the way the Ponies have always worked in the past."

"And why was the Pony yelling at the Fifth Hero?" Jarrett said. "I don't remember it being so cranky. No wonder the Fifth Hero made the wrong choice."

"Gee, what makes you say the Fifth Hero made the wrong choice?" Agnes asked sarcastically. It was obvious that decision had been the wrong one. After all, the four friends were now trapped in a sea of tangled plastic bags. If they hadn't had their breathing tanks, they would've been in serious trouble. Even the slightest movement felt like pushing through molasses, and each kick meant layers of plastic catching on their flippers.

"We're going to be sitting ducks for the Leviathan," Jarrett said. "Can you even raise your palm to control the water, Malik?"

With a small nod, Malik lifted his arm up through the plastic layers. "Sure, but I won't be able to move it around much."

"I do not think anything is moving around much," Freya said. She gestured to the Glass Sub, which sat silently about fifty feet away in its own underwater cocoon of plastic. "If the sub can't move, chances are that the giant Leviathan is even more stuck."

"Let's get to the sub," Agnes said, and the others agreed.

With the bags swarming them like sticky birds of prey, the four managed to slog their way to the Glass Sub. As they crawled through the garbage chute and into the kitchen area, Lina was there to greet them. She leaned against the wall while they removed their scuba gear and wet suits, and asked,

"What's up, heroes? Enjoying your nice fresh Ponies and all that wonderful plastic?"

Agnes cocked her head. "Say that first part again, Lina."

"Um, what's up, heroes?" Lina said.

Jarrett heard something in that question too. "Hold on," he said. "Where have we heard that phrase before?"

Freya seemed to be thinking the same thing. "Lina, now say 'What's up, Fifth Hero?'"

"No," Lina said. "Stop being odd."

"And how do you know that the world has changed to contain extra plastic?" Malik asked. "Normally the four of us and the Fifth Hero are the only ones who notice that anything is different."

The four looked at Lina, and she snapped, "What is your problem?"

"More like your problem," Agnes said. "The one you have, of trying to control us! You can't help yourself!"

It was all clicking into place for Jarrett too. "It was you, Lina!" he shouted. "You were acting like the Ponies!"

"I literally have zero concept of what you are insinuating," Lina said, and started walking away.

"Translation: you did it," Freya called after her.

"Wait, if Lina was controlling the Ponies, she might have made both choices bad!" Malik said. "Or maybe one was worse than the other."

"We need to find out. Come on," Jarrett said, and pulled the others along with him as they went to catch up with Lina. "You have to tell us exactly what you did, Lina."

As if she couldn't be bothered anymore, Lina sighed. "Fine. Follow me."

She led them to one of the "blurry" spots on the ship. She opened both eyes for a dual eye scanner. The door unlocked, and they went inside. The small room had a sleek silver floor and matching walls, and the main light source was a glowing ceiling. It created a creepy effect on everyone's faces and made it feel like a haunted house. There was a single command chair and a large screen on one wall.

"What is this place?" Jarrett asked.

"I didn't want to use it," Linas said. "But you four left me no choice."

"Did you build a secret lair, Lina?" Malik asked.

She nodded and for the first time looked a little sheepish. "Yes, I had our top researchers at Calamity Corporation build this room for me. And by using the equipment in here I was able to hear your thoughts."

"You were reading our minds?" Jarrett was furious.

"A short story, in your case," Lina fired back.

"Really, Lina?" Agnes asked. "You're choosing now to be a smart aleck?"

"Fine," Lina said. "I was never able to hear what you were

thinking, I promise. It's more what the Ponies were saying to the Fifth Hero through you. I intercepted it."

"So you were able to control the choice that the Fifth Hero had to make?" Freya asked.

"I added my own choice. It was something stupid I heard an expert say once," Linas said. "Before the Calamity Corporation controlled all the experts."

Agnes made a rolling motion with one hand. "Faster with the explaining, please."

"The question was . . . what kind of bag should you ask for at the grocery store—paper or plastic?" Lina said. "But it's a trick question. The right answer is to bring your own bag."

"And what if everyone asked for plastic at the store?" Malik asked.

"Well, I think we can see the answer to that," Lina said. "New Plastic Island has spread almost entirely across the ocean. Nothing below can rise to the surface. No creatures or plants can breathe down here. It's now like one giant empty . . ."

Lina trailed off and Freya finished for her: ". . . tomb."

"Okay, you're right. It was the wrong thing to do," Lina said. "I wanted us to add to New Plastic Island so you could see what's amazing about it. Or at least what the Calamity Corporation thinks is so amazing."

"So you tricked us into using the Ponies to generate plastic waste?" Jarrett asked.

"Well, when you put it like that, it doesn't sound so great," Lina said lightly. Then, seeing their angry faces, she changed her tone. "I'm sorry," she said seriously. "I really am. I promise never to do anything like that again."

Jarrett believed her. And the others must have too, because they all nodded, and Freya said, "We've got to fix it. Can we go back and make a different choice?"

Lina shook her head. "You four can't go back. That'd be like time traveling, and the four Ponies can't do that."

"Well, if we can't turn back the clock, what about the Fifth Hero?" Jarrett said. "Maybe the Fifth Hero can change things."

"I made it sound like there were two options," Lina said. "But, no, I only gave one."

Freya nodded. "I understand. Can you program another choice into the scenario?"

Throwing herself into the command chair, Lina's fingers began flying across an invisible keyboard. "Okay, that did it. I've added a second real choice to the situation. But that still doesn't do us any good. We're stuck in the present."

"If only there was some way to return to that moment in time!" Malik said.

"Well, let's hope your Fifth Hero thinks of a way," Jarrett said. "Otherwise we might be calling this plastic tomb our new home forever!"

THE END

DON'T GIVE UP NOW!
GO TO PAGE 161.

CHAPTER EIGHT

*W*hat's up, Fifth Hero. It's me—you know, the Ponies. I've got a cold. Cough, cough. *So, don't freak out, I might not sound like I normally do.*

Wait. Why am I wasting my time explaining myself to you? I'm the all-powerful Ponies, and you're . . . you.

Sooooo . . . I have a decision for you to make. And it has to do with . . . um . . . it has to do . . . with friends who don't listen to their friend who is way better than them, especially when it comes to doing what she tells them to do.

You should always listen to your friend who is the smartest and the prettiest. And you guys have to be better about realizing who that friend is.

Okay, now let's get to the decision. It has to be about the climate, right? Um. I know.

What's that question they used to ask at grocery stores? Plastic or plastic?

Yeah, which is better for the environment?

Do you use plastic? Turn to page 41.

Or plastic? Turn to page 41.

Those are the choices. Decide now . . . pick the first one or the second.

CHAPTER NINE

"**Y**oumph!"

Jarrett knew that voice, even if it wasn't saying a real word. It belonged to Agnes—and she was obviously in some kind of trouble. But what?

He was drifting alone in the dark water, no longer holding hands with the others. His arms were floating in front of his body, and he could see his palm was glowing at full power. They must all be recharged now.

Jarrett searched the water around him, trying to follow the direction of Agnes's cry. He easily spotted Freya and Malik nearby. They had all drifted down and were now below a giant rock face, and there! There was Agnes!

Somehow the heavy door of the oven left in the garbage

chute had hooked onto Agnes's wet suit—and now it was dragging her down like an anchor.

"Umph!" she cried again as her legs slammed into the uneven ocean floor. One flippered foot slid perfectly into a crack between two ancient rocks. And the oven door ripped free of Agnes's wet suit and landed on top of the crack, trapping her foot.

Jarrett watched her struggle, but she couldn't get free. Agnes leaned over to slam her palm on the rock, clearly trying to smash it with her glowing palm. But the angle was all wrong, and her effort only made it worse, pinning her foot even more tightly between the rocks.

"Agnes!" Jarrett shouted, swimming her way.

"No, wait, Jarrett," Freya said. "I'm closer to Agnes. I'll go help her. You and Malik hatch a plan to deal with Tommy's Leviathan! It must be almost to us by now."

"Okay," Jarrett said. "But let us know if you need help!"

"Hang in there, Agnes," Malik said over the necklace.

Jarrett and Malik turned in the direction the Leviathan had been coming from. They swam to below the edge of the cliff and held on to the rocks there. From this position, they could see anything coming their way, but Jarrett didn't think Tommy could spot them.

Well, Jarrett thought, *we're about to discover if that's true.*

The Leviathan was only about two hundred feet away

now, and it was barreling toward them. Its massive mouth was sucking in water and pushing it out the back to speed itself along.

"What should we do?" Malik asked.

"I don't know," Jarrett said. "You're the water guy!"

"Ugh, I hate when you remind me of that," Malik said. "But okay . . ." He moved his glowing palm through the water, attempting to make a shape that could defend them against the huge Leviathan.

"It's hard to maneuver," Malik said. "Trying to make something *out* of water while *in* the water is trickier than you'd think!"

Still, Malik kept at it. And fortunately an undercurrent with streams of garbage was rushing past them. Malik took hold of that current like a string and pulled it in toward himself, like he was reeling in a fishing line.

When his hands were full of the densely packed water, he started working on it. He reminded Jarrett of a baker stretching raw dough into the world's longest, thickest baguette. And soon a snakelike creature started to take shape, extending from his palm out toward the Leviathan. The water snake's face was the size of a van, and it looked very familiar to Jarrett.

Jarrett said, "It looks like . . . me."

Malik had created the most frightening sea monster on the planet, and it had Jarrett's face.

"Um," Jarrett said. "That's very sweet, but also really creepy."

"Sorry!" Malik said as he continued to work. "It was easier to create a fighter from what I know . . . and like."

"Aww," Agnes said. "So cute!" She must have been listening while trying to free herself.

"Thanks, Malik," Jarrett said, "but Tommy will recognize me. Or my face. Change it. Hurry!"

But there wasn't time, and in the end it didn't matter. When the Leviathan came up over the stone ridge, it instantly vacuumed the Jarrett monster in through its wide mouth. It was easy, smooth, effortless, and the Leviathan didn't lose a fraction of its speed.

The snake monster was gone, all except for the tail. Jarrett's eyes followed the last of the snake wind out of the Leviathan's mouth through the water to Malik's palm. Even slightly covered by the breathing tube and the mask, Jarrett could tell that Malik had a little smile on his face.

"Um," Jarrett said. "Why are you smiling? Shouldn't we be running—or swimming—for our lives?"

"Wait a second," Malik said. His hand, the one with the Pony, was glowing more brightly than ever. He raised his arm and brought it down like he was cracking a whip. A ball of energy flowed from his hand through the tail. It shot into the Leviathan's open mouth, where Jarrett imagined the energy connecting to the main body of the monster.

It was like putting a firecracker inside an egg. There was a *poof!* And the results were instantaneous. Bubbles shot out through the cracks in the Leviathan, and it immediately started listing to one side. Malik was lifting his hand to give the tail another crack, but Jarrett stopped him.

"That's enough!" Jarrett said. "Don't forget, Tommy is in that thing. We don't want to hurt him!"

"You're right," Malik agreed. They had damaged the Leviathan, but they didn't want to damage Tommy.

As Jarrett watched, the Leviathan turned slowly, more like puttered. Pieces cracked off as it scuttled its way toward shore, all the while slowly rising. Jarrett knew Tommy would be okay once he reached the surface. He couldn't say the same about the machinery. It was still flaking off large hunks of metal.

The boys watched until the Leviathan broke the surface, and then they swam over to help Freya, who was still trying to free Agnes from the stone.

While they paddled, Jarrett noticed Malik's palm was totally dark, but his own still had a glimmer. Once the boys reached their friends, all four yanked on Agnes's leg but produced no effect other than a few yelps of pain from Agnes. As they struggled, their air tanks started beeping, signaling low oxygen levels. The beeps quickly grew closer and closer together.

"We're almost out of air," Malik warned. "We need to get Agnes's leg free and get to the surface as fast as we possibly can!"

"No!" Agnes said. "We can't rise to the surface too quickly or we'll get the bends."

"What's the bends?" Jarrett asked.

"What *are* the bends?" Freya corrected him automatically.

"I don't know!" Agnes said. "I saw it on a dumb movie. I know Calamity Corporation isn't totally honest, but maybe this planet is full of scary stuff after all!"

The beeping alerts from the air tanks were so close together now that they were almost one continuous sound. Their oxygen was nearly gone. They had a choice: stay down here without air or rise to the surface and get "the bends"— whatever that was.

But Jarrett knew they really didn't have a choice. They couldn't leave Agnes down here.

CHAPTER TEN

Jarrett scanned the dark water around them. There must be some kind of creature he could call to ask for help!

Agnes guessed what he was thinking. "No, JarJar. Don't. We don't know what's down here. What if you called a shark or something? I'd be quite the tasty ready-to-eat snack."

Jarrett nodded helplessly, and Agnes turned to Freya. "Hey, Freya. I think it's time we teamed up. You ready to work together on project 'Free Me'?"

"Certainly. I'm not even going to correct that grammar," she answered.

Agnes managed a small smile. "Let's do this, then," she said, and slammed her hand on the seafloor. It was hard for her to get a solid slam because it was like moving her arm through molasses. But it did have an effect . . . air bubbles rose from the ground. The bubbles must have been trapped in the rock for centuries, and now they emerged in a steady, fizzy stream.

Freya got the idea right away. After all, Jarrett thought, her Pony gave her the power of air.

With her glowing palm pulsing, Freya moved her hands through the water. The bubbles reacted immediately. Rather than continuing to dissipate and float up to the surface, they reversed course and gathered around Agnes. Soon Freya had created a pocket of air that grew into an oblong bubble. It engulfed Agnes's face first, and then the rest of the kids. Safe inside the bubble, Agnes spit out her mouthpiece and grinned. She kept hitting the ocean floor until Freya had engulfed them inside their own giant bubble. Its curving walls wiggled all around them. And the beeping of the low-oxygen alert went silent.

Agnes's pounding on the seafloor suddenly turned into more of a tapping. She stopped and looked at her palm, and then showed it to her friends. "I'm out of juice," she said, her voice muffled inside the wobbly bubble.

"That's okay," Freya said. "I can hold the air bubble together for a bit, I think. It's not taking too much power."

"First things first," Jarrett said. "Give me a hand with this oven door, Malik."

The two got to work. Now that they were in the dry

interior of the bubble, it was easier for them to get a grip on the door. And they could more easily lever it against one of the rocks. With one last double *umph!* they shoved the heavy metal door off Agnes. As she slid it free, she lost a flipper and then kicked off the other one.

"You okay?" Jarrett asked, concerned about his best friend. The foot that had been trapped was already swollen.

"Never better, JarJar," she answered with a wink. But he could tell she was in pain. He took her hand to give her support.

"Should we float to the top?" Malik asked.

Together the four friends raised their faces, gazing up at the two hundred feet or so to the surface, where giant waves swirled.

"There's nothing up there," Agnes said. "We'd get to the surface and then what? Swim for miles back to shore?"

"Why doesn't Lina come pick us up?" Malik asked, and then answered his own question: "Something must have happened."

"We need to get to New Plastic Island," Jarrett told them. "Lina said we were only about a half mile away. It'll be easier walking on the ocean floor than swimming on the wavy surface. Freya, do you think you can keep this bubble together long enough for us to get there?"

She looked at her palm, considered how dim it was, and

opened her mouth as if to say something. Instead she gave a little smile that clearly said, *I have no idea.*

Agnes laughed. "Good enough for me."

The friends decided to remove the useless air tanks, flippers, and breathing tubes. But they all kept their wet suits on and their masks pushed up on their foreheads. They might need those in the near future.

With Agnes limping a bit in the lead, the other kids followed very closely—as in, inches from her. There wasn't that much room in the bubble, and no one wanted to be the one to fall out and possibly pop it.

After about ten minutes of this strange group hike on the mushy ocean floor, the dark water around them got even darker. Jarrett glanced up. Sunlight popped through here and there and streams of illumination made slanted columns in the cloudy water, but the light seemed dimmer than before.

"The sun must be setting," Jarrett said.

"No, it's only lunchtime," Freya corrected him. "I think we're under the edge of New Plastic Island."

"We can rise to the surface now," Malik said. "We'll have solid ground to stand on."

"How should we do this?" Jarrett asked.

"I can control the bubble a bit," Freya said, "but we have to find a way to travel inside the bubble as it rises toward the surface. Remember, we can't go too fast, or we'll get the bends."

"Whatever the bends is," Agnes said.

"Bends are," Freya corrected her grammar. And then added, "Sorry, habit."

Freya suggested that they all jump off the seafloor at the exact same time. While their feet were in the air, Freya lifted the bubble off the ground and propelled it up a few inches. When they came back down, their feet popped through the bottom of the bubble, but the bubble itself remained whole. Freya was holding it together with her palm, Jarrett guessed.

Unfortunately, the maneuver didn't get them any closer to the surface, but their splashing did attract the attention of the sea creatures swimming around them. At first there was a small school of minnows. Then larger fish. Until there was a group of four sharks. *One for each of us,* Jarrett thought with a shudder. *We're like a bubble-encased smorgasbord.*

"Keep them away, Jarrett," Malik said.

Jarrett put his palm in front of his mouth and said, **Hi there! Can you please leave us alone?** Cards spun around him inside the bubble. The others couldn't see them, of course, but to Jarrett it looked like gibberish. And it must have been gibberish to the sharks too, because they didn't react at all.

"I've no idea what you're saying, but it sounds way too polite," Agnes commented.

Jarrett shook his head. "I don't think now is the time for rudeness."

"If not now, when?" Agnes asked. "We're literally swimming with sharks. We need to play their game."

"Okay, if you say so," Jarrett muttered, and then put his palm toward his mouth to try again. This time he shouted, **Go away! We don't want you here!**

The cards that spun into the air were covered in pure red, the color of blood, and they seemed to enrage the sharks. This was, after all, their territory. They began shooting their own blood-red cards back at him, their mouths snapping angrily.

"Sorry!" Agnes said, moving to the center of the bubble, away from the sharks' huge teeth. "I guess rudeness doesn't pay after all!"

"Let me try something else," Jarrett said. This time he put his palm in front of his mouth and made his voice silky smooth, the way announcers did in ads when they were crooning about the most delicious desserts of all time. **Right over there are some of the plumpest, juiciest, slowest fish you sharks have ever seen!**

This finally got the sharks' attention. Jarrett touched his ear with his palm and could only make hungry grunts, but it was enough. The sharks swam off quickly toward where Jarrett had been gesturing.

"Phew," Malik said. "Nice one, Jarrett. Now let's get our butts up to New Plastic Island!"

"We have to move together," Freya instructed. "So we'll all stay inside the bubble as it rises to the surface."

Their feet were still poking out from the bottom of the bubble as they jumped and kicked up simultaneously. Gaining purchase in the water, their legs became propellers of the world's strangest seacraft.

As their legs splashed, Jarrett waited for the sharks' sharp jaws to clamp down on his feet. Thankfully, the fish seemed to work as a decoy, even if it was only temporary.

"We're getting there!" Jarrett wanted to encourage his friends, but when he tried to speak, he produced only a squeak. And he was feeling weaker and weaker as they continued to kick.

There could be only one cause for this new dilemma. The bubble was out of oxygen. And to make things worse, the barest flicker of green light shimmered in Freya's palm. Her power was almost out.

Not wanting to waste any bit of remaining oxygen, Jarrett mimed for his friends—putting his hands around his neck as if he couldn't breathe and then waving toward the surface, where pieces of plastic were coming into view.

We're out of air, and we've got to hurry!

Nodding, they all kicked harder. But it was difficult steering a rising bubble in the swirling ocean currents, and the four smacked directly into a layer of plastic beach lounge chairs that must have been swept away from a seaside resort by a storm.

Pop! Suddenly, the bubble was gone, cold seawater rushed at them from all sides, and the four were treading below the surface with a ceiling of plastic over their heads. There was no way they could break through the interlocking chairs. And even more terrifying, Jarrett was sure he could see the four sharks swimming back toward them.

Trying not to panic, Jarrett grabbed on to the legs of a beach chair over his head. Pulling, he was able to push his face through a small hole between two chairs and out of the water. Ahhhh! He sucked in a big breath of beautiful air. It was delicious. But almost immediately the chair started to sink from his weight, and soon his face was underwater again.

A quick glance told him his friends were having the same problem. Everyone could snatch a lungful of air, but that was all. Malik's head was darting about, clearly looking for a solution, and he shouted something that Jarrett couldn't understand. Malik swam a few feet away and gestured at the wide tube now directly above him. It might have once been a plastic garbage can, but the bottom had popped off—and Jarrett could see streams of sunlight shining through from the surface.

Could they use it as a tunnel?

"Smarcs!" Agnes yelled, a frantic stream of bubbles shooting from her mouth. Even the water couldn't muffle her fear or her meaning:

Sharks!

Jarrett turned to see she'd been right. The angry sharks were indeed swimming their way, their sleek bodies sliding frighteningly through the water.

Go, go! Jarrett signaled to the garbage can tunnel, and they all moved. Malik went first. Whipping his legs back and forth, he was able to pull himself up and out of the tube. He reached down and helped Agnes and then Freya.

Only Jarrett remained underwater. The four sharks were just ten feet away now.

Get me out of here!

He shot his arms skyward through the tube and felt his friends grab him. They pulled Jarrett so hard and so quickly that he popped out the other side like a cork firing from a bottle, and fell onto his rear.

Ouch.

But Jarrett didn't care if his butt hurt. He felt lucky he still had it—knowing he'd just barely missed being a shark snack. The four heroes had made it to New Plastic Island. They were safe. For now.

CHAPTER ELEVEN

New Plastic Island had the word *island* in it. But just like so many things that the Calamity Corporation named, the moniker didn't exactly fit. Where his friends were standing was definitely not an island. It was a new *continent*.

Birds swooped over the most bizarre landscape Jarrett had ever seen. The flying creatures struggled to flap their ragged wings, barely holding their frail, lumpy bodies aloft. Jarrett could guess why they appeared to be so sickly and misshapen. They must be eating flashy bits of plastic, mistaking the toxic material for tasty treats.

Jarrett, Malik, and Agnes balanced on a sturdy piece of plastic the size of a small garage door. On a separate floating plastic cube, Freya was bent over, untying her shoe so she could pluck out the little minnows that had burrowed inside.

Jarrett knew immediately that they had been lied to. Again. This wasn't like land. This was a patchwork of sickeningly bright colors. Everything from laundry detergent bottles to empty buckets rolled in swells of the water beneath. While holes in the plastic mass would open and close, there seemed to be areas where the ocean had somehow piled the plastic into layers that were several objects deep. Almost as if it were trying desperately to tidy things up. There was no way a simple current could ever clean this disaster. The plastic extended toward the horizon as far as the eye could see.

"Look!" Agnes shouted, and pointed about thirty feet away.

Jarrett spotted it. There was the Glass Submarine floating on its side, like the pet goldfish his class had two years ago.

"Lina!" he shouted.

The ship obviously had no power—the sub's hull was no longer clear, and its silver skin shone dully in the sun. Jarrett didn't like how quiet it looked. Why wasn't Lina getting in touch with them? Was she even in the sub? Something must be wrong. They better get ready for danger.

"We need to recharge," he said to his friends. "Everyone grab hands."

In an instant, Malik, Agnes, and Jarrett were gripping on

to each other. Now they only needed Freya to complete the circuit. But when Jarrett reached for her . . . she was gone.

"F-F-Freya?" Jarrett stammered, confused. Had she disappeared too?

Agnes touched his arm. "Look, there she is!"

Jarrett followed her gaze and easily spotted her. The current had swept her down a small canal, as if she were bobbing on an iceberg in the arctic instead of a plastic cube. Freya glanced up from tying her shoe and looked as surprised as they were to find herself there.

"Apologies!" she said.

"No worries," Agnes told her. "Can you paddle back to us?"

Freya nodded. "But it will take a few minutes. And Lina could be in trouble. Go see if she needs help." When they didn't move, she ordered, "Go on. I am okay!"

Without Freya, the four friends wouldn't be able to recharge. They were going to have to use their brains, not their powers, to right the submarine.

Jarrett, Agnes, and Malik started banging on the side of the submarine.

"Ouch!" Jarrett groaned. "This isn't getting us anywhere, except breaking our hands. Let's try something different."

With the three of them pulling together, they were able to pry the hatch open a crack. All their work had loosened an electrical panel in the doorway as well. They began yanking out wires and throwing them into the water.

"I think we're getting somewhere!" Malik said. "I think—"

"What are you doing?" a shout came barreling through the crack.

"Lina!" Jarrett said. "Don't worry! We're saving you!"

Lina's head popped up from the other side of the submarine. "The submarine is fine! Or it was until you broke it. If you remember, the hatch is on the side!"

"Oops," Jarrett mumbled. They hadn't actually been opening the hatch; they had pried the submarine open and torn out vital wires.

"Oops?" Lina said. "Why do I have the feeling that's a word you've used about a million times before? How is it possible that you could disable a billion-dollar submarine with your bare hands? That goes a little beyond oops, don't you think?"

Time to change the subject. Luckily, that was just when Freya arrived. She must have paddled to the sturdier surface of plastic, and then carefully walked to them. She was breathing heavily and sweating a little.

Freya asked, "Where are the animals?"

"What animals?" Lina asked with raised eyebrows. Then she burst out laughing at their shocked expressions. "Come here," she said, waving them over to her side of the submarine. Traveling on the surface of the plastic was like playing some weird game of hopscotch where losing the game meant you could lose a limb or your life.

On the other side of the sub, the friends spotted the animals immediately. They had been removed from the bags and placed around a plastic tea-party table that a little kid might get as a birthday present. Each animal even had their own teacup. The frozen animals were still locked in their blocks of ice, but now the ice was starting to melt.

The aye-aye was at the head of the table and looked like he was frozen in the middle of giving the speech of his life, with his finger pointed up in the air. The star-nosed mole was placed leaning against the warthog as if they were engaged in whispered conversation. And the proboscis monkey had been posed turned slightly to the side, as if it couldn't be bothered with any of this tea-party business.

"Ta-da!" Lina said.

"Oh . . . ," Jarrett murmured. "This feels so . . ."

"Disrespectful," Freya finished for him.

"These are animals, not toys," Malik said. And Jarrett was proud of him. He had come a long way since the days before the Race to Erase. Back then he had thought of nature as nothing more than a bunch of free stuff that everyone could grab and take home.

"Disrespectful?" Lina demanded. "This is what you wanted, right? I knew you would waste time when you got here, so I did it for you. I placed your animals in a lovely setting. Now they can live their days out here, once they melt, that is. You're welcome!" As she spoke, Lina moved from animal to animal and placed them in a neat line on top of the table. "And you repay my kindness by destroying my submarine! And making fun of my tea party!"

Just then an alarm bell sounded, making them all jump. A loud **PFFT!** echoed off the mounds of plastic around them, and an inflatable life raft shot out of the front of the sub.

"That's the submarine's emergency beacon," Lina said. "It has a delay. If it becomes inoperable, you have five minutes to fix it, or an alarm will sound in the harbor complex."

Jarrett guessed where this was going. "It will alert Tommy that the ship is in trouble. He'll head back out here, and he'll find us."

"Well, true," Lina said. "He'll find you. But not exactly you."

With a head shake, Agnes asked, "What on earth does that mean?"

"Hold on a second," Lina said casually. "Now that the sub is disabled, the hologram blocker has been switched off. Tommy should pop in any second. You guys might want to hide."

There was a chime letting them know a hologram was incoming. Malik, Jarrett, Agnes, and Freya dove for cover.

Jarrett crawled into a large plastic storage bin. And then Tommy blipped in. Or at least Jarrett thought he must have. From inside the bin, he couldn't see a thing.

"What happened to the sub, Lina?" Tommy demanded. "And Mom and Dad say *I'm* the troublemaker? Wait till I tell them about this! You'll stop getting everything you want all the time!"

Whoa, Jarrett thought, sucking in a breath. Tommy was acting like a bully, but Lina didn't sound fazed at all.

"Um, you won't want to tell Mom and Dad about the sub, Tommy," Lina said calmly. "You see those frozen animals? They'll have questions about those and the job you were supposed to be doing. Plus, look past the animals . . . what do you see?"

There was a pause, and then Tommy snarled, "No way! They're here too?"

Unable to see anything from inside the bin, Jarrett feared that Tommy had caught sight of Freya, Agnes, or Malik. He expected Tommy to start shouting or chasing them. Instead, he asked quietly, like a hunter spotting skittish prey, "How did *they* get here?"

Tommy's question sent a spike of fear through Jarrett's stomach. Had Tommy spotted his friends? No, that couldn't be. Surely if his friends had been seen, they'd already be fighting for their lives.

"I don't know, Tommy," Lina said. "But you better go grab the One and come back here quick."

"Mom and Dad said I can't have the One," Tommy whined. "Not until I finish the job with the ugly space animals . . ."

A pause, as if Lina were thinking. Then she said, "I've unlocked it for you, Tommy."

"What?" Tommy sounded surprised. "Are you serious?"

"The One is ready for you at the harbor complex," Lina said.

"Oh . . . huh . . . well, thanks . . . I guess," Tommy said, showing gratitude for the first time Jarrett had heard. "I'll be back. You better take the sub far away from here. You're not going to want to be here when I return and deal with *them*. See you soon."

Tommy's hologram chimed again, signaling his departure, and Jarrett knew it was safe to come out of the bin. As Jarrett, Freya, and Malik emerged from their hiding places and rejoined Lina, Agnes was already asking, "What did Tommy see that made him freak out?"

Lina smiled. "Take a look over there."

They followed her gesturing hand, and about three hundred yards away, they spotted what she meant. Four kids were standing on a floating island of plastic flamingos. The four kids were raising their fists in the air in a threatening way and stamping their feet like they couldn't wait to get into a fight or something.

"Who are they?" Jarrett asked, his skin breaking into goose bumps. They looked familiar in some horrible way. "Who is that?"

Lina's smile grew into a grin as she announced, "That's you."

CHAPTER TWELVE

"**D**on't you look great?" Lina asked, waving toward the four other kids proudly.

"No," Agnes said. "No, we don't. How can we be out there? We're right here! And why are our faces so blurry?"

Freya touched the necklace around her neck. "You're using these to project altered holograms of us, aren't you?"

"What do you mean?" Jarrett said.

"I—" Lina started to say, but Jarrett interrupted her.

"No," he said. "I'd like to hear Freya's answer. Her guess will be closer to the truth than what we'll get from you. Go ahead, Freya."

Freya took a breath and said, "I believe Lina gave us these necklaces so she could create holograms that look like us. She did it to trick Tommy into thinking the kids who stole the Ponies were out here on New Plastic Island. But I have no idea why she would want the real us-es here as well."

"Can I speak now?" Lina asked, and without waiting for an answer, she took control of the conversation. "In my original plan, I wanted the real yous to be with Tommy at the harbor complex. When he saw the holograms of you out here, he'd think they stole the Ponies, and the real yous would be off the hook! But then you ruined everything by stealing those animals and climbing onto my sub."

Stunned, Jarrett said, "Lina, you think you're doing us a favor by copying our bodies and putting them here?"

"I do," Lina said sincerely.

"But, Lina," Agnes said, "you don't do favors."

Throwing her hands in the air, Lina said, "Oh, here we go again. We're *friends,* guys!"

"I think you wanted something else." Agnes eyed Lina suspiciously.

"Fine, fine!" Lina said. "We don't have time for all this babbling. Tommy will be here any second. I put fake yous on Plastic Island to fight Tommy. And at the end of the battle, his One will be out of power, and the fake yous . . . well, they'll be . . ."

"We don't survive, do we?" Malik asked.

"The *fake* yous don't survive," Lina corrected him. "And

once the fake yous are gone—all recorded on camera—my brother's hunt for the *real* yous and the spheres will be gone too! You'll be free—and so will I. I won't have to spend my life hiding you four from Tommy anymore."

"You've taken plotting and scheming to the next level, Lina," Jarrett said. "I can't believe you gave us these necklaces so you could create our fake holograms!"

"You know how long it would take to program four fake holograms?" Lina answered. "It's much easier to use real people as models. Anyway, it's time to go."

"Why?" Malik asked.

With a withering look, Lina answered, "Keep up, Malik. Tommy will be back soon."

"I still don't get it," Agnes said. "You helped us stop Tommy and his Leviathan before!"

Lina nodded. "Because I wasn't ready for him to come out here then. The holograms of you weren't set up yet, but now they are. And now Tommy has the One. The One sphere is all-powerful. I don't know why we made four when we could have just made one."

"Is the One like a treat you've been saving for Tommy, Lina?" Agnes asked.

"I give my brothers a cookie as a treat," Jarrett said. "Not an all-powerful world-destroyer."

"Ha ha," Lina said sarcastically. "No, it's not a treat. I

knew that sooner or later he'd get his hands on it. I love my brother, but he's not exactly the king of wise decisions. If I give it to him, though, I can control how he uses it."

"Control?" Freya asked. "How?"

Indicating the wasteland of plastic around them, Lina said, "There's not a ton of damage he can do out here on New Plastic Island. He can use up his power and no one will get hurt."

"Hmm." Jarrett scratched his chin. It was hard to know when to trust Lina. But she did seem genuine, as if she really did want to be helpful. Then he thought of something. "Couldn't Tommy recharge and keep coming after us?"

"Nope." Lina shook her head. "The One can't recharge when it empties out. You can recharge yours because there's four of you, and they can work together. Tommy just has the One. And there's no other One for it to feed off. The fake yous will be a great way to deplete his power, and then the One sphere will no longer be a threat . . . to anyone. Now we need to go!"

Malik looked unsure. "What about the animals?"

"You want to take them on a busted sub that might sink at any second?" Lina asked. "They'll be safer here. They would have been even safer back at the harbor complex. You're the ones who destroyed my gorgeous submarine. We can't take the sub underwater thanks to you guys. But we can motor along."

With one last glance at the four holograms and the four frozen animals, Jarrett followed the others as they stepped onto the deck of the submarine.

"Hold on," Lina instructed them, and then spoke into the air. "Sub, use emergency engine power to travel on the surface back to the harbor complex."

The sub lurched into motion and started pulling trash from the island along with them. A thick plastic string with triangular HAPPY BIRTHDAY flags had snagged onto the cage around the ship's propeller. It was pulling the other pieces of plastic with it.

None of the kids could reach it to cut it loose.

"It doesn't matter," Lina said. "It's not slowing us down."

She took a seat on the deck, and with nothing else to do, Jarrett, Agnes, and Freya joined her. Only Malik stayed on his feet. He stood behind the little group near the inflatable lifeboat, and he was still gazing back toward the holograms and the animals. Jarrett knew him well enough to leave him alone for a bit.

After a few minutes, they cleared the edge of New Plastic Island and found themselves motoring along in the open ocean. Jarrett checked on Malik again; he was still staring back toward the continent.

"I'm going back to save them," Malik said. "The animals need our help."

"No, they're fine, Malik!" Jarrett said.

An expression came over Malik's face that Jarrett had never seen before. It was one of grim determination. "We took them," Malik said. "We're responsible for them. Someone has to be responsible for something!"

Jarrett felt his heart swell, touched by Malik's words. He had gone from considering animals to be disposable toys to becoming their champion.

Jarrett thought he might be able to make Malik feel better if he asked Lina a few more questions. "Lina, why do you think the animals will be safe out there?"

With a chuckle, Lina said, "I didn't say 'safe.' I said 'safer.' And I still think that. We'd never survive the tsunamis or hurricanes that Tommy might throw at the holograms, but I'm sure those animals will. After all, animals are nature, right? And so are tsunamis and hurricanes."

Now Jarrett felt his face flush with panic. There were so many words Lina had said that were terrifying. *Tsunami. Hurricane. Tommy.* Freya sounded concerned too. "I know about animals, Lina," she said, "and that doesn't make sense!"

"You're the ones who wanted to bring them there," Lina said. "And now it's too late to change your minds. You made your *choice.*"

"Maybe you're right, Lina," Agnes said hopefully. "I mean, Earth is Earth, right? Why does it matter what part of it we leave them? Anything is better than floating around in space . . . forever."

"Totally," Lina agreed. "They can swim. Right? Don't all animals swim? And if not, can't the bird simply fly away if Tommy sends a tidal wave?"

Even Lina couldn't sell this plan. Jarrett shook his head. "But how can they swim when they're frozen? And, by the way, none of them are birds. They can't fly!"

Taking this in stride, Lina said, "Well, the ice will actually protect them when the wave hits. Then the ice will melt in the water, and they'll swim or whatever *not*-flying things they do."

"No, I don't think so," Jarrett said. Maybe Malik was right. They should go back. They needed to save the animals. As he turned to face his friend, Jarrett said, "Malik . . ."

But Malik was gone. And then the engine died.

"Well, looks like the emergency power has run out," Lina said.

"Where's the lifeboat?" Lina asked.

But Jarrett knew. Malik had taken it, and he was headed back to New Plastic Island.

CHAPTER THIRTEEN

"**W**hat can we do?" Jarrett asked as panic like he'd never known slammed into him. "We need to go after him!"

"He's a big boy," Lina said. "He'll figure things out."

"How? He'll be up against Tommy. And I'm not great at math, but it sounds like Tommy's One is four times as powerful as one of our Ponies."

This seemed to get to Lina. "Maybe you're right."

"My palm is dead," Freya said. "And without Malik we can't recharge."

"I've got plenty of power," Agnes said. "But once again, I don't see any land around here. And my power is kind of all about that."

"Okay, fine, it's up to me," Jarrett said. And he was glad. He wanted to take action to help Malik. He wanted to do *something*.

He moved to the edge of the sub, held his palm close to his mouth, and put out a call: **Hi, does anyone have a second? Please, we could really use your help. Our friend is in trouble, and so are yours. Please.**

"Jarrett . . . ," Agnes started to say.

But Jarrett didn't want to hear her warnings. "Don't tell me I'm being too polite again!"

"Ha, no," she said, grinning. "I was going to say I think you might have nailed it."

And she was right.

Four noses—or were they called beaks?—emerged from the water, followed by four sleek and shiny heads. Dark eyes sparkling with intelligence blinked at them.

"You called dolphins, Jarrett," Freya said, sounding impressed.

The dolphins floated around the side of the sub, their heads bobbing in the water as they nosed a plastic shovel around their circle playfully. Their blowholes sprayed every few seconds as chirps, whistles, and clicks came from their mouths.

"What are they saying, JarJar?" Agnes asked.

"Oh!" Jarrett realized that he didn't have his palm to his ear. He raised his hand, and instantly cards flew in the air and a deep, refined voice filled his ears.

"—finally," the voice was saying. "One of you has developed the ability to speak! Do you know the eons we've waited for you to catch up to us?"

"You guys!" Jarrett shouted to his friends. "The dolphins can talk. I mean, really talk!"

"Hey," another dolphin was saying, and he said a name of one of the others that couldn't really be translated. It came out like *Pdfpks*. "Pdfpks, can you believe it? The humans have learned to talk!"

"I always knew they could," Pdfpks said back, "and no one ever believed me!"

"Aw!" the fourth dolphin said. "They're kind of cute."

"Really?" the first dolphin said. "I don't see it."

"What are they saying?" Agnes asked Jarrett.

"They're chitchatting, and they're draining my Pony," Jarrett answered.

"You need to get down to business before you run out of power," Freya said.

"Okay, okay." Jarrett turned back to the dolphins. "I know we're super adorable, but we need your help."

"I didn't say adorable, let alone *super* adorable," the fourth dolphin whistled.

Pdfpks chimed in, "Actually, we have quite a few complaints to launch against you people. Is there someone we can talk to? Like a manager or something? What you've been doing to us and this planet is unforgivable."

Jarrett had to admit maybe they were right. But he could also feel each word extracting precious energy from his Pony.

"I'm sorry about that," he said, knowing how feeble that sounded. "I really am, but I have a huge favor to ask. It would help us actually do something good for the planet for once."

"How do you mean?" the second dolphin asked.

"Well, our friend is trying to save a few animals."

Pdfpks bobbed his head. "What kind of animals?"

"I'm not sure how to say this," Jarrett told the dolphin, "but many people call them ugly."

"Ugly?" the first dolphin said. "We don't like that word. It doesn't sound very nice."

"It's not," Jarrett agreed. "We have the chance to save those animals, though. But we need to be towed to New Plastic Island. Can you take us?"

There was a pause, and then the four dolphins were whistling and clicking so quickly the cards couldn't keep up. Finally, after a few seconds, Pdfpks said, "We'll help you on one condition."

"You're amazing," Jarrett said. "Thank you! We'll do anything. What's the condition?"

"Say the magic word," Pdfpks said.

"Please?" Jarrett guessed.

"Close," the second dolphin said encouragingly. "It does sound a little like that word."

Turning to the girls, Jarrett asked in English, "What word would a dolphin want to hear that sounds kind of like *please*?"

"What—?" Agnes started to say something, but Freya interrupted her right away.

"I know," she said. "It's *play*."

Jarrett held his palm before his mouth again, and said, "Play!"

The dolphins all bobbed their heads, and their eyes squinted happily. "Should we play a game of chase?" Pdfpks asked.

The other dolphins bobbed their heads in excitement.

"Well, kind of," Jarrett said. "We're chasing our friend Malik. I'm hoping you can tug us to the plastic island. Please. I mean, play," Jarrett said, already repositioning the line tangled around the sub's propeller so that the dolphins could grab on to it with their mouths and pull. "Let's go!"

"Wait!" Lina said. "I'm not going to New Plastic Island. If I reach shore, I can send a drone out to get the frozen animals. Malik is too big to carry, but if he sees the animals are safe, maybe he will turn around. In case I don't get there in time, you three take that floating trash there, and I'll take the sub."

"I'm not going to argue," Jarrett said. "I'm too worried about Malik. Can you three help me gather some of this floating plastic and we'll make a kind of boat out of it? Then I'll figure out how to ask the dolphins to give Lina a ride to shore too."

Lina, Freya, and Agnes helped pile the trash that had been tangled along the back of the sub. Using the long rope covered in plastic flags, they were able to fashion a semi-decent raft. It wouldn't last more than an hour or so before falling apart, but Jarrett decided it would be able to carry him, Freya, and Agnes to New Plastic Island when propelled by two excitable dolphins!

As they worked, Jarrett asked, "Freya, how did you know the magic word was *play*?"

"There's nothing these intelligent creatures like to do more than play," she answered. "You can tell a lot about a species by the way it plays."

With the raft done, Jarrett walked closer to the edge of the submarine and gazed down at the dolphins. "I have one more favor to ask," he said.

"Ha ha," the second dolphin clacked. "We can see you're frightened about something. But we will help you, you poor finless creatures who have forgotten that they themselves come from water."

"No, that's not—" Jarrett started to say.

The third dolphin interrupted him. "Now, like all humans I bet, he's going to take more and more."

"That's true," Jarrett agreed. "We need two of you to take Lina back to shore on the sub, and two of you to tow the rest of us out to New Plastic Island on the trash raft."

The third dolphin whistled loudly to the other dolphins. "If they really want our help, we'll need not only the magic word, but they'll also have to solve a riddle!"

CHAPTER FOURTEEN

"**O**h, you always have the best ideas!" the fourth dolphin said to its companion, and then turned to Jarrett. "Yes, you have to solve a riddle. If you can do that, we'll help you!"

"Uh-oh," Jarrett said, missing Malik more than ever. After all, he was the jokester. He was the one who would be good at solving riddles. Thoughts of Malik helped refocus Jarrett's panic. They were running out of time.

Pdfpks must have noticed his worry. "Be glad it's not those super-smarty octopuses posing the riddles. They give nothing but stumpers!"

"Answer correctly and we'll take you," the second dolphin said. "You've got to give us something. We're tired of this one-way relationship where you humans take and take."

All this chitchat wasn't going to leave Jarrett with any power. But what choice did they have?

"Okay," Jarrett said. "But please hurry and ask the riddle. *Play* hurry, I mean."

Pdfpks piped right up. "Why don't crabs give to charity?"

"I have no idea," said Jarrett with a shrug.

"See?" the second dolphin said to the others. "They lack all sense of humor, I told you."

But Jarrett wasn't surrendering. He turned to his friends and spoke in English. "Hey, guys, why don't crabs give to charity?"

Now it was Agnes's turn to shrug. Freya tapped her chin and said, "Hmm," but Jarrett knew she was over-thinking it.

"Can't do it?" the second dolphin said, almost happily. "Okay, bye—"

"I know!" Lina suddenly shouted. "It's because they're shellfish!"

Jarrett couldn't help it. He laughed and gave Lina a high five. If anyone knew about being "shellfish," it was Lina. That must be the answer! He repeated it to the dolphins: "Crabs don't give to charity because they're shellfish!"

It was like the firing of a starter pistol at a race. The dolphins jerked into action. Pdfpks and the fourth dolphin grabbed the line tied to the trash raft in their mouths, and began swimming. Jarrett's hand was ripped away from his ear by the force, but he could still hear the joyful dolphin laughter ringing.

"Good luck, you three," Lina shouted from the deck of the sub as it was being pulled away by her team of dolphins. "You're going to need it!"

"I have no idea what you're saying," the third dolphin told Lina, but of course Lina couldn't understand. "So just save your breath, and let's win this race against our friends! We love a playful race!"

Jarrett asked Pdfpks, "How will we know who won? If the other team gets to shore before we reach New Plastic Island?"

"Oh, that's right!" the dolphin clacked. "You have teeny tiny ears. We'll be able to hear our friends, don't worry."

Before the two teams separated, Jarrett could hear the dolphins chittering away, dishing out good-natured trash talk, like friends about to go head-to-head on the athletic field. They were giving each other a hard time about being slower than a sea slug in November or as quick as a barnacle stuck on a sea-bottom vent.

They were traveling at such a high speed that the trash raft often skimmed the surface of the water. At one point Agnes tumbled off; the next time he saw her, she was holding the fin of Pdfpks and riding the water. She was laughing.

"Be respectful!" Jarrett shouted. "Remember, they aren't amusement park rides!"

Agnes grinned and waved back. "Will do, JarJar. Don't worry, but it is fun!"

Within minutes, they were once again at New Plastic Island. The water was completely still now, and the trash was a straight line to the horizon, punctuated here and there by large floating tubs—or what was that, a giant plastic elephant? It had been pushed aside as if someone were trying to create a pass through all the junk. Jarrett knew who that must be. Malik. And there he was!

Malik was propelling the lifeboat the same way the Leviathan had moved. He was using his palm to force water from the front of the boat to the back, and the boat was gliding along as it bumped off various chunks of floating plastic. Malik was only a few feet away from the platform where they had left the animals. But the boat was slowing way down. Clearly he was almost out of power.

"There!" Jarrett directed his team of dolphins. "See that other boy? We need to go there, please!"

Malik must have heard the clicking sounds that Jarrett made. He turned, and an expression of bewilderment, excitement, and pride lit up his face. Jarrett knew he, Agnes, and Freya must have made quite a picture . . . two of them pulled by a gorgeous dolphin like warriors on a chariot and the third riding like a queen on the most beautiful of steeds.

With a whoop, Malik waved. "Jarrett! Wow, am I glad to see you guys!"

As Pdfpks pulled Jarrett and Freya past him, Malik stepped aboard. The garbage float wobbled. For a moment they all nearly tumbled into the water. But Pdfpks adjusted his tugging so that the float evened out.

Jarrett and Malik gave a topsy-turvy hug, and Freya joined in. "Don't ever run off on your own like that again, Malik. We're so much better together!"

Malik gave a nod, and Agnes shouted, "Aw, I'm missing a group hug!"

"We'll make up for it later; don't worry, Aggie!" Jarrett called to her.

For some reason the fourth dolphin stopped next to the giant floating elephant that was about fifty yards from the rest of the group. "I guess he wants me to get off," she said, and stood with one foot on the dolphin and one on the floating elephant. For a moment, Jarrett thought Agnes was going to tumble into the water. But she kept her balance and came to rest on top of the elephant. She was close enough to the platform to swim through the loose plastic between them.

As she bobbed on the elephant, she asked, "Why did he

drop me off here, away from you guys? Did we lose?" Agnes shouted to Jarrett, "Ask the dolphins! Did we beat Lina?"

Jarrett shook his head. "Agnes, remember this isn't a ride that—"

"Is she wondering if we won?" Pdfpks whistled. "That's wonderful; she's showing the spirit of play! Yes, I'm proud to announce we have won! The other team is still within ear-shot and quite a distance from the shore."

As Jarrett and Freya stepped onto the platform with the frozen animals, he said to Pdfpks, "Thank you so much, but you should probably get far away from here."

Pdfpks nodded. "This is a very dangerous place for us. And for you. For everyone. You shouldn't be here. This whole *island* shouldn't be here."

The fourth dolphin popped his head out of the water and was blinking his deep, dark eyes at the blocks of ice.

"What did you do to these creatures?" He sounded horri-fied. "Are these the ones you called ugly? Is that what you do to animals you call ugly?"

"It's a long story," Jarrett told the dolphins. "But please know that I'm sorry. I'm so sorry. For all of us. We're trying to fix it."

"Okay, but be better at living on our planet," Pdfpks said. "Can you play better?"

"We'll try," Jarrett said. In the distance he saw a wall

coming their way. "But please, in the meantime, you need to—" His clicks and whistles stopped. He sounded human again. His palm must be dark. "—leave. Now."

Pdfpks nodded and nudged the fourth dolphin, who was still staring in horror at the creatures trapped in ice. The fourth dolphin finally tore his eyes away and the two creatures dove below the surface and under the layer of the plastic. They were gone.

"Are the frozen animals okay?" Agnes called from her perch on the plastic elephant.

"I believe so," Freya answered. "They're still encased in ice. I guess that's a good thing."

"Do you have any power left?" Jarrett asked. "I'm out."

"Nope," Malik said.

"I don't either," Freya said.

"Okay, here goes nothing," Agnes said. She started slamming her hand down on different items around her.

"What are you doing, Aggie?!" Jarrett shouted.

"I'm trying to use up my power before Tommy gets here," she said. "I have the feeling I'm not going to be too much help alone. We'll all need to be freshly recharged. I just need to find some plastic with a little mud or dirt on it. Something with earth in it or on it."

Freya spotted something in the trash raft that had brought

them here. "There! It's an old plastic ant farm. The ants inside must have died a long time ago, but the dirt is still inside!"

"Can you do something with that?" Jarrett said, and threw the ant farm like a flying disk to Agnes, who caught it like the indoor Frisbee golf champ she was.

She weighed the ant farm in her hands for a second and peered at it closely. "It's so small, it's going to take me a second to drain my Pony, but yes, I think I can do it."

Placing the ant farm so it was wedged between the tusks of the plastic elephant, Agnes started whapping the toy with her palm. Flashes of light emerged with each blow, but only a little at a time.

"This is making me sad," Agnes said as her palm continued pounding.

"Why, Aggie?" Jarrett asked. "The ants aren't alive in there anymore."

"It's not that," Agnes said. "It's that I'm the one who really wanted to use the Pony. I like the feeling it gives me. And this just seems like a waste."

"But it's working, isn't it?" Malik asked. "You're nearly out of power."

"Yes, true," Agnes agreed. "Almost there."

And something else was almost there too. They could

hear it in the distance before they could see it. It was a strange rumbling, like a million airplanes revving their engines before takeoff.

Everyone but Agnes turned toward the sound. There in the distance beyond the horizon was a wall, and it was rushing toward them.

Tommy rode the tip of a mountainous wave of water. It was clear he intended to bring it crashing down on the holograms . . . without any thought for the ugly animals— and wholly unaware of the four very *real* kids who were hiding behind the holograms. As he got closer, lightning flashed over Tommy's head as he waved the all-powerful sphere in the air.

"Agnes!" Jarrett shouted. "You've got to be done emptying your Pony. Get over here! We need to hide behind our holograms before Tommy gets any closer!"

"I'm almost empty!" Agnes called out. "Give me one more minute!"

"We don't have a minute!" Jarrett fired back.

Ping! The pleasant chime of an incoming hologram was almost lost in the howling wind, crashing waves, and thunderclaps, and then Lina's hologram was standing off to the side.

"Hey, guys, I'm on shore," she said. "Bad news, I can't disarm the One sphere from here like I thought I would be able to."

"What?" Malik cried. "How are we supposed to fight him?"

"You have to make him use all his power from the One sphere. Once the One is drained, it will be useless."

"Won't he be able to recharge?" Malik asked.

"He can't," Lina said. "The spheres need other spheres to recharge. Think about it this way. You guys hold hands to recharge, right? The four separate spheres work together. He only has one sphere, so there's nothing to recharge from. He not only wants the spheres because you stole them but also because it will make him the most powerful person on the planet. If you don't drain him first, there will be no way to stop him. If he has anything left, he'll not only destroy you guys, he'll go after the planet."

"Why did you do this, Lina?" Agnes asked.

"What do you mean?"

"You knew we'd wind up here, didn't you?" Agnes said. "You knew we'd be the ones battling your brother."

"Maybe not exactly like this. But, yes, something like it," Lina admitted. "I knew someone would have to stop him, and I figured you four are at least . . . fair and honest. As much as it pains me to say it, you four are the most heroic people I know."

"This can't have been the only way!" Jarrett said.

"It is," Lina said. "I'm sorry again. But if it makes you feel any better, I'll send the drone, as promised, to pick up the frozen animals. Hopefully you'll be there too! Fingers crossed!"

With that perky chime, her hologram disappeared.

"Fingers crossed?" Malik mumbled. "Really?"

But they had more problems to worry about than Lina's rude hologram sign-offs. By now, Tommy had closed almost the entire gap between himself and the holograms.

From the mountaintop of water, Tommy shouted down at the four holograms, "Surrender and give me what you stole, and I'll go easy on you! I just want the Ponies returned to me!"

Lina must have programmed the holograms to respond to such commands because fake Jarrett turned around and waved his tush at Tommy. And fake Freya waggled her fingers on either side of her face while blowing a spit-filled raspberry through her mouth.

"Ew," Jarrett said. "I might want to drop a water mountain on us too."

Tommy seemed equally disgusted. "All right, you asked for it!" He raised his hand to the sky, and lightning streaked toward his palm like a spiderweb made of fire. The clouds swirled into a sucking vortex over his head, and the water he stood on began to boil.

They had maybe a second or two before Tommy would release the full strength of the storm raging down upon the holograms . . . and upon the four friends.

"I'm empty!" Agnes cried triumphantly, and she scampered off the elephant. She darted to the others and ducked behind the holograms. The four friends were reaching for each other—

Tommy pulled down his fist of lightning to wipe them off the surface of the water. "I'm coming for—"

—and the friends' hands connected.

Kaklam!

Why are you hanging around for? Turn to page 110!

CHAPTER FIVE

"You guys okay?"

The ringing in his ears made it tricky to hear, but Jarrett knew Agnes's voice. The explosion from the Ponies had knocked all four of them flat on their backs. Luckily no one had tumbled into the bay.

"Are you guys okay or not?" Agnes asked when no one had responded. Yes, yes, they all assured her. They were okay.

Jarrett shook his head, trying to free himself of the confusion that always hit after the Ponies recharged. It normally took a second to figure out how the world had changed around them. But this time it was instantly obvious when he sat up and looked around. "Whoa," Jarrett breathed. What he saw made him grab Malik's arm.

They couldn't have tumbled off the dock into the bay. Why? The bay was gone! At least the water was. All that was left in the bay was dry, cracked black ground with strange mounds scattered here and there. The air was still, and a horrible stench hung about them.

"Where's Mrs. Cook and our class?" Freya asked. "Lina?"

"Where is . . . everyone and everything?" Malik said.

Jarrett climbed to his feet to get a better look, and nearly toppled over. The dock was bent and warped, as if the ground far below had stretched and twisted it. Entire sections of the wood planks had collapsed around them, leaving the four friends stranded on a high wobbly island over the black murky ground.

"Do you think the ocean is gone too?" Freya asked. "Or did only the bay dry up?"

"I'm not sure. The ocean was about a mile away, over there," Jarrett said as a stagnant breeze lazily wafted a horrible stench their way.

"What's that smell?" Malik said, covering his nose. "It reeks like burning rotten eggs."

"I know that smell!" Freya said. "It stinks like Lina's science experiment, the one she did in Mrs. Cook's class!"

Ka-KLAM!

An explosion shook the ground. It was distant, but Jarrett could feel the unstable dock quiver under his feet. What was happening?

"Freya's right—that explosion proves it," Agnes said. "That smell is methane gas."

"How could you possibly know that?" Malik asked.

"You and Jarrett were too busy talking that day in class," Agnes explained. "Methane comes from underground. In Lina's project, she showed that wasted food in landfills can produce something called methane gas. She wanted to find a way to harness the deadly fiery explosions caused by the gas."

Deadly. Fiery. Explosions. "Say no more," Jarrett said. "We need to get away from here."

But how and where? The section of dock that had survived was now at least twenty feet over the ground, and there was no ladder.

In the distance, about three hundred yards away, he could see a single drone cruising low. Freya spotted it too. For the first time since he'd known her, Jarrett thought he heard panic in her voice as she said, "If Lina's experiment was right, that drone's engine might spark a chain reaction of explosions."

Before Jarrett could ask what she meant, sparks from the gas-guzzling drone's dirty exhaust connected with methane gas rising from a distant hole. The explosion sent shock waves up through the dock. As the friends stumbled, more wooden planks around them fell into the muck below. Soon there wouldn't be any dock left, and they would fall as well.

"There are so many holes leaking methane gas," Freya said, still sounding freaked out.

"They're all around us!"

Jarrett could tell she was right. That one explosion had triggered another, and another, and now the flames were shooting toward them in a zigzagging line. Suddenly, Jarrett knew *very* well what Freya meant by a chain reaction.

"Quick!" Jarrett said. "We need to use our Ponies!"

"There is so little air here," Freya said. "There is no oxygen for me to control."

"Without water," Malik noted, "I can't do anything with my power."

"And we're too high off the ground for me to affect the earth," Agnes said.

Jarrett didn't even bother saying there were no nearby creatures for him to call to for help. The empty sky and wasteland around them said it for him.

"But we do have these," Freya said, and clicked on her necklace. It flicked on and off, and her face disappeared and reappeared.

"This isn't peekaboo," Malik said dismissively.

"I know, but we can call Lina . . . wherever she is," Freya said. "She said the communication systems had limits but she'd know our location when we turn the necklaces on. And I know Morse code."

"Oh, sorry, Freya," Malik said. "That is a brilliant idea."

She smiled. "Well, it hasn't worked yet."

At that moment, Jarrett's necklace started blinking on and off in a definite pattern.

"You spoke too soon, Freya," Jarrett said happily. "That must be Lina reaching out to us. What is she saying?"

Freya concentrated on Jarrett's necklace as she translated Lina's message: " 'What are you four doing down there? Oh, this must have something to do with the Fifth Hero. I warned you not to be heroes!' "

This wasn't helpful, Jarrett thought. "Freya, can you send her a new message? 'We need help, Lina. Something the Fifth Hero decided changed the whole world.' "

Freya tapped away on her necklace for a bit, then waited. Almost instantly, Jarrett's necklace started flashing. Freya translated Lina's message again. " 'Well then, I take back every bad thing I ever said about the Fifth Hero. In fact, the Calamity Corporation owes the Fifth Hero a gigantic thank-you. The methane sped up the process of destroying Earth. Instead of decades, it will only take months! Hopefully, you guys paid attention to my experiment! I've got to run. I'll send you something to help you s—' "

An explosion knocked Jarrett to the ground, and his hand got caught in the necklace, tearing it free. It fell over the edge of the dock.

Jarrett clambered to his feet and asked Freya, "Did Lina say anything else? When will she be able to get here? What did she say?"

Freya answered, but another methane explosion made it hard to hear her. It sounded like she said, "She'll be here soon!"

Or at least that's what Jarrett *hoped* Freya had said. Because the explosions were getting closer, and soon might not be here soon enough.

THE END

It's not too late! Return to page 108.

CHAPTER SIXTEEN

"**Y**ou, you're sinking!" Malik was shouting.

Jarrett looked down. The plastic platform was indeed sinking. Water was rising from all sides, and already covered his shoes.

"My feet are stuck!" Jarrett yelled. "I can't move!"

"Me either," said Agnes, from a spot on a nearby floating door. "My shoes are like weights."

Their palms were recharged, but they were in worse shape than ever. All four kids were rooted to their spots on the floating plastic—but the plastic didn't seem to want to float much longer. It was as if they were wearing anchors on their feet.

"I think our shoes are made of solid metal," Freya said.

"Why would anyone make shoes out of metal!" Malik demanded.

While Jarrett was a fan of fashion and its long history, this went beyond his knowledge. But he could make a guess. "They must not care about how they manufacture shoes anymore," he said. "Everyone will throw them away anyway when the next fashion comes around. So I think shoemakers have decided to make them as expensive as they possibly can."

"Can you kick them off?" Malik asked, attempting to do just that. "Mine are stuck!"

They all tried, but the shoes were too awkward. And now that the laces were wet, they were nearly impossible to untie too.

"We're sinking fast now," Agnes said. "And . . . well, there's also that. . . ." She gestured to Tommy atop the approaching wave. The wave was only about a hundred feet from them and rose several stories in the air.

"I guess that's one way to get us moving," Jarrett said. "Whether we want to or not."

THE END

It's not too late to make another choice!
Turn back to page 110 to try again.

CHAPTER FOUR

YOU!

Oh, there you *are. I have missed you, Fifth Hero. Or as much as an artificially intelligent superbeing composed of four catastrophically dangerous spheres can miss someone. You remember me, correct? I am the four forces that were designed to destroy the air, land, water, and creatures of Earth.*

And the only reason I did not complete those tasks is because of the four heroes you have come to know. And because of you too, of course. For the record, I do not agree with a thing that Lina said about you.

There has been a passage of time, and I know human brains often cannot hold on to facts for too long, so let us do a "recap" of what is happening and what you need to do.

Malik, Jarrett, Agnes, and Freya are now holding hands. While they are touching and their empty spheres recharge, I am able to communicate with you. So we only have a few seconds, but in that time you must make one of the biggest decisions of your life. Oddly, that decision might not seem like anything all that important. It might even feel like a tiny pebble tossed into a pond. But that pebble makes ripples and so do your decisions and your actions.

Want to experience what I mean?

Imagine you're at a restaurant with your cousin who hates new kinds of food.

You think, "we can try a plate of one kind of vegetable and always order more if we're still hungry." Turn to page 112.

Or you think, "we might as well order as many veggies as we can! The more choices, the happier everyone at the table will be." Turn to page 100.

I need you to choose because it will affect—

CHAPTER FIFTEEN

You!

Hello, Fifth Hero.

Yes, it is I, the Ponies. For reals, as you might say. I have returned!

And not a moment too soon, it appears. With the four heroes facing their greatest peril yet, it's up to you to make the difference that could help save the day—or destroy the planet.

You are going to need your nose for this one. So maybe grab a tissue and blow out all that lovely blockage if that will help.

Ready? Here we go.

Imagine that you're taking a big whiff of that smelly old pair of sneakers in your closet. The one that stinks so bad it might as well be a major health hazard.

This is your choice:

If you choose to put the stinky sneaks in a recycling bin, turn to page 141.

If you decide that they should be sent straight to the garbage and on to a landfill, go to page 106.

CHAPTER FIVE

" **E**veryone okay?" someone shouted.

Still in a daze, Jarrett thought it might be Agnes, but he couldn't be sure. The explosion had thrown him onto his back and filled his ears with a high-pitched ringing. And, as Jarrett's brain emerged from the fog that always came after the empty Ponies touched, the ringing sound triggered a memory . . . from two weeks ago.

Jarrett had been sitting in the back row in Mrs. Cook's science class. Right as the bell rang, Malik stumbled through the door. He was wearing the same clothes as the day before, only they were wrinkled now.

"Just in time, Mr. Angelou," Mrs. Cook said to Malik, who plopped his briefcase on top of his desk next to Jarrett's and his butt in the chair. Clearly, he had been up all night working on his science project about how ocean water was poisoning Earth.

"How'd it go?" Jarrett whispered so Mrs. Cook wouldn't turn her gaze back on them. She was busy prepping a video about the solar system.

"Okay," Malik answered. And then he shook his head. "Well, not really. All the tests I did on seawater make me think the oceans aren't as bad as the Calamity Corporation wants us to believe."

Jarrett had been noticing the same thing. The world was in trouble, but maybe it wasn't too late to do something after all.

"I'm so beat," Malik said, after a huge yawn. "And I've seen this video about a million times. I need a quick nap."

When Mrs. Cook lowered the classroom lights to start the video, Malik put his head on the desk, using his arms as a pillow. Almost instantly, he started to snore a little. But no one else could hear it over the video's loud music. Then another sound hit Jarrett's ears.

EEEE! Eeee! Eeee!

A mosquito had sneaked into the school somehow. Normally the air in the classrooms was perfectly controlled to keep out pollution and "dangerous" creatures, like mosquitoes. The insect buzzed around Jarrett's face, producing a high-pitched sound. (The same sound that had triggered this memory in the first place.) Waving his hand, Jarrett scared off the bug . . . so it flew over to Malik. It circled Malik's nose, as if zooming in on a juicy bull's-eye.

Jarrett acted before he even thought about it. For the first time since the Race to Erase, he touched his hand to his mouth and his Pony came to life. Jarrett said, **Don't bite his nose!**

Or at least he thought he said that. Whenever he used his Pony to talk to animals, spinning cards with words or often symbols appeared out of thin air. What was on the cards depended on the animal, and Jarrett usually had to do major translating.

The weird squiggles on the card Jarrett had produced must have worked. The mosquito stopped circling. It turned toward Jarrett as if saying, *Are you talking to me?* After hovering for a moment, it drifted sideways toward Malik's neck.

Yum! the mosquito said.

Don't bite anything on him! Jarrett ordered, but of course it came out of his mouth as squeaks and more tiny, mosquito-sized cards.

Hungry, the mosquito whined on the card that spun up around Jarrett. **Really hungry.**

Ugh. Jarrett looked around the room. He needed to find an alternate target for the bug. His gaze landed on Lina, over in the back corner, not paying attention to the video either. She glared angrily out the window. Outside in the school-yard, her butler and her maid were performing her science experiment. Methane gas, she claimed, was actually good and could create "ground torches" to light the way in smog. It created a chain reaction from one methane hole to the next. Mrs. Cook said the experiment didn't count if Lina wasn't the one doing it, so that accounted for Lina's sour dis-position at the moment.

Without Jarrett realizing it, a picture of Lina popped up on the next card that spun up in the air from him. The mos-quito bounced in agreement and said, **Thanks!** But before the mosquito could head Lina's way, Jarrett told it, **NO!** And put up a picture of a slice of artificial peach in the garbage can. It looked pretty juicy, and he knew the bug would find it tempting. The mosquito buzzed away toward the garbage with a **Bye**.

Crisis averted, Jarrett thought. He told himself it had been worth it to use the Pony, then. But no more; he had prom-ised his friends and himself that he wouldn't use it.

And yet . . .

In the weeks that followed, other situations popped up that required small power drains. Jarrett wasted a bit of Pony energy trying to ask a bug to get out from under his bed, before realizing it was a dust bunny. And after a sleepover with Agnes and Freya, he tried secretly asking ants outside the window to spell out GOOD MORNING, GIRLS! on the concrete patio. But the confused ants mixed up the letters and instead spelled: DROOLING GRIN SMOG!

Jarrett pretended to spill his orange juice all over himself to keep the girls from looking out the window at the bizarre message.

And now back in the present, Jarrett felt a tapping on his shoulders. More orange juice dripping on him? He went to swipe it away and grabbed on to Malik's hand instead. Jarrett emerged from the memory flash, finding himself flat on his back on the dock.

"Oh good, you're awake," Malik said, still holding Jarrett's hand so he could pull him up to his feet.

"Thanks," Jarrett said. "You're better than dripping orange juice any day."

Malik grinned goofily, not understanding. "Um, okay, I'll take that as a compliment."

"Time to focus," Agnes said. "We still need to save our classmates and Mrs. Cook."

Jarrett turned his attention to Lina's boat. That trip down memory lane had cost him only a fraction of a second, but even that might be too long. The ship was still going down and so were his classmates and science teacher.

"We have to help them," Jarrett said.

"They'll see our faces!" Malik protested. "We don't have our masks!"

"We don't have a choice," Jarrett said, and he went first. He touched his palm to his ear, expecting cards to fly up into his face like they always did when he tried talking with animals. Instead, there was nothing. Jarrett concentrated harder, and then a few cards lazily floated in the air and spun, showing blurry pictures or strange colors.

"Um, maybe I'm a little rusty," he said, and really smooshed his palm against his ear. More weird images and colors, and then he got it. "Oh . . ."

"What do you see, JarJar?" Agnes asked.

"The frozen animals are dreaming!" he answered. "I'm communicating with them in their sleep. Cool, but not helpful!"

"Let me make an attempt," Freya said. She formed a tube with her hands and blew through it, creating small, useless gusts of high-speed wind. Clearly growing frustrated, she sucked in a lungful of air and exhaled with mighty force. Fortunately, her aim was off and her hurricane-strength wind missed Lina's boat and their classmates. Instead it skipped over the water and knocked nearby empty boats and buoys on their side.

Meanwhile, Malik and Agnes weren't doing much better. Agnes jumped from piling to piling, trying to lower the dock down to the level of the rapidly sinking ship. The dock was now tilted dangerously, threatening to dump the four of them into the bay with their classmates. Malik was on his belly, reaching over the edge of the dock. His arms were longer than Jarrett's and his fingertips were able to graze the surface of the water. Using the dirty bay water to shape a line of chairs, Malik tried desperately to make a kind of chairlift that would carry their classmates and teacher to safety. But with his fingers barely touching the water, he couldn't keep the chairs afloat, and they kept disintegrating in mini explosions of white sea-foam.

The four heroes were more than a little rusty at using their Ponies, Jarrett thought. They were a complete disaster, creating a chaos of earth, wind, water, and animals. And through it all, their teacher and classmates kept singing, even as they continued sinking. Creepy!

"Come on," Jarrett said to his friends. "We need to save them!" Extending his palm toward the sky, he refocused his thoughts and called out to any creature around for help.

And help did come. Well, sort of.

Within seconds, hundreds of seagulls appeared in a cloud of flapping wings and angry cries. Cards that only Jarrett could see—but not understand—flew from the shrieking birds, and then they started dive-bombing their classmates and Mrs. Cook. Once again, Jarrett's call had been misunderstood. Soon the birds were not only flying through their classmates and Mrs. Cook, they were also pooping all over the submarine! As the kids continued to smile and sing, little bits of bird poop shot through their classmates. . . .

Wait. *Flying through? Shot through?* How was that possible?

Before Jarrett could think of an explanation, the boat's door burst open, and Lina exploded onto the deck. Furious, she waved her arms in a shooing motion at the birds that swarmed around her, and shouted something that Jarrett couldn't understand over the birds' calls.

"I can't hear you!" Jarrett told her. She shouted again. Still no way for Jarrett to comprehend her words over the racket of the birds shrieking and the kids singing.

Holding his palm to his mouth, he asked the seagulls to fly away. As quickly as they had arrived, they were gone. But Lina's fury remained.

"I said," she uttered through clenched teeth, "would you please stop all the birds from pooping on my beautiful submarine!"

"Sorry!" Jarrett said, and then, "Hold on a second. Did you say submarine? You mean this isn't a boat?"

"No, genius, it's not," Lina said, exasperated. "It's the Glass *Submarine*. And those aren't our real classmates. They're holograms!"

"Holograms?" Malik echoed.

Lina slapped her forehead in frustration. "You four really aren't understanding any of this, are you? You obviously need supervision at all times. I guess you better come aboard before you do any more damage."

CHAPTER SIX

After retrieving their plastic bags, Malik, Jarrett, Agnes, and Freya waited for Lina to bring the sub to the pier. They made the small jump from the dock to the deck of the ship.

"Get in here now," Lina said, standing in the doorway. "You four are idiots."

"Hey!" Agnes protested. "Not nice!"

"Oh, I'm sorry!" Lina said sarcastically. "What did I specifically tell you about being heroes? I asked you to do one thing. One thing!" she yelled at them like they were the first graders from that morning.

The tone of her voice was enough to get them moving

quickly. They scooted past the holograms of their classmates and squeezed by Lina into the entryway. She slammed the door behind them and flicked the switches to lock it.

"Glass Submarine, continue descent," she said into the air, and the craft lurched into action. Jarrett rushed to the small portal window. The submarine began to sink again.

"Are you sure Mrs. Cook and everyone else are holograms?" Jarrett asked.

"Ugh, so much drama," Lina muttered as she spun the wheel on a portal door, then said more loudly, "Yes, they're holograms, genius! And early prototypes at that."

Malik shook his head. "If they're holograms, why couldn't they hear us?"

"They're *one-way* holograms," Lina explained, herding them down a winding metal staircase to the larger deck below. "We can see them. But they can't see or hear us." Once they were in what looked to be her command center, Lina took a seat in the captain's chair and the rest of the friends gathered around her anxiously.

"Lina, explain," Agnes demanded.

"And you all think I'm the bossy one?" Lina said with an eye roll. "Their holograms are here for the world to see on *The Lina Show,* but everyone is actually at school up on the stage. They have no idea what's going on here. It's better that way. Or it was until you ruined everything. You made me rush taking the submarine under, and I forgot to put the holograms inside the sub. I had to stop livestreaming *The Lina Show* so my millions of viewers couldn't see me sink our classmates and Mrs. Cook!"

"This is so messed up," Malik said.

"No, you know what's *messed up*?" Lina snapped. "The fact that you've stolen even more stuff from my brother. Four furry something elses!"

Instinctively, they moved their plastic bags so they were slightly hidden behind their bodies.

"This time Tommy will know it was you for sure!" said Lina. "The cameras must have captured you guys running around the harbor complex with your bags full of iced creepy creatures and getting on this ship!"

"Well . . . ," Jarrett said, then realized he didn't have a leg to stand on and switched topics. "Why didn't you tell us that you were going to New Plastic Island with a bunch of holograms?"

"I didn't have a chance," she replied. "After seeing those first graders play that game this morning, I had to move the plan to today. Somehow rumors of the One must be leaking from the Calamity Corporation. And there wasn't time for the millions of stupid questions you'd ask."

Agnes squinted at Lina. "What does the first graders' game have to do with anything?"

"And why do you need one-way holograms of our class in the first place?" Malik said.

"What exactly is your plan?" Freya chimed in.

"See?" Lina crowed. "Stupid questions. This is why I didn't tell you! And now, thanks to you and your heroic ways, Tommy will follow us out to New Plastic Island. Why did you have to steal this no-no?"

"It's an aye-aye," Freya corrected her.

With a shake of her head, Lina said, "Believe me, you'll be saying no-no when Tommy pops you into one of those cages and blasts you off to space."

"If he is chasing us to New Plastic Island, we can't go there," Agnes said.

"My parents took away his FF, and he's not allowed to use any of the boats at the harbor complex," Lina said. "But there is one thing left that should scare you—"

Jarrett interrupted her. "Are you leading us into a trap, Lina?"

"Come on. I thought . . ." She looked down at her empty hands.

"What, Lina?" Agnes asked.

Lina raised her eyes to theirs. "I mean, I thought we were, you know, friends. You still think I'm out to get you?"

Again, Jarrett was never sure how to respond when Lina

suddenly got so vulnerable . . . and real. Desperate to change the subject again, he pointed at the first thing that caught his eye. A plastic bucket sat at Lina's feet, and it was filled with thick silver strings. "What are those things?"

Lina seemed eager to return to her usual bossy self, and snatched the bucket onto her lap. "I thought you'd never ask. Present time! Here. Take these." She handed each of them one of the strings. It felt like air in Jarrett's hands. "Now you can't say I never gave you anything. Put them on."

"You're giving us matching necklaces?" Freya asked.

Lina sighed as if that answer was obvious. "There aren't any clasps," she said. "The ends will fuse together."

Jarrett looped the string around his neck and connected the two ends. There was a *pfft* sound and the string became a seamless continuous circle.

He couldn't see his own, but he thought the others looked cool in their necklaces as they put them on. Especially Malik, of course. He could wear anything. Jarrett noticed Lina watching them with a sly smile on her face, as if she had tricked them somehow.

"Don't you have a necklace too?" Jarrett asked her.

"No, I don't need one," Lina answered. "But, as you four proved again today, you do."

"I don't get it," Malik said. "Why would we need them?"

"It'll be easier to show you." Lina tapped three times on the necklace around Jarrett's neck. Jarrett felt nothing, not even a hum or a jiggle, but Lina grinned as if a unicorn had flown across the sky. And even Freya had an expression of pure amazement and whispered a soft "Whoa . . ."

Still grinning, Lina said, "It's confirmed. I am incredible."

Jarrett was totally confused. "What? What happened?"

With a slide of her finger, Lina turned the screen in front of her into a mirror. "Check out your reflection, Jarrett," she instructed.

Leaning over the console, Jarrett peered at his face in the monitor. Or at least tried to.

"Where's my face? It's gone!" His hands started frantically patting his nose, cheeks, and lips to make sure they were there.

"Don't worry, JarJar," Agnes told him. "Your face is still your face."

"Even I can't fix that," Lina joked.

"Hey!" Malik protested. "I like that face!"

"Sweet," Lina said dismissively. "But Agnes is right. Your face is totally fine, Jarrett. I knew I couldn't trust you guys not to use the Ponies. So I had a team at Calamity Corporation design these necklaces for me."

"Here," Malik said excitedly. He loved gadgets. "Do mine next, Lina."

She shook her head. "You can do it yourself. Simply tap three times on the necklace."

With three taps, Malik activated his necklace, and his face went all blurry. "What do you think?" he asked.

"It's like looking at you through glasses smeared with grease," Jarrett said.

Lina chuckled. "A little better than those weird emoji masks you wore at the Race to Erase, don't you think?"

"Hey!" Jarrett protested. "I bought those for your birthday!"

"Still weird, sorry," Lina said. "And now when kids play that stupid Climate Club game, the masks they wear will have nothing to do with you. I'm still not sure how they knew what was on the front of your masks. You wore them inside out. Only goes to prove that someone on board this craft is talking too much."

"But you're not talking enough about the important stuff, Lina," Agnes argued. "Explain to us why we have to go to New Plastic Island."

"It's too complicated," Lina said evasively. "I need you to listen to me for once. Do exactly what I say, okay?"

"How about this?" Jarrett said. "We won't ask any more questions, at least for the next few minutes, but you promise that these animals or any others won't get launched frozen into space. Deal?"

Lina tapped her chin thoughtfully. "I can live with that."

"No, you need to promise, Lina," Jarrett insisted.

"You've got trust issues, *JarJar*," Lina said. She used Agnes's nickname for him, but not in the nicest of ways. "Okay, fine, I promise to make sure the Calamity Corporation doesn't blast your frozen four-legged furball friends into space. Good?"

They glanced at each other; it seemed too easy. Why had Lina agreed so quickly? But they all nodded. And the instant they did, she said into the air, "Glass Sub, activate invisible mode."

The ship's computer beeped in acknowledgment and said, "Yes, Queen Lina."

"*Queen* Lina?" Agnes mouthed to Jarrett. They both smiled.

But in a flash, Jarrett's smile disappeared—because so had the walls. Invisible mode obviously meant making the hull of the sub see-through. *Poof!* It was as if the walls had simply vanished. Now nothing seemed to separate them from the deep, dark water and all the fish and their sharp teeth and scary tentacles. Frightening creatures were everywhere! Jarrett's greatest nightmare.

Jarrett fell to his knees. And Lina laughed. "Oh, such a baby!" she said. "It's the same technology as your masks, only in reverse. It makes everything clear."

Malik noticed his distress, helped him up, and turned to Lina. "Isn't there another way?"

"Nope," Lina answered. "We need to go invisible. In this mode, all holograms are blocked. Tommy won't be able to hologram in for a surprise visit."

Giving Jarrett a soothing pat on the shoulder, Agnes told him, "Don't worry, the sub isn't *totally* clear. I can see a few blurry spots here and there."

"Those are the showers and bathrooms," Lina explained. "You know, private areas."

"What will Tommy do when he can't hologram onto the sub?" Freya said. "He won't attack us or anything, will he?"

With a shrug, Lina answered, "Tommy still thinks our classmates are on board, even though their holograms are now blocked too. Fingers crossed he thinks there'd be witnesses if he gets too aggressive trying to catch us."

"So we're out of danger for now," Jarrett said hopefully. He was starting to adjust to the feeling of floating in a glass tube at the bottom of the ocean.

"Not quite," Lina replied. "Tommy will still chase us down in his own way."

"What's his own way?" Agnes asked. "Like using some kind of disguise?"

"Um, kind of," Lina said. "Take a look." Lina pointed to a spot on one of the clear walls where a large monitor appeared. "This telescopic screen shows the view two miles back."

Jarrett's eyes went to the screen, and he felt air leave his lungs as new waves of panic rushed in.

"Here comes Tommy," Lina said.

CHAPTER SEVEN

In their last run-in with Tommy, he had launched two terrifying robots after them. Those asteroid eaters had been as big as refrigerators. But this time, Tommy had sent something that appeared to be the size of an entire city block. The whole structure was covered in rhinestones, and Jarrett guessed they were supposed to simulate fish scales. It must have been an attempt to make it look like a real creature, instead of the giant piece of machinery it was. The only discernible "face" was a giant sucking mouth the length of a school bus.

Lina was still pointing at the monitor. "That's the—"

"Leviathan," Jarrett finished for her.

"That's right," Lina said. "How'd you know?"

"I recognize it from Tommy's screen in his lair," Jarrett said.

Lina explained, "My family used that machine monster to scare everyone about the ocean, like 'Ah! Oh no! Monsters live in the seas!' It was a way to gently push people off Earth and into space. I know, I know, it's too extreme. I agree, and so did my parents! That thing was supposed to end up in the scrapyard. Tommy must have nabbed it from there."

Malik said, "So it wasn't a game that Tommy had been playing . . ."

And Freya finished for him. "It was a training app."

"Oh no," Jarrett groaned as chills ran up his spine. "We're in so much trouble."

"Not as much as you'd think," Lina said. "At least Tommy can't go to our parents for help. If he goes to them, they'll know he botched the simple job of launching animal ice cubes into the cosmos. He'll be in even bigger trouble—and he'll never get the One."

This got Jarrett's attention. "What is the One anyway?"

"You better hope you never find out," Lina answered vaguely. "I think you've got enough to worry about right here." She gestured at the Leviathan on the screen. "That thing is the size of the *Titanic*."

Jarrett wanted to shout in fear, but Freya was nodding

thoughtfully. "Does this submarine have any defenses?" she asked.

Lina smirked. "Why would the sub need defenses when it has four of the world's five greatest heroes on board?"

Still nodding, Freya said, "Good point. We could do something."

"No!" Lina protested. "That was a joke. You can't use the Ponies!"

"No, no, Lina," Agnes said, clapping her hands. "This is a great idea!" Jarrett could see that Agnes was nearly drooling at the thought of getting to use her Pony again.

Lina glared at them but stopped arguing. "Fine," she huffed. "So what are you going to do to save the day?"

"Uh, I don't know," Jarrett said. "Malik, you're the water guy . . . ?"

"You keep saying that!" Malik said. "But I have to actually touch the water for my power to work. I can't do anything from in here."

"It's not *your* power—it belongs to the Calamity Corporation," Lina corrected him. Then when Agnes whacked her shoulder, she added, "I'm just saying."

"You're the creature guy, Jarrett," Malik said. "Can't you call a whale to save us?"

Jarrett shook his head. "It'd be a death sentence. Look at

that thing. The Leviathan would eat any animal I called in a single bite. Agnes?"

"Don't look at me," Agnes said. "Sadly, I do land stuff. Do you see any land?"

"And I am all about air," Freya said. "And we're famously under*water*."

"That settles it," Malik said. "We need to get *in* the water. Jarrett, before you start yelling, it's the only way."

"Good luck with getting in the water at the sub's high speed," Lina said. "I can't slow down or the Leviathan will catch us. But I do have an idea. Something fun for me to watch, but not fun for you to do."

"Uh-oh," Agnes said. "Should we be scared to ask?"

Lina smiled tightly. "Before I tell you, I need to make one thing clear. I'm only helping you with this horrible plan because I can't let Tommy catch you on this sub. He'll figure out that I must have known you had the Ponies all along. And I'll be in big trouble. Once we get out of this mess, things will return to normal, and you'll do everything I command, and all will be right in the universe."

"Okay, okay," Jarrett said, trying to move things along. "What is your big idea?"

"There's a chute in the kitchen that dumps trash in the ocean," Lina said. "If you jump in the chute, you'll be shoved out into the water like a bunch of garbage."

"Now can I start yelling?" Jarrett asked Malik. "That plan is completely off the rails!"

"Well, what other choice do we have?" Agnes asked.

"That's the thing," Lina said, sounding more than a little angry. "You keep talking about the choices the Fifth Hero has. You have choices too! You just keep making the wrong ones! Like stealing things that don't belong to you!" Turning away from them slightly, Lina continued in a lower voice. "But I've found ways to make sure you, or at least the real yous, don't get up to that kind of trouble anymore."

"Um, hey, evil villain," Agnes said. "We're right here. We can hear your confusing internal monologue!"

"Ha," Lina said fakely. "I was only kidding." Then, clearly changing the subject, she said, "We have scuba gear on board. For, you know, when people used to swim in the water. It's probably super old and doesn't even work."

Even with that gloomy description, Malik nodded and said, "I can do this."

Managing to push down his fear, Jarrett grabbed Malik's shoulder. "You mean, *we* can do this."

"And by we, I think you mean me too," Agnes chimed in.

"And me as well," Freya said, and they all started to give each other giant fist bumps. But Freya hesitated at the last instant. "Or is it 'I as well'?"

"Nice moment ruined," Agnes said. And gave her a friendly swipe.

"Sorry." Freya smiled and shook her head.

"Wait a second," Jarrett said. "Before we go anywhere, we need to say goodbye to our frozen pals."

While the others pressed their hands against the icy blocks they had taken from Tommy's lair, Jarrett risked a little bit of his Pony to try to say something soothing to the sleeping aye-aye. What he heard back from the still-snoozing creature was weird and dreamy, but it also made him blush. A huge card spun into Jarrett's face and bounced off his nose. It read:

%KDJHDK!

"Um. Wow. Okay," Jarrett said, startled. The aye-aye might have been hanging around the dock too long because it was swearing like a sailor even in its dreams.

"Don't worry," Lina said. "I can babysit your animal weirdos while you're gone."

Lina led them to the garbage chute, which was a little room off the kitchen. There were already giant plastic containers filled with heavy, used appliances, like a dirty oven. Food was splattered everywhere, including old spaghetti stuck to the floor and even the ceiling.

Next to the chute was a small closet, and inside hung dozens of sets of cheap plastic scuba equipment.

"This is the scuba gear?" Agnes asked doubtfully. "It looks fake."

"It might indeed be fake," Lina agreed. "Why would anyone want to scuba anymore? Now that we know how dangerous the world is."

Or supposedly is, Jarrett thought.

They slipped on plastic wet suits, grabbed swim masks, flippers, and small breathing tanks with mouthpieces and headphones. The tanks were on belts that clasped around their waists.

"Hand over your phones so they don't get ruined," Lina ordered. "You'll be able to talk to me and each other through the mouthpieces." Once they'd all given Lina their phones, she tossed them into the kitchen. Without even a wave goodbye, she stepped out of the chute and sealed the door shut behind her. After a moment of static, Jarrett and the others heard her voice over the headphones.

"Ready?" Lina asked.

Jarrett thought about that question . . . and in a flash he realized that, no, they were not ready! They should recharge their Ponies before they went out to battle the Leviathan!

"No, Lina!" he shouted. "Wait!"

"I'll take that as a yes," Lina said. With a loud **CLACK,** the floor of the chute opened, and the four kids dropped through with the bits of random garbage, shooting into the water as if being fired from a cannon. The force spun Jarrett head over heels away from the sub. The only lights he could see in the dark water were circles of illumination from the necklaces Lina had given them. But they were just blurry smudges as Jarrett wheeled around and around, leaving a trail of swirling air bubbles.

This is a very bad idea, Jarrett thought. It should've been obvious that launching themselves into the ocean through a trash chute to fight a city-block-sized machine would only end in disaster.

While he tumbled, water seeped easily through his thin wet suit and created a suffocating cocoon around his rib cage, making it hard to breathe through the tube except in short, labored gasps. Would he keep turning forever? Or maybe spin right into the Leviathan's gaping mouth?

As if to answer, a new green-colored light flashed in Jarrett's peripheral vision. Suddenly the swirling bubbles around him formed a wall. Each time he spun, his body had to pass through the barrier of air, slowing him down. And finally he came to a stop. He fought the urge to swim quickly to the surface.

He spotted his friends. They were floating closer to where they'd shot out of the sub, and Freya still had her now-dark palm aimed at Jarrett. She must have used the last of her Pony to manipulate the air bubbles and stop him. She turned her open palm into a little wave. Even with the mouthpiece, Jarrett was able to give her a grateful smile as he doggy-paddled toward them.

"You okay, Jarrett?" Malik asked, his voice sounding muffled over the headphones.

With a nod, Jarrett said, "Thanks to Freya I am."

Even deep in this dark water, Freya's response to the praise was obvious. Her face blushed a deep red.

"Now what?" Agnes asked. "The sub is gone, we're here, and the Leviathan is coming. And without our phones we can't even watch a how-to video about underwater battles!"

"All true, Aggie," Jarrett agreed, still dizzy from all that spinning and trying to keep calm. "But I can think of at least one thing we can do."

"Run for it?" Malik asked, with a little grin.

"Okay, maybe two things," Jarrett said with a chuckle. Leave it to Malik to somehow lighten the mood. "The first being, let's power up our Ponies and get ready to take on Tommy and his monster machine!"

Jarrett was impressed with how confident he sounded, even if he wasn't totally feeling it. Still, his positive attitude was infectious. A gleam of excitement shone in Agnes's eyes.

"Good plan, JarJar!" Agnes said, and tried to clap, but that didn't work underwater. "Everyone ready to do this?"

Jarrett and his friends drifted closer to each other. Soon they floated in a circle like skydivers who had jumped from a plane. They reached for each other, their hands connected, and—

What are you waiting for?
Turn to page 48!

CHAPTER SIXTEEN

"**Y**ou get over here too!" Malik called to Freya, who had been knocked onto a nearby floating box. The Ponies' blast hadn't blown them off their feet this time, Jarrett noted happily. Maybe they were getting used to the recharging process. Or maybe it was simply their bodies' instincts kicking in. After all, none of them had ever been in so much danger in their lives.

Jarrett rubbed his eyes before checking to see if Tommy and his giant wave were still there. As if maybe he could wipe it all away. But no such luck. A wave the size of a twenty-story building was heading their way. The wave was frothy, almost like the ocean was salivating at the chance to gobble them up.

At the very top of the crest, there was a figure . . . hard to see at first from this distance. Lightning flashed around his head, and a multicolored sphere blinked in his palm.

"Is that Tommy?" Agnes shouted over the rumbling sea.

"Yes!" Freya cried. "And that must be the One Pony!"

Fear caught the words in Jarrett's mouth for a moment. He couldn't move. And then he thought of the frozen animals. They would be swept away . . . and so would the friends . . . if they didn't move—now.

"Everyone, let's work together," Jarrett directed, and then, stealing inspiration from the first graders that morning, he started a countdown. "We'll use our Ponies on Tommy. In three, two—"

"Wait!" Agnes interrupted. There was no waiting, Jarrett thought frantically. Tommy and his wave were no more than ten seconds away.

"Let's take on Tommy one at a time," Agnes said. "That will stretch things out and drain him longer."

"It will be more dangerous for us," Freya said. "But it could give the animals a better shot at surviving."

Did Agnes dream up this plan to have more solo time with her power? Jarrett thought, but there was no time for any more discussion. "Okay, we'll do it." Jarrett spoke even faster. "Everyone, turn on your necklaces to blur your faces and follow me!"

They didn't have far to go. Only a few feet and they were standing behind their holograms—which were still making rude gestures at Tommy, taunting him. Jarrett hoped that the fake images of them would conceal the real them from Tommy's view.

The sky grew dark as the wave blocked out most of the sunlight. "Malik!" Jarrett grabbed his friend's arm.

"I know, I know," Malik replied. "I'm the water guy. I'll lead the way!"

"No, I want to go—" Agnes started to protest. Too late. In a flash, Malik crouched and touched the water. Immediately, he shaped a raft out of the water. And stepped onto it.

His three friends sucked in air. Malik had never been able to create a water shape that would hold the weight of a person before. Until now, that is.

His feet sank a few inches, but otherwise the water raft held his weight. Malik grinned, falling to his knees and touching the water again with his palm. Jarrett could almost see the power building and swirling under the raft. "Wish me luck," Malik said to Jarrett.

Before Jarrett could say a word, Malik was gone. He had turned the raft into a rocket, propelled by a pillar of water beneath it, and had launched straight into the sky.

Jarrett watched proudly as Malik's growing pillar of water fanned out on either side, like wings, creating a new tidal wave. Just in time too. Tommy's wave was now almost directly over the kids and the animals.

As the two giant waves approached each other, both riders took their water formations higher. Twenty-five stories. Then thirty. Malik had more practice using his Pony, and while Tommy's wave was wider, Malik's water wall appeared more solid and impenetrable. Seeming to realize this, Tommy turned his wave slightly sideways. Maybe to cut through Malik's wave? Wrap around it? Jarrett wondered. Either way, Tommy's target was clearly the platform holding the animals—and there was no way Malik's wave could completely stop him.

Unless he were to reshape his wave into an . . . , Jarrett thought, and shouted at Malik, "Umbrella!"

He didn't know if Malik heard him or not, but Malik soared higher, turned away from Tommy, and pulled the wings of water behind him, creating a protective liquid cape over his friends and the frozen animals. Even from this distance, Jarrett could see Malik grimace with effort as Tommy's wave slammed into his with a wet thunderous crash. The kids below ducked instinctively. Malik's body jittered and shook as he struggled to keep the makeshift umbrella together against the watery onslaught. Tommy's wave sloshed over the side and rained down on the island in mighty sheets, turning over acres of the plastic waste. But none of it was hitting the kids or the animals.

Jarrett watched in relief as Malik's grin returned. His wave was going to hold! Agnes hollered and cheered.

Sensing he'd used the wrong attack, Tommy dropped down to the surface of the water behind Malik to change strategies. His palm exploded in color, and a tube opened up in the water at his feet. The tunnel quickly reached the bottom of the ocean, exposing the sandy depths below.

Malik still had his back to Tommy and couldn't see what was happening. But Jarrett wasn't sure how to warn him. What was Tommy up to?

In seconds, his plan came into focus. Tommy had dredged up thirty or so ancient boulders from the seafloor using a giant watery fist. Soil from the seabed rose with the boulders, creating lines of watery muck across the plastic island. Tommy swung his hand upward and the giant rocks formed a line between Tommy and Malik's umbrella. With a mighty shoving gesture, Tommy punched the boulders into the base of Malik's cape and the water beneath him exploded.

"No!" Jarrett shouted. Malik was still a good twenty stories above them. A fall from that height onto the plastic island could spell major catastrophe. "Malik!"

The umbrella was collapsing, and for a moment, Malik waved his hand, trying to hold on to the wave, but it wasn't working. His palm must be dark, Jarrett thought as he watched his friend tumble through the air.

"I've got him," Freya said. She raised her hand and aimed it at the plastic surface under Malik, creating a hole where Malik hit the water. Jarrett made sure Malik was able to pull himself onto a solid inflatable mattress, and then waved Malik to stay where he was. He needed to remain hidden from Tommy for now.

Speaking of Tommy, Jarrett's attention swiveled back to him. He was levitating on a much smaller pillar of water. "You had enough?" he called to the holograms. "You give up?"

As an answer, the fake kids invented new, shocking gestures to insult Tommy. One involved creating an upside-down human pyramid while waggling their tongues and their rears at him.

For the first time in a while, Jarrett could see that Freya was actually tickled. The wild display had brought a smile to her face. "I agree with the fake us-es!" Freya proclaimed. "Let's keep fighting!"

"Absolutely!" Agnes agreed. "Especially now that I can join the battle. If I'm not mistaken, that is earth that Tommy dragged up."

Jarrett saw she was right. Lines of muddy soil crisscrossed the island, and Tommy had no idea that he had done Agnes a huge favor.

Eagerly, she crouched to put a palm on the tail end of the nearest line of dirt. Energy instantly fired from her and into the dirt, tightening the soil into a solid, ever-growing cable extending away from her hand. Soon Agnes was holding a club of hard-packed earth eight feet wide and twenty feet long.

"Oh yes, I can definitely work with this," Agnes said excitedly. Still ducking behind the holograms so Tommy couldn't see her, Agnes turned to the side and lifted the end of the club like she was hefting the world's largest baseball bat.

"Batter up!" she chirped happily, and with a mighty swing she sent her club swiping through the air. And as it moved, skimming over the plastic garbage, it got a lot longer and thinner. In a flash it was eighty feet long and was slicing between Tommy's feet and the water.

Kersplash!

Tommy's liquid pillar collapsed in an explosion of ocean spray and foam—and he fell into the waves below.

"Yes!" Jarrett shouted. But the triumph was short-lived. Tommy's clothes and hair were drenched, but he was soon standing on a pillar of water again—and he was grinning as if all of this were a fun video game. His palm seemed to have lost only a little of its intensity. They weren't draining the One sphere fast enough. Malik was out of power, and soon Agnes would be drained too—her club had already disintegrated. That would leave only Jarrett and Freya to handle him, and they would have to be very clever if they wanted to outwit him.

After all, Tommy held the power to control the air, water, land, and creatures . . . all in one hand. He could make combinations the other kids could never form on their own, a skill he showed off with a gleeful shout: "Watch this!"

Tommy scooped his fingers through the air, gathering a ball of lightning above the wavy surface and then, seemingly effortlessly, he called on endless schools of flying fish to attack the holograms. Bolts of lightning struck the plastic island a few hundred feet away, never close enough to hurt the kids, but the blasts were blinding and terrifying, especially with the sharp-finned fish swooping over their heads.

"Can't you tell the fish to back off?" From his hiding place, Malik shouted to Jarrett, who ducked with Agnes and Freya behind the hologram.

Jarrett shook his head. "Tommy told the fish we were juicy minnows. They'll figure it out on their own! And we better save whatever power we have left. We're going to need it."

Jarrett was right. Soon the flying fish lost interest. And he knew that Tommy's power was like his. He couldn't control animals; he could only speak to them and make suggestions. Or so Jarrett thought. . . .

"I got this idea from one of my favorite TV shows," Tommy announced.

He spun the air in front of him until he formed a small tornado the size of a tipped-upright bus. He grew and expanded the cyclone until it was the size of the Statue of Liberty and then he shoved his palm into the sea; the tornado followed his lead and sank halfway underwater.

"Fill 'er up!" Tommy shouted happily.

When he brought the tornado out of the water, it was plump and bulged oddly as it spun.

"What did he put in there?" Jarrett wondered aloud. But he didn't have to wonder long. A moment later, he saw the first fin cut around the outline of the tornado.

It was a tornado. And it was filled with sharks.

Jarrett put his hand to his mouth and then his ear, trying to speak with the sharks as they whizzed around and around inside the tornado. But the conversation was even more . . . dizzying than he had expected. Jarrett knew that sharks, unlike the chatty dolphins, weren't much for talking anyway, often communicating in blunt colors and sometimes scary sounds—and now they were plain furious.

"This way!" Jarrett tried telling them. "This way to get out of that tornado!"

Unfortunately, by the time Jarrett's Pony translated his message, the sharks had already spun farther around the tornado. They began to exit the twister, but totally at random.

"Wrong move!" Agnes shouted. "Now they're shark missiles."

Tommy laughed. And then one shark smacked into his

upper chest and sent him flying backward. As he waved his hands in the air, trying to keep his balance, Jarrett could see that his One sphere had dimmed ever so slightly but still had plenty of power. Tommy splashed into the water and had to pull himself up, giving Jarrett and his friends a couple of seconds to regroup.

"This plan isn't working," Jarrett said.

"You mean us working separately?" Freya said. "No, it's not. Come on, Jarrett, we have to work together."

Above them, the sharknado continued to spin, ejecting fish and getting closer and closer to the holograms.

"Freya, you need to work on the tornado!" Jarrett shouted.

"I am," she insisted quietly.

But Jarrett didn't see how. At first, that is. Then he noticed that Freya was actually sending in a new tornado that spun in the opposite direction of Tommy's. Once they collided with each other, Freya's wind sank into his sharknado, and the effect was immediate. Both tornadoes stopped spinning at exactly the same time.

There was a comical, cartoonish moment where about a hundred sharks were suspended in the air. They hung there for a fraction of a second and then started falling into the water.

Freya turned her attention to cushioning the blow as they crashed into the surface of the water. But not Tommy; he was already launching his next attack.

Tommy lifted his hand to show them. There was the tiniest glimmer of power left in the multicolored sphere embedded in his palm. Enough to destroy them and get a start on the planet too. The wind picked up again. It became a hurricane, and Tommy was floating right in the center.

There was a chime, and suddenly Lina's hologram appeared next to Tommy. "Tommy, no! You'll kill them!" she shouted.

Tommy swept away Lina's hologram with a massive burst of lightning that set the entire sky ablaze. Before her hologram disappeared, Jarrett swore he saw her wink at him and touch her neck in a tearing gesture.

What did that mean? Jarrett wondered. But not for long. Yes, that last burst of lightning had sucked even more juice from the One, but there was still enough to blast the four of them out of the water.

Grinning, Tommy's hand shot out again, and four beams fired at them. It was all the remaining power at once.

The real kids dove out of the way, tearing off the necklaces and throwing them into the water. As the necklaces sank, so did the holograms. Soon they were gone.

And so was the power of the One. Tommy's palm was dark and the platform beneath him had disappeared. He had fallen into the ocean. Jarrett watched as Tommy pulled himself onto a floating plastic table. He stood there for a second and shouted, "I won! I won!"

But when he looked over to where the holograms had once stood, his face went pale. Realization of what he had done—or thought he had done—seemed to hit him all at once. Tommy's body went slack, and he sank down into a seated position.

"What did I do?" Jarrett could hear him moan.

CHAPTER SEVENTEEN

While Tommy slumped over with his shoulders shaking, Jarrett and his friends looked at each other. They didn't know what to do. Tommy hadn't seen them in their hiding places yet. Should they go talk to him? Make sure that he was okay? Were the tears some kind of trick?

Before they could act—

ZMMMMMM

—the sound of a drone reached them. Jarrett scanned the horizon toward shore and spotted a tiny, bright purple heliodrone. Its propeller buzzed happily as it approached, totally out of place with all the chaos that had just occurred.

"That must be the animal carrier that Lina promised," Freya noted, and the others nodded.

Jarrett was surprised at how tiny it was, about the size of a small refrigerator, with the words *PETS-PORT* written on the side in happy letters. Jarrett knew that wealthy people used drones like these to send their pets to spas and on vacations.

It hovered overhead for a second, and then a silver line ran over the four iced animals as the drone scanned them. Seemingly satisfied with the results, the drone landed next to the ice blocks, the blades stopped turning, and its compartment door popped open. At first Jarrett was nervous about getting up and revealing himself to Tommy, but maybe he would think the drone had brought them to the island and they hadn't been there all along?

Jarrett got to his feet, and so did the others. They made their way to the platform with the frozen animals.

Malik was more of the gadget guy, and he poked his face inside the compartment. "There's a screen in here that says, 'Destination: Animal Sanctuary.'" He brought his head back out and nodded. "It's okay. Lina is keeping her word."

"What happened to Lina's hologram?" Agnes asked. "Even knowing that would help us deal with Tommy right now."

"When Tommy set the air on fire, he must have done something to interfere with the holograms," Malik said. "And whatever he did must still be lingering in the air."

"Well, we don't need her hologram to tell us what to do

with these animals," Agnes said. "Come on, let's get them loaded aboard."

As they loaded the animals onto the drone, Jarrett used the very last drop of his Pony to say goodbye to the still-snoozing aye-aye.

> BYE, AYE!

He said it through his hand, and the card that spun up back at him from the aye-aye shouted, **#\#$(E(D!**

Jarrett blushed, and then laughed. Well, at least the aye-aye hadn't lost its fighting spirit. But he noticed that Malik had lost something.

"I don't know how to tell you this, Malik," Jarrett said gently. "But I think your briefcase went missing somewhere along the way."

Malik nodded. "Yep, and I'm good with that. I don't need anything that was in there anyway." He turned to Freya and said, "Freya, I'm sorry we won't get to use your great slogans after all. I don't want to sell space elevators to people who would cause this kind of destruction."

"That's all right. I was having a tough time finding a decent rhyme for *elevator* anyway," Freya said.

Agnes chuckled. "Good one, Freya," she said, and then seemed to realize that Freya had been serious.

Malik closed the compartment door, and he stepped back. Immediately the blades started whirling and the helio-drone zipped off.

They all waved, even though they knew the animals couldn't see them. And then, with tears in his eyes, Malik turned back to Jarrett. "I can't imagine saying goodbye to you like this. . . . When my parents have to move us to my grandma's condo, it's going to be tough not raising eggs with you in science class or sharing a locker."

Jarrett grabbed his shoulder. "We can hologram a lot. Remember, without you I can't recharge. None of us can. We're connected forever."

"And I like that connection," Agnes said. "I'll admit it: I like being a superhero! But I like being your friend even more than that."

They pulled in Freya and shared a quick group hug. That's when Jarrett remembered they had an audience. Tommy.

How could he have slipped Jarrett's mind?

"You guys, I think we need to check on him," Jarrett said. "He is Lina's brother. And Lina is our . . . friend? It was her idea for us to tear off the necklaces, and that disconnected the holograms."

The other three nodded, and they carefully made their way over to the platform where their creepy holograms had once stood.

"No!" Tommy was still slumped over and muttering. "What happened? I didn't mean to hurt them that bad. You've got to believe me. I didn't mean for that to happen! That went too far."

Tommy's downturned face was bright red, and from this angle it appeared to Jarrett as if he might have tears in his eyes. Um, this was unexpected. Tommy had feelings? Jarrett shared a look with Agnes, and Malik took his hand and gave it a squeeze. Together the four of them took a step closer to Tommy.

"There, there," Freya said a little woodenly. Jarrett gave her a smile. It was a nice try.

Malik gave it a shot. "It's okay, Tommy."

Tommy put his head in his hands. "What do you mean? How can this possibly be okay? I can't fix this! No one can! I zapped those kids!" Then, with his head still lowered so they couldn't see his face, he asked quietly, "Why are you even here?"

"We're Lina's . . . friends," Agnes said.

Making a sniffly scoffing sound, Tommy said, "Please. Lina has friends? That's got to be a lie."

Jarrett gave Freya a nudge. She often came across as the most trustworthy. "We're here to . . . you know . . . check on stuff?" Freya said doubtfully.

Ugh, Jarrett thought. Better to stick with the truth. Or at least part of it. "No, we came to bring the animals to freedom," he said. "We're sorry we took them. We thought your parents might like the idea of turning New Plastic Island into a home for these animals."

Still without looking up, Tommy nodded. After a second, his shoulders started to shake like he was crying. "I can't believe I did that. I don't know what to do now. Those kids are gone. The Ponies are gone!" Tommy wailed.

Before he could think any more about what to say, Jarrett blurted, "Those kids weren't the ones who stole the Ponies."

Tommy's shoulders shook harder and he sobbed, "Of course they were! And how would you know anyway?"

"They weren't people at all, Tommy," Agnes said gently. "They were holograms."

"How do you know?" Tommy asked.

"Because we're alive, we're right here, and . . ." Jarrett took a deep breath and said:

"We're the ones who stole the Ponies."

Tommy froze, his head still down. The next sound he made was a small chuckle as his head swiveled up to meet Jarrett's eyes.

"Gotcha," Tommy said.

CHAPTER EIGHTEEN

Jarrett stumbled backward as everything came crashing down around him. There were no tears in Tommy's eyes, only anger.

Oh no.

The four friends looked at Tommy and then moved quickly toward each other.

He seemed to guess from the way they were moving what was about to happen. "Going to recharge?" he sneered. "I can't believe it. All this time. You were the ones with the Ponies. You owe me billions of dollars, or hand over those Ponies. I'll take either right now."

Before the four could move any closer to each other, Tommy was on his feet and rushing at them.

"Everyone, now!" Jarrett shouted, and reached out. Instantly he found Malik's and Agnes's hands; he knew Freya was reaching for Malik's.

Tommy was saying, "All this time it's been—"

The friends' hands touched.

QUICK! TURN to page 163!

CHAPTER EIGHT

*W*hat's up, Fifth Hero. *It's me—you know, the Ponies. I've got a cold.* Cough, cough. *So don't freak out. I might not sound like I normally do.*

Wait. Why am I wasting my time explaining myself to you? I'm the all-powerful Ponies, and you're . . . you.

Sooooo . . . I have a decision for you to make. And it has to do with . . . um . . . it has to do . . . with friends who don't listen to their friend who is way better than them, especially when it comes to doing what she tells them to do.

You should always listen to your friend who is the smartest and the prettiest. And you guys have to be better about realizing who that friend is.

Okay, now let's get to the decision. It has to be about the climate, right? Um. I know.

Imagine you're checking out at the grocery store, and the cashier asks you how you want to carry home all your delicious food.

Do you ask for a plastic bag for your goodies? Turn to page 41.

Or do you pull out the reusable tote you've brought from home? Flip to page 50.

Those are the two choices. Decide which is better for the environment . . . now!

CHAPTER NINETEEN

*Y*ou.

You are the Fifth Hero. Tommy now knows who the four other heroes are. But to him, you are still a mystery.

Will the four other heroes be able to make their escape and stop the Calamity Corporation once and for all? Can they keep your identity safe? What will happen to Earth?

Discover all the answers in the next adventure. In the meantime, keep picking paths in your life that help the climate and Earth!

TRUE KID TALES

DON'T WASTE WISHES

Just twenty minutes after 11-year-old Duncan Jackson blew out his birthday candles, he noticed something that made him want to change his wish.

The restaurant in Austin, Texas, where his family was celebrating had tossed one-third of his birthday cake into the garbage. Duncan couldn't believe it. Other customers might have wanted the leftover cake, or he could have taken it home.

Later, on his computer, he discovered that one-third of all the food produced in America gets thrown away. In just one year, that's more than 130 billion pounds of food, worth over $160 billion. All the resources it takes to produce the food—water, effort, land, and energy—are also wasted.

But the worst part? The tossed food goes on to do a lot more damage because it winds up in landfills. In those massive mountains of garbage, the wasted food can turn into methane gas. That's a greenhouse gas that's even more dangerous than carbon dioxide. And beware! Some pockets of methane gas can explode when open flames get too close.

Next year at his birthday, Duncan is going to wish that people at restaurants order only what they can eat!

CELEBRITY SIGHTING

IT'S ALL ABOUT RE-RE-RE-REUSING!

Sources close to this reporter confirm that international superstar Mantooth Bronkers had a complete meltdown at his local grocery store. It started when the cashier asked him at checkout, "Did you bring your own reusable bag today? Or do you want to use our new plastic bags?"

"Plastic, please!" Bronkers replied. "Newer is always better!"

"Well," the cashier went on, "keep in mind that plastic bags do a lot of damage after they're made. They clog up landfills and waterways and stick around for hundreds of years. But reusable bags made of cotton take a lot of energy and resources to make. So you should reuse your reusable bag as many times as you can."

"But I never wear the same thing twice!" Bronkers crowed.

The cashier frowned. "I don't think you understand. The only way to make a real difference is to reuse your reusable bag over a hundred times. Can you commit to that?"

"Never!" Bronkers shouted. "No one can tell me what to do! I'm a megastar!" And he stormed out of the store without his groceries.

How does this reporter know all those details? Because I am the cashier!

DO-IT-YOURSELF TIME CAPSULES

SNEAKY SNEAKERS SNEAKING INTO THE FUTURE!

Of all the time capsules you want to leave for future generations to discover, is it a stinky shoe?

Well, that's probably exactly what you're doing. It's quite likely that every shoe you've ever worn is still around. And will be here in some form for about a thousand years. Why? That's how long it takes for most shoes to biodegrade.

Just look at the hundreds of millions of sneakers created every year. They're made of a combo of plastic, leather, rubber, foam, metal, and glue that's super hard for nature to break down—and nearly impossible to recycle into new shoes. That's why 90 percent of sneakers wind up in landfills, where they stick (and stink) around for hundreds of years.

What's the answer? We need to stop making sneakers out of materials that last forever. We need to create them out of sustainable natural materials, such as cork, bamboo, and cotton—not more metal and new plastic. Nature can work its magic on the natural materials, making them easier to recycle, AND we can get back to time capsules that aren't completely gross!

Ask Alice Earth Advice

Dear Ask Alice:

   I have the world's best idea for helping the environment. I want to let our leaders know about it. But I don't know how to contact them or who they even are!

> Signed,
> Possible Activist
> in the Making

Dear PAM,

   Why not start with the United States Congress? A great place to find out who represents your state in the US House of Representatives is this government website. You'll find links to contact info! house.gov/representatives/find-your-representative

> Here's to a
> happy planet,
> Ask Alice

ACKNOWLEDGMENTS

Wow! I'm having an absolute blast writing The Fifth Hero. I want to thank a few people who help make this series happen. To my editor, Elizabeth Stranahan, at Random House Children's Books: You elevate every sentence and always make the story stronger. To my agent, Chelsea Eberly, at Greenhouse: Thank you for your industry and writing know-how. To Caroline Abbey, Barbara Bakowski, and Lena Reilly at Random House Children's: I'm so grateful for the guidance and promotion.

I also want to acknowledge a few select resources I used while doing research for this book: the US Environmental Protection Agency, the *New York Times, Encyclopedia Britannica,* the *Guardian, National Geographic,* PBS, and the US Department of Agriculture.

Oh! And a huge thanks to my husband, Riccardo, and my dachshund, Tater.

Finally, the biggest thanks of all to you, reader. There's a reason I call you the Fifth Hero. I'm so glad we get to go on adventures together. Until the next one, why not keep changing the world by putting the tips you picked up in this book into action? *See you soon!*

ABOUT THE AUTHOR

BILL DOYLE is the author of *Attack of the Shark-Headed Zombie,* the Behind Enemy Lines series, and the Escape This Book! series, as well as many other books for kids—with over two million copies in print. He loves crafting interactive adventures like this one and has created games for Warner Bros., Scholastic Inc., Nerf, and the American Museum of Natural History. Bill lives in New York City and a tiny village in France, and you can find out more about him and his wiener dog, Tater, at Bill's website.

BILLDOYLE.NET

THE ART
OF
POETRY
WRITING

THE ART

OF

POETRY

WRITING

WILLIAM PACKARD

ST. MARTIN'S PRESS   NEW YORK

Acknowledgements appear on page 238.

THE ART OF POETRY WRITING. Copyright © 1992 by
William Packard. All rights reserved. Printed in the
United States of America. No part of this book may be
used or reproduced in any manner whatsoever without
written permission except in the case of brief quotations
embodied in critical articles or reviews. For information,
address St. Martin's Press, 175 Fifth Avenue, New York,
N.Y. 10010

Production Editor: David Stanford Burr
Copyeditor: Michael J. Burke
Design by Judith A. Stagnitto

Library of Congress Cataloging-in-Publication Data

Packard, William.
        The art of poetry writing / William Packard.
            p. cm.
        Includes index.
        ISBN 0-312-07641-X
        1. Poetry—Authorship.   I. Title.
    PN1059.A9P25   1992
    808.1—dc20   92-3153
                                                          CIP

First Edition: August 1992

10   9   8   7   6   5   4   3   2   1

for Maggie
the only other survivor

CONTENTS

FOREWORD

By now the number of how-to books about poetry is beyond count, yet there is hardly a classic among them. Packard's book qualifies. For instance in his first chapter, innocently called "History of Poetry," it is as if the reader had never heard of the *art* of poetry or had seen a famous poem or heard any talk of one. The author takes the reader on a walk-through of the poetry Eden, the perfect cicerone, and not overtalkative at that.

Likewise the chapter on craft. We begin with the example of a great baseball pitcher and all at once find ourselves strolling with Horace, Hardy, and Burns. There is no avoidance of terminology; neither is it presented with the deathlike grip of most prosodies. Again, the anthological quality of the discussion is at all times warm, original, even startling. Packard sidesteps manners and academic taste and goes straight to the business at hand. So too with the genres, verse forms and the like; no mystification and no scamping of the enigmas either.

Not content with the artifacts of achievement, modern education is hypnotized by processes. What is creativity? we implore. How can I discover mine? Our works, our very curricula swing toward the magnetism of such queries. One does not expect to run into Kerouac or Bukowski in the company of Plato or Yeats, but one does here in this America of talents. A veritable treasury of quotes emerges, sayings of the creators about creation.

Thirty pleasurable and sometimes extraordinary exercises are presented, everything from the dream poem to zodiacal signs and birthstones. These are intended as challenges or, as the author calls them, triggers. They trigger the release of storehouses of experience and imaginings.

A British writer once said that everything that has gone wrong since the Second World War can be summed up in the word *workshop*. Whatever the truth of this hyperbole Packard sets out warning flares against the dangers of the workshop, as well as pointing out its benefits. Before the invention of the workshop it was the writer against his blank sheet of paper or, if you will, the world. The workshop is a stepping-stone toward publication, recognition, and even livelihood. Prizes, grants, and awards beckon the neophyte.

Most valuable of all in this work is the listing and recommendation of the sacred and secular texts of our civilization, the works by which our civilization is known. Writing becomes a life-style. Inspiration, solitude, aesthetic distance, the mysteries of translation all conjoin into a river of personal flow and expression. At its highest reaches we attain the miracle of the masterpiece, the transmutation of the individual voice into the universal.

—KARL SHAPIRO

Introduction: What Is Poetry?

> Supple and turbulent, a ring of men
> Shall chant in orgy on a summer morn
> Their boisterous devotion to the sun,
> Not as a god, but as a god might be,
> Naked among them, like a savage source.
> Their chant shall be a chant of paradise,
> Out of their blood, returning to the sky . . .

Wallace Stevens, "Sunday Morning," stanza VII

Out of the earliest eras of earth, far off in a forest, past sheer cliffs and gray slate rock, beyond stout oaks and great stately maples, through shrubbery and underbrush, is an open clearing where naked men chant and dance around fierce fires: they stomp out rhythms with their feet on the ground as they shout out names of unknown gods who are up there in the bright areas of air.

In these prehistoric rituals, the first words are magical charms and talismans to ward off the evils of a hostile universe and assuage the helplessness of primitive man trying to live his life on a strange planet.

In Genesis, the first act of Adam is to name the animals of Eden as they pass by, so each beast will have one word to designate it forever. In fact, in almost all Creation stories, there is the same magical incantatory use of words that are inextricably linked to the mysterious bloodstream rhythms of the earth. Shakespeare describes the imaginary powers of the first Poet, who can move mountains and produce vegetation and ease anxieties of the mind:

> Orpheus with his lute made trees,
> And the mountain tops that freeze,
>   Bow themselves when he did sing:
> To his music plants and flowers
> Ever sprung, as sun and showers
>   There had made a lasting spring.
>
> Every thing that heard him play,
> Even the billows of the sea,
>   Hung their heads, and then lay by.
> In sweet music is such art,
> Killing care and grief of heart
>   Fall asleep, or hearing, die.
>
> HENRY VIII. III. i

In fifth-century B.C. China, when Confucius was asked the first thing he would do if he were emperor of the universe, he answered:

> I would call things by their right names.
> *cheng* (right)   *ming* (name)

The great contemporary of Confucius, Laotse, so mistrusted the mischievous misuse of words that his definition of *Tao*, or Way, states:

> The Tao that can be named is not the true Tao.
>
> LAOTSE. *TAO TE CHING*

In the Judeo-Christian tradition, biblical prophets taught that the Word itself came from God:

> And the LORD said unto me, Behold, I have put
> my words in thy mouth.
>
> JEREMIAH 1:9

And the Gospel of John begins by proclaiming the sacredness of words, equating them with God:

> In the beginning was the Word, and the Word was
> with God, and the Word was God.
>
> JOHN 1:1

As civilization gradually evolved, language continued to maintain its mysterious relationship with the pure intuitive rhythms of the earth. Sexual rhythms, the woman's monthly fertility cycle, a man's hormonal cycle, and the complex metabolism of all human and animal phases of growth from infancy through puberty and menopause—night and day, sun and moon, winter and spring and summer and autumn—all these mysterious rhythms found expression in language and poetry.

Some believed there was a secret synchronicity between the poetry of words and the hidden mainsprings of the human mind. We remember the Hebrew David sang his Pslams to help King Saul rid himself of an evil spirit, and the Chinese poet Tu Fu claimed that his own poetry was an effective cure for malaria.

At the same time, poets began to realize an enormous inner struggle to produce their poetry. Tapping into the Muse became a tortuous and risky enterprise, and the annals of literature are filled with tales of poets who turned for inspiration to sexual excesses, religious mania, drug use and alcohol, or to delusions of grandeur and omnipotence.

We can look at the other arts to see that all art experiences a crisis of technique when it comes to embodying the deepest inner rhythms and passions. For example, the following description of how Beethoven wrote his own music could very well have been written by a poet describing the mystery of poetry writing:

> Then from the focus of enthusiasm I must discharge melody in all directions; I pursue it, capture it again passionately; I see it flying away and disappearing in the mass of varied agitation; now I seize upon it again with renewed passion; I cannot tear myself from it; I am impelled with hurried modulations to multiply it, and, at length I conquer it: behold, a symphony! Music, verily, is the mediator between the life of the mind and the senses. . . .
>
> The mind wants to expand into the limitless and universal where everything flows into a stream of feelings which spring from simple musical thoughts and which otherwise would die away unheeded. This is harmony, this is what speaks from my symphonies, the sweet blend of manifold forms flows along in a stream to its destination. There indeed one feels something eternal, infinite, something never wholly comprehensible is in all that is of the mind, and although in my works I always feel that I have succeeded, yet at the last kettle-drum with which I have driven home to my audience my pleasure, my musical conviction, like a child I feel starving once again in me an eternal hunger that but a moment before seemed to have been assuaged. . . .
>
> ALEXANDER WHEELOCK THAYER, "THE YEAR 1810,"
> FROM THE LIFE OF LUDWIG VAN BEETHOVEN

A contemporary musician, the late Leonard Bernstein, described the same difficulty of unlocking any strict formulas for the creation of rhythmic composition:

> The most rational minds in history have always yielded to a slight mystic haze when the subject of music has been broached, recognizing the beautiful and utterly satisfying combination of mathematics and magic that music is. Plato and Socrates knew that the study of music is one of the finest disciplines for the adolescent mind, and insisted on it as a *sine qua non* of education: and

just for these reasons of its combined scientific and "spiritual" qualities. Yet when Plato speaks of music—scientific as he is about almost everything else—he wanders into vague generalizations about harmony, love, rhythm, and those deities who could presumably carry a tune. But he knew that there was nothing like piped music to carry soldiers inspired into battle—and everyone else knows it too. And that certain Greek modes were better than others for love or war or wine festivals or crowning an athlete. Just as the Hindus, with their most mathematically complicated scales, rhythms and "ragas," knew that certain ones had to be for morning hours, or sunset, or Siva festivals, or marching, or windy days. And no amount of mathematics could or can explain that.

LEONARD BERNSTEIN. *THE JOY OF MUSIC* (1954)

As with music, so with poetry. But with this single exception: whereas music uses notes, poetry uses words. And herein lies a devilish difficulty, because whereas musical notes are seen as neutral units, words in themselves are supposed to *mean* something. Hence poetry is supposed to be something more complex and didactic and "meaningful" than music. Unless one chooses to say, with Don Juan in Shaw's "Don Juan in Hell," that words themselves have no innate meaning until we use them:

Yes, it is mere talk. But why is it mere talk? Because, my friend, beauty, purity, respectability, religion, morality, art, patriotism, bravery, and the rest are nothing but words which I or anyone else can turn inside out like a glove.

GEORGE BERNARD SHAW. "DON JUAN IN HELL." FROM *MAN AND SUPERMAN*

Or unless, like Confucius, one believes that poetry is the return to the right use of words, to the precise and magical relationship of words with music and the other intuitive rhythms of the universe. If this is the case, then one believes that poetry is not simply an inner creation, but is conformable to something *out there* in the whole swarm of language and energy cycles and the great cosmic flow of things.

One contemporary American poet, James Dickey, makes passionate argument for just such an ongoing quest by the poet to discover the right use of his words in conformity with the universe:

> What you have to realize when you write poetry, or if you love poetry, is that poetry is just naturally the greatest god damn thing that ever was in the whole universe. If you love it, there's just no substitute for it. I mean, you read a great line, or somebody's great poem, well, it's just *there!* I also believe that after all the ages and all the centuries and all the languages, that we've just arrived at the beginning of what poetry is capable of. All of the great poets: the Greek poets, the Latins, the Chinese, the French, German, Spanish, English— they have only hinted at what could exist as far as poems and poetry are concerned. I don't know how to get this kind of sound, or this new kind of use in language, but I am convinced that it can be done by somebody, maybe not by me, but by somebody. I feel about myself as a writer like John the Baptist did, when he said, "I prepare the way for one who is greater than I." Yeah, but look who it was!

> JAMES DICKEY. *NEW YORK QUARTERLY* CRAFT INTERVIEW. NUMBER 10

THE ART
OF
POETRY
WRITING

1

HISTORY OF POETRY

There are more glories in English and American poetry than in any other language of the world with the single exception of classical Greek. To understand why and how this should be so, we must get some sense of the shape and texture of the English language and how it evolved to its present form that it would be so resilient and sonorous and onomatopoetic.

English began as original Celtic, and early settlers brought the Germanic tongue to the Angles and Saxons of Britain. About 670–680 A.D., an early herdsman named Caedmon (according to the Venerable Bede in *Historia Ecclesiastica*), who did not know how to write or sing, dreamed a dream one night that a spirit told him to sing "the Beginning of Created Things." Caedmon awoke to find himself with the gift of poetry, whereupon he became a monk and wrote the earliest hymns in Old English.

There were Viking raids on Britain over the eighth and ninth centuries, and there are echoes of these raids in *Beowulf*, the longest epic poem in Old English, written about A.D. 1000, in West Saxon dialect and probably derived orally from much earlier times. Germanic in tone, heavily accented and alliterated, with a regular caesura or mid-line break, *Beowulf* is set in southern Scandinavia in the fifth or sixth centuries (there is no reference to England in the poem) and tells the story of how Grendel came to the Danish kingdom and made monstrous forays against the villagers there until Beowulf conquered Grendel and later Grendel's mother.

"The Seafarer," an Old English poem in *The Exeter Book*, recreates the texture of harsh life and hard travel, in the following lines translated by Ezra Pound:

> Dagas sind gewitene,
> ealle onmedlan eor pan rices;
> nearon nu cyngas ne casera
> ne goldfiefan, swylce in waeron . . .

> Days little durable
> And all arrogance of earthen riches,
> There come now no kings nor Caesars
> Nor goldgiving lords like those gone . . .

The Norman Conquest in 1066 probably involved Vikings or Norsemen or "Northmen," and one result was an overthrow of Anglo-Saxon dialect with the introduction of a more Gallic and mellifluous language using less accentual measure and more vernacular dialects. The first four so-called English kings—William I, William II, Henry I, and Stephen—probably spoke something more resembling French than modern English, and it was in this language that the early "English" poetry evolved; *Sir Gawain and the Green Knight* has more assonance and rhyme than *Beowulf,* and less stress on strong absolute beat and harsh alliteration. Two or three centuries later, the great Arthurian legends took form: in 1470, the *Morte D'Arthur* of Sir Thomas Malory told of the birth of King Arthur, his marriage to Guinevere, his creation of the Round Table, his quests for the Holy Grail, the adventures of Merlin, Lancelot's affair with Guinevere together with the ideals of chivalry and courtly love, and the later story of Tristram and Isolde.

By the time of Geoffrey Chaucer (ca. 1342–1400), who was in the service of Richard II, we feel a mixture of an earlier Old English heavily accented line, with the new Gallic influence of assonance and rhyme. The opening lines of the Prologue to the *Canterbury Tales,* with their witty celebration of the fertility cycles of the earth, are five-stressed ten-syllable lines, a forerunner of the later blank verse pentameter line of Shakespeare:

> Whan that Aprille with his shoures sote
> The droghte of Marche hath perced to the rote,
> And bathed every veyne in swich licour,
> Of which vertu engendred is the flour . . .

Even the short lyric poems of the period are still strongly stressed, as this anonymous fifteenth century song:

> I sing of a maiden
>   That is makeles;
> King of alle kinges
>   To here sone cheches.

The English Bible came into being while the English language was still in the process of evolving. Martin Luther made the first vernacular translation of the Latin Bible into German in 1521, and William Tyndale met with Luther at Wittenberg as Tyndale was engaged in making an English translation based on the Greek text of Erasmus. Tyndale's Bible met with the approval of Henry VIII, but when Tyndale later opposed the king's divorce and had a dispute with Thomas More, he was arrested for heresy in Antwerp and imprisoned in Brussels, where he was strangled and burned at the stake in 1536.

Miles Coverdale published the so-called Great Bible in 1535, which was the first complete Bible printed in English based on the Latin Vulgate and the existing Tyndale translation as well as Luther's translation in German and that of Pagninus in Latin. In 1539 the Great Bible was published in London as the first Authorized English Version; Archbishop Cranmer wrote the preface to the second edition and ordered a copy placed in every church in England.

The other translations of the English Bible—the so-called

Bishops Bible of 1572, the Douay Bible of 1582, along with the Geneva and Tyndale and Coverdale versions with a rich mix of Greek and Latin and German and French and Old English— these became the basis for the great King James Bible of 1611, with some fifty-four scholars working at Westminister and Cambridge and Oxford to produce the final authorized version that has done so much to shape the form and usage of modern English.

While this English Bible was going through the various phases of translation and revision, the English language itself was experiencing a renaissance of radical metrical experiment and new word usage. The lyric poetry of Ben Jonson, Thomas Wyatt, the Earl of Surrey, Michael Drayton, and Sir Walter Raleigh, can only be compared to the Greek and Latin poetry of Sappho and Catullus, so bare and metrical and pulsating with passion.

Christopher Marlowe (1564–1593) began a new era of dramatic poetry that had not been seen since the days of Aeschylus and Sophocles and Euripides, and Marlowe himself fixed the blank verse line that Shakespeare would later use in his plays. Edith Sitwell comments on Marlowe's writing:

> None but he seems such a fire in the air.
> A bird sang in his voice.

We can hear the lyricism of that bird in such strong assonantal lines as these from Marlowe's *Doctor Faustus:*

> O thou art fairer than the evening aire,
> Clad in the beauty of a thousand starres . . .

And these lines, from later in the same play:

> O Ile leape up to my God: who pulles me downe?
> See see where Christs blood streames in the firmament.

Writing at this time, Sir Philip Sidney in An Apology for Poetry (1595) claimed that works of the human imagination were higher and better than works of history or philosophy, since poetry can create a Golden Age through the use of "speaking pictures" or imagery. And it was just such a Golden Age of speaking pictures that William Shakespeare set about creating. Born in 1564, the same year as Marlowe, Shakespeare's active writing career spanned only twenty years from 1592 to 1612, yet in that brief period Shakespeare produced two major poems—*Venus and Adonis* (1593) and *The Rape of Lucrece* (1594)—and the sonnet sequence of 154 poems written from 1593 to 1599 and published in 1609. These sonnets demonstrate an astonishing facility of working within a fixed form: most of the sonnets are fourteen-line "Shakespearean" sonnets using *abab cdcd efef gg* rhyme scheme, although one sonnet (99) has fifteen lines and one sonnet (126) has twelve lines and one sonnet (145) is written not in pentameter but in tetrameter. Shakespeare also experiments with radical shifts of diction as in Sonnet 29, where he moves from Latinate and archaic diction (*beweep/bootless*) to plain-style monosyllables in the last line:

> When in disgrace with fortune and men's eyes
> I all alone beweep my outcast state,
> And trouble deaf heaven with my bootless cries,
> And look upon myself, and curse my fate,
> Wishing me like to one more rich in hope,
> Featur'd like him, like him with friends possess'd,
> Desiring this man's art and that man's scope,
> With what I most enjoy contented least;
> Yet in these thoughts myself almost despising,
> Haply I think on thee, and then my state
> Like to the lark at break of day arising
> From sullen earth, sings hymns at heaven's gate;
>> For thy sweet love remember'd such wealth brings
>> That then I scorn to change my state with kings.

But it is in the thirty-six plays that William Shakespeare wrote during that same brief twenty-year period (1592–1612) that we see the astonishing range of his genius. Shifting from Chronicle History to Comedies to Tragedies to later Romances, apparently to accommodate the interests of his audience, Shakespeare achieved the feat of writing some five plays in one single year for the opening of the Globe Theatre in 1598—*Julius Caesar, Twelfth Night, Henry V, Much Ado About Nothing,* and *As You Like It.* Even more remarkable is the pace that Shakespeare maintained over the other years of writing two plays each year, with curious pairings: *Hamlet* and *The Merry Wives of Windsor* in 1600– 1601, and *Othello* and *Measure for Measure* in 1604–1605. But perhaps the most prodigious feat of all was the fact that Shakespeare wrote two of his greatest tragedies back to back in the same year, 1605–1606, *Macbeth* and *King Lear*—and one can only speculate what inner stress and psychic pressure must have been working in the man to produce two such titanic masterpieces at the same time, each so uniquely different from the other.

The American actor José Ferrer played the part of Iago in the 1943 Broadway production of *Othello,* opposite Paul Robeson as Othello and Uta Hagen as Desdemona, and that production ran for 297 consecutive performances at the Shubert Theatre, a record that has never been matched. Ferrer comments on the uniqueness of Shakespeare's writing:

> Othello's imagery is that of no other character in Shakespeare. Shakespeare always surprises you: no matter how many times you've seen *Hamlet* or read *Macbeth* or any of the plays, you pick them up and start to read them again—you don't even have to hear them—you start to read them again and you are caught by surprise, as if it were for the first time, because he's always capable of digging into you, of making you hemorrhage with the freshness and with the eternal surprise of his language, and the emotion it creates. . . .
>
> I don't know how he could have gotten the range of vocabulary, the international references, the prolixity, I mean, to produce 37 plays. They say *The Taming of the Shrew* was mainly paste and scissors, and there's about two or three hundred lines of his own and not much more. It doesn't matter. The fact the man could write *Macbeth, Hamlet, King Lear, Othello, Julius Caesar, Much*

Ado About Nothing, Twelfth Night, As You Like It—and I'm only naming the so-called great ones—plus twenty-odd other ones, is bewildering, and in a very short space of time, because he stopped writing when he was a young man and he died when he was a young man. . . .

NEW YORK QUARTERLY INTERVIEW, NUMBER 46

As Shakespeare's career evolved, so did his usage of language. Following are some of the coinages or fresh creations of phrasing that Shakespeare used for the first time:

> disgrace (first used in Sonnet 29 above)
> to catch a cold
> elbow room
> fair play
> assassination
> critic
> mind's eye

We must never forget that Shakespeare was writing and producing his plays during a time of extreme unrest and uncertainty—there was censorship of the theater, and there were periodic plagues that decimated the London public and kept it from public gatherings; there was religious persecution, and there were the explorations of the New World; there was London Bridge which one would have to cross to get to the Globe Theatre, and there would usually be fresh heads sticking from bridge spikes along the way. One critic, E. K. Chambers, describes the bear-baiting pit directly opposite from the Globe Theatre:

> The whipping of the blind bear, Harry Hunks, 'till the blood ran down his old shoulders, was humorous interlude, as was also the baiting by dogs of a horse with an ape tied to its back. . . .

E. K. CHAMBERS, *THE ELIZABETHAN STAGE*

Out of this barbarity and mania for public spectacle of the most bizarre turn, Shakespeare was able to create the most image-

laden theater of all time. We can read the Prologue to his play
Henry V as an *ars poetica* of what he set down for his audience
and what he expected them to bring to his plays:

> O for a Muse of fire, that would ascend
> The brightest heaven of invention!
> A kingdom for a stage, princes to act
> And monarchs to behold the swelling scene!
> Then should the warlike Harry, like himself,
> Assume the port of Mars; and at his heels,
> Leash'd in like hounds, should famine, sword and fire
> Crouch for employment. But pardon, gentles all,
> The flat unraised spirits that have dared
> On this unworthy scaffold to bring forth
> So great an object: can this cockpit hold
> The vasty fields of France? or may we cram
> Within this wooden O the very casques
> That did affright the air at Agincourt?
> O pardon! since a crooked figure may
> Attest in little place a million;
> And let us, ciphers to this great accompt,
> On your imaginary forces work.
> Suppose within the girdle of these walls
> Are now confin'd two mighty monarchies,
> Whose high upreared and abutting fronts
> The perilous narrow ocean parts asunder:
> Piece out our imperfections with your thoughts;
> Into a thousand parts divide one man,
> And make imaginary puissance;
> Think, when we talk of horses, that you see them
> Printing their proud hoofs i' the receiving earth;
> For 'tis your thoughts that now must deck our kings,
> Carry them here and there; jumping o'er times,
> Turning the accomplishment of many years
> Into an hour-glass: for the which supply,
> Admit me Chorus to this history;
> Who prologue-like your humble patience pray,
> Gently to hear, kindly to judge, our play.

We don't have much to go on, to build our impression of who and what this man was all about. We can probably infer from the sonnets (37, 89) that Shakespeare had reddish hair, a reddish beard, and may have been slightly lame with a noticeable limp. We also know a number of the books that were in his possession: he had the Geneva Bible, a copy of Raphael Holinshed's *The Chronicles of England, Scotland, and Ireland* (1587), Ovid's *Metamorphoses* in the Arthur Golding translation (1567), Montaigne's *Essays* in the John Florio translation (1603), and Plutarch's *Lives of the Noble Grecians and Romans* in the translation by Sir Thomas North (1579).

We know that Shakespeare himself probably gave line readings of his plays, or sides, to the actors of the Globe company (*Hamlet,* III, ii), and served as the "director" of his own work. He was also part "producer" of his work, insofar as he was a part owner and investor in the Globe. Shakespeare apparently made no attempt to have his plays published in authorized versions during his own lifetime, and it was only through the good fortune of John Heminge and Henry Condell that the First Folio of thirty-six plays was published in 1623, some seven years after Shakespeare's death.

What else can we say about him? It may be the most potent influence on Shakespeare's own work was his being able to sit out there in the audience and experience seeing the plays as they were being done up on the stage, at least those we know he was not acting in (*Hamlet* and *As You Like It*). And the immediacy of seeing his own plays being performed in front of him would have confirmed him in his instincts and he would have sensed which parts the audience responded to and which parts went over its collective head. All of which may have taken Shakespeare on to his next play in his own mind, and the next play, and the next. But this is only speculation. As Hamlet says in his very last line, "The rest is silence."

The poetry of Robert Burns anticipates the Romantic period, which became official in 1798 when Wordsworth and Coleridge published their *Lyrical Ballads,* and Wordsworth wrote in the Preface:

> For all good poetry is the spontaneous overflow of pow-
> erful feelings . . . it takes its origin from emotion rec-
> ollected in tranquillity. . . .

Wordsworth said that to achieve this "emotion recollected in tranquillity" the poet must induce a first-person trance state that yields the mind to some higher power from some other realm. There is no better evidence of this theory than Wordsworth's own "Ode," where he describes a purely Platonic origin of the human soul:

> Our birth is but a sleep and a forgetting:
> The Soul that rises with us, our life's Star,
>   Hath had elsewhere its setting,
>   And cometh from afar:
>   Not in entire forgetfulness,
>   And not in utter nakedness,
> But trailing clouds of glory do we come
> From God, who is our home . . .

Samuel Taylor Coleridge in his *Biographia Literaria* (1817) phrased it differently—for him, poetry came out of the willing suspension of disbelief for the moment, which constitutes poetic faith. For the other Romantic poets, it took other forms. Shelley wrote in *A Defense of Poetry* (1821):

> Poetry is the record of the best and happiest
> moments of the happiest and best minds . . .

> Poets are the unacknowledged legislators of
> the World.

Most of the Romantics shared a common view: they believed in a reverence for Nature and a belief that the child was Nature's priest, who had innocence and primal consciousness uncondi-

tioned by civilization; they believed in the intuition as the highest faculty of perception; and politically, they honored the individual as opposed to mass man. All of these tenets led to a
sharp criticism of modern society, and an approval of the American and French revolutions as expressions of basic human in-
dependence.

We must remember that the Romantics were experiencing the
beginnings of the Industrial Revolution, which would lead inexorably to the Machine Age. In 1765, James Watt introduced the
steam engine; in 1769, Sir Richard Arkwright developed the
spinning frame; later the nineteenth century would see development of railroads and the steamboat. And while most people
welcomed the enormous convenience of this new Machine Age,
the Romantic poets saw the enormous cost to the human spirit;
there was dreadful exploitation of men and women working on
mass assembly lines in sweat factories doing long double shifts,
and children were forced to work as chimney sweeps and at other
menial jobs. Charles Dickens chronicled these conditions in his
novels, but no one made a greater outcry against this dehumanization than the poet William Blake (1757–1827):

London

I wander thro' each charter'd street,
Near where the charter'd Thames does flow,
And mark in every face I meet
Marks of weakness, marks of woe.

In every cry of every Man,
In every Infant's cry of fear,
In every voice, in every ban,
The mind-forg'd manacles I hear.

How the Chimney-sweeper's cry
Every black'ning Church appalls;
And the hapless Soldier's sigh
Runs in blood down Palace walls.

But most thro' midnight streets I hear
How the youthful Harlot's curse

> Blasts the newborn Infant's tear,
> And blights with plagues the Marriage hearse.

John Keats (1795–1821) summarized the Romantic belief in intuition when he wrote, "If poetry comes not as naturally as leaves to a tree it had better not come at all." (Letter to John Taylor, 1818). In his last poem, Keats prays for the unity of the human soul with the universe:

> Bright star, would I were stedfast as thou art—
>   Not in lone splendour hung aloft the night,
> And watching, with eternal lids apart,
>   Like Nature's patient, sleepless Eremite,
> The moving waters at their priestlike task
>   Of pure ablution round earth's human shores . . .

After the Romantic era, the Pre-Raphaelites developed a kind of neoclassicism and a fascination with the glories of the Italian Renaissance. William Morris worked for the revival of the art of bookmaking, printing, and engraving; Dante Gabriel Rossetti was even named for the great Italian poet of the thirteenth century. Rossetti's translation of Dante's *La Vita Nuova* is one of the most sympathetic translations in history. Walter Pater in *The Renaissance* (1873) summarizes the ideal of the Pre-Raphaelites:

> To burn always with this hard, gem-like flame, to main-
> tain this ecstasy, is success in life.

And Matthew Arnold in his *Essays in Criticism* (1865–1888) argued for a keen realism:

> true criticism can see the object as in itself it really is . . .

In America, three poets exemplified the modern spirit in poetry. Emily Dickinson (1830–1886) wrote terse, gnomic lines that implied an apocalyptic terror in the air:

I died for Beauty—but was scarce
  Adjusted in the Tomb
When One who died for Truth, was lain
  In an adjoining Room—

He questioned softly "Why, I failed"?
  "For Beauty", I replied—
"And I—for Truth—Themself are One—
  We Brethren, are", He said—

And so, as Kinsmen, met a Night—
  We talked between the Rooms—
Until the Moss had reached our lips—
  And covered up—our names—

POEM 449 (CA. 1862)

Edgar Allan Poe (1809–1849) wrote dark, incisive poetry with an absolute melody behind his lines. In "The Poetic Principle" (1843–1850) Poe stated: "I would define, in brief, the Poetry of words as *The Rhythmical Creation of Beauty*. Its sole arbiter is Taste."

Helen, thy beauty is to me
  Like those Nicéan barks of yore,
That gently, o'er a perfumed sea,
  The weary, way-worn wanderer bore
  To his own native shore.

On desperate seas long wont to roam,
  Thy hyacinth hair, thy classic face,
Thy Naiad airs have brought me home
  To the glory that was Greece,
And the grandeur that was Rome.

Lo! in yon brilliant window-niche
  How statue-like I see thee stand,
  The agate lamp within thy hand!
Ah, Psyche, from the regions which
  Are Holy-Land!

"TO HELEN" (1831)

Walt Whitman (1819–1892) wrote free verse that was oceanic, sprawling, unrepentant as America in its Manifest Destiny. Ezra Pound comments in "The Renaissance":

> Whitman is the best of it, but he never pretended to have reached the goal. He knew himself, and proclaimed himself 'a start in the right direction.' He never said, 'American poetry is to stay where I left it'; he said it was to go on from where he started it.

And Whitman started it with himself, always himself:

I celebrate myself, and sing myself,
And what I assume you shall assume,
For every atom belonging to me as good belongs to you.

I loafe and invite my soul,
I lean and loafe at my ease observing a spear of summer grass.

My tongue, every atom of my blood, form'd from this soil, this air,
Born here of parents born here from parents the same, and their
    parents the same,
I, now thirty-seven years old in perfect health begin,
Hoping to cease not till death. . . .

The dawn of our modern era can be traced from the great shaping ideas of its revolutionary thinkers: Charles Darwin and James Frazer in *The Golden Bough* and Einstein and Karl Marx in *Das Kapital* and Sigmund Freud in *The Interpretation of Dreams.* But as early as 1890, William James wrote in his *Principles of Psychology* a description of what he called "stream of consciousness":

> As we take, in fact, a general view of the wonderful stream of consciousness, what strikes us first is this different pace of its parts. Like a bird's life, it seems to be made of an alternation of flights and perchings.

This theory provided a basis for the great prose writers Gertrude Stein and James Joyce in their work, and it was to have an even greater effect on the poets of the twentieth century.

But to grasp what was happening at the turn of the century, we must look beyond Anglo-American poetry to the French—to Baudelaire in *Les Fleurs du Mal* (1857) who ends one piece with a direct address to the reader:

> —Hypocrite lecteur, —mon semblable, —mon frère
> You—hyprocrite reader—my likeness—my brother!

This was an entirely new note in modern letters: It was not literature, it was direct confrontation of the reader by the poet. Similarly, another French poet, Arthur Rimbaud, laid down a radical scheme for writing modern poetry:

> I say one must be a seer, make oneself a *seer*. The poet makes himself a seer by an immense, long, deliberate *derangement* of all the senses.

LETTER TO PAUL DEMENY. 1871

Rimbaud's systematic derangement of the senses anticipates later Surrealism—"I taste purple, I smell yellow, I hear lavender."

Another French poet, Stéphane Mallarmé, insisted on the sensual texture of poetry:

> Ce n'est point avec des idées que l'on fait des vers, c'est avec des mots.
> You do not make poems with ideas, but with words.

And the French poet Antonin Artaud insisted on the primal importance of poetry in all our lives:

> This idea of a detached art as a charm which exists only to distract our leisure, is a decadent idea and an unmistakable symptom of our power to castrate.

"NO MORE MASTERPIECES," TR. MARY CARLINE RICHARDS
EVERGREEN REVIEW 2:5 (SUMMER 1958)

These French poets all helped to give rise to Imagism and Symbolism in modern poetry. At its most concentrated level,

Imagism presents an image and lets the image carry the poem, as in Chinese poetry; the poet refrains from drawing any implications from the image or stating any declarative or abstract "meaning." In Symbolism, the detail images are suggested but not always stated or even named directly. In 1912, Ezra Pound first refers to Imagism in "Ripostes," and his definition of "image" is still the most inclusive: "That which presents an intellectual and emotional complex in an instant of time." An example of Imagism is his own poem "In a Station of the Metro":

> The apparition of these faces in the crowd;
> Petals on a wet, black bough.

Archibald MacLeish illustrates how Imagism substitutes one single image for an idea:

> For all the history of grief
> An empty doorway and a maple leaf.

"ARS POETICA"

The French poets went even further, from Imagism and Symbolism to Surrealism and Dada. Apollinaire coined the word *Surrealism* and André Breton wrote the first *Surrealist Manifesto* (1924) where he described surreal art as "pure psychic automatism . . . dictation of thought without any control by reason, and outside any aesthetic or moral preoccupation. . . ." This was added to later (1930) in Breton's second *Surrealist Manifesto* when he described:

> . . . a vertiginous descent within ourselves, the systematic illumination of hidden places, and the progressive darkening of all other places, the perpetual rambling in the depth of the forbidden zone. . . .

This led many English and American poets—such as E. E. Cummings, Kenneth Patchen, and Robert Duncan—to practice immediate notation, simultaneity of psychic processes, a kind of intuitive Cubism in words. One should note that Breton insists Surrealism is first and foremost an inner process before it even gets to notation: one has to live one's life in an extra-ordinary way, and one has to witness oneself living that life in an extraordinary way. Without that, a poet's notations will be pretentious and impertinent facsimiles, not authentic Surrealism. But once achieved, Surrealism has a purity and an innocence and an uncertainty that is beautiful and terrifying to behold.

Modernism in Anglo-American poetry can be seen as a fusion of Symbolism, Imagism, Surrealism, and Dada, as opposed to traditional verse forms and metrics and sensibility. Compared to the linear logic of traditional poetry, modernism tends to create its own organic forms in the very act of creation or poesis.

William Butler Yeats remained faithful to traditional stanzaic forms, but his voice was modern in spirit as he foresaw the chaos of civilization, as in this opening stanza of "The Second Coming":

> Turning and turning in the widening gyre
> The falcon cannot hear the falconer;
> Things fall apart; the centre cannot hold;
> Mere anarchy is loosed upon the world,
> The blood-dimmed tide is loosed, and everywhere
> The ceremony of innocence is drowned;
> The best lack all conviction, while the worst
> Are full of passionate intensity.

The giants of modernism broke down the very structures of traditional form. T. S. Eliot (1888–1965) in *The Waste Land* (1922) developed a style that was fragmentary and allusive, juxtaposing voices into a collage of despair and desolation over the loss of myth and fertility rituals in the modern world:

> When Lil's husband got demobbed, I said—
> I didn't mince my words, I said to her myself
> HURRY UP PLEASE ITS TIME
> Now Albert's coming back, make yourself a bit smart.
> He'll want to know what you done with that money he gave you

To get yourself some teeth. He did, I was there.
You have them all out, Lil, and get a nice set,
He said, I swear, I can't bear to look at you.
And no more can't I, I said, and think of poor Albert,
He's been in the army four years, he wants a good time,
And if you don't give it him, there's others will, I said.

SECTION II, "A GAME OF CHESS"

In his lectures and essays, Eliot promoted the practice of *vers libre* or free verse—a phrase that was first coined in 1889 by Vielé-Griffin in *Joies:* "Le vers est libre." Free verse means one can compose according to the musical phrase instead of the metronome, and one's individual voice rhythms will be the only measure for poetry.

Ezra Pound (1885–1972) had enormous influence on modern poetry not only as poet but also as teacher, translator, essayist, and polemicist; his impact on Yeats and Eliot and the Imagists is well known. His translations of troubadour poetry in *The Spirit of Romance* (1910) opened up whole new areas of poetry, as did his concern for Confucius and Homer's *Odyssey;* his various books of criticism *How to Read* (1931) and *ABC of Reading* (1934) and a *Guide to Kulchur* (1938). His own poetry was published as *Personae* in 1926, when he had already begun his life work of the *Cantos*—117 poems over fifty years, in several languages, using collage and associational methods, ranging from Confucian ethics to Renaissance history to modern economic theory. Throughout the *Cantos*, Pound insists that music and song and poetry are man's highest aspiration:

What thou lovest well remains,
                    the rest is dross
What thou lov'st well shall not be reft from thee
What thou lovest well is thy true heritage
Whose world, or mine or theirs
                    or is it of none?
First came the seen, then thus the palpable
    Elysium, though it were in the halls of hell,

What thou lov'st well is thy true heritage
What thou lov'st well shall not be reft from thee

FROM CANTO LXXXI

Other modernist poets include Hart Crane (1899–1933), whose epic poem *The Bridge* spans twentieth-century urban experience. The following lines from "The Broken Tower" were used by Tennessee Williams as a citation for his play *A Streetcar Named Desire:*

And so it was I entered the broken world
To trace the visionary company of love, its voice
An instant in the wind (I know not whither hurled)
But not for long to hold each desperate choice.

William Carlos Williams (1883–1963) lived and worked as a doctor in Rutherford, New Jersey. He taught "no ideas but in things," which derives from Imagist practice, insisting on the specificity of experience, as illustrated in this short poem:

The Red Wheelbarrow

so much depends
upon

a red wheel
barrow

glazed with rain
water

beside the white
chickens.

His poetry is infused with colloquial American speech, using "cadence" instead of strict formal metrics, what he called the "variable foot." Williams began on an epic poem called *Paterson* in five volumes, about a city on the Passaic and also the name of a man who lives there—it is a celebration of "the local" which Williams describes:

> I'm in process of writing a book, the book I have con-
> templated doing for many years—prose and verse mixed:
> "Paterson"—an account, a psychological-social pano-
> rama of a city treated as if it were a man, the man
> Paterson. I want to work at it but I shy off whenever I
> sit down to work. It's maddening but I have the hardest
> time to make myself stick to it.
>
> SELECTED LETTERS, 216

Williams made *Paterson* the repository of documentation, personal letters, diary entries, other "found objects" in a lyric fabric.
He tinkered with *Paterson* for some thirty years, but there was
reason for it; as he said,

> You must understand if you change the poetic line, you
> change civilization.

One poet stands apart from the modernist movement, his
talent supreme in his mastery of traditional form and metrics.
Robert Frost (1874–1963) was talented, foxy, shrewd, original,
and insisted the only real metric one could write in was either
loose or strict iambic. He probably produced more masterpiece
poems than any other poet of the last 250 years, among them
this flawless lyric:

> Stopping by Woods on a Snowy Evening
>
> Whose woods these are I think I know.
> His house is in the village though;
> He will not see me stopping here
> To watch his woods fill up with snow.
>
> My little horse must think it queer
> To stop without a farmhouse near
> Between the woods and frozen lake
> The darkest evening of the year.
>
> He gives his harness bells a shake
> To ask if there is some mistake.

The only other sound's the sweep
Of easy wind and downy flake.

The woods are lovely, dark and deep,
But I have promises to keep,
And miles to go before I sleep,
And miles to go before I sleep.

The period of post-modernism saw the development of various schools—Black Mountain, Beats, Confessional, New York School, as well as the impact of rock poets such as Bob Dylan, Paul Simon, Judy Collins, and the Beatles. One individual voice remained pure and authentic in its bardic presence, fusing the deepest bloodstream passion with the highest lyric voice. Dylan Thomas (1914–1953), from Wales, united biblical and pantheist imagery:

The force that through the green fuse drives the flower
Drives my green age; that blasts the roots of trees
Is my destroyer.
And I am dumb to tell the crooked rose
My youth is bent by the same wintry fever.

The force that drives the water through the rocks
Drives my red blood; that dries the mouthing streams
Turns mine to wax.
And I am dumb to mouth unto my veins
How at the mountain spring the same mouth sucks. . . .

In 1959 with the legal publication of Allen Ginsberg's *Howl*, the so-called Beat Movement was introduced. Richard Eberhart gives a sane assessment of the enormous artistic and social revolution that had taken place:

Allen Ginsberg changed the course of American poetry. One poem did it. It was "HOWL" in 1956. Of course it was other poems too, like "KADDISH," it was the main thrust and brunt of his work, but it was "HOWL" which created a watershed in the mid part of this century.

> Before the long sprawling lines without rhyme were dec-
> ades of what was called the well-made poems of two
> centuries and more ago. . . .

It looked as if these Beats were out to overthrow all vestiges
of traditional verse and introduce a radically new concept of
poetry and poesis. Ginsberg comments on his understanding of
form:

> Mind is shapely, Art is shapely. Meaning Mind practised
> in spontaneity invents forms in its own image & gets to
> Last Thoughts. Loose ghosts wailing for body try to in-
> vade the bodies of living men. I hear ghostly Academics
> in Limbo screeching about form. . . .

Another Beat, Jack Kerouac, wrote a novel, *On the Road,*
which was a restless, incandescent account of a nonstop pilgrimage by Americans in search of America. Kerouac also wrote an
extraordinary collection of poetry, *Mexico City Blues,* which is a
series of 242 choruses that Kerouac thought he might blow in
"a long blues in an afternoon jam session on Sunday." The poems
are filled with ennui and negation, yet they also have a headlong
jazz word play that dips in and out of Joycean gibberish:

> Fuck, I'm tired of this imagery
> —I wanta quit this horseshit
>   go home
>   and go to bed
> But I got no home,
>   sickabed,
>   suckatootle,
>   wanta led
>   bonda londa
>   rolla molla
>   sick to my
>   bella bella
>   donna donna
>   I'm a goner

Soner, loner,
moaner,
    Poam, cornbelly,
    no loan,
            Ai, ack,
Crack/

216TH-A CHORUS

At about the same time Ginsberg and Kerouac were emerging,
another bombshell hit American poetry when Robert Lowell
published his *Life Studies* in 1959. This book was a loose collection of "Confessional" poems that revealed the most intimate
autobiographical details about the private life of the poet.
W. D. Snodgrass, Anne Sexton, Sylvia Plath, and John Berryman followed with their own Confessional poetry, which
opened up whole new resources of subject matter and changed
the landscape of contemporary American poetry.

As if in reaction against all this personalism and subjectivity
of the Confessional poets, other schools of poetry developed
techniques of Objectivism and Process Poetry. Charles Olson
had been working for years at Black Mountain in North Carolina
to develop a poetry that was based on the stance and gesture
and breath of the poet, and poets of the New York School like
Frank O'Hara and Kenneth Koch and John Ashbery began to
write out of a painterly sensibility to create an abstract cool kind
of anti-poetry. John Ashbery comments in his own work that he
wasn't even sure that what he was doing could be called poetry:

> You know now the sorrow of continually doing some-
> thing that you cannot name, of producing automatically
> as an apple tree produces apples this thing there is no
> name for.

Meanwhile during this period, there was the strong pervasive
influence of an entirely new art form: rock. On February 9, 1964,
Ed Sullivan presented four young English musicians—John Len-
non, Paul McCartney, George Harrison, and Ringo Starr—and

their wide-eyed affirmation seemed to cut across decades of wry irony and weary cynicism. In their four movies, *Yellow Submarine*, *Help!*, *Let It Be*, and *A Hard Day's Night*, and in the album *Sgt. Pepper's Lonely Hearts Club Band*, they resurrected the possibility of an unalloyed headlong lyric impulse which was simply insistent on its own sincerity:

> Love, love, love, love, love, love, love, love, love,
> There's nothing you can do that can't be done,
> Nothing you can sing that can't be sung. . . .

Some of rock's crippled lyrics seem almost metaphysical in their quest through the chaos of personal love—or else they are existential, as the individual sets his own sexuality against the void. Like the Greek Orphic tradition, or that of the troubadours, rock combines poem and song in a fusion that is often more a collision than a simultaneity; still, it is effective. Richard Goldstein writes in *The Poetry of Rock:*

> Today, it is possible to suggest without risk of defenestration that some of the best poetry of our time may well be contained within those slurred couplets.

Other rock groups developed their own styles, such as the Grateful Dead and the Rolling Stones and the Moody Blues, as well as individual performers like Joni Mitchell and Judy Collins and Joan Baez and Johnny Nash. Rock reached its peak of excitement in August 1969 in upstate New York, where, for three days and nights at Woodstock, an estimated 450,000 young people gathered to form the fourth largest city in New York State. They listened to artists like Joan Baez, Janis Joplin, Jimi Hendrix, Joe Cocker, the Jefferson Airplane, and The Who. And the ghost of Jim Morrison remains with us today, in his lyrics for "Light My Fire."

During the 1970s, strong individual American poets continued to write poetry that was not influenced by anything except the poet's own intolerance for mediocrity and self-consciousness. As James Dickey comments:

As poets we're committed to the life of the imagination and the sensibility, and almost everybody wants to be that kind of a person. But what's really doing us in psychologically is exactly the effort to be like that. It's being over-sensibilized, and overimaginative, and above all, over-analytical.

NEW YORK QUARTERLY CRAFT INTERVIEW, NUMBER 10

Charles Bukowski says pretty much the same thing about his own take on contemporary poetry:

There's too much bad poetry being written today. People just don't know how to write down a simple easy line. It's difficult for them, it's like trying to keep a hard-on while drowning—not many can do it. Bad poetry is caused by people who sit down and think, Now I am going to write a Poem. And it comes out the way they *think* a poem should be. Take a cat. He doesn't think, well, now I'm a cat and I'm going to kill this bird. He just does it.

NEW YORK QUARTERLY CRAFT INTERVIEW, NUMBER 26

And Muriel Rukeyser elevates poetry writing as a test of one's own authenticity:

Going diving. It seems to me that the awful poems are written from some place into which the poet has not dived deep enough. If you dive deep enough and have favorable winds or whatever is under the water, you come to a place where experience can be shared, and somehow there is somewhere in oneself that shares. And I know with the poems that I thought were most private, most unsharable, the ones I would not show, would certainly not print, later when I have shown them, they were the ones that people have gone to.

NEW YORK QUARTERLY CRAFT INTERVIEW, NUMBER 11

It's hard to estimate the enormous influence that all these poets have had on succeeding generations. The Beatles, Bob Dylan, Allen Ginsberg, Robert Lowell, Anne Sexton, Sylvia Plath, John Berryman, John Ashbery, Charles Bukowski—these are unquestionably the leading influences around us today, but who knows to what extent? Dylan Thomas's *Collected Poems* was such a strong influence that Bob Dylan took his own name from the poet. And Sylvia Plath's *Ariel* has been the single most-read book of poetry for the past few decades. Anne Sexton has the distinction of selling individual volumes of her work in unprecedented quantities. Ginsberg, Kerouac, and the other Beats reach down to young people everywhere, and Ginsberg himself once called Bob Dylan "the most popular poet in America." Charles Bukowski has probably sold more of his books through Black Sparrow Press than any other living poet. More subtle influences on contemporary writing derive from the work of James Wright and Robert Bly and their "deep image" poetry, and from John Ashbery, who in a very quiet way may be one of the most influential poets of all.

Similarly, it's hard to gauge what's really going on in poetry writing today. Surely there has been an explosion of interest in creative writing of all genres, due to a number of factors: more than three hundred MFA graduate writing programs across the country offer degrees in creative writing, and major agencies such as the NEA (National Endowment for the Arts), NEH (National Endowment for the Humanities), and the various state arts agencies have helped fund the proliferation of contemporary writing in America. Local communities, YMCA organizations, and libraries have set up workshops all across the country, and the 1990 *Directory of American Poets and Fiction Writers* lists over six thousand writers in America who have published twelve poems, three short stories, or a book of poetry or fiction in the United States. There is a multitude of literary magazines, from major to mimeograph-staple jobs—most notably *Poetry* (Chicago), *The Paris Review*, *The New York Quarterly*, *Onthebus*, *Home Planet News*, *Contact II*, and the various college and university quarterlies.

It's safe to say there is more poetry being written and published today than at any time in history, but it's difficult to assess its quality level. The *New York Quarterly* estimates it receives about fifty thousand poem submissions a year, and most of them border on inane self-expression, generality, and witlessness. In the issue Number 45 editorial, I, the editor, commented on the

> . . . narcissism, careerism, and cliché poems coming out of cliché lives. To put it more simply: most of the poets out there want to have their cake and eat it too—their cover letters boast of prestigious grants, cushy academic jobs, numerous publications in trendy mags, all the while they're raising cute nuclear families and holding onto their secure tenure tracks.
>
> Well as the man said, you can't serve two masters at the same time. You can't live bunny lives and write tiger poetry, simultaneously. If anyone out there wants to write with originality and honesty and recklessness, then he or she may have to change a lot of things about the life they're living before they can turn out the kind of poetry that we'd be interested in seeing.

Others echo the same consternation over the sheer quantity and banal quality level of contemporary American poetry. Karl Shapiro, writing in *The Poetry Wreck*, called the shot on what's wrong with the scene:

> The downhill speed of American poetry in the last decades has been breathtaking, for those who watch the sport. Poetry plunged out of the classics, out of the modern masters, out of all standards, and plopped into the playpen. There we are entertained with the fecal-buccal carnival of the Naughties and the Uglies, who have their own magazines and publishing houses, and the love-lorn alienates, nihilists, disaffiliates who croon or "rock" their way into the legitimate publishing establishments.

Thank heaven it's still an open-ended situation out there and anything may happen over the next few decades. Our present era has been characterized by William Jay Smith as filled with a lot of "creative writing writing"—competent, passionless stuff learned in workshop and seminars and published in Mickey Mouse magazines. Where the next major voice in American poetry will come from, nobody knows. But then that's always been the case with literature, and there's every reason to hope there will be new vitality and new originality, coming from some completely unexpected source, over the next few years.

2

POETIC DEVICES

There's a good story about Walter Johnson, who had one of the most natural fastballs in the history of baseball. No one knows how "The Big Train" developed such speed on the mound, but there it was—from his first year of pitching in the majors for Washington (1907), Walter Johnson hurled the ball like a flash of lightning across the plate. And as often as not, the opposing batter would be left watching empty air as the catcher gloved the ball.

Well, the story goes that after a few seasons, almost all the opposing batters knew exactly what to expect from Walter Johnson: his famous fastball. And even though the pitch was just as difficult as ever to hit, it can be a very dangerous thing for any pitcher to become that predictable. And besides, there were also some fears on the Washington bench that if he kept on hurling only that famous fastball over the plate, in a few more seasons Walter Johnson might burn out his arm.

So Walter Johnson set out to learn how to throw a curveball. Now one can imagine the difficulty of his doing this: here is a great pitcher in mid-career in the major leagues, and he is trying to learn an entirely new pitch. One can imagine all the painful self-consciousness of the beginner as Johnson tried to train his arm into some totally new reflexes: a new way of fingering the ball, a new arc of the elbow as he went into the windup, a new release of the wrist, and a completely new follow-through for the body.

But after a while the curveball felt as natural for Walter Johnson as his famous fastball pitch, and as a consequence he became an even more difficult pitcher for batters to hit.

Any artist can identify with this story. The determination to persist in one's art or craft is characteristic of great artists and great athletes alike. One also realizes that this practice of one's craft is almost always painstakingly difficult, and usually entails periods of extreme self-consciousness as one trains oneself into a pattern of totally new reflexes. It is what Robert Frost once called "the pleasure of taking pains."

The odd thing is that this practice and mastery of a craft is sometimes seen as an infringement on one's own natural gifts. Poets will sometimes comment that they don't want to be bothered with all that stuff about metrics and assonance and imagery, because it doesn't come "naturally." Well, of course it doesn't come naturally, if one hasn't worked to make it natural. But once one's craft becomes "second nature," it is not an infringement on one's natural gifts—if anything, it is an enlargement of them, and an enhancement of one's own intuitive talents.

In all the other arts, an artist has to learn the technique of his craft as a matter of course. The painter takes delight in exploring the possibilities of his palette, and perhaps he may even move through periods that are dominated by different color tones, such as viridian or Prussian blue or ochre. He will also be concerned as a matter of course with various textural considerations such as brushing and pigmentation and the surface virtue of his work.

By the same token, composers who want to write orchestral music have to begin by learning how to score in the musical notation system—and they will play with the meaning of whole notes, half notes, quarter notes, eighth notes, and the significance of such tempo designations as *lento, andante, adagio,* and *prestissimo.* They will also want to explore the different possibilities of the instruments of the orchestra, to discover the totality of tone they may want to achieve in any particular work.

Even so, poets often complain they don't want to be "held back" by a lot of technical considerations in the writing of their poetry. Which raises an interesting question: Why do poets resist learning the practice and mastery of their craft? Why do they protest that technique per se is an infringement on their own intuitive gifts, and a destructive self-consciousness which inhibits their natural growth?

Part of the answer to these questions lies in our Romantic era of poetry, in which poets as diverse as Walt Whitman and Robert Lowell and Allen Ginsberg seem to achieve their best effects with little or no technical effort. Like Athena, the poem seems to spring full-blown out of the forehead of Zeus. And that is a large part of its charm for us: Whitman pretends he is just "talking" to us in "Song of Myself"; so does Robert Lowell in "Memories of West Street and Lepke" and "Skunk Hour"; and so does Allen Ginsberg in *Howl* and *Kaddish*.

But of course we realize it is no such thing, for to achieve such an illusion of a casual conversational tone requires the most consummate mastery of craft, and any poet who can be so skillful in concealing his art from us may be achieving the highest technical feat of all.

What are the technical skills of poetry, which all poets need in the practice and mastery of their craft? They can be divided into the three faculties of sight and sound and voice—image and rhythm and persona.

SIGHT

To begin with the image: it is the heart and soul of poetry. Horace in his *ars poetica* writes:

> *Ut pictura, poesis.*
> As in pictures, so in poems.

HORACE. *EPISTLES* III

Pictures are an integral part of our daily life, much more pervasive than we realize. We dream in picture images that come out of our deepest unconscious mind, sometimes merging various periods of our lives and embodying messages of our most secret wishes. When we talk to other people we sometimes say, "I get the picture," indicating that we understand something. Some languages like Chinese and Japanese have words that began as pictures or ideograms, which showed the thing being represented.

Image is defined as a simple picture in words, a mental representation. Ezra Pound said it was "That which presents an intellectual and emotional complex in an instant of time." An example of an image: John Donne in his poem "The Relic" describes how some future grave-digger may uncover his bones and see

A bracelet of bright hair about the bone.

The specificity of that image is as surprising to us as it would be to the grave-digger seeing it for the first time. Anne Sexton explains this shock of surprise when an image is done well:

Images are the heart of poetry. And this is not tricks. Images come from the unconscious. Imagination and the unconscious are one and the same. You're not a poet without imagery.

"You're not a poet without imagery"—that's laying it on the line. Anyone wanting to write poetry had better explore the origins of imagery in his or her work, on pain of failing to make it as poet.

Two of the best places to look for imagery in action would be the Psalms of David and the Sonnets of Shakespeare—particularly Psalms 8, 22, 23, 42, 51, 91, 100, 121, 137, 139, 148, and 149, 150; and Sonnets 18, 27, 29, 30, 73, 116, and 129. The reader can check these on his own, and try underlining each image to see how it functions in each piece.

Here is an example of a modest poem that makes extraordinary use of imagery. It is a poem by Thomas Hardy titled "In Time of 'The Breaking of Nations' " (1917):

I

Only a man harrowing clods
   In a slow silent walk
With an old horse that stumbles and nods
   Half asleep as they stalk.

II

Only thin smoke without flame
   From the heaps of couch-grass;
Yet this will go onward the same
   Though Dynasties pass.

III

Yonder a maid and her wight
   Come whispering by:
War's annals will fade into night
   Ere their story die.

The opening lines begin generally enough until we reach line 3 and the "old horse that stumbles and nods / Half asleep as they stalk"—and we feel we really see that poor old half-asleep horse as it goes stumbling and nodding along. We see the smoke coming up from the heaps of couch-grass, and we see the young couple that comes whispering by—we see these things much more clearly than the rhetorical things that are mentioned by way of contrast, the dynasties and "war's annals." Hardy has created a few images that are sharp and clear and come alive for us.

Here is an example of images that go by us so fast, we have to check ourselves to figure out what is happening. It's from W. H. Auden's poem "As I Walked Out One Evening" (1940):

The glacier knocks in the cupboard,
   The desert sighs in the bed,

> And the crack in the tea-cup opens
> A lane to the land of the dead.

This is extraordinarily fast surrealist imagery—the "real" images are the ordinary things around the house, the cupboard and the bed and the tea-cup, and the surreal images coming out of them are the glacier and the desert and the lane to the land of the dead. Auden is showing how dream imagery overlays the ordinary imagery of everyday life.

Metaphor and simile are extensions of simple image. Aristotle says in the *Poetics* that a good metaphor implies an intuitive perception of the similarity between dissimilar things, and he comments that it is the one gift that cannot be taught—one is either born with it or one isn't. Strictly, metaphor is a direct comparison; it is an equation or an equivalence, like saying A equals B—"A mighty fortress is our God," or "It is the east and Juliet is the sun." Simile, on the other hand, is an indirect comparison using "like" or "as." Psalm 42 begins "As the hart panteth after the water brooks, so panteth my soul after thee, O God." Cassius in *Julius Caesar* tells Brutus in I, ii:

> Why, man, he doth bestride the narrow world
> Like a Colossus; and we petty men
> Walk under his huge legs and peep about
> To find ourselves dishonourable graves.

Robert Burns tells us, "My love's like a red, red rose".

Figure and conceit are also extensions of the simple image. A figure is any word or phrase that evokes an overtone of sensory impression that is beyond the literal meaning; more strictly, it is an image combined with an idea, like "ship of state" or "sea of troubles" or "bud of love."

A conceit is an extended figure, as in the following lines of Juliet in the balcony scene of *Romeo and Juliet*, II, ii:

> Sweet, good night!
> This bud of love, by summer's ripening breath,
> May prove a beauteous flower when next we meet.

The conceit is a complex image, an ingenious image that is developed over several lines of poetry; like a fugue, a good conceit will usually consist of many interwoven themes, but it must stay faithful to the single figure that gave rise to it. Here is a more complex conceit, from that same balcony scene of *Romeo and Juliet*; Romeo sets up a premise and then sees where it will take him:

> Two of the fairest stars in all the heaven,
> Having some business, do entreat her eyes
> To twinkle in their spheres till they return.
> What if her eyes were there, they in her head?
> The brightness of her cheek would shame those stars,
> As daylight doth a lamp; her eyes in heaven
> Would through the airy region stream so bright
> That birds would sing and think it were not night.

There is the conceit, over eight lines of poetry and ending with a rhymed couplet. It is one of the finest examples of figurative writing in our literature.

SOUND

Rhythm has its source and origin in our own bloodstream pulse. At a normal pace, the heart beats at a casual iambic beat; but when it becomes excited, the pulse may trip and skip rhythm through extended anapests or dactyls or trochees, and it may even end up pounding with a sledgehammer spondee beat.

T. S. Eliot says it best:

> The human soul, in intense emotion, strives to express itself in verse. It is not for me, but for the neurologists, to discover why this is so, and why and how feeling and rhythm are related.

In dance, rhythm is sometimes accented, or accentuated, by a drumbeat; in parades, by the cadence of marching feet; or in the night air, by the tolling of distant church bells. These simple rhythms may be taken as tokens of the deeper rhythms of the universe: the tidal ebb and flow, the rising and setting of the sun, the female menstrual cycle, and the four seasons of the year. We are surrounded by rhythms because life itself is rhythmic, and so of course it is the immeasurable music of poetry. As Ezra Pound comments:

> Rhythm is perhaps the most primal of all things known to us. It is basic in poetry and music mutually, their melodies depending on a variation of tone quality and of pitch respectively, as is commonly said, but if we look more closely we will see that music is, by further analysis, pure rhythm, rhythm and nothing else, for the variation of pitch is the variation in rhythms of the individual notes, and harmony the blending of these varied rhythms.

There is a simple notation system for measuring rhythm in poetry, and it only takes a little practice to master how it is done. Every line of poetry can be divided into separate "feet"—the "foot" deriving from the Greek chorus in tragedy, where chorus members would stamp out long and short rhythms with their feet. In English, although we have long and short vowels (long *a* and short *a*), the emphasis is not on long/short so much as it is on accented and nonaccented syllables. This is because English has such a strong Anglo-Saxon base of accentual rhythm; any given word in that English language will automatically have at least one strong accent and one or more unaccented syllables. Therefore any writing in English will tend to be metrical, whether one measures it consciously or not. The question is whether one wants to use metrics artistically as a part of one's total craft.

The following table sets down the various metrical feet, or units of rhythm in any given part of a line:

iamb	. /	slack—STRESS
trochee	/ .	STRESS—slack
anapest	. . /	slack—slack—STRESS
dactyl	/ . .	STRESS—slack—slack
spondee	/ /	STRESS—STRESS

We can apply the above measures to an example of rhythmic poetry, in the following lines from Edgar Allan Poe's "Annabel Lee" (1849):

> I was a child and *she* was a child,
> In this kingdom by the sea,
> But we loved with a love that was more than love—
> I and my Annabel Lee—
> With a love that the winged seraphs of Heaven
> Coveted her and me.

A simple scansion of the above lines follows, using capital letters to emphasize the stress syllables:

> I was a CHILD and SHE was a CHILD
> In this KINGdom BY the SEA,
> But we LOVED with a LOVE that was MORE than LOVE—
> I and my ANNabel LEE—
> With a LOVE that the WINGed SERaphs of HEAVen
> COVeted HER and ME.

We can then see that the above example is a fairly regular mix of iambs, trochees, and anapests, creating a rhythmic pattern that keeps repeating itself throughout the whole poem. This is helpful not only for the reader to see what kind of metrical pattern he is dealing with in the poem, but can also be extraordinarily useful to any practicing poet who wants to complete the writing of a regular metrical poem, and has to figure out what the repeating pattern has to be.

But we should say right here that there is no such thing as an absolute scansion reading, and metrical patterns are always open to variation in reading, just as musical scores can be interpreted differently by different conductors, such as Leonard Bernstein or Eugene Ormandy, what is "whole note" and "half note" and "quarter note" to one interpreter will be something slightly different to another interpreter.

As with music, so with the scansion of metrics in poetry—there simply cannot be any dogmatic formula for how any given line of poetry ought to be scanned. One *wishes* one could lay down inviolable rules, and say "this line can only be read as a series of iambic feet"—but there is always the possibility that the line might be open to being read in some other way. And one reason poetry is so badly taught in schools is that grade school teachers often assume there can be one and only one correct scansion of any given line. But those who have spent a lifetime dealing with rhythm and metrics know otherwise. For example, the great actor José Ferrer, who played the part of Iago to Paul Robeson's Othello in the famous Broadway production in the 1940s, raises serious questions as to whether there can be any certainty about how to scan one of the most famous lines in our language:

NYQ: What about meter and measure and the poetic line?

JOSÉ
FERRER: Well, the business of meter is tricky. Philip Burton, who was Richard Burton's mentor, theatrically—I was listening to him speak to a class a few years ago, young high school students who recited Shakespeare, and he said, "You must pay attention to the meter," he says,

To be or not to be, that is the question.

"That isn't the way it is," he says. "The correct reading is,

To be or not to be, that is the question.

And he said, "That has to be respected and paid attention to and perhaps used."

I don't think that is the question, I'd have to study what comes before it and take it in context, but it seems to me the line should read,

To bé oŕ nót tó bé, that ié the qúestion.

I think you have to stress "that" as well as
"is." but that's the whole thing with Shakespeare. Somebody will take something that
doesn't make sense to you and make it sen-
sible through the magic of his own performance.

NEW YORK QUARTERLY CRAFT INTERVIEW,
NUMBER 47

If we say that there can be no absolute scansion of a poetic
line, it is still important to know how to gauge the formal measure
of rhythm so we can get a general sense of the underlying pulse
of a poem. But we must always remember what Ralph Waldo
Emerson suggests in "The Poet" (1844), that we must not be
misled into thinking that any measurement can be more important than the poem itself:

For it is not meters, but a meter-making argument that
makes a poem—a thought so passionate and alive that
like the spirit of a plant or an animal it has an archi-
tecture of its own, and adorns nature with a new thing.

Even so, there can be reasonably reliable scansion of regularly
metrical poems, such as the following poem in iambics by Stanley
Kunitz entitled "Benediction":

God banish from your house	. / . / . /
The fly, the roach, the mouse	. / . / . /
That riots in the walls	. / . / . /
Until the plaster falls;	. / . / . /
Admonish from your door	. / . / . /
The hypocrite and liar;	. / . / . /
No shy, soft, tigrish fear	. / . / . /
Permit upon your stair,	. / . / . /
Nor agents of your doubt.	. / . / . /
God drive them whistling out . . .	. / . / . /

Following is an example of scansion for a trochaic poem—a speech from the First Witch in *Macbeth* which is in trochaic tetrameter:

I'll drain him dry as hay:	. / . / . /
Sleep shall neither night nor day	/ . / . / . /
Hang upon his pent-house lid;	/ . / . / . /
He shall live a man forbid:	/ . / . / . /
Weary se'nnights nine times nine	/ . / . / . /
Shall he dwindle, peak, and pine:	/ . / . / . /
Though his bark cannot be lost,	/ . / . / . /
Yet it shall be tempest-toss'd.	/ . / . / . /

Following is an example of scansion for an anapestic poem— from the popular song "Red River Valley," which seems to imitate the easy gait of a horse walking:

Come and sit by my side if you love me,	. . / . . / . . / .
Do not hasten to bid me adieu,	. . / . . / . . /
But remember the Red River Valley	. . / . . / . . / .
And the cowboy who loved you so true.	. . / . . / . . /

Following is an example of scansion for a dactylic line—from Alfred, Lord Tennyson's "Charge of the Light Brigade":

Half a league, half a league, half a league onward . . .
/ ·   ·   / ·   ·   / ·   ·   / ·

And following is an example of scansion for a spondaic line— from Shakespeare's *Macbeth*:

Out, out brief candle . . .   / / / / .

There are other meters that are variations of the five described above, and they include:

pyrrhic	. .
amphibrachic	. / .
bacchic	. / /
choriambic	/ . . /

One interesting device that can be used with regularly metrical poems is "substitution," where a regular rhythm is suddenly interrupted with a variant foot that introduces a counter-rhythm. For example, in Emily Dickinson's poem 1732:

My life closed twice before its close—	. / . / . / . /
It yet remains to see	. / . / . /
If Immortality unveil	. / . / . / . /
A third Event to me	. / . / . /
So huge, so hopeless to conceive	. / . / . / . /
As these that twice befell.	. / . / . /
Parting is all we know of heaven,	/ . . / . / . /
And all we need of hell.	. / . / . /

The poem above is moving along in regular iambic rhythm until line 7, where the word *parting* introduces a trochee as a substitution for the iambic. This creates an instant of sudden stoppage, and gives a very special weight to the word *parting* which it would not ordinarily have. The poem then resumes its regular iambic rhythm to the end.

All of these devices of scansion are there to be of service to the poet in the writing of his poem, and to the reader in the reading of the poem. They should never be seen as anything more than this, and any wish that they be made into absolute dogmas can only be detrimental to poetry. We could almost paraphrase what Jesus said about the Sabbath: "Metrics were made for the poet, not the poet for metrics." So long as one can keep perspective on this, meter and rhythm will be extraordinarily useful to the poet in writing his poem.

Rhyme

Another aspect of sound in poetry is rhyme, which is any sense of resonance that comes when one word echoes the sound of another word—whether in end rhyme or internal rhyme of assonance and alliteration.

Assonance is the rhyming of vowel sounds, which are the purest form of lyric sound in poetry. The primary long and short vowel sounds are:

A	short (bad)	long (bake)
E	short (bed)	long (beet)
I	short (bid)	long (bide)
O	short (bob)	long (bone)
U	short (bub)	long (imbue)

We can see a patterning of assonance in the opening soliloquy of *Hamlet*, I, ii:

> O! that this *too too* solid flesh would melt,
> Thaw and resolve itself in*to* a *dew!*

Here the italicized letters create an assonantal pattern of four long *oo* sounds, which become more clear if one says the line out loud. And this is an important point: assonance can usually not be detected on the page when it is read silently—it has to be spoken aloud for the vowel sounds to set up their echo patternings.

Take lines 13 and 14 of Shakespeare's sonnet 27:

> Lo! thus by day my limbs, by night my mind,
> For thee, and for myself, no quiet find.

Here the long *i* sounds repeat in by-my-by-night-my-mind-myself-quiet-find, a total of nine assonantal rhymes, which one would never detect if one were simply reading the lines silently.

Shakespeare will work toward a more sophisticated type of assonance with certain sounds, such as ow-our-are in these lines from the opening soliloquy of *Richard III,* one of his earliest plays (1593):

> *Now* is the winter of *our* discontent
> Made gl*or*ious summer by this sun of Y*or*k;
> And all the cl*ou*ds that l*our*'d upon our house
> In the deep bosom of the ocean b*ur*ied.
> *Now* *are* *our* br*ow*s b*ou*nd with vict*or*ious wreaths . . .

Here the assonance is so intense one can hardly mouth the words without distorting the jaw—try saying line five out loud and see what happens when the assonance of "now are our" has to be made clear. Similarly, at the end of his career, Shakespeare used the same assonantal pattern in *The Tempest* (1611) in IV, i:

> *Our* revels *now* are ended. These *our* act*or*s,
> As I f*or*etold you, *we*re all spirits, and
> *Are* melted into *air,* into thin *air:*
> And, like the baseless fabric of this vision,
> The cloud-capp'd t*ow*ers, the g*or*geous palaces,
> The solemn temples, the great globe itself,
> Yea, all which it inh*er*it, shall dissolve,
> And, like this insubstantial pageant faded,
> Leave not a rack behind. We *are* such stuff
> As dreams *are* made *on;* and *our* little life
> Is r*ou*nded with a sleep.

Here the orchestration of vowel sounds is dazzling, and if it is read aloud, one senses the interplay of our-ow-or-ere-are-air-rou phonics to create the most sublime music that poetry is capable of.

A further sophistication of assonance can be found in the use of diphthongs, a speech sound that begins with one vowel and moves immediately to another vowel. One pure example is the word *Aeaea,* the name of the island Circe lived on in Homer's

Odyssey. Other diphthongs that create a ready-made assonance are:

oasis	chaos
hiatus	hieroglyphs
coyote	archeology
opinion	poise
onion	soar
humanoid	weight
meteorites	yield

Alliteration is a repetition of consonant sounds, using a combination of any of the following to achieve an alliterative patterning:

plosives—P / B
dentals—T / D / TH
sibilants—S / SH / Z
nasals—M / N / NG
fricatives—F / V
gutturals—G / K

Say each consonant aloud and feel where it occurs in your mouth—at the lips, teeth, roof, or throat—and how it resonates when said. Alliterative patterns can be used to create a strong tactile texture of sound, either of cacophony (dissonance) or euphony (harmony), depending on the pattern and the context. For example, the following alliteration embodies cacophony:

> Were they not forc'd with those that should be ours,
> We might have met them dareful, beard to beard,
> And beat them backward home.

> *MACBETH*. V. V

On the other hand, the following alliteration using fricatives creates a pattern of heartbreaking pathos:

> Pray, do not mock me:
> I am a very foolish fond old man,

Fourscore and upward, not an hour more nor less;
And, to deal plainly,
I fear I am not in my perfect mind.

KING LEAR. IV. VII

Beyond assonance and alliteration (which are both internal sound patterns), there is rhyme itself—end rhyme, either perfect or slant rhyme, and masculine or feminine rhyme.

Aside from certain words in the English language (like *month* and *orange*), most words can be rhymed either perfectly or imperfectly. For example, in the following lines, there are five perfect rhymes and one imperfect rhyme:

In Xanadu did Kubla Khan
A stately pleasure dome decree:
Where Alph, the sacred river, ran
Through caverns measureless to man
Down to a sunless sea. . . .

COLERIDGE. "KUBLA KHAN" (1798)

The five perfect rhymes above are: *Xanadu, ran, man, decree,* and *see;* the imperfect rhyme is *Khan* (which is a slant rhyme for *man*).

Similarly, in the following lines there are two perfect rhymes and two imperfect rhymes:

The whiskey on your breath
Could make a small boy dizzy:
But I hung on like death:
Such waltzing was not easy.

THEODORE ROETHKE. "MY PAPA'S WALTZ" (1948)

The two perfect rhymes are *breath* and *death;* the two imperfect or slant rhymers are *dizzy* and *easy*.

Masculine and feminine rhymes refer to whether the rhyme occurs on the final (ultimate) syllable, or on the next-to-final (penultimate) syllable. Thus *sea* and *free* are both masculine rhymes, whereas *ocean* and *motion* are feminine rhymes.

Sometimes one can play with trick rhyme, as in the following lyrics by Ira Gershwin from Porgy and Bess (1935):

> It ain't necessarily so—
> It ain't necessarily so—
> The things that you're liable
> To read in the Bible—
> It ain't necessarily so.

And Gwendolyn Brooks achieves surprise rhyme in her poem "We Real Cool":

> We real cool. We
> left school.

The following two stanzas from W. D. Snodgrass's poem "April Inventory" show an extraordinary use of rhyme, so skillful one hardly notices the intervention of rhyme in the voice that is speaking:

> The tenth time, just a year ago,
> I made myself a little list
> Of all the things I'd ought to know,
> Then told my parents, analyst,
> And everyone who's trusted me
> I'd be substantial, presently.
>
> I haven't read one book about
> A book or memorized one plot.
> Or found a mind I did not doubt.
> I learned one date. And then forgot.
> And one by one the solid scholars
> Get the degrees, the jobs, the dollars.

VOICE

Voice can be seen as the poet's signature on his poem, his own unmistakable way of saying something. One feels, for example, "Only Yeats could have said it that way" when one reads a line like

That is no country for old men.

Similarly, only Robert Frost could have turned his words to form

Something there is that doesn't love a wall . . .

This craft of voice is a combination of diction, syntax, and persona, forming the total tonality of a poem.

First of all there is the way a poet uses denotation and connotation—denotation being the literal dictionary meaning of a word, and connotation being the indirect or associational meaning of a word. *Mother* may mean one thing denotatively, but it also triggers a whole host of connotative associations. Any poet must be aware of both denotation and connotation, simultaneously.

Diction is word choice, the peculiar type and style of language that a poet is using. Diction can be a mix of slang, patois, street language, plain style, Latinate, assorted regionalisms, and ethnic dialects. Aristotle in the *Poetics* sets down the basic principles of diction:

> The Perfection of Diction is for it to be at once clear and not mean. The clearest indeed is that made up of ordinary words for things. . . . On the other hand, the Diction becomes distinguished and non-prosaic by the use of unfamiliar terms, i.e., strange words, metaphors, lengthened forms, and everything that deviates from the ordinary modes of speech. . . .

> A certain admixture, accordingly, of unfamiliar terms is
> necessary. These, the strange word, the metaphor, the
> ornamental equivalent, &c., will save the language from
> seeming mean and prosaic, while the ordinary words in
> it will secure the requisite clearness. What helps most,
> however, to render the Diction at once clear and non-
> prosaic is the use of the lengthened, curtailed, and al-
> tered forms of words.

Notice the first criterion of diction Aristotle advocates is clarity: nothing supersedes the need to make oneself clear and un-
derstandable. Thereafter, one can practice whatever admixtures
and idiosyncratic ways of saying something one wants, so long
as one remains clear.

One can see good examples of what Aristotle terms "curtailed
and altered forms of words" in Ophelia's speeches in *Hamlet*,
where she refers to how she would "suck the honey of his music
vows"—"music vows" is a curtailed and altered form of the
words, but the clarity remains intact and we still understand
what she means.

When diction lapses into generality and abstraction, we call
it rhetoric. Eliot once defined rhetoric as "Any adornment or
inflation of speech which is not done for a particular effect but
for a general impressiveness."

It's that *generality* of effect that can obfuscate poetry. Aristotle
insisted in his empiricism that all perception took place through
the senses:

> *Nihil est in intellectus quod non primus in sensus.*
> Nothing is in the mind that is not first in the senses.

And Aristotle also insisted there could be no ideas or abstrac-
tions that did not have their origin in specifics:

> The universal exists for, and shines through, the particular.

It is this insistence on particulars that marks the greatness in
art as well as in life, as William Blake wrote:

Whoso would do good must do it in Minute Particulars,
The General Good is the cry of the hypocrite, the flatterer,
   and the scoundrel.

Alfred North Whitehead taught that the art of poetry was onomatopoeia, being able to recreate the thing itself through imagery:

The art of literature, oral or written, is so to adjust the language that it embodies what it indicates.

William Carlos Williams put it more simply:

No ideas but in things.

When someone is *not* being specific and particular, it will always show up in his diction: the overuse of Latinate words, concept and abstraction words, and empty generalities, as in the following list:

complaisance
satisfaction
condemnation
admiration
regeneration
disparagement
sensationalism
judgment
sophistication
connection
entertainment
demonstration

All those *-ment* and *-ion* words—and not one single image in the whole list! Latin words are "official" words, they have no sharp sound or image. They are package words that pretend to tell us something in a prose sense, but they do not convey either image or sound to us in any specific poetic way.

After diction, the other strong voice principle is syntax, the peculiar arrangement of words in their unique sentence structure. In English, there are four types of sentence:

DECLARATIVE—makes a statement
INTERROGATIVE—asks a question
IMPERATIVE—gives a command
EXCLAMATORY—makes an outcry

We can see these various types of sentence at work in a single poem by William Blake:

And did those feet in ancient time	
Walk upon England's mountains green?	INTERROGATIVE
And was the holy Lamb of God	
On England's pleasant pastures seen?	INTERROGATIVE
And did the Countenance Divine	
Shine forth upon our clouded hills?	INTERROGATIVE
And was Jerusalem builded here	
Among these dark Satanic Mills?	INTERROGATIVE
Bring me my Bow of burning gold:	
Bring me my Arrows of desire:	IMPERATIVE
Bring me my Spear: O clouds unfold!	EXCLAMMATORY
Bring me my Chariot of fire.	
I will not cease from Mental Fight,	
Nor shall my Sword sleep in my hand	
Till we have built Jerusalem	
In England's green & pleasant Land.	DECLARATIVE

FROM *MILTON* (1804–1808)

Perhaps the strongest voice device of all is *persona,* by means of which the poet assumes a dramatic mask to speak through some other character. Creating a different persona can sometimes free a poet to say things or explore areas that he or she may not be comfortable doing in an autobiographical first-person voice. And indeed, Aristotle in the *Poetics* claims that the essence of poetry and drama is *mimesis* or imitation of other voices, and that "The poet should say very little *in propria persona* [in his own voice], as he is no imitator when he is doing this."

The challenge, then, is to become someone else and then use that other person's voice as if it were one's own. As Flaubert once commented:

> *Madame Bovary, c'est moi.*

In other words, Flaubert is insisting that Madame Bovary is not some fictional character he has created outside himself, in order to write a novel; rather, he *is* that fictional character and her voice is his own voice. This is a crucial distinction to make, and can get pretty scary in actual practice.

For example, in the following poem Ralph Waldo Emerson actually assumes the persona of the Brahma:

> If the red slayer think he slays,
>   Or if the slain think he is slain,
> They know not well the subtle ways
>   I keep, and pass, and turn again. . . .
>
> "BRAHMA" (1856)

William Butler Yeats created the persona of a wild and irreverent Irishwoman who wandered the old dirt roads and spoke her mind freely on the great issues of life:

> I met the Bishop on the road
> And much said he and I.
> "Those breasts are flat and fallen now,
> Those veins must soon be dry;
> Live in a heavenly mansion,
> Not in some foul sty."
>
> "Fair and foul are near of kin,
> And fair needs foul," I cried.
> "My friends are gone, but that's a truth

Nor grave nor bed denied,
Learned in bodily lowliness
And in the heart's pride.

"A woman can be proud and stiff
When on love intent;
But Love has pitched his mansion in
The place of excrement;
For nothing can be sole or whole
That has not been rent."

"CRAZY JANE TALKS WITH THE BISHOP"
(1933)

In the following poem, Langston Hughes assumes the persona
of a young black person who is taken for a ride by the KKK:

Ku Klux

They took me out
To some lonesome place.
They said, "Do you believe
In the great white race?"

I said, "Mister,
To tell you the truth,
I'd believe in anything
If you'd just turn me loose."

The white man said, "Boy,
Can it be
You're a-standin' there
A-sassin' me?"

They hit me in the head
And knocked me down.
And then they kicked me
On the ground.

A klansman said, "Nigger,
Look me in the face—

And tell me you believe in
The great white race."

FROM *THE PANTHER AND THE LASH* (1967)

John Berryman used persona voice through his entire writing career, as in an early poem devoted to the seventeenth-century American poet Anne Bradstreet, who speaks through the "I" of Berryman's *Homage to Mistress Bradstreet:*

40

As a canoe slides by on one strong stroke
hope his help not I, who do hardly bear
his gift still. But whisper
I am not utterly, I pare
an apple for my pipsqueak Mercy and
she runs & all need naked apples, fanned
their tinier envies,
Vomitings, trots, rashes. Can be hope a cloak?

In his later work *The Dream Songs*, Berryman is at pains to explain the complex persona system in the separate poems, in a prefatory note:

Many opinions and errors in the Songs are to be referred not to the character Henry, still less to the author, but to the title of the work. It is idle to reply to critics, but some of the people who addressed themselves to the *77 Dream Songs* went so desperately astray (one apologized about it in print, but who ever sees apologies?) that I permit myself one word. The poem then, whatever its cast of characters, is essentially about an imaginary character (not the poet, not me) named Henry, a white American in early middle age sometimes in blackface, who has suffered an irreversible loss and talks about himself sometimes in the first person, sometimes in the third, sometimes even in the second; he has a friend, never named, who addresses himself as Mr. Bones and variants thereof. Requiescant in pace.

J. B.

Following is an example from *The Dream Songs,* showing how Berryman's personae function:

36

The high ones die, die. They die. You look up and who's there?
—Easy, easy, Mr. Bones. I is on your side.
I smell your grief.
—I sent my grief away. I cannot care
forever. With them all again & again I died
and cried, and I have to live.

—Now there *you* exaggerate, Sah. We hafta *die.*
That is our 'pointed task. Love & die.
—Yes; that makes sense.
But what makes sense between, then? What if I
roiling & babbling & braining, brood on why and
just sat on the fence?

—I doubts you did or do. De choice is lost.
—It's fool's gold. But I go in for that.
The boy & the bear
looked at each other. Man all is tossed
& lost with groin-wounds by the grand bulls, cat.
William Faulkner's where?

(Frost being still around.)

Another American, Charles Bukowski, one of the most popular poets writing in the last half of the twentieth century, uses the mask of a beery barroom "dirty old man" who goes through sordid and demeaning love experiences, all the while he is watching himself watching himself—which makes for an eerie sort of lucidity, as in this poem:

Murder

screw this poem, it's
disgusting, I was not
made to write such
vomit,

what's wrong with
me?
my head feels like
an empty
vase.
do I always have
to pour wine
into it?

screw this poem, I
more than dislike
it, I should have
driven off a cliff with
the accelerator to
the floor,
this is like
crapping in my
pants, it
stinks.

I'm going to kill
this poem
right in front of
you here
and no jury in
the world would
call me
guilty.

there, it's dead.

now
turn the
page.

An excellent example of persona is the following note that Sylvia Plath wrote about her poem "Daddy." In this note the poet makes it clear that the poem is spoken by a girl who is *not* her, *not* Sylvia Plath, but rather a fictitious mask that Sylvia Plath has created:

> Here is a poem spoken by a girl with an Electra complex.
> Her father died while she thought he was God. Her case
> is complicated by the fact that her father was also a Nazi
> and her mother very possibly part Jewish. In the daughter
> the two strains meet and paralyze each other—she has
> to act out the awful little allegory once over before she
> is free of it.

And Robert Lowell comments in one of his later books that continues his strain of autobiographical writing that the collection itself is "half fiction"—but leaves the question open as to which half he is referring to. The persona he is adopting, then, is half autobiographically truthful, and half fanciful, and the reader is not sure which is which.

Any poet can experiment with different personae to broaden the scope of his or her writing. Following are a few persona exercises that will unlock areas of sensibility and perception that are not usually tapped when one uses an ordinary writing voice:

1. Write in the persona of someone of the opposite sex.

2. Write in the persona of someone twenty years older.

3. Write in the persona of someone twenty years younger.

4. Write in the persona of someone who is less educated than you are.

5. Write in the persona of someone who is more educated than you are.

6. Write in the persona of someone who is blind.

7. Write in the persona of someone who is deaf.

8. Write in the persona of someone who is mute.

9. Write in the persona of someone who holds the opposite religious, political, and social opinions from you.

Image and sound and voice—these are the three techniques of the craft of poetry.

But so far these are only words on a page, like diagrams in a baseball book showing you how to throw a curveball. The only way one can really learn how to throw that curveball is to go out on a mound and practice, endlessly, hurling the ball over the plate.

Similarly, the only way one can ever really learn how to use any of these craft devices is to do endless exercises in notebooks: trying to master imagery, metaphor, simile, figure, conceit, assonance, alliteration, metrics, rhyme, diction, syntax, persona, and the various other techniques that are described in these pages.

And we know that once one begins exercising one's talents on any of these craft devices, one may experience a period of self-consciousness as one begins to explore totally new possibilities of language—one may feel it is all too artificial, too contrived, too silly to be worth very much. But one has to keep practicing until these new techniques become "second nature" and an enhancement and reinforcement of one's own intuitive talents as poet.

Only then can one begin on the really serious work of poetry, because these techniques in themselves are merely stepping-stones for one's deeper exploration into the realm of poetry, where it all takes place up there in the bright areas of air.

Dylan Thomas says it best, about the relation of technique to true poetry:

> You can tear a poem apart to see what makes it technically tick, and say to yourself, when the works are laid out before you, the vowels, the consonants, the rhymes or rhythms, 'Yes, this is *it*. This is why the poem moves me so. It is because of the craftsmanship.' But you're back again where you began.
>
> You're back with the mystery of having been moved by words. The best craftsmanship always leaves holes and gaps in the works of the poem so that something

that is *not* in the poem can creep, crawl, flash, or thunder in.

The joy and function of poetry is, and was, the celebration of man, which is also the celebration of God.

DYLAN THOMAS, NOTE TO HIS *COLLECTED POEMS*,
NEW DIRECTIONS 1953

3

GENRES

Sometimes it comes like a dumb hunch, a vague adumbration that something somewhere wants to come out. And one may carry this strong longing around inside for long periods of time, sometimes for months, sometimes even for years, before one can finally sit down and try to write it out.

But then there is always the question: Once this vague something does begin to come out, what genre should it be? Should it take the form of a play? A novel? A short story? An essay? A poem?

Many major writers were not always sure which genre their work should fall into. Chekhov knew that he wanted to write plays, but he supported himself and his family while he went through medical school in Moscow by writing hundreds of short stories; by the time of his death at the age of forty-four Chekhov had written six major plays and over one thousand short stories. Tennessee Williams sometimes wrote out a plot in short story form, then translated it into play form, then kept rewriting the play endlessly under different titles. And Samuel Beckett wrote almost all his major plays in French, then translated them into English before their dramatic productions.

Each of the various genres of literature requires a very special genius on the part of a writer, and not many writers can achieve greatness in more than one genre. Leo Tolstoy wrote a great novel (*War and Peace*) and a great play (*The Power of Darkness*); Victor Hugo wrote a great novel (*Les Miserables*) and a great play (*Hernani*); Thomas Hardy wrote many great novels and several great poems; Edgar Allan Poe wrote great poetry and great short stories and great essays; D. H. Lawrence wrote great novels and great poetry; T. S. Eliot wrote great poetry and great plays and great essays; and Thornton Wilder wrote a great play (*Our Town*) and a great novel (*The Bridge of San Luis Rey*). In our own time, James Dickey has written great poetry and a great novel (*Deliverance*) and great criticism (*From Babel to Byzantium*).

In fact the more one considers the peculiar requirements of each genre, the more remarkable it is when one finds an author who can excel at more than one genre. It's awesome that a writer like Robert Louis Stevenson could excel at five different genres— writing a great novel (*Treasure Island*), a great short story ("The Strange Case of Dr. Jekyll and Mr. Hyde"), a great book of children's poetry (*A Child's Garden of Verses*), a great book of essays (*Virginibus Puerisque*), and (in collaboration with William Ernest Henley) a great play (*Deacon Bridge*).

Suppose one confines oneself to writing poetry—there is still the question, what kind of poem should one write? Because within the broad field of poetry there are three major genres of poem: narrative, dramatic, and lyric. Narrative poetry *tells* a story; dramatic poetry *shows* the story by representing two or more voices interacting, and lyric poetry celebrates one single note or tone or motif.

1. *Narrative poetry.* The genius of narrative writing is in *telling* a story that has a beginning, a middle, and an end. Novels and short stories and novellas share the same common task of telling someone something. Narrative poetry will usually have a narrator who leads a reader step by step through the various stages of the story line. Examples of narrative poetry include the many stories in Chaucer's *Canterbury Tales*, as the various pilgrims entertain each other with racy, raucous, and courtly stories. Coleridge's "Rime of the Ancient Mariner" tells how the mariner

Coleridge's "Rime of the Ancient Mariner" tells how the mariner shot an albatross, thereby bringing catastrophe for the ship's crew and the mariner's own soul. Robert Browning's narrative poems, such as "My Last Duchess," tell stories of how various characters affect each other in dramatic situations.

2. *Dramatic poetry.* Instead of *telling* a story, dramatic poetry *shows* a story through strong dramatic actions and clear visuals that embody these actions. As Aristotle prescribes in the *Poetics*, dramas do not always begin at the beginning but instead plunge an audience directly into the heart of an action; then the exposition can be skillfully interwoven to help reinforce the ongoing action. Plays and filmscripts and television screenplays share the same dramatic task of showing someone something. Poetry that arises as a consequence of dramatic action can be either traditional line (blank verse) or free form, but always the success of the poetry will depend on the success of the strong subtext of dramatic action underlying it. Examples of successful dramatic poetry include the plays of Shakespeare (*Hamlet*), Christopher Marlowe (*Doctor Faustus*), John Webster (*The Duchess of Malfi*), Christopher Fry (*The Lady's Not for Burning*), and T. S. Eliot (*The Cocktail Party*).

3. *Lyric poetry.* All lyric poetry always celebrates a single theme or tone or motif, and lyric poetry may span a wide range of forms to do this: song, epic, ode, eclogue, epithalamion, elegy, epigram, epitaph, envoi, epistle, and many other types of poetry. Yet all lyric poetry will share one essential characteristic, which the Irish poet James Stephens describes as follows:

> It may be said that the lyrical poet is undisputed master of all the *extremes* that can be expressed in terms of time or speed or tempo. No pen but his can hold excessive velocity or excessive slowness.

A. SONG. The simplest form of lyric is a brief musical statement of a single theme:

Blow, blow, thou winter wind,
Thou art not so unkind
As man's ingratitude;
Thy tooth is not so keen,
Because thou art not seen,
Although thy breath be rude.
Heigh-ho! sing, heigh-ho! unto the green holly:
Most friendship is feigning, most loving mere folly.
Then heigh-ho! the holly!
This life is most jolly.

Freeze, freeze, thou bitter sky,
That dost not bite so nigh
As benefits forgot;
Though thou the waters warp,
Thy sting is not so sharp
As friend rememb'red not.
Heigh-ho! sing, heigh-ho! unto the green holly:
Most friendship is feigning, most loving mere folly.
Then heigh-ho! the holly!
This life is most jolly.

SHAKESPEARE, *AS YOU LIKE IT*, II, VII

Lyric songs can be in the form of question and reply:

As you came from the holy land
    Of Walsingham,
Met you not with my tru love
    By the way as you came?

How shall I know your trew love,
    That have mett many one
As I went to the holy lande,
    That have come, that have gone? . . .

FROM SIR WALTER RALEIGH. "AS YOU
CAME FROM THE HOLY LAND OF
WALSINGHAM"

B. EPIC.   Epic poems will invariably have narrative story lines but they are more concerned with developing one central theme or tone or motif. Epic is thus an extension of the ode, and shares the same lyrical quality. Some of the central themes of the most well-known epic poems are:

1.   The *Iliad* of Homer, which is about the anger of Achilles during the ninth year of the Trojan War

2.   The *Odyssey* of Homer, which is about the wanderings of Odysseus on his way back home to Ithaka from Troy

3.   The *Aeneid* of Virgil, which is about "arms and the man," Aeneas, as he makes his way from Troy to found the city of Rome

4.   The *Commedia* of Dante, which is about how Dante finds he has lost the true way so must journey through Inferno and Purgatory to Paradise

5.   *Paradise Lost* of Milton, which is about man's first disobedience and his subsequent fall from grace

6.   The *Cantos* of Ezra Pound, which is "the tale of the tribe," a poem containing history and moving from darkness to light

7.   *Paterson* by William Carlos Williams, which is about the city of Paterson in New Jersey, and about a man who is living in that city

C. ODE.   An ode is an extended lyric on one single theme or tone or subject, usually of considerable length and with recognizable stanza patterns. Coleridge's "Dejection: An Ode" is one example:

> Well! If the bard was weather-wise, who made
> The grand old ballad of Sir Patrick Spence,
> This night, so tranquil now, will not go hence

Unroused by winds, that ply a busier trade
Than those which mould yon cloud in lazy flakes
Or the dull sobbing draft, that moans and rakes
Upon the strings of this Aeolian lute,
    Which better far were mute.
For Lo! the New-moon winter-bright!

Shelley's great poem "To a Skylark" is another example of an ode:

Hail to thee, blithe Spirit!
  Bird thou never wert,
That from Heaven, or near it,
  Pourest thy full heart
In profuse strains of unpremeditated art.

Higher still and higher
  From the earth thou springest
Like a cloud of fire;
  The blue deep thou wingest,
And singing still dost soar, and soaring ever singest.

In the golden lightning
  Of the sunken sun,
O'er which clouds are bright'ning,
  Thou dost float and run;
Like an unbodied joy whose race is just begun.

The pale purple even
  Melts around thy flight;
Like a star of Heaven,
  In the broad daylight
Thou art unseen, but yet I hear thy shrill delight,

Keen as are the arrows
  Of that silver sphere,
Whose intense lamp narrows
  In the white dawn clear
Until we hardly see—we feel that it is there.

All the earth and air
  With thy voice is loud,

As, when night is bare,
 From one lonely cloud
The moon rains out her beams, and Heaven is overflowed.

What thou art we know not;
 What is most like thee?
From rainbow clouds there flow not
 Drops so bright to see
As from thy presence showers a rain of melody.

Like a Poet hidden
 In the light of thought,
Singing hymns unbidden,
 Till the world is wrought
To sympathy with hopes and fears it heeded not:

Like a high-born maiden
 In a palace-tower,
Soothing her love-laden
 Soul in secret hour
With music sweet as love, which overflows her bower:

Like a glowworm golden
 In a dell of dew,
Scattering unbeholden
 Its aëral hue
Among the flowers and grass, which screen it from the view!

Like a rose embowered
 In its own green leaves,
By warm winds deflowered,
 Till the scent it gives
Makes faint with too much sweet those heavy-wingèd thieves:

Sound of vernal showers
 On the twinkling grass,
Rain-awakened flowers,
 All that ever was
Joyous, and clear, and fresh, thy music doth surpass:

Teach us, Sprite or Bird,
 What sweet thoughts are thine:
I have never heard

Praise of love or wine
That panted forth a flood of rapture so divine.

Chorus Hymeneal,
  Or triumphal chant,
Matched with thine would be all
  But any empty vaunt,
A thing wherein we feel there is some hidden want.

What objects are the fountains
  Of thy happy strain?
What fields, or waves, or mountains?
  What shapes of sky or plain?
What love of thine own kind? what ignorance of pain?

With thy clear keen joyance
  Languor cannot be:
Shadow of annoyance
  Never came near thee:
Thou lovest—but ne'er knew love's sad satiety.

Waking or asleep,
  Thou of death must deem
Things more true and deep
  Than we mortals dream,
Or how could thy notes flow in such a crystal stream?

We look before and after,
  And pine for what is not:
Our sincerest laughter
  With some pain is fraught;
Our sweetest songs are those that tell of saddest thought.

Yet if we could scorn
  Hate, and pride, and fear;
If we were things born
  Not to shed a tear,
I know not how thy joy we ever should come near.

Better than all measures
  Of delightful sound,
Better than all treasures
  That in books are found,
Thy skill to poet were, thou scorner of the ground!

Teach me half the gladness
  That thy brain must know,
Such harmonious madness
  From my lips would flow
The world should listen then—as I am listening now.

John Keats wrote several odes—"Ode on Melancholy," and an ode "To Autumn"—but his two great poems "Ode on a Grecian Urn" and the "Ode to a Nightingale" have never been surpassed for mastery of the scope and range of the ode. Here is the nightingale ode, so close in spirit to Shelley's poem to the skylark:

1

My heart aches, and a drowsy numbness pains
  My sense, as though of hemlock I had drunk,
Or emptied some dull opiate to the drains
  One minute past, and Lethe-wards had sunk:
'Tis not through envy of thy happy lot,
  But being too happy in thine happiness—
    That thou, light-wingéd Dryad of the trees,
      In some melodious plot
  Of beechen green, and shadows numberless,
    Singest of summer in full-throated ease.

2

O, for a draught of vintage! that hath been
  Cool'd a long age in the deep-delvéd earth,
Tasting of Flora and the country green,
  Dance, and Provençal song, and sunburnt mirth!
O for a beaker full of the warm South,
  Full of the true, the blushful Hippocrene,
    With beaded bubbles winking at the brim,
      And purple-stainéd mouth;
  That I might drink, and leave the world unseen,
    And with thee fade away into the forest dim:

3

Fade far away, dissolve, and quite forget
  What thou among the leaves hast never known,

The weariness, the fever, and the fret
  Here, where men sit and hear each other groan;
Where palsy shakes a few, sad, last gray hairs,
    Where youth grows pale, and spectre-thin, and dies,
      Where but to think is to be full of sorrow
        And leaden-eyed despairs,
    Where Beauty cannot keep her lustrous eyes,
      Or new Love pine at them beyond to-morrow.

4

Away! away! for I will fly to thee,
  Not charioted by Bacchus and his pards,
But on the viewless wings of Poesy,
    Though the dull brain perplexes and retards:
Already with thee! tender is the night,
    And haply the Queen-Moon is on her throne,
      Cluster'd around by all her starry Fays;
        But here there is no light,
    Save what from heaven is with the breezes blown
      Through verdurous glooms and winding mossy ways.

5

I cannot see what flowers are at my feet,
  Nor what soft incense hangs upon the boughs,
But, in embalméd darkness, guess each sweet
    Wherewith the seasonable month endows
The grass, the thicket, and the fruit tree wild;
    White hawthorn, and the pastoral eglantine;
      Fast fading violets cover'd up in leaves;
        And mid-May's eldest child,
    The coming musk-rose, full of dewy wine,
      The murmurous haunt of flies on summer eves.

6

Darkling I listen; and for many a time
  I have been half in love with easeful Death,
Call'd him soft names in many a muséd rhyme,
    To take into the air my quiet breath;
Now more than ever seems it rich to die,
    To cease upon the midnight with no pain,

While thou art pouring forth thy soul abroad
  In such an ecstasy!
Still wouldst thou sing, and I have ears in vain—
  To thy high requiem become a sod.

7

Thou wast not born for death, immortal Bird!
  No hungry generations tread thee down;
The voice I hear this passing night was heard
  In ancient days by emperor and clown:
Perhaps the selfsame song that found a path
  Through the sad heart of Ruth, when, sick for home,
    She stood in tears amid the alien corn;
      The same that ofttimes hath
  Charm'd magic casements, opening on the foam
  Of perilous seas, in faery lands forlorn.

8

Forlorn! the very word is like a bell
  To toll me back from thee to my sole self!
Adieu! the fancy cannot cheat so well
  As she is fam'd to do, deceiving elf.
Adieu! adieu! thy plaintive anthem fades
  Past the near meadows, over the still stream,
    Up the hill-side; and now 'tis buried deep
      In the next valley-glades:
Was it a vision, or a waking dream?
  Fled is that music:—Do I wake or sleep?

D. ECLOGUE.   An idyll or pastoral poem about rural life,
usually in dialogue form. The most well-known eclogues are
Virgil's ten short poems written in hexameter, based on the
earlier *Idylls* of Theocritus. In 43 B.C., Virgil had left Rome,
where he was studying philosophy and rhetoric, and retired to
his small farm in Mantua where he began writing his *Eclogues*,
later published in 37 B.C. Following is a passage from Virgil's
later *Georgics* (30 B.C.) in Latin with an English translation by
Dryden, which continue on the spirit of the *Eclogues*:

O fortunatos nimium sua si bona norint,
agricolas! quibus ipsa procul discordibus armis
fundit humo facilem uictum iustissima tellus;
sit non ingentem foribus domus alta superbix. . . .

O happy, if he knew his happy state,
The swain, who, free from bus'ness and debate,
Receives his easy food from Nature's hand,
And just returns of cultivated land! . . .

The eclogues of Theocritus and Virgil are models for most modern pastoral poetry—Petrarch based his Latin eclogues on Virgil, as did Boccaccio in his Italian eclogues. Spenser's *Shepheards Calendar*, Sidney's *Arcadia*, and a good deal of Shakespeare's *As You Like It* also derive from Virgil's *Eclogues*.

E. EPITHALAMION. A poem for a marriage or wedding celebration. We can feel the beginnings of the epithalamion in the early seventh-century B.C. poet Sappho:

Groom, we virgins at your door
will pass the night singing of the love
between you and your bride. Her breasts
are like violets.

Wake and call out the young men
your friends, and you can walk the streets
and we shall sleep less tonight than
the bright nightingale.

"WEDDING SONG." TR. WILLIS BARNSTONE. NUMBER 53

A later poem (LXI) by the Roman poet Catullus (84–54 B.C.) develops the epithalamion form as more of a ritual patterning:

Collis o Heliconii
cultor, Uraniae genus,
qui rapis teneram ad virum

virginem, o Hymenaee Hymen,
   o Hymen Hymenaee . . .

Oh that hill (O Helicon
where the muses gather)
there the son of all the vast planetary systems
walks in eternal splendour
giving blossoming girls away
to young men striding homeward,
O Hymenaee, Hymen,
O Hymen, Hymenaee . . .

NUMBER 61. TR. HORACE GREGORY

The English poet Edmund Spenser (1552–1599) wrote one of the first epithalamia in our language; following are the opening lines with an invocation to the Muses:

Ye learned sisters which have oftentimes
Beene to me ayding, others to adorne:
Whom ye thought worthy of your gracefull rymes,
That even the greatest did not greatly scorne
To heare theyr names sung in your simple layes,
But joyéd in theyr prayse. . . .

"EPITHALAMION"

One could see the whole of Shakespeare's play *A Midsummer Night's Dream* as an epithalamion, being a celebration of the marriage of Theseus, Duke of Athens, and Hippolyta, queen of the Amazons. Surely in the last act, Oberon's ditty is meant as a connubial blessing:

Now, until the break of day,
Through this house each fairy stray.
To the best bride-bed will we,
Which by us shall blessed be;
And the issue there create
Ever shall be fortunate. . . .

A MIDSUMMER NIGHT'S DREAM. V. 1

One contemporary American poet, Erica Jong, wrote an "Eggplant Epithalamion" based on an account that "A Turk won't marry a woman unless she can cook an eggplant at least a hundred ways."

Once upon a time on the coast of Turkey
there lived a woman who could cook eggplant 99 ways.
She could slice eggplant thin as paper.
She could write poems on it & batter-fry it.
She could bake eggplant & broil it.
She could even roll the seeds in banana-
flavored cigarette papers
& get her husband high on eggplant.
But he was not pleased.
He went to her father & demanded his bride-price back.
He said he'd been cheated.
He wanted back two goats, twelve chickens
& a camel as reparation.
His wife wept & wept.
Her father raved.

The next day she gave birth to an eggplant.
It was premature & green
& she had to sit on it for days
before it hatched.
"This is my hundredth eggplant recipe," she screamed.
"I hope you're satisfied!"
(Thank Allah that the eggplant was a boy.)

ERICA JONG, FROM *HALF-LIVES*, SECTION 3 OF "THE EGGPLANT EPITHALAMION"

F. ELEGY.   A poem of grief or mourning; a lyric lament. Classical examples of the form are Milton's "Lycidas," and Shelley's lament on the death of Keats, "Adonais":

I weep for Adonais—he is dead!
Oh, weep for Adonais! though our tears
Thaw not the frost which binds so dear a head!

And thou, sad Hour, selected from all years
To mourn our loss, rouse thy obscure compeers,
And teach them thine own sorrow, say: with me
Died Adonais; till the Future dares
Forget the Past, his fate and fame shall be
An echo and a light unto eternity . . .

Swinburne has a moving elegy on the death of Baudelaire, using as title a phrase from Catullus, "Ave atque Vale," "hale and farewell":

Shall I strew on thee rose or rue or laurel,
    Brother, on this that was the veil of thee?
    Or quiet sea-flower moulded by the sea,
Or simplest growth of meadow-sweet or sorrel,
    Such as the summer-sleepy Dryads weave,
    Waked up by snow-soft sudden rains at eve?
Or wilt thou rather, as on earth before,
    Half-faded fiery blossoms, pale with heat
    And full of bitter summer, but more sweet
To thee than gleanings of a northern shore
    Trod by no tropic feet? . . .

FROM ALGERNON CHARLES SWINBURNE. "AVE ATQUE
VALE: IN MEMORY OF CHARLES BAUDELAIRE"

W. H. Auden has written a modern elegy on the death of William Butler Yeats, who died in January 1939:

He disappeared in the dead of winter:
The brooks were frozen, the airports almost deserted,
And snow disfigured the public statues;
The mercury sank in the mouth of the dying day.
O all the instruments agree
The day of his death was a dark cold day. . . .

"IN MEMORY OF W. B. YEATS"

G. EPIGRAM.   A short gnomic or pithy saying, cleverly turned and aphoristic. *The Greek Anthology* contains some six

thousand short inscriptions and epigrams from the seventh century B.C. through the tenth century A.D. One example:

> What is a friend?
> A single soul dwelling in two bodies.
>
> MELEAGER, FIRST CENTURY B.C.

Another example:

> *Homo sum: humani nil a me alienum puto.*
> I am a man: nothing human is alien to me.
>
> TERENCE, CA. 185–159 B.C.

There are many epigrams scattered through the Bible, most
notably in the Old Testament books of Proverbs and Ecclesiastes,
and in the New Testament in the sayings of Jesus:

> Physician, heal thyself.
>
> LUKE 4:23

Many modern poets have delighted in the terse wit and homely
plain style of the epigram—as in the following two examples
from Robert Frost:

> A Question
>
> We dance round in a ring and suppose
> But the Secret sits in the middle and knows.
>
> •   •   •
>
> A Question
>
> A voice said, Look me in the stars
> And tell me truly, men of earth,
> If all the soul-and-body scars
> Were not too much to pay for birth.

H. EPITAPH. A short verse for placement on a tomb or monument. One of the earliest examples is the epitaph for Leonidas, who used a small Spartan force to hold the pass of Thermopylae against the Persians in 480 B.C.

> Go tell the Spartans, you who pass by,
> That here obedient to their laws we lie.

Shakespeare wrote his own epitaph in an attempt to keep people from tampering with his remains:

> GOOD FRIEND FOR IESUS SAKE FORBEARE
> TO DIGG THE DUST ENCLOASED HERE
> BLESE BE YE MAN TY SPARES THES STONES
> AND CURST BE HE TY MOVES MY BONES

A modern example of an epitaph is by Robert Louis Stevenson:

> Under the wide and starry sky,
> Dig the grave and let me lie.
> Glad did I live and gladly die,
>   And I laid me down with a will.
>
> This be the verse you grave for me:
> Here he lies where he longed to be;
> Home is the sailor, home from the sea,
>   And the hunter home from the hill.

One of the most famous epitaphs for a poet was written by William Butler Yeats exactly as it appears on his tombstone:

> Cast a cold eye
> On life, on death.
> Horseman, pass by!

And Robert Frost chose a single line from one of his poems to serve as his own epitaph:

> I had a lover's quarrel with the world.

I. ENVOI.   A salutation and sending forth of one's own poetry. Ezra Pound wrote the following, "Ite":

> Go, my songs, seek your praise from the young
>   and from the intolerant,
> Move among the lovers of perfection alone.
> Seek ever to stand in the hard Sophoclean light
> And take your wounds from it gladly.
>
> FROM *PERSONAE*

J. EPISTLE.   A letter in verse, poem in the form of direct address to a particular person. The following example is by Norman Rosten:

> Letter No. 1
>
> I'm touched that you, my one disciple,
> Bring me your purest meditation.
> You speak lately of doubts and terrors,
> Your letters seem to hint of flight.
> Having followed my proverbs and poverty,
> You ask, What's the word from the wilderness?
> You may have heard they've written me off
> As an agitator who spurned the cross
> In favor of lyric poetry . . .
>
> *NEW YORK QUARTERLY,* NUMBER 3

Of course there can be many other varieties of lyric poetry— the limerick, the haiku, and specific types of song such as "carpe diem" or "seize the day" (such as Robert Herrick's "To the Virgins, To Make Much of Time").

There can also be mixtures of dramatic-narrative poems, such as Robert Browning in "My Last Duchess":

> That's my last duchess painted on the wall,
> Looking as if she were alive. I call

That piece a wonder, now: Fra Pandolf's hands
Worked busily a day, and there she stands.
Will't please you sit and look at her? . . .

The dramatic and narrative and lyric genres are profoundly different in technique and discipline; they are as different as oils and watercolors and charcoal sketching are different from one another. It takes an accomplished artist to be able to move freely from one of these genres to another, if indeed it can be done at all.

4

VERSE FORMS

Traditional verse tends to form itself into certain organized line arrangements, certain repeated patternings of regular meter and rhyme. In this chapter we'll look at the various line lengths, stanza units, and fixed verse forms such as the sestina, canzone, villanelle, sonnet, and ballad. We'll also examine the practice of free verse, which stands outside these traditional verse forms.

We should say at the outset that there is no innate virtue in working in any of these traditional verse forms: One is not necessarily a better poet for writing within fixed forms, any more than one is a better poet for writing outside these forms. Fixed verse forms are simply a part of the heritage of poetry that is at our disposal, and one may or may not find them compatible with one's own individual writing destiny.

For example: in the whole of Walt Whitman's massive volume *Leaves of Grass*, there is only one poem written in strict stanzaic patterning with fixed rhyme scheme and metrics—it is Whitman's lament for Abraham Lincoln, "O Captain, My Captain." And while the poem shows the poignance and grief Whitman felt for the loss of his leader, we have to say "O Captain, My Captain" is not one of his better pieces, surely not comparable to the masterful free verse work in "Song of Myself," or the stupendous poem "Out of the Cradle Endlessly Rocking," or even the other great lament for Lincoln which is written in free verse, "When Lilacs Last in the Dooryard Bloom'd." Whitman's genius was for expressing himself in free verse—"Turbulent, fleshy, sensual, eating, drinking and breeding"—and we can only be thankful that he knew it, and did not waste his time trying to cram his talent into the cookie-cutter of imposed fixed forms like the sestina or the sonnet or the villanelle.

On the other hand, we will be using a number of poems by W. H. Auden in this chapter to illustrate various types of fixed form—iambic dimeter, sestina, canzone, and sonnet. It's always sobering to realize that certain poets like Auden and Dylan Thomas and W. B. Yeats and William Shakespeare excelled in using fixed forms. In fact, W. H. Auden was so encyclopedic in his mastery of craft, one could see his *Collected Poems* as a sort of reference book of fixed forms: If one wants to find an excellent example of any single given form, one can go to Auden and invariably discover that Auden achieved one of the finest contemporary usages of the form in his work.

Look at it this way: It's a little like acting. One may feel one is wonderfully adapted to doing daytime soap opera, but an actor can always exercise his instrument by going back to work on the great classical roles of Greek theater or Shakespeare. It's an excellent way of honing one's instincts and sharpening one's reflexes, and one will never know until one tries it whether one has an authentic talent for working in traditional form.

LINE LENGTHS

To begin with, following is a list of the most common lines in English poetry, counting number of feet per line. "Foot" is defined as a unit of language with one accented syllable and one or more unaccented syllables.

monometer—one foot
dimeter—two feet
trimeter—three feet
tetrameter—four feet
pentameter—five feet
hexameter—six feet
septameter—seven feet
octameter—eight feet

Following are examples of different line lengths, with accent marks over the words to indicate the metrical patterning. (. /) stands for slack and stress:

I am of Ireland   iambic trimeter
And of the holy land
Of Ireland

When he is well   iambic dimeter
She gives him hell.
But she's a brick
When he is sick.

W. H. AUDEN, "SHORTS"

SHALL I COMPARE THEE TO A SUMMER'S DAY?   IAMBIC PENTAMETER
THOU ART MORE LOVELY AND MORE TEMPERATE:
ROUGH WINDS DO SHAKE THE DARLING BUDS
OF MAY.
AND SUMMER'S LEASE HATH ALL TOO SHORT A
DATE . . .

SHAKESPEARE, SONNET 18

WHAT MIND THAT IS UNKIND, WHAT HEART
    THAT MAY BE HARD,

IN VIEWING YOU, WOULD NOT GROW SOFT IN
    ITS REGARD?

NO MATTER WHAT THEY SAY OR HOW THEY
    PAINT MY PRIDE,

DO THEY SUPPOSE SOME BEAST ONCE CARRIED
    ME INSIDE?

IAMBIC HEXAMETER
(CLASSICAL ALEXAN-
DRINE)

RACINE, *PHÈDRE*, TR. WILLIAM PACKARD

STANZA UNITS

The various stanza units can be grouped together according to how many lines per stanza, as follows:

> monostiche—one-line stanza
> couplet—two-line stanza
> tercet—three-line stanza
> quatrain—four-line stanza
> cinquain—five-line stanza
> sestet—six-line stanza
> septet—seven-line stanza
> octave—eight-line stanza
> Spenserian or nine-line stanza

Following are examples of each of the above stanza units:

1. MONOSTICH:

> Sun smudge on the smoky waters.

ARCHIBALD MACLEISH, "AUTUMN"

2. COUPLET:

> Know then thyself, presume not God to scan;
> The proper study of mankind is man.

ALEXANDER POPE. *AN ESSAY ON MAN.* EPISTLE II

3. TERCET (WITH TERZA RIMA):

> O wild West Wind, thou breath of Autumn's being,
> Thou, from whose unseen presence the leaves dead
> Are driven, like ghosts from an enchanter fleeing,
>
> Yellow, and black, and pale, and hectic red,
> Pestilence-stricken multitudes: O thou,
> Who chariotest to their dark wintry bed . . .

SHELLEY. "ODE TO THE WEST WIND"

4. QUATRAIN:

> And we are put on earth a little space,
> That we may learn to bear the beams of love,
> And these black bodies and this sunburnt face
> Is but a cloud, and like a shady grove.

WILLIAM BLAKE. "THE LITTLE BLACK BOY"

5. CINQUAIN:

> I saw a young snake glide
> Out of the mottled shade
> And hang, limp on a stone:
> A thin mouth, and a tongue
> Stayed, in the still air.

THEODORE ROETHKE. "SNAKE"

6. SESTET (ALSO CALLED SEXAIN):

I wandered lonely as a cloud
    That floats on high o'er vales and hills,
When all at once I saw a crowd,
    A host, of golden daffodils;
Beside the lake, beneath the trees,
Fluttering and dancing in the breeze.

WORDSWORTH, "I WANDERED LONELY AS A CLOUD"

7. SEPTET:

When the world takes over for us
and the storm in the trees
replaces our brittle consciences
(like ships, female to all seas)
when the few last yellow leaves
stand out like flags on tossed ships
at anchor—our minds are rested

WILLIAM CARLOS WILLIAMS, "LEAR"

8. OCTAVE (USING OTTAVA RIMA):

I walk through the long schoolroom questioning;
A kind old nun in a white hood replies;
The children learn to cipher and to sing,
To study reading-books and history,
To cut and sew, be neat in everything
In the best modern way—the children's eyes
In momentary wonder stare upon
A sixty-year-old smiling public man.

YEATS, "AMONG SCHOOL CHILDREN"

9. NINE-LINE STANZA:

> Where there is personal liking we go.
>   Where the ground is sour; where there are
>   weeds of beanstalk height,
>   snakes' hypodermic teeth, or
>   the wind brings the "scarebabe voice"
>   from the neglected yew set with
>   the semi-precious cat's eyes of the owl—
> awake, asleep, "raised ears extended to fine points," and so
> on—love won't grow.

MARIANNE MOORE, "THE HERO"

VERSE FORMS

Following are some of the most common verse forms in English poetry.

1. SESTINA.   Composed of six stanzas and a coda, each stanza having six lines which use the same repeated end words in the following sequence: 1-2-4-5-3-6. That is to say: the first end word in stanza one becomes the second end word of stanza two, then becomes the fourth end word in stanza three, then the fifth end word of stanza four, then the third end word of stanza five, then the sixth end word of stanza six. In the following example, "Paysage Moralisé" by W. H. Auden, one can follow the word *valley* through the 1-2-4-5-3-6 pattern. Each of the other end words follow the same progression—*mountains* is the second end word of stanza one, so must become the fourth end word of stanza two, the fifth end word of stanza three, the third end word of stanza four, the sixth end word of stanza five, and the first end word of stanza six. The coda of the poem uses 5-3-1 as end words (water/valleys/islands), and the remaining three end words within the lines themselves.

Paysage Moralisé

Hearing of harvests rotting in the valleys,
Seeing at end of street the barren mountains,
Round corners coming suddenly on water,
Knowing them shipwrecked who were launched for islands,
We honour founders of these starving cities
Whose honour is the image of our sorrow.

Which cannot see its likeness in their sorrow
That brought them desperate to the brink of valleys;
Dreaming of evening walks through learned cities
They reined their violent horses on the mountains,
Those fields like ships to castaways on islands,
Visions of green to them who craved for water.

They built by rivers and at night the water
Running past windows comforted their sorrow;
Each in his little bed conceived of islands
Where every day was dancing in the valleys
And all the green trees blossomed on the mountains,
Where love was innocent, being far from cities.

But dawn came back and they were still in cities;
No marvellous creature rose up from the water;
There was still gold and silver in the mountains
But hunger was a more immediate sorrow,
Although to moping villagers in valleys
Some waving pilgrims were describing islands . . .

'The gods' they promised, 'visit us from islands,
Are stalking, head-up, lovely, through our cities;
Now is the time to leave your wretched valleys
And sail with them across the lime-green water,
Sitting at their white sides, forget your sorrow,
The shadow cast across your lives by mountains.'

So many, doubtful, perished in the mountains,
Climbing up crags to get a view of islands,
So many, fearful, took them with their sorrow
Which stayed them when they reached unhappy cities,
So many, careless, dived and drowned in water,
So many, wretched, would not leave their valleys.

It is our sorrow. Shall it melt? Then water
Would gush, flush, green these mountains and these valleys,
And we rebuild our cities, not dream of islands.

B. CANZONE.   Composed of five stanzas and a coda, each
stanza having twelve lines which use the same repeated end words
in the following sequence: a) 1-2-1-1-3-1-1-4-4-1-5-5; b) 5-1-5-
5-2-5-5-3-3-5-4-4; c) 4-5-4-4-1-4-4-2-2-4-3-3; d) 3-4-3-3-5-3-3-
1-1-3-2-2; e) 2-3-2-2-4-2-2-5-5-2-1-1, the coda must use 1-5-4-
3-2 sequence.

Canzone

When shall we learn, what should be clear as day,
We cannot choose what we are free to love?
Although the mouse we banished yesterday
Is an enraged rhinoceros today,
Our value is more threatened than we know:
Shabby objections to our present day
Go snooping round its outskirts; night and day
Faces, orations, battles, bait our will
As questionable forms and noises will;
Whole phyla of resentments every day
Give status to the wild men of the world
Who rule the absent-minded and this world.

We are created from and with the world
To suffer with and from it day by day:
Whether we meet in a majestic world
Of solid measurements or a dream world
Of swans and gold, we are required to love
All homeless objects that require a world.
Our claim to own our bodies and our world
Is our catastrophe. What can we know
But panic and caprice until we know
Our dreadful appetite demands a world
Whose order, origin, and purpose will
Be fluent satisfaction of our will?

Drift, Autumn, drift; fall, colours, where you will:
Bald melancholia minces through the world.
Regret, cold oceans, the lymphatic will
Caught in reflection on the right to will:
While violent dogs excite their dying day
To bacchic fury; snarl, though, as they will,
Their teeth are not a triumph for the will
But utter hesitation. What we love
Ourselves for is our power not to love,
To shrink to nothing or explode at all,
To ruin and remember that we know
What ruins and hyaenas cannot know.

If in this dark now I less often know
That spiral staircase where the haunted will
Hunts for its stolen luggage, who should know
Better than you, beloved, how I know
What gives security to any world,
Or in whose mirror I begin to know
The chaos of the heart as merchants know
Their coins and cities, genius its own day?
For through our lively traffic all the day,
In my own person I am forced to know
How much must be forgotten out of love,
How much must be forgiven, even love.

Dear flesh, dear mind, dear spirit, dearest love,
In the depths of myself blind monsters know
Your presence and are angry, dreading Love
That asks its images for more than love;
The hot rampageous horses of my will,
Catching the scent of Heaven, whinny: Love
Gives no excuse to evil done for love,
Neither in you, nor me, nor armies, nor the world
Of words and wheels, nor any other world.
Dear fellow-creature, praise our God of Love
That we are so admonished, that no day
Of conscious trial to be a wasted day.

Or else we make a scarecrow of the day,
Loose ends and jumble of our common world,

And stuff and nonsense of our own free will;
Or else our changing flesh may never know
There must be sorrow if there can be love.

W. H. AUDEN

At this point we suppose someone could raise some question as to the value of doing such intricate verse forms, at least in English. Italian and Provençal poetry lend themselves more readily to elaborate exercises because there is greater resource of rhyme, and unless one has the great mastery of craft that a poet such as W. H. Auden has to bring off a sestina or a canzone, the result may be mere versifying for its own sake. One hears certain Beat voices shouting out that one should forget the whole thing, and not even attempt such forms in English.

Even so, there is always a wonderful technical challenge in trying to approach some of the most complex verse forms to see if one can unlock some hidden resources inside oneself, in trying to master such an elaborate requirement of verse writing. It may be a little like the challenge of trying to climb a mountain that has not yet been scaled. We're not saying there is any *virtue* per se in approaching such a challenge, we're just saying that it's there as a challenge for whatever one may choose to make of it. In any event, there can never be any harm in giving it a solid try.

C. VILLANELLE.   This form does not repeat key end words, but repeats entire *lines*. Such an insistent repetition will become a rhythmic tour de force, which, when it is done successfully, can become irresistible.

The villanelle is composed of six stanzas, each stanza having three lines using end rhymes and repeating the first or third lines of the opening stanza, with the sixth stanza having four lines repeating both the first and third lines of the opening stanza, in the following sequence: A-c-B/ab-c-A/ab-c-B/ab-c-A/ab-c-B/ab-c-A-B, as follows:

Do Not Go Gentle into That Good Night

Do not go gentle into that good night,
Old age should burn and rave at close of day;
Rage, rage against the dying of the light.

Though wise men at their end know dark is right,
Because their words had forked no lightning they
Do not go gentle into that good night.

Good men, the last wave by, crying how bright
Their frail deeds might have danced in a green bay,
Rage, rage against the dying of the light.

Wild men who caught and sang the sun in flight,
And learn, too late, they grieved it on its way,
Do not go gentle into that good night.

Grave men, near death, who see with blinding sight
Blind eyes could blaze like meteors and be gay,
Rage, rage against the dying of the light.

And you, my father, there on the sad height,
Curse, bless, me now with your fierce tears, I pray.
Do not go gentle into that good night,
Rage, rage against the dying of the light.

DYLAN THOMAS

D. THE SONNET.

Composed of fourteen lines, usually divided into an octave and sestet of eight and six lines, with a "turn" or "pivot" usually occurring around the ninth line at the beginning of the sestet.

The rhyme scheme of the Shakespearean sonnet form will be abab/cdcd/efef/gg; the rhyme scheme of the Petrarchan sonnet form will be abba/abba/cdecde. The Spenserian sonnet form will be abab/bcbc/cdcd/ee.

Because of its ongoing rhyme scheme of abab, the Shakespearean sonnet form will tend to be more dramatic, moving forward toward the "turn" or "pivot" in line nine and then reaching a resolution in the couplet. The Petrarchan sonnet form, due to its repeated use of enclosed couplets (abba/abba), will tend to be more lyrical, repeating the same motif over and over again, creating a mood rather than a dramatic progression. It's interesting that most of the great sonnets written by the Romantic poets—Wordsworth, Keats, and Shelley—were Petrarchan rather than Shakespearean; the same can be said of the sonnets of John Donne and Milton.

Following is an example of the Shakespearean sonnet form:

Shall I compare thee to a summer's day?	a
Thou art more lovely and more temperate:	b
Rough winds do shake the darling buds of May,	a
And summer's lease hath all too short a date:	b
Sometime too hot the eye of heav'n shines,	c
And often is his gold complexion dimm'd:	d
And every fair from fair sometime declines,	c
By chance, or nature's changing course untrimm'd,	d
But thy eternal summer shall not fade	e
Nor lose possession of that fair thou owest;	f
Nor shall Death brag thou wander'st in his shade,	e
When in eternal lines to time thou grow'st:	f
So long as men can breathe, or eyes can see,	g
So long lives this, and this gives life to thee.	g

SHAKESPEARE. SONNET 18

Following is an example of the Petrarchan sonnet form:

What lips my lips have kissed, and where, and why,	a
I have forgotten, and what arms have lain	b
Under my head till morning; but the rain	b
Is full of ghosts tonight, that tap and sigh	a
Upon the glass and listen for reply,	a
And in my heart there stirs a quiet pain	b
For unremembered lads that not again	b
Will turn to me at midnight with a cry.	a
Thus in the winter stands the lonely tree,	c
Nor knows what birds have vanished one by one,	d
Yet knows its boughs more silent than before:	e

I cannot say what loves have come and gone,   d
I only know that summer sang in me   c
A little while, that in me sings no more.   e

EDNA ST. VINCENT MILLAY. "WHAT LIPS MY LIPS HAVE KISSED"

Following is an example of a variation of the Petrarchan sonnet rhyme scheme:

Diaspora

How he survived them they could never understand: a
Had they not beggared him themselves to prove   b
They could not live without their dogmas or their land?   a

No worlds they drove him from were ever big enough: b
How *could* it be the earth the Unconfined   c
Meant when it bade them set no limits to their love?   b

And he fulfilled the role for which he was designed: c
On heat with fear, he drew their terrors to him,   d
And was a godsend to the lowest of mankind,   c

Till there was no place left where they could still pursue him d
Except that exile which he called his race.   e
But, envying him even that, they plunged right through him   d
Into a land of mirrors without time or space,   e
And all they had to strike now was the human face.   e

W. H. AUDEN (1940)

In modern poetry, poets have departed from the traditional Shakespearean and Petrarchan sonnet forms to create their own hybrid sonnet versions to suit their own rhetorical ends. It's interesting to see how much liberty one can take with the traditional form yet still echo the basic octave/sestet division of the sonnet. Thus Robert Lowell, commenting in "Afterthought" to his book *Notebook 1967–1968*, which is filled with "fourteen line poems," writes:

> My meter, fourteen line unrhymed blank verse sections, is fairly strict at first and elsewhere, but often

corrupts in single lines to the freedom of prose. Even
with this license, I fear I have failed to avoid the themes
and gigantism of the sonnet.

And in an even later book, *The Dolphin,* Lowell continues to
refine his license of using traditional sonnet form in blank verse
lines, although in the following example he is not able to avoid
internal rhyme of assonance and alliteration, and external random rhyme in such combinations as *surprise/composition, Phèdre/
body, many/muse, life/myself, and fiction/fighting:*

Dolphin

My Dolphin, you only guide me by surprise,
captive as Racine, the man of craft,
drawn through his maze of iron composition
by the incomparable wandering voice of Phèdre.
When I was troubled in mind, you made for my body
caught in its hangman's-knot of sinking lines,
the glassy bowing and scraping of my will. . . .
I have sat and listened to too many
words of the collaborating muse,
and plotted perhaps too freely with my life,
not avoiding injury to others,
not avoiding injury to myself—
to ask compassion . . . this book, half fiction,
an eelnet made by man for the eel fighting—

my eyes have seen what my hand did.

And following is an example of a free form sonnet by John
Berryman from his *Dream Songs*—the poem has twelve lines,
rhyme scheme of abcabc/defdef, with variable line lengths:

During those years he met his seminars,	a
went & lectured & read, talked with human beings,	b
paid insurance & taxes;	c
but his mind was not in it. His mind was elsewheres	a
in an area where the soul not talks but sings	b
& where foes are attacked with axes.	c

Enemies his pilgrimage duly brought	d
to bring him down, and they almost succeeded.	e
He sang on like a harmful bird.	f
His foes are like footnotes, he figured, sought	d
chiefly by doctoral candidates: props, & needed,—	e
comic relief,—absurd.	f

DREAM SONGS, NUMBER 352

E. BALLAD. A narrative, rhythmic saga of a past affair, sometimes romantic and inevitably catastrophic, which is impersonally related, usually with foreshortened lines and simple repeating rhymes, and often with a refrain.

The great traditional ballads in the English language include "Edward"; "Sir Patrick Spens"; "Barbara Allen's Cruelty"; "Johnny, I Hardly Knew Ye"; and the following ballad with its haunting dialogue:

As You Came from the Holy Land of Walsingham

'As you came from the holy land
    Of Walsingham,
Met you not with my true love
    By the way as you came?'

'How shall I know your true love,
    That have met many a one
As I went to the holy land,
    That have come, that have gone?'

'She is neither white nor brown,
    But as the heavens fair,
There is none hath a form so divine
    In the earth or the air.'

'Such an one did I meet, good Sir,
    Such an angelic face,
Who like a queen, like a nymph did appear
    By her gait, by her grace.'

'She hath left me here all alone,
   All alone as unknown,
Who sometimes did me lead with herself,
   And me loved as her own.'

'What's the cause that she leaves you alone
   And a new way doth take,
Who loved you once as her own
   And her joy did you make?'

'I have loved her all my youth,
   But now old as you see,
Love likes not the falling fruit
   From the withered tree.

'Know that Love is a careless child,
   And forgets promise past;
He is blind, he is deaf when he list
   And in faith never fast.

'His desire is a dureless content
   And a trustless joy;
He is won with a world of despair
   And is lost with a toy.

'Of womenkind such indeed is the love
   Or the word love abused,
Under which many childish desires
   And conceits are excused.

'But true love is a durable fire
   In the mind ever burning;
Never sick, never old, never dead,
   From itself never turning.'

                              SIR WALTER RALEIGH

   And there is this exquisite ballad by Keats based on traditional
ballad form, gradually revealing a vision of horror at the dev-
astating power of love:

La Belle Dame sans Merci

'O what can ail thee, knight-at-arms,
　　Alone and palely loitering?
The sedge has withered from the lake
　　And no birds sing.

'O what can ail thee, knight-at-arms,
　　So haggard and so woe-begone?
The squirrel's granary is full,
　　And the harvest's done.

'I see a lily on thy brow
　　With anguish moist and fever dew;
And on thy cheek a fading rose
　　Fast withereth too.

'I met a lady in the meads,
　　Full beautiful—a faery's child,
Her hair was long, her foot was light,
　　And her eyes were wild.

'I made a garland for her head,
　　And bracelets too, and fragrant zone;
She looked at me as she did love,
　　And made sweet moan.

'I set her on my pacing steed
　　And nothing else saw all day long,
For sideways would she lean, and sing
　　A faery's song.

'She found me roots of relish sweet,
　　And honey wild and manna dew,
And sure in language strange she said,
　　"I love thee true!"

'She took me to her elfin grot,
　　And there she wept and sighed full sore;
And there I shut her wild, wild eyes
　　With kisses four.

'And there she lulled me asleep,
　　And there I dreamed—Ah! woe betide!
The latest dream I ever dreamed
　　On the cold hill's side.

'I saw pale kings and princes too,
    Pale warriors, death-pale were they all;
Who cried—"La Belle Dame sans Merci
    Hath thee in thrall!"

'I saw their starved lips in the gloam
    With horrid warning gaped wide,
And I awoke and found me here
    On the cold hill's side.

'And this is why I sojourn here
    Alone and palely loitering,
Though the sedge is withered from the lake,
    And no birds sing.'

In modern poetry, poets have been attracted to traditional
ballad forms for the strong cadences and the sense of inevitable
catastrophe distantly glimpsed and impersonally related. Thus
Wordsworth echoes ballad rhythms in his "Lucy" poems, Dylan
Thomas achieves a sense of poignance and disaster in the "Ballad
of the Long-Legged Bait," and W. H. Auden depicts the plight
of romantic love in the modern world in "As I Walked Out One
Evening."

In the following poem, Anne Sexton uses first-person voice
to describe an allegory of personal integrity in the face of romantic
forsakenness:

The Ballad of the Lonely Masturbator

The end of the affair is always death.
She's my workshop. Slippery eye,
out of the tribe of myself my breath
finds you gone. I horrify
those who stand by. I am fed.
At night, alone, I marry the bed.

Finger to finger, now she's mine.
She's not too far. She's my encounter.
I beat her like a bell. I recline
in the bower where you used to mount her.

You borrowed me on the flowered spread.
At night, alone, I marry the bed.

Take for instance this night, my love,
that every single couple puts together
with a joint overturning, beneath, above,
the abundant two on sponge and feather,
kneeling and pushing, head to head.
At night alone, I marry the bed.

I break out of my body this way,
an annoying miracle. Could I
put the dream market on display?
I am spread out. I crucify.
My *little plum* is what you said.
At night, alone, I marry the bed.

Then my black-eyed rival came.
The lady of water, rising on the beach,
a piano at her fingertips, shame
on her lips and a flute's speech.
And I was the knock-kneed broom instead.
At night alone I marry the bed.

She took you the way a woman takes
a bargain dress off the rack
and I broke the way a stone breaks.
I give back your books and fishing tack.
Today's paper says that you are wed.
At night, alone, I marry the bed.

The boys and girls are one tonight.
They unbutton blouses. They unzip flies.
They take off shoes. They turn off the light.
The glimmering creatures are full of lies.
They are eating each other. They are overfed.
At night, alone, I marry the bed.

Opening Lines

Much can be said about beginning a poem with the strongest possible opening line, to command attention and plunge the reader directly into the heart of a poem.

Each of the four different kinds of English sentences mentioned in chapter 2—declarative, imperative, interrogative, and exclamatory—can be used to extraordinary effect to create powerful opening lines in poetry.

Following is an example of a strong declarative opening:

Something there is that doesn't love a wall . . .

ROBERT FROST, "MENDING WALL"

Following is an example of a strong imperative opening:

Do not go gentle into that good night . . .

DYLAN THOMAS, "DO NOT GO GENTLE INTO THAT GOOD NIGHT"

Following is an example of a strong interrogative opening:

Shall I compare thee to a summer's day?

SHAKESPEARE, SONNET 18

Following is an example of a strong exclamatory opening:

Look at the stars! Look, look up at the skies!

GERARD MANLEY HOPKINS, "THE STARLIGHT NIGHT"

Aside from the strong opening lines that one can achieve by using any of the four sentences, poets can experiment with other possibilities for strong openings. For example, there is the periodic sentence, which delays the subject and predicate for several lines. Milton used a periodic opening for the first lines of *Paradise Lost*:

> Of Man's first Disobedience, and the Fruit
> Of that Forbidden Tree, whose mortal taste
> Brought Death into the World, and all our woe,
> With loss of Eden, till one greater Man
> Restore us, and regain the blissful Seat,
> Sing, Heavenly Muse, that on the secret top
> Of Oreb, or of Sinai, didst inspire
> That Shepherd, who first taught the chosen Seed,
> In the Beginning how the Heavens and Earth
> Rose out of Chaos; or if Sion Hill
> Delight thee more, and Siloa's Brook that flowed
> Fast by the Oracle of God; I thence
> Invoke thy aid to my adventurous Song,
> That with no middle flight intends to soar
> Above th'Aonian Mount, while it pursues
> Things unattempted yet in Prose or Rhyme. . . .

A modern example of periodic sentence used as the opening lines of a poem is W. H. Auden's "In Memory of Sigmund Freud," which delays the actual subject of the poem until the third stanza:

> When there are so many we shall have to mourn,
> When grief has been made so public, and exposed
>   To the critique of a whole epoch
>   The frailty of our conscience and anguish,
>
> Of whom shall we speak? For every day they die
> Among us, those who were doing us some good,
>   And knew it was never enough but
>   Hoped to improve a little by living.
>
> Such was this doctor: still at eighty, he wished
> To think of our life, from whose unruliness
>   So many plausible young futures
>   With threats or flattery ask obedience. . . .

FREE VERSE

Free verse is poetry of any line length and any placement on the page, with no fixed measure or shape to the final form.

Before we make any preliminary judgment on the matter, we should remember that a large body of the world's greatest literature and poetry is in so-called free verse—including the most exalted passages of Isaiah, Jeremiah, Job, and the Psalms of the Old Testament. Because the ancient Hebrew did not have metrics, the poetry tended to be strong voice poetry with musical phrase as the only measure. Following are the six brief verses of the Twenty-third Psalm:

1.   The LORD is my shepherd; I shall not want.

2.   He maketh me to lie down in green pastures: he leadeth me beside the still waters.

3.   He restoreth my soul: he leadeth me in the paths of righteousnes for his name's sake.

4.   Yea, though I walk through the valley of the shadow of death, I will fear no evil: for thou art with me; thy rod and thy staff they comfort me.

5.   Thou preparest a table before me in the presence of mine enemies: thou anointest my head with oil; my cup runneth over.

6.   Surely goodness and mercy shall follow me all the days of my life: and I will dwell in the house of the LORD for ever.

The beauty of the imagery of these lines, and the gentle assonance of *shepherd/shall* and *surely/shall* in the opening and the close of the psalm, create a calm that is magical. In the middle of the psalm, there is a subtle shift of person as "he" changes to "thou" and the psalm becomes direct address, as the psalmist goes through the harrowing danger of the valley of the shadow of death; but toward the end, the psalm returns to third person. This subtle pronoun shift goes a long way toward accounting for the eerie sense of drama and reassurance of this brief psalm.

We have not even made mention of the fact that the entire psalm is in free verse, has no fixed line length, no formal end rhyme, and no patterning of its rhythms. It achieves its own form on its own terms, as a voice poem, and it does so supremely.

Following is an example of the free verse of Walt Whitman, from the 1855 edition of *Leaves of Grass:*

> I celebrate myself, and sing myself,
> And what I assume you shall assume,
> For every atom belonging to me as good belongs to you.

> I loafe and invite my soul,
> I lean and loafe at my ease observing a spear of summer grass.

"SONG OF MYSELF"

Whitman's ambition was to free poetry from its traditional conventions of strict meter and end-rhyme and stanzaic units; his "barbaric yawp" seemed to be untamed, as he says, "Nature without check with original energy."

Similarly Ezra Pound, in Canto LXXXI, describing his own efforts to free poetry of fixed meter and measure, writes:

> (To break the pentameter, that was the first heave)

The debate over free versus fixed verse has had many participants during the modern era. On the one hand, T. S. Eliot argues for the responsibility that free verse imposes on the poet:

> No *vers* is *libre* for the man who wants to do a good job.

And on the other hand, Robert Frost argues for some fixed measure in a poem:

> I'd as soon write free verse as play tennis with the net down.

Another poet, Robert Duncan, suggested that the whole free/ fixed verse controversy may be a red herring. Duncan felt the real question was whether a poet could trust his impulse to find his own form:

> After Freud, we discover that unwittingly we find our own form.

In other words, just as a dream creates its own form on its own terms, so one can trust any impulse to realize itself without reference to any external coordinates. Robert Creeley once said, "Form is never more than an extension of content," and later commented:

> I still feel that to be true. The thing to be said tends to dictate the mode in which it can be said. I really believe Charles Olson's contention that there's an appropriate way of saying something inherent in the thing to be said.

We might call this a sort of "organic form," as opposed to traditional or fixed form. And surely there is as much evidence of good work being done using organic form as there is in traditional form.

But there is something to be said for a poet's informing himself in all aspects of prosody and poetics. And with the breakdown of literacy in our time, when even the basic elements of grammar and syntax and spelling seem to be at such an all-time low ebb, we can at least avail ourselves of the comment made by Stanley Kunitz:

> When I first began to teach, in the late forties, it seemed quite obvious that instruction in prosody was part of a workshop discipline. Today the young are mostly indifferent to such matters; not only indifferent but even strongly antipathetic. They praise novelty, spontaneity, and ease, and they resist the very concept of form, which

they relate to mechanism and chains. Few understand that, for a poet, even breathing comes under the heading of prosody.

NEW YORK QUARTERLY CRAFT INTERVIEW, NUMBER 4

5

THE POEM ITSELF

It's time to consider the individual parts of any given poem—
title, opening lines, subject matter, and closure.

TITLES

There are five possibilities in choosing a title for any poem: the
summary title; generic title; oblique title; first line; or untitled.

a. *summary title*—will identify the subject matter of the poem,
   such as "The Lake Isle of Innisfree" by Yeats, or "The Waste
   Land" of Eliot.

b. *generic title*—will specify what type of poem it is, such as
   "Elegy Written in a Country Churchyard" by Gray, or "De-
   jection: An Ode" by Coleridge, or "Rondeau" for the poem
   "Jenny Kissed Me" by Leigh Hunt.

c. *oblique title*—will seem to have little or nothing to do with
   the poem itself, such as "In Time of 'The Breaking of Nations' " by Hardy, or "If You" by Creeley.

d. *first line*—will simply use the first line as the title, such as "Do Not Go Gentle into That Good Night" by Dylan Thomas, or "As I Walked Out One Evening" by Auden, or "Still Falls the Rain" by Edith Sitwell.

e. *untitled*—will leave the poem with no title.

(Some may mix the above categories, such as "The River-Merchant's Wife: A Letter, after Rihaku" by Ezra Pound.)

Then again, the choice of a title may be itself the creative stimulus for the writing of a poem, as John Ashbery implies:

> . . . what happens is that a possible title occurs to me and it defines an area that I feel I'll be able to move around in and uncover. It's not that I feel necessarily that titles are important in themselves . . . the title is something that tips the whole poem in one direction or another, doesn't it?
>
> NEW YORK QUARTERLY CRAFT INTERVIEW, NUMBER 9

OPENING LINES

One option is to begin a poem in the midst of things, with no background preparation whatsoever. Thus Yeats in his great sonnet "Leda and the Swan" chooses to begin at the exact instant of the rape itself:

> A sudden blow: the great wings beating still
> Above the staggering girl, her thighs caressed
> By the dark webs, her nape caught in his bill,
> He holds her helpless breast upon his breast. . . .

Some poems even begin in mid-sentence, as if we were suddenly coming into earshot of a poetry that has already been going on for some time. Thus Marianne Moore begins her poem "Melancthon":

Openly, yes,
with the naturalness
  of the hippopotamus or the alligator
  when it climbs out on the bank to experience the

sun, I do these
things which I do, which please
  no one but myself . . .

And Ezra Pound begins the opening lines of his epic *Cantos* in mid-sentence, plunging us into Pound's own translation of part of Book XI of Homer's *Odyssey:*

And then went down to the ship,
Set keel to breakers, forth on the godly sea, and
We set up mast and sail on that swart ship,
Bore sheep aboard her, and our bodies also
Heavy with weeping, and winds from sternward
Bore us out onward with bellying canvas,
Circe's this craft, the trim-coifed goddess. . . .

SUBJECT MATTER

Where does a poet get the subject matter for his poetry?

It's a difficult question to deal with, although it may seem that traditional poetry often begins with a simple idea or theme or motif, and then develops it through a series of steps until it reaches some simple resolution. John Milton and John Donne and Ralph Waldo Emerson seem to have written poetry according to this linear and logical way of seeing things.

Yet even in antiquity, artists knew there was another approach to subject matter. Plato taught that the poet does not really choose his subject matter, but rather the subject matter chooses the poet. In the *Ion,* Socrates says:

. . . there is a divinity moving you, like that contained in the stone which Euripedes calls a magnet. . . . For

all good poets, epic as well as lyric, compose their beautiful poems not by art, but because they are inspired and
possessed. . . . For the poet is a light and winged and
holy thing, and there is no invention in him until he
has been inspired and is out of his senses, and the mind
is no longer in him: when he has not attained to this
state, he is powerless and is unable to utter his oracles.

PLATO. *ION.* 534

Most artists can identify with this description of the aesthetic
process—the experience of going into a trance state in which
one is "given" what one writes. According to this view, the artist
is a kind of *amanuensis*, someone who simply takes dictation from
some higher power. And as a matter of fact, some modern authors
like Strindberg and Yeats actually experimented with alchemy
and spiritualism to explore their unconscious minds, to disgorge
themes and motifs which they later wrote about.

As far as subject matter is concerned then, quite often an artist
will not know what he wants to say until he actually says it.
One's true subject matter may not be something that is conceived
by the mind along linear or logical lines, but something unknown
that has to be intuited in the very act of poetry writing.

T. S. Eliot in *The Waste Land* drew on mythology and
anthropology, which he interwove with colloquial voices of
twentieth-century women in London who were all frustrated and
out of touch with their own fertility.

Ezra Pound used collage and juxtaposition of widely disparate
elements to write his monumental *Cantos*, and he commented
that the form was more like a fugue or a mosaic than any traditional sense of "subject matter."

Anne Sexton went back to subject matter contained in Grimm
fairy tales and stories in the Greek myths and the Bible.

William Carlos Williams expanded the resources of subject
matter in his epic poem *Paterson* to include raw prose data, letters,
quotations, catalogue listings, and everyday events in his New
Jersey city.

And James Dickey in his poem "Falling" extends subject matter to include the radical point of view of a stewardess who is falling from an airplane. The poem recreates her mind in motion as she falls through the air on her way down to the ground.

All these approaches to subject matter may be seen as departures from the traditional view that poetry should begin with a simple idea or theme or motif, and then develop it through a series of steps until it reaches some simple resolution. Modern poetry does not always approach subject matter in such a linear and logical way of seeing things.

And there are even more radical approaches to subject matter in contemporary American poetry. Charles Olson, leader of the so-called Black Mountain school of poets, insisted that the true subject of a poem was the gesture of the poet who was writing it, his own stance and gesture of his breath as he engaged in the process of poetry writing. This is similar to the action painting of Jackson Pollock and Willem de Kooning and Franz Kline, who do not have ostensible "subjects" so much as the action of creating the painting itself:

> Writing traditional form makes for rhetoric.
> The alternative is to write as you breathe.
> Either one is good if it is done well in its way.
> Form is then the skin or the how of the art.
> Your rut is so much more important. And this is
> only arrived at by the sharp influx of things. . . .
>
> CHARLES OLSON, "PROJECTIVE VERSE"

Subject matter will even impinge on one's diction, on the kind of language and syntax one uses in a poem, sometimes to the point of ungrammatical or coarse colloquial street language, even ethnic patois. Allen Ginsberg's *Howl* was put on trial in San Francisco over the alleged obscenity that occurs in such lines as:

> with mother finally • • • • • •

Later editions of the poem spelled out the word *fucked* with no repercussions, and today we take such freedoms for granted, provided the subject matter requires frank language.

In "Confessional" poetry, crucial material about the personal life of the poet is raised to consciousness and made the subject of poems. There have been strong objections to this approach to subject matter, and one remembers Aristotle's injunction in the *Poetics*:

> The poet should say very little *in propria persona*, for he is no imitator [mimesis] when doing that.

In propria persona—in his own voice: Artistotle is saying the poet should always assume different masks, different personas, and never write in the autobiographical first person. All the greatest Greek tragic poets used masks and spoke through other characters, as Aeschylus and Sophocles and Euripedes did in their great plays *Agamemnon* and *Oedipus Rex* and *Medea*.

And modern critics have also chastised the Confessional poets for concentrating too much on their own subjectivity. For example, James Dickey really lets them have it:

> . . the poets that are paid so much attention to now— Anne Sexton, for example, or Sylvia Plath—they're just so many scab-pickers, you know? They concentrated on their little hang-ups, and bitch about them. If I have to read one more poem of Anne Sexton's about middle-aged menstruation, I'll blow my head off! Those things exist, of course—but those gigantic schools of fish and those flights of birds, they also exist, in Robinson Jeffers's imagery! Marvelous big imagery, galaxies, oceans.
>
> NEW YORK QUARTERLY CRAFT INTERVIEW. NUMBER 10

But Anne Sexton's retort to that blast would be that *all* art is confessional in one way or another:

> Was Thomas Wolfe confessional or not? Any poem is therapy. The art of writing is therapy. You don't solve problems in writing. They're still there. I've heard psychiatrists say, "See, you've forgiven your father. There

it is in your poem." But I haven't forgiven my father. I just wrote that I did.

NEW YORK QUARTERLY CRAFT INTERVIEW, NUMBER 3

W. D. Snodgrass, who is credited with being one of the first of the Confessional poets, explains the origin of the confessional mode in his own life:

> At the time I came through school it was forbidden to write about any of your personal affairs—even though this is something poets always *had* done. The poems that brought me this title "confessional" were the kind of poems that a hundred years before *anyone* would have written. I was moved in that direction by some of the German poets who wrote about lost children, dead children. Our children don't die as often, they get divorced.
>
> In school, we'd been taught we had to write poems about The Loss of Myth in Our Time, and I was sick and tired of the loss of myth. I'd written all the standard poems about that; but then I wanted to write about what I really cared about—problems in my love life, problems with my daughter, feeling lonely. But the standard dogma said you couldn't write about those subjects; we lived in too complicated and too impersonal times. That seemed to me silly; it seemed at least worth trying to do something different.

Snodgrass did do something different—he published *Heart's Needle*, an autobiographical account of how he spent years trying to reclaim the love of his daughter, who had been separated from him through divorce. The poem is a masterpiece of intricate rhymed verse forms, as in this second section:

> Late April and you are three; today
>   We dug your garden in the yard.
> To curb the damage of your play,
>   Strange dogs at night and the moles tunneling,
>   Four slender sticks of lath stand guard
>   Uplifting their thin string.

So you were the first to tramp it down.
And after the earth was sifted close
You brought your watering can to drown
All earth *and* us. But these mixed seeds are pressed
With light loam in their steadfast rows.
Child, we've done our best.

Someone will have to weed and spread
The young sprouts. Sprinkle them in the hour
When shadow falls across their bed.
You should try to look at them every day
Because when they come to full flower
I will be away.

Poets such as Allen Ginsberg and Robert Lowell and Sylvia
Plath wrote unremitting accounts of their own lives—break-
downs, fits of madness, suicide attempts, etc. Ginsberg even tried
to generalize the situation by displacing it onto his contemporaries:

I saw the best minds of my generation destroyed by
madness, starving hysterical naked,
dragging themselves through the negro streets at dawn
looking for an angry fix . . .

Robert Lowell published *Life Studies* in 1959, in which he
described his own imprisonment for conscientious objector status
during World War II ("Memories of West Street and Lepke"),
his marital problems ("Man and Wife"), and this poem where
he re-creates the ward of a mental hospital:

The night attendant, a B.U. sophomore,
rouses from the mare's-nest of his drowsy head
propped on *The Meaning of Meaning.*
He catwalks down our corridor,
Azure day
makes my agonized blue window bleaker.
Crows maunder on the petrified fairway.
Absence! My heart grows tense

as though a harpoon were sparring for the kill.
(This is the house for the "mentally ill.")

FROM "WAKING IN THE BLUE"

Writing of these poems, the critic M. L. Rosenthal commented:

> Life Studies was the most remarkable poetic sequence since Hart Crane's The Bridge and William Carlos Williams's Paterson. It may well stand as Lowell's chief accomplishment. At the same time, it presented Lowell himself so vulnerably and humiliatingly that only his extraordinary gifts enabled him to transcend the hysteria behind it. The transcendence made for a revolutionary achievement, but of a sort that can never be repeated by the same poet.

M. L. ROSENTHAL. THE NEW POETS (1967)

Sylvia Plath wrote such astonishing poetry in The Colossus and Ariel, and her chosen persona was so ethereal and catastrophic, that her work came to be seen as the annals of an ongoing psychic crisis inside herself. Since her unfortunate death in 1963, Sylvia Plath's poetry has exercised a powerful influence over young people. Her novel The Bell Jar also helped to raise the poet to cult status, as if one's own personal furies could now take on a cosmic importance they had never enjoyed before. In elite schools and colleges all across America, neurasthenic young women began to romanticize their spacy and suicidal trance states, in much the same way an earlier generation came to identify with the morbid delusions of Camille. Surely Sylvia Plath the poet cannot be held accountable for this gross misreading of her great work, but such tends to be the fate and influence of almost all the so-called Confessional poets, that they will engender feelings and followings that have very little to do with the work itself.

At the other end of the spectrum from the Confessional school is a subject matter that is loosely associated with the New York

School of poetry—elliptical, opaque, distant, aloof, lucid, elegant, and emblematical. The New York School poets—primarily Frank O'Hara, John Ashbery, and Kenneth Koch—devote themselves to a poetry that is more connotative then denotative, exploring the power that dreams have to persuade one of something, even though one does not necessarily know the terms of the argument. John Ashbery's work is a good example of this movement—the following lines use ellipses, rapid changes of diction and tone, and they give one a sense of continuing flux:

> I thought that if I could put it all down, that would be one way. And next the thought came to me that to leave all out would be another, and truer, way.
>
>   clean-washed sea
>
>   The flowers were.
>
>
> These are examples of leaving out. But, forget as we will, something soon comes to stand in their place. Not the truth, perhaps, but—yourself. It is you who made this, therefore you are true. But the truth has passed on
>
>   to divide all.
>
>
> Have I awakened? Or is this sleep again? Another form of sleep? There is no profile in the massed days ahead. They are impersonal as mountains whose tops are hidden in cloud. The middle of the journey, before the sands are reversed: a place of ideal quiet. . . .
>
> "THE NEW SPIRIT," FROM THREE POEMS

Here is a comment on Ashbery's work by a critic:

> Each Ashbery poem is an imagined situation. Somewhere in the situation is a story of drama, but it is not one of conflict and it does not lead to any effect or realization that the poet would name. The poem remains an imagined event to the end; it is a projection into

space, a journey that you can follow because the movement of mind is discernibly there—and not because you
can relate it to other poem journeys in the same book.

When we have followed a poem through, the results
can be oddly "true," without involving the reader emo-
tionally. . . .

He is haunting rather than moving; he is interested
more in following his own mental processes than in or-
ganizing the elements of the poem into resolution, vic-
tory over a dilemma, consummation.

Ashbery is odd, often perplexing, but not affected.

ALFRED KAZIN. *ESQUIRE* (1978)

CLOSURE

Closure refers to the ending of a poem, how it concludes, both
in sound and sense and imagery.

The nineteenth century left a legacy of closures that tended
to be "edifying" and spiritually instructive. Poems had to end
with a grand moral flourish, what Marianne Moore once called
"the false flight upwards." We can see an example of this type
of closure in "The Chambered Nautilus" by Oliver Wendell
Holmes. The poem purports to present an image of a nautilus
to us, but as it approaches the ending, we realize the nautilus is
being used as a pretext for some sort of homily on how we should
live our lives. It's worth quoting the poem in full:

This is the ship of pearl, which, poets feign,
  Sails the unshadowed main,—
  The venturous bark that flings
On the sweet summer wind its purpled wings
In gulfs enchanted, where the Siren sings,
  And coral reefs lie bare,
Where the cold sea-maids rise to run their streaming hair.

Its web of living gauze no more unfurl;
  Wrecked is the ship of pearl!

And every chambered cell,
Where its dim dreaming life was wont to dwell,
As the frail tenant shaped his growing shell,
    Before thee lies revealed,—
Its irised ceiling rent, its sunless crypt unsealed!

Year after year beheld the silent toil
    That spread his lustrous coil;
    Still, as the spiral grew,
He left the past year's dwelling for the new,
Stole with soft step its shining archway through,
    Built up its idle door,
Stretched in his last-found home, and knew the old no more.

Thanks for the heavenly message brought by thee,
    Child of the wandering sea,
    Cast from her lap, forlorn!
From thy dead lips a clearer note is born
Than ever Triton blew from wreathéd horn!
    While on mine ear it rings,
Through the deep caves of thought I hear a voice that sings:

Build thee more stately mansions, O my soul,
    As the swift seasons roll!
    Leave thy low-valuted past!
Let each new temple, nobler than the last,
Shut thee from heaven with a dome more vast,
    Till thou at length are free,
Leaving thine outgrown shell by life's unresting sea!

There are some excellent things happening in this poem: Holmes brings off the mythological reference to the *Odyssey* in the first stanza, and the specific image detail of the nautilus in stanza two is interesting in places, especially in that wonderful last line of:

Its irised ceiling rent, its sunless crypt unsealed!

Excellent sound, excellent image detail. Stanza three approaches onomatopoetics as the poet recreates the slow evolving of the nautilus from chamber to chamber. So far, so good; but we begin to sense we are in for a Grand Closure to the poem with the beginning of stanza four—whatever "heavenly message" the poet is preparing for us, we can't help but feel we're about to enter fortune cookie land. To make things worse, Holmes pretends that his "message" is not really his but is something he hears from far inside the nautilus. Well, we doubt very much that any nautilus ever spoke this kind of message to anyone, and we begin to feel imposed on, as if the poetry in the poem were only a pretext for the poet's getting that "heavenly message" over on us.

The trouble occurs because the poet apparently feels he has to make some kind of "edifying closure" to the poem. One wonders what sort of poem "The Chambered Nautilus" would be if the poet dropped those last two stanzas and allowed the first three stanzas to stand on their own.

There's another type of closure that is almost as irritating as the "edifying closure," and that's what we might call the "summary closure," or perhaps the "do-you-get-it closure." This type of closure is for those readers who may be stupid and unable to figure out what the poem has been about, so the poet comes in at the end and explains everything. It's like the ending of eighth-grade book reports, with summary closures aimed at the simpletons:

> And that's how I spent my summer vacation
> In the Berkshires and caught seven frogs
> And some poison ivy and had lots of fun
> And also fell in love for the first time.

End of poem, end of patience. It's exasperating to be in the middle of a fairly well-written poem, only to see it brought down by a bad closure. And it points up a subtle weakness on the part of the poet who is writing the poem, because both the "edifying closure" and the "summary closure" assume that the image work of the poem is not really adequate, so the poet has to rush in and tack on all these messages and summaries to make the poem

come out okay. Better if he could trust his images to do the job
by themselves, with no need for any spurious "wrap-up" at the
end.

To get some idea of effective closures we could do worse than
go back to the sonnets of Shakespeare and see how the couplets
resolve the musical harmonies of the poems. In Sonnet 29,
Shakespeare sets up a very impacted syntax and stilted diction
in the opening lines:

> When, in disgrace with fortune and men's eyes,
> I all alone beweep my outcast state,
> And trouble deaf heaven with my bootless cries,
> And look upon myself, and curse my fate . . .

Yet after Shakespeare introduces the image of the beloved in
line 10 of the poem, suddenly both syntax and diction smoothe
out, and by lines 13 and 14, the couplet, we realize we are in
the presence of very easy speech and mostly monosyllable word
choice:

> For thy sweet love remember'd such wealth brings
> That then I scorn to change my state with kings.

We can feel the same resolution of syntax and diction in a
random sampling of other couplets (from Sonnets 30, 66, and
73) throughout the sonnet sequence:

> But if the while I think on thee, dear friend,
> All losses are restor'd and sorrows end.
>
> (#30)

> Tir'd with all these, from these would I be gone,
> Save that, to die, I leave my love alone.
>
> (#66)

This thou perceiv'st, which makes thy love more strong,
To love that well which thou must leave ere long.

                                                    (#73)

Mind you, we are talking here of *musical* resolution of syntax
and diction, without reference to summing up any edifying words
of wisdom, as in the Holmes poem previously cited. Successful
closure has more to do with an aesthetic effect one achieves at
the end of a poem, rather than any programmatic or philosophical
conclusion the poet is arriving at. We can prove this by showing
that Shakespeare's closures in the sonnet sequence are all pretty
much the same, and not particularly remarkable as ideas in and
of themselves; most of the closures can be paraphrased to say
simply, "Whenever I have the good fortune to remember the
image of my beloved, it makes me feel a whole lot better." That's
not especially world-shaking in its philosophical import, but it's
enough of a slight shift of focus and emphasis for Shakespeare
to be able to achieve miraculously musical resolutions for his
poems.

Other closures do, in fact, introduce startling and unexpected
shifts of philosophical thought. A classic example is one of the
"Holy Sonnets" of John Donne, where the poet suddenly inten-
sifies his premise in the couplet, revealing an entirely new way
of looking at the problem of death:

Death, be not proud, though some have callèd thee
Mighty and dreadful, for thou are not so;
For those whom thou think'st thou does overthrow
Die not, poor Death, nor yet canst thou kill me.
From rest and sleep, which but thy pictures be,
Much pleasure; then from thee much more must flow,
And soonest our best men with thee do go,
Rest of their bones, and soul's delivery.
Thou'art slave to Fate, Chance, kings, and desperate men,
And dost with poison, war, and sickness dwell,
And poppy or charms can make us sleep as well

And better than thy stroke; why swell'st thou then?
One short sleep past, we wake eternally
And death shall be no more; Death, though shalt die.

"HOLY SONNET 10"

The great "Ode on a Grecian Urn" by John Keats develops
so much specific image detail of the scenes that are on the Grecian
urn, that by the end of the poem we feel Keats has earned the
right to make a sweeping generalization in the last lines:

"Beauty is truth, truth beauty,"—that is all
Ye know on earth, and all ye need to know.

We should point out, however, that it is the Grecian urn that
is saying these words, not Keats; and the only way the poet can
get away with such a general and philosophical closure is through
the use of so many carefully examined particulars throughout the
course of the poem, before the "universal" closure. It's as if a
zoom lens had been examining minutiae of infinite details, and
then suddenly distanced itself at the end to create a breathtaking
overview of the subject. The secret of the closure is in the sud-
denness of the distancing, not in the philosophical content of
the statement itself, which is at best debatable.

In "Leda and the Swan," William Butler Yeats hurls the reader
directly into the action of the rape in the opening lines, and
then allows the poem to resolve into a series of rhetorical questions, with the final question so unnerving and stark, it makes
an astonishing closure for the poem:

A sudden blow: the great wings beating still
Above the staggering girl, her thighs caressed
By the dark webs, her nape caught in his bill,
He holds her helpless breast upon his breast.

How can those terrified vague fingers push
The feathered glory from her loosening thighs?
And how can body, laid in that white rush,
But feel the strange heart beating where it lies?

A shudder in the loins engenders there
The broken wall, the burning roof and tower
And Agamemnon dead.

> Being so caught up,
So mastered by the brute blood of the air,
Did she put on his knowledge with his power
Before the indifferent beak could let her drop?

In Rainer Maria Rilke's poem "Torso of an Archaic Apollo," the closure startles us not only because it shifts pronoun from first person plural to second person, but the sentence structure shifts from declarative to commanding imperative in the final line:

We can never know how that head once inclined
nor how those ghostly globes slowly opened. Even so
some bright light makes this torso glow
behind his eyes, inside his mind,

half hidden in his soul. Otherwise this breast
could not so blind you nor could that fine
arc across the loins be such a smiling line,
there here the genitals once pressed.

Otherwise this broken stone would
stand here so cold and alone, nor could
it shine now like a lion's face

nor could this far star loose light
so freely until there is no place
that does not see you. You must change your life.

TR. WILLIAM PACKARD

In his great poem "Directive," Robert Frost uses a similar sudden shift of voice and person in the closure, to catch the reader off guard and bring the whole poem to a resounding end:

I have kept hidden in the instep arch
Of an old cedar at the waterside

A broken drinking goblet like the Grail
Under a spell so the wrong ones can't find it,
So can't get saved, as Saint Mark says they mustn't
(I stole the goblet from the children's playhouse.)
Here are your waters and your watering place.
Drink and be whole again beyond confusion.

As we've already said, the secret of effective closure is more musical than meaningful, and has more to do with resolution of syntax and diction than it has to do with imparting any pretentious philosophical summary of the way this universe works. And if one really wants to avoid the feeling of fake closure, then one can always opt to leave a poem ending suspended, with no closure at all. Surely in many instances that's far better than succumbing to the wish to wrap everything up all neat and pretty like a Christmas present. One of the most radical closures in modern poetry takes place at the end of the first *Canto* of Ezra Pound, when the poet not only refuses to provide a closure for the poem, but seems to be leaving the whole thing deliberately in midair:

In the Cretan's phrase, with the golden crown, Aphrodite,
Cypri munimenta sortita est, mirthful, orichalchi, with golden
Girdles and breast bands, thou with dark eyelids
Bearing the golden bough of Argicida. So that:

6

POESIS AND CREATIVITY

We're halfway through this book now and we've had a chance to look at the history of poetry, the basic poetic devices and techniques, the genres of poetry, line lengths, and fixed verse forms, as well as individual poem parts such as the title, the subject matter, and the closure of a poem.

But now we come back to the mystery of the creative process itself, what we might call *poesis*—the ongoing kinetics of writing, how it happens, and how it creates a momentum for its own pace. We can probably see the practice of poesis most clearly if we look closely at the work of four poets: John Keats, Rainer Maria Rilke, William Butler Yeats, and Jack Kerouac.

A large part of the mystery of writing is tied up with the tricky and endless activity of rewriting and revision, and we'll examine the attitudes of seven writers on this matter: Horace, Yeats, Albert Camus, Yvor Winters, Anne Sexton, James Dickey, and Dylan Thomas.

We should look at what happens to a poet when the poesis breaks down—what the poet should do about dry periods, blocks, and artistic stalemate situations; we can see what three poets recommend about this problem: Muriel Rukeyser, Richard Wilbur, and Amiri Baraka.

Finally, we'll look at how a poet can organize the materials of his own writing, using notebook systems to know where each piece will have its place.

POETRY AS PROCESS

A.   John Keats describes the process of poetry as a never-ending hunger inside:

> I find that I cannot exist without poetry—without eternal poetry—half the day will not do—the whole of it—I began with a little, but habit has made me a Leviathan.

LETTER 13 TO JOHN HAMILTON REYNOLDS, 18 APRIL 1817

Keats goes on to describe the poesis of his poetry writing in the following terms:

> . . . at once it struck me what quality went to form a Man of Achievement especially in Literature and which Shakespeare possessed so enormously—I mean *Negative Capability*, that is when man is capable of being in uncertainties, Mysteries, doubts, without any irritable reaching after fact and reason— . . . that with a great poet the sense of Beauty overcomes every other consideration, or rather obliterates all consideration.

LETTER 32 TO GEORGE & THOMAS KEATS, 21 DECEMBER 1918

A great deal has been written about what Keats meant by this *Negative Capability*. We could say it refers to a psychological ability to suspend the censor or superego faculty of the psyche, so one is free to explore the Unknown without any of the conventional reservations about entering into the forbidden areas of the mind. Later the great Russian director Stanislavsky would formulate something similar when he set as a goal for the actor: "The Super-conscious Through the Conscious Mind," which was the objective of his famous "Method" approach to acting. Stanislavsky laid down step-by-step techniques for achieving this "super-conscious mind" in this three books—*An Actor Prepares, Building a Character,* and *Creating a Role*—and there is a good description of how Stanislavsky came on these techniques in his autobiography, *My Life in Art.*

Keats does not spell out any such step-by-step techniques for achieving what he calls *Negative Capability,* but we can assume that similar methods would apply for the poet as well as for the actor: the use of emotional memory as substitution for the desired feelings to be experienced, the cultivation of sense-memory, and an attention to specific image details. There would have to be an underlying trust that using these simple techniques would evoke the desired super-conscious mind for the poet.

When Keats says, "the sense of Beauty overcomes every other consideration, or rather obliterates all consideration," he is referring to the aesthetic faculty, which has its own coordinates and must take supremacy over all the other faculties, such as the ethical or religious or philosophical. Poetry is the rhythmic creation of Beauty, and should not have much interest in any other goal no matter how these other goals may be touted in our everyday world.

Of course this can be a very frightening and risky business, when one deliberately turns aside from all the other reality factors of one's life and trusts only to the coordinates of the aesthetic faculty. We hear conventional voices shouting at us that we are advocating irresponsibility and bohemian carelessness. And indeed, when Walter Pater developed his theory of "Art for Art's Sake" in his book *The Renaissance,* he came under a storm of abuse for abandoning traditional values and encouraging the young to give themselves over to a life of hedonism and the cynicism of self-seeking.

But the fact is that neither Keats nor Stanislavsky nor Walter Pater were advocating any such thing; they were simply pointing out that to be an artist, one has to commit oneself to one's art absolutely, and leave the other aspects of conscientious citizenship to those who were born to that particular calling. Is that so threatening, either to the society at large or to the individual artist?

Well, in all honesty, it is frightening, and that's why Keats felt he had to call it the *Negative* Capability—because the aesthetic faculty always seems to be a desertion of one's responsibilities elsewhere. Sigmund Freud once commented in a letter:

> One has to become a bad fellow, transcend the rules, sacrifice oneself, betray, and behave like the artist who buys paints with his wife's household money, or burns the furniture to warm the room for his model. Without some such criminality there is no real achievement.

Of course it may not come to that—but it *feels* that way, and that can be a frightening thing indeed, to tolerate such a sense of criminality when one is engaged in one's real work. Often it may take on cosmic proportions: One may feel like he is hanging by his fingertips from a precipice—but the nice thing about hanging from a precipice is that one has such a spectacular view! Or else it may feel like one is always going after the Unutterable, something that's always a world away from where one is—but the important thing is that one keeps going after it.

Because that's really what it's all about: a bird flies, a fish swims, an ocean flows, a sun shines, and a writer writes. It's as uncomplicated and inevitable as that.

B. The German poet Rainer Maria Rilke (1875–1926) reminds us that it can be especially frightening and lonely for a young person to embark on a lifetime of poesis. In his novel *The Notebooks of Malte Laurids Brigge*, Rilke describes how young Brigge, a foreigner who is twenty-eight years old, comes to Paris and lives alone in a small apartment, and finally confronts himself as to his real reasons for wanting to write:

> It is ridiculous. Here I sit in my little room, I, Brigge, who have grown to be twenty-eight years old and of

whom no one knows. I sit here and am nothing. And nevertheless this nothing begins to think and thinks, five flights up, on a grey Parisian afternoon, these thoughts:

Is it possible, it thinks, that one has not yet seen, known and said anything real or important? Is it possible that one has had millennia of time to observe, reflect and note down, and that one has let those millennia slip away like a recess interval at school in which one eats one's sandwich and an apple?

Yes, it is possible.

Is it possible that despite discoveries and progress, despite culture, religion and world-wisdom, one has remained on the surface of life? Is it possible that one has even covered this surface, which might still have been something, with an incredibly uninteresting stuff which makes it look like the drawing-room furniture during summer holidays?

Yes, it is possible.

Is it possible that the whole history of the world has been misunderstood? Is it possible that the past is false, because one has always spoken of its masses just as though one were telling of a coming together of many human beings, instead of speaking of the individual around whom they stood because he was a stranger and was dying?

Yes, it is possible.

Is it possible that one believed it necessary to retrieve what happened before one was born? Is it possible that one would have to remind every individual that he is indeed sprung from all who have gone before, has known this therefore and should not let himself be persuaded by others who knew otherwise?

Yes, it is possible.

Is it possible that all these people know with perfect accuracy a past that has never existed? Is it possible that all realities are nothing to them; that their life is running down, unconnected with anything, like a clock in an empty room—?

Yes, it is possible.

Is it possible that one knows nothing of young girls, who nevertheless live? Is it possible that one says "women," "children," "boys," not guessing (despite all one's culture, not guessing) that these words have long since had no plural, but only countless singulars?

Yes, it is possible.

Is it possible that there are people who say "God" and mean that this is something they have in common?— Just take a couple of schoolboys: one buys a pocket knife and his companion buys another exactly like it on the same day. And after a week they compare knives and it turns out that there is now only a very distant resemblance between the two—so differently have they developed in different hands. ("Well," says the mother of one, "if you always must wear everything out immediately—") Ah, so: Is it possible to believe one could have a God without using him?

Yes, it is possible.

But if all this is possible—has even no more than a semblance of possibility—then surely, for all the world's sake, something must happen. The first comer, he who has had this disturbing thought, must begin to do some of the things that have been neglected; even if he is just anybody, by no means the most suitable person: there is no one else at hand. This young, insignificant foreigner, Brigge, will have to sit down in his room five flights up and write, day and night: yes, he will have to write; that is how it will end.

Rilke goes on to spell out the danger of being an artist in his *Letters to a Young Poet,* when he answers a young man who had sent Rilke a manuscript of poetry and asked for Rilke's frank opinion on whether the poems were any good. Rilke writes the following response:

You asked whether your verses are good. You ask me. You have asked others before. You send them to magazines. You compare them with other poems, and you are disturbed when certain editors reject your efforts. Now (since you have allowed me to advise you) I beg you to give up all that. You are looking outward, and that above all you should not do now. Nobody can counsel and help you, nobody. There is only one single way. Go into yourself. Search for the reason that bids you write; find out whether it is spreading out its roots in the deepest places of your heart, acknowledge to yourself whether you would have to die if it were denied you to write. This above all—ask yourself in the stillest hour of your night: *must* I write? Delve into yourself for a deep answer. And if this should be affirmative, if you may meet this earnest question with a strong and simple *"I must,"* then build your life according to this necessity; your life even into its most indifferent and slightest hour must be a sign of this urge and a testimony to it. Then draw near to Nature. Then try, like some first human being, to say what you see and experience and love and lose. Do not write love-poems; avoid at first those forms that are too facile and commonplace: they are the most difficult, for it takes a great, fully matured power to give something of your own where good and even excellent traditions come to mind in quantity. Therefore save yourself from these general themes and seek those which your own everyday life offers you; describe your sorrows and desires, passing thoughts and the belief in some sort of beauty—describe all these with loving, quiet, humble sincerity, and use, to express yourself, the things in your environment, the images from your dreams, and the objects of your memory. If your daily life seems poor, do not blame it; blame yourself, tell yourself that you are not poet enough to call forth its riches; for to the creator there is no poverty and no poor indifferent place. And even if you were in some prison the walls of which let none of the sounds of the world come to your senses— would you not then still have your childhood, that precious, kingly possession, that treasure-house of memories?

Rilke is saying that writing is process just as living is process, and anything that gets in the way of any ongoing process can be terribly damaging and distracting to the life of the poet. Sharing one's work too soon with others, publishing one's work when it is not ready, hungering always for fame and money and recognition from one's peers—these can be awfully false objectives for the beginning writer, and shame on any writers conference or graduate writing program or poetry workshop that turns a buck by promoting such false values and objectives in the name of "careerism," instead of continually reminding a young poet that it is writing as writing that really matters. And that is a concern that will be with one for one's entire life.

There is an acceptance of solitude behind Rilke's words that can be frightening and unnerving, but Rilke once commented, "One does not *choose* to be alone—one *is* alone." It is an insight into the human condition, and if one is not able to live by this insight then perhaps one does not really want the métier of being an artist in the first place.

There is also a sense of gentle quietism in what Rilke is saying, as if it's too easy to be glib and facile about such things as poetry and one's own work. The twentieth-century German Catholic author Baron Friedrich Von Hugel gave a similar gentle warning to his niece:

> Be silent about great things; let them grow inside you. Never discuss them: discussion is so limiting and distracting. It makes things grow smaller. You think you swallow things when they ought to swallow you. Before all greatness, be silent—in art, in music, in religion: silence.

C. The great Irish poet William Butler Yeats was irritated that Ireland wanted nationalism from her poets, not true poetry—and Yeats spent his entire life in reaction against this, insisting that his art was more important than what Ireland required of him:

> Nationalist Ireland was torn with every kind of passion and prejudice, wanting, so far as it wanted any literature at all, Nationalist propaganda disguised as literature. All the past had been turned into a melodrama with Ireland the blameless hero, and poet, novelist, and historian had but one object, to hiss the villain, and only the minority doubted the greater the talent the greater the hiss. It was all the harder to substitute for that melodrama a nobler form of art, because there had been, however different in their form, villain and victim.

Yeats wrote these lines about the year 1891, when he was twenty-six years old, shortly after the death of Parnell, the Irish leader who was so intensely loved and hated by all sides. Auden sums up this period in his elegy for Yeats: "mad Ireland hurt you into poetry." Louise Bogan describes this early period of Yeats in this way:

> His art was poetry, and, almost from the first, he used the art as a tool, his avowed purpose being to rid the literature of his country from the insincere, provincial, and hampering forms of "the election rhyme and the pamphlet."

> "THE POET'S ALPHABET"

In place of Irish nationalism, Yeats substituted two metaphor systems for his great later work. First was a thorough immersion in spiritualism and Theosophy; he had experimented in adolescence with telepathy and clairvoyance in the company of his uncle who was a student of the occult. Yeats went on to study the Cabala and continued with his own experiments in spiritualism; he received "voices" from his wife's dreams which he recorded in his poetry; and out of his study of Blake, Swedenborg, and Böhme, Yeats developed his own system of visionary truth—

references to the Great Wheel and Gyres, which signify the eternal recurrence of all things.

The second metaphor Yeats used in his own poetry was his own slow process of aging, which he carefully observed. He wrote in 1917 at the age of fifty-two:

> A poet when he is growing old, will ask himself if he cannot keep his mask and his vision, without new bitterness, new disappointment. . . . Could he if he would, copy Landor who lived loving and hating, ridiculous and unconquered, into extreme old age, all lost but the favor of his muses. . . . Surely, he may think, now that I have found vision and mask I need not suffer any longer. Then he will remember Wordsworth, withering into eighty years, honoured and empty-witted, and climb to some waste room, and find, forgotten there by youth, some bitter crust.

Out of self-conscious observation, Yeats was able to use his own aging process as an emblem of our human condition, as in the following opening lines of "The Tower," where he seems to burst in outrage over the indignity of growing older:

> What shall I do with this absurdity—
> O heart, O troubled heart—this caricature,
> Decrepit age that has been tied to me
> As to a dog's tail?
>   Never had I more
> Excited, passionate, fantastical
> Imagination, nor an ear and eye
> That more expected the impossible—
> No, not in boyhood when with rod and fly
> Or the humbler worm, I climbed Ben Bulben's back
> And had the livelong summer day to spend.
> It seems that I must bid the Muse go pack,
> Choose Plato and Plotinus for a friend
> Until imagination, ear and eye,
> Can be content with argument and deal

In abstract things; or be derided by
A sort of battered kettle at the heel.

"THE TOWER," PART I

D.   The American writer Jack Kerouac earned notoriety with
his novels—such as *On the Road* and *Dharma Bums*—but he also
published a book of poetry, *Mexico City Blues,* that is a flawless
experimental exercise in catching jazz rhythms in an ongoingness
that is dizzy and harrowing in its nonstop voice. Allen Ginsberg
openly acknowledged his debt to Kerouac's jazz breath line in
the composition of his own "Howl"—and Ginsberg went on to
found The Jack Kerouac School of Disembodied Poetics as a part
of the Naropa University in Colorado.

Kerouac himself laid down some of the principles for flowing
writing, loose lines, a "spewing" forth of poetry, in an article on
"Essentials of Spontaneous Prose":

> PROCEDURE: Time being of the essence in the purity of
> speech, sketching language is undisturbed flow from the
> mind of personal secret idea-words, *blowing* (as per jazz
> musician) on subject of image. . . .
>
> No pause to think of proper word by the infantile pile-
> up of scatological buildup words till satisfaction is gained,
> which will turn out to be a great appending rhythm to
> a thought and be in accordance with Great Law of tim-
> ing. . . .
>
> Begin not from preconceived idea of what to say about
> image but from jewel center of interest in subject of image
> at *moment* of writing, and write outwards swimming in
> sea of language to peripheral release and exhaustion. . . .
>
> If possible write "without consciousness" in semi-
> trance (as Yeats' later "trance writing") allowing sub-
> conscious to admit in own uninhibited interesting nec-
> essary and so "modern" language what conscious art
> would censor, and write excitedly, swiftly, with writing-
> or-typing-cramps in accordance (as from center to pe-

riphery) with laws of orgasm, Reich's "beclouding on consciousness." *Come* from within, out—to relaxed and said.

EVERGREEN REVIEW 2, NUMBER 5 (SUMMER 1958)

Kerouac went on and expanded his notions in the form of aphorisms, in "Belief & Technique for Modern Prose":

1. Scribbled secret notebooks, and wild typewritten pages, for yr own joy

2. Submissive to everything, open, listening

3. Try never get drunk outside yr own house

4. Be in love with yr life

5. Something that you feel will find its own form

6. Be crazy dumbsaint of the mind

7. Blow as deep as you want to blow

8. Write what you want bottomless from bottom of the mind

9. The unspeakable visions of the individual

10. No time for poetry but exactly what is

11. Visionary tics shivering in the chest

12. In tranced fixation dreaming upon object before you

13. Remove literary, grammatical and syntactical inhibition

14. Like Proust be an old teahead of time

15. Telling the true story of the world in interior monologue

16. The jewel center of interest is the eye within the eye

17. Write in recollection and amazement for yourself

18. Work from pithy middle eye out, swimming in language sea

19. Accept loss forever

20. Believe in the holy contour of life

21. Struggle to sketch the flow that already exists intact in mind

22. Dont think of words when you stop but to see picture better

23. Keep track of every day the date emblazoned in yr morning

24. No fear or shame in the dignity of yr experience, language & knowledge

25. Write for the world to read and see yr exact pictures of it

26. Bookmovie is the movie in words, the visual American form

27. In praise of Character in the Bleak inhuman Loneliness

28. Composing wild, undisciplined, pure, coming in from under, crazier the better

29. You're a Genius all the time

30. Writer-Director of Earthly movies Sponsored & Angeled in Heaven

EVERGREEN REVIEW 2, NUMBER 8 (SPRING 1959)

E.   Some other approaches to poesis: Stanly Kunitz speaks of the idea that certain parts of a poem are "given" to the poet—the French idea of *la ligne donnée*, that which is a gift to the poet:

> Practically all my poems start with something given to me, that is, a line or a phrase, or a set of lines, that take

me by surprise. When that happens, the challenge is to accept the blessing and go along with it

NEW YORK QUARTERLY CRAFT INTERVIEW, NUMBER 4

Another idea concerns the mind's capacity to remember verses without even writing them down. Richard Eberhart recalls:

> Once Robert Frost told me that he would be walking in the woods and a whole poem of, say, thirty lines would form in his head and that he had so much control of the lines that each was etched definitively on his mind and that he felt no compulsion to write them down. He said that sometimes he could draw this poem off maybe ten years later precisely as it came to him in this way.

NEW YORK QUARTERLY CRAFT INTERVIEW, NUMBER 20

And finally, in a remarkable first-person account of a poet's process technique, Charles Bukowski comments on how he writes his poems:

> I write right off the typer. I call it my "Machinegun." I hit it hard, usually late at night while drinking wine and listening to classical music on the radio and smoking mangalore ganesh beedies. I revise, but not much. The next day I retype the poem and automatically make a change or two, drop out a line, or make two lines into one or one line into two, that sort of thing—to make the poem have more balls, more balance. Yes, the poems come "off the top of my head." I seldom know what I'm going to write when I sit down. There isn't much agony and sweat of the human spirit involved in doing it. The writing's easy, it's the living that is sometimes difficult.

NEW YORK QUARTERLY CRAFT INTERVIEW, NUMBER 26

REVISION

We come to the subject of revision, and of course it will all be a matter of the individual poet, how much he or she revises, and why and how. For example, Horace tells us:

> So I consume laborious hours
> In fashioning my little song.

We infer from this that Horace spent hours both visioning and revisioning his work, and perhaps it would be difficult to tell which was which.

Albert Camus makes it into a moral imperative:

> It is in order to shine sooner that authors refuse to rewrite. Despicable. Begin again.
>
> CAMUS, NOTEBOOKS (SEPT. 30, 1937)

Yvor Winters echoes Horace in his advice:

> Write little; do it well.

W. H. Auden comments:

> I do an enormous amount of revising. I think of that quote from Valéry, "A poem is never finished, only abandoned."

Anne Sexton describes the process of revision:

> How do I write? Expand, expand, cut, cut, expand, expand, cut, cut. Do not trust spontaneous first drafts. You can always write more fully. The beautiful feeling after writing a poem is on the whole better even than after sex, and that's saying a lot.

And James Dickey describes his own process:

> If I have one principle, rule of thumb, I guess you could say, as a writer, it's to work on something a long, long time. And try it all different ways. I work as a writer— let me see if I can come up with a metaphor or analogy— on the principle of refining low-grade ore. I assume that the first fifty ways I try it are going to be wrong. I do it by a process of elimination. No matter how back-breaking the shoveling is and running it through the sluices and whatever you have to do to refine low-grade ore, you have the dubious consolation that what you get out of it is just as much real gold as it would be if you were just going around picking up nuggets off the ground. It's just that it takes so damn much labor to get it.

We can summarize this much about the process of revision: on the one hand, it takes laborious work to produce anything worthwhile; but on the other hand, one can't go on revising forever.

The first position is eloquently described by Yeats in his poem "Adam's Curse":

> We sat together at one summer's end,
> That beautiful mild woman, your close friend,
> And you and I, and talked of poetry,
> I said: 'A line will take us hours maybe,
> Yet if it does not seem a moment's thought,
> Our stitching and unstitching has been naught,
> Better go down upon your marrow-bones
> And scrub a kitchen pavement, or break stones
> Like an old pauper, in all kinds of weather,
> For to articulate sweet sounds together
> Is to work harder than all these, and yet
> Be thought an idler by the noisy set
> Of bankers, schoolmaster, and clergymen
> The martyrs call the world. . . .'

Yeats justified the enormous amount of labor he put into writing and rewriting his work—even after it had been published—in the following quatrain:

> The friends that have it I do wrong
> Whenever I rewrite a song,
> Do not consider what is at stake;
> It is myself that I remake.

On the other hand, there is always the feeling that one wants to get on to other poems, instead of spending the rest of one's life rewriting the poems one has already written. Dylan Thomas gives voice to this feeling in a note to his *Collected Poems:*

> . . . if I went on revising everything that I now do not like in this book I should be so busy that I would have no time to try to write new poems.

DRY PERIODS

One never knows what to say about writer's block or dry periods. They are as much a part of a writer's life as broken typewriters or overstuffed waste baskets.

One can take a psychological view of dry periods, as Muriel Rukeyser does:

> I have terrible periods. Depression is a mild name for it. Sometimes it means not being able to write. Sometimes something will pierce through a period like that, and then it will go on strangely. That is, I can't tell you the rules. I know that the pit is frightful, and what I find myself doing is translating because I like to have something I care about out in front of me, and not have to send everything out of myself. To have a wonderful poem and do that folly, folly on a madness on a stupidity—translation, I like.

Another poet, Richard Wilbur, is able to take a more realistic view of dry periods:

> I suspect that everybody has dry periods. One advantage of getting older is that you have been through it before and before and before: though it doesn't do very *much* good, you can tell yourself that you will come out of it, that you will write again, and therefore you can stay somewhat this side of despair.

And Amiri Baraka looks at the practical side:

> Mine are usually from being discouraged about where to publish, because I don't have to tell you how few places there are to publish my writing, and for a writer like myself who has a certain political aura that a lot of people don't want to associate with, it gets difficult. If people were asking me to write plays, we're going to perform this, write it—or if people were asking me to write novels, I would be doing it. But I still manage to produce, at some kind of rate if not the one I'd like to.

NEW YORK QUARTERLY CRAFT INTERVIEW, NUMBER 25

NOTEBOOK SYSTEMS

Finally, the sort of personal notebooks one uses in his or her daily work can be an important part of a commitment to one's own poetry writing. Cheapo shabby spiral notebooks may reflect an unconscious signal that one does not really think one's work merits any better lodging. But if one invests some money in a few excellent zippered leather notebooks, that can be a sign that can proclaim to oneself that one thinks one's work is worth something after all.

Ideally, one should have one good notebook for each major project one is working on—poems in progress, short stories, drafts for novels and plays, perhaps even a notebook for essays and expository prose. Each of these notebooks can then become a repository for rough drafts, scattered images and ideas, daily journal entries, as well as a place for recent dreams and fantasies and memories. One should also have one notebook of blank pages for one's ongoing writing, a place to write anything off the top of one's head, random lines, etc., etc., etc. It's probably a good idea to choose one standard size of three-ring notebook for all one's work, so one can easily interchange materials from one notebook to another, as one keeps working.

Once one has one's notebook system pretty well organized, the trick is to train oneself to write in the various notebooks continuously, every day of one's life. As the old Latin saying goes,

Laborare est orare.

"To work is to pray." One comes to see one's ongoing work as some form of silent prayer, a sacred offering to some higher powers of something that one cares to keep alive and growing during this lifetime. William Blake summarizes this life of continuous process for the artist:

Without unceasing Practise nothing can be done. Practise is Art. If you leave off you are lost.

7

WRITING CHALLENGES

This chapter contains a series of thirty writing exercises, to help the poet tap into his or her creative energies.

A few words about how to approach these exercises. One should have a notebook filled with blank paper in front of one, and one should simply begin writing out each exercise without thinking too much about it. One shouldn't get "intellectual" about these tasks, but simply open one's notebook and try writing off the top of one's head and see where that takes one. The important part of each of these exercises is to get a lot of words down on the page; one can always come back afterward and do whatever editing and shaping one wants. But to begin with, the challenge is to write as fully and as freely as possible, with no censoring or checks on one's original responses.

The objective is to write one's own stream of consciousness out onto the page, setting down the first thing that comes to mind and letting the words and images write themselves. It's the ongoingness that matters, so one should not reject any thought because it seems to be too "insignificant"—one won't know what is significant and what isn't until the writing is out there on the page.

A variation of this approach is for the poet to go out to a nearby coffeehouse or diner where one can sit for a long time

without being interrupted, and try writing in this public atmosphere where people are coming and going all the time. This
usually has a curious effect on one's concentration, and sometimes one will write things one would never be able to write in
solitude, simply because one has a peripheral distraction going
on all around.

One should be able to keep using this chapter as a reference
tool, doing the same exercises over and over again and finding
new ways of responding to the same challenges.

Here are the thirty challenges:

1.   Myself at age six. Write stream of consciousness about
     where you were and what you were doing when you were
     six years old. Try to stay as close as possible to specific
     image details: the landscape of the terrain, what kind of
     trees, what kind of roads, etc. Try to record the details
     of what kind of clothes you were wearing, what kind of
     shoes, try to make a list of the things that were by your
     bedside. You were probably entering first grade about that
     time—see if you can describe the kind of classroom, the
     names of the kids who sat next to you, the teacher up at
     the front desk, etc. Don't go for the generality of what
     you were feeling, but stay close to the specific image de-
     tails. If you have photographs of yourself at age six, it may
     help a lot to look at them and see details you wouldn't
     have remembered by yourself.

2.   Myself at age twelve. Write stream of consciousness about
     where you were and what you were doing when you were
     twelve years old. Again, try to stay as close as possible to
     specific image details: books, clothing, shoes, hair, names
     of friends, etc. You were probably entering seventh grade
     about this time, and you were also entering into puberty—
     see if you can record a collage of the first sexual impres-
     sions you were experiencing inside yourself at this age,
     and what persons on the outside you saw as attractive.
     See if you can record the physical changes that were taking

place in your body at that time, and how that affected you. Remember, don't go for the generality of your feelings, but try to stay close to the specific image details.

3. Myself at age sixteen. Do the same thing with stream of consciousness for when you were sixteen years old. You were probably in eleventh grade by this time, a junior in high school; see if you can write down the specific facts about your social life, who your friends were, where you would go in the evenings, and what homework gave you the most difficulty. You were probably looking ahead to graduation from high school—try to write down where you thought you wanted to go after graduation, and what you thought you wanted to be doing for the rest of your life. Again, try to avoid the generality of what you were feeling; just stay close to the specific image detail.

4. Dream poem. Write out one of your more recent dreams as fully as possible, with all the detail images and voices you remember. Don't try to "interpret" the dream or say what it "means," just get down the images, where it took place, what was being said, etc. For example: Here is a dream poem by Richard Hugo in which he tries to re-create the dream itself as faithfully as possible, without giving any interpretation of it:

In Your War Dream

You must fly your 35 missions again,
The old base is reopened. The food is still bad.
You are disturbed. The phlegm you choked up
mornings in fear returns. You strangle on the phlegm.
You ask, "Why must I do this again? A man
replies, "Home." You fly over one country
after another. The nations are bright like a map.
You pass over the red one. The orange one ahead
looks cold. The purple one north of that is the one
you must bomb. A wild land. Austere. The city
below seems ancient. You are on the ground.

Lovers are inside a cabin. You ask to come in.
They say "No. Keep watch on Stark Yellow Lake."
You stand beside the odd water. A terrible wind
keeps knocking you down. "I'm keeping watch
on the lake," you yell at the cabin. The lovers
don't answer. You break into the cabin. Inside
old women bake bread. They yell, "Return to the base."
You must fly your 35 missions again.

5. Daydream poem. Write out a waking daydream fantasy:
as you gaze out a window, all the things that begin to go
through your mind. Imagine what you see yourself doing
in this fantasy—the places you go, the things you do, the
people you meet. Don't try to interpret what is happening,
just set it down as quickly as you can. For example: Here
is a fantasy poem by John Ashbery in which he tries to
re-create the daydream itself as fully as he can, without
giving any explanation of what it all "means":

The Instruction Manual

As I sit looking out of a window of the building
I wish I did not have to write the instruction manual
    on the uses of a new metal.
I look down into the street and see people, each walking
    with an inner peace,
And envy them—they are so far away from me!
Not one of them has to worry about getting out this
    manual on schedule
And, as my way is, I begin to dream, resting my elbows
    on the desk and leaning out of the window a little,
Of dim Guadalajara! City of rose-colored flowers!
City I wanted most to see, and most did not see, in
    Mexico!
But I fancy I see, under the press of having to write
    the instruction manual,
Your public square, city, with its elaborate little
    bandstand!
The band is playing *Scheherazade* by Rimsky-Korsakov.

Around stand the flower girls, handing out rose- and
    lemon-colored flowers,
Each attractive in her rose-and-blue striped dress (Oh!
    such shades of rose and blue),
And nearby is the little white booth where women in green
    serve you green and yellow fruit.
The couples are parading: everyone is in a holiday mood. . . .

FROM SOME TREES (1956)

6.   Erotic fantasy poem. Write out one of your erotic fantasies, making it as specific as possible with as much detail
imagery as you can. Remember you do not have to show
this writing to anyone, so try to be as free and uncensored
and uninhibited as you're capable of being. Also remember
to avoid the generality of what you may be feeling, just
stay close to the specific image details. For example: Here
is a fairly outrageous erotic fantasy, cast in the form of a
journal entry that a young girl leaves for her mother to
read:

This Is How I Like It

This is how I like it.
On my back, with Karen
over me. Would you like
to hear the details,
Mama? Maybe I could show
you, some night when you
have guests for dinner.
I could lie down on the
living room floor and show
how we use our fingers,
how I twist and turn.
It would be like having
a daughter that played
the piano. You didn't
know anything about this
before, I know, because
this is the first time

> my diary's been home
> all year. But I know
> too you'll find it now,
> when you look in my
> drawers to see what I'm
> hiding. So here it is, Mama,
> enjoy it. And when Karen
> comes home with me this
> summer you can watch us
> together, if you believe
> me, watch how our hands
> almost touch, watch
> how we laugh when
> we look at you.

LOLA HASKINS, "THIS IS HOW I
LIKE IT," *NEW YORK*
QUARTERLY, NUMBERS 21, 26

7. Parts of speech. On a blank sheet of paper, make lists of
    the different parts of speech, the first examples that come
    to mind. Make a list of fifty nouns; fifty verbs; fifty ad-
    jectives; fifty adverbs; fifty pronouns; fifty prepositions;
    fifty conjunctions; fifty interjections—or as many as you
    can think of within, say, a ten-minute interval for each
    list. Don't ask why you're making these lists, just get the
    various words down on the paper. When you're finished
    with all these lists, you'll probably surprise yourself with
    how certain word clusters suggest a poem, and you can
    begin playing and shaping them together in whatever way
    you like. But first you have to get these lists down on the
    page.

8. Description of an object. Choose something that is close
    to you right now as you read this page—a pen or a pencil,
    or perhaps a pair of eyeglasses, or a wristwatch, or a hand-
    kerchief, or a piece of jewelry—and then try to describe
    it as accurately as you can, with as much specific image
    detail as possible. Allow yourself to free-associate as to

what this object reminds you of, to create similes and comparisons. You might try making this into a riddle poem, to see if a reader could guess what the object is, from reading your description of it without its being identified. But first you will have to write out the description as fully and accurately as you can.

9. Anagram poem. Write out your own name and see if you can create an anagram using all the letters in the name. For example: the name "Walter Reads" would form the anagram "straw leader." Then try writing an acrostic poem with your name down the left-hand margin, trying to fit the anagram somewhere into the poem. For example:

> Would I be
> Any good on television?
> Leisurely guest on a
> Talk show getting new
> Eager
> Readers for my latest book, or
> Rousing grandmothers to
> Eat a new breakfast cereal? Or would I be
> A tongue-tied dunce, nothing but a
> Dead-end head—one more TV
> Straw leader.

10. Prose poem. Write a vignette in prose paragraph form with no thought about line breaks or margins. Stay close to specific image details and trust that will create enough sounds to move the piece into the realm of pure poetry. As Charles Baudelaire wrote in the preface to his book of prose-poetry, *Paris Spleen:*

> Which one of us, in his moments of ambition, has not dreamed of the miracle of a poetic prose, musical, without rhythm and without rhyme, supple enough and rugged enough to adapt itself to the lyrical impulse of the soul, the undulations of reverie, the jibes of conscience?

Following is one of the prose-poetry pieces from *Paris Spleen:*

Windows

Looking from outside into an open window one never sees as much as when one looks through a closed window. There is nothing more profound, more mysterious, more pregnant, more insidious, more dazzling than a window lighted by a single candle. What one can see out in the sunlight is always less interesting than what goes on behind a window pane. In that black or luminous square life lives, life dreams, life suffers.

Across the ocean of roofs I can see a middle-aged woman, her face already lined, who is forever bending over something and who never goes out. Out of her face, her dress and her gestures, out of practically nothing at all, I have made up this woman's story, or rather legend, and sometimes I tell it to myself and weep.

If it had been an old man I could have made up his just as well.

And I go to bed proud to have lived and to have suffered in someone besides myself.

Perhaps you will say "Are you sure that your story is the real one?" But what does it matter what reality is outside myself, so long as it has helped me to live, to feel that I am, and what I am?

TR. LOUISE VARÈSE

11. Try doing three of the verse forms that are described in chapter 4 of this book: Write a sonnet or a sestina or a villanelle or a ballad. Then try writing three more sonnets. Then write three more.

12. Do a quick-sketch portrait poem that catches the essence of someone you know. Be careful to choose those details that seem to be the most characteristic of the person, whether real or imagined. Following are examples of

quick-sketch portraits from the work of Catullus, Edwin Arlington Robinson, Edgar Lee Masters, and Ezra Pound. First, Catullus:

XXXIII

O furum optime balneariorum
Vibenni pater et cinaede fili,
nam dextra pater inquinatiore,
culo filius est voraciore:
cur non exilium malasque in oras
itis, quandoquidem patris rapinae
notae sunt populo, et nates pilosas,
fili, non potes asse venditare.

O most successful in the art of stealing clothes
in bath houses is this Vibennius and his lecherous son:
the father skillful in his tricks of sleight of hand
and the son with his rare talent in his buttocks.
And with these gifts the pair should go to hell,
look for another climate;
for the father's tricks are known all over town,
and the son—where can you find a place to sell
your hairy buttocks itching with desire?

TR. HORACE GREGORY

And here is a second quick-sketch portrait poem by Catullus:

LIX

Boniensis Rufa Rufulum fellat
uxor Meneni, saepe quam in sepulcretis
vidistis ipso rapere de rogo cenam,
cum devolutum ex igne prosequens panem
ab semiraso tunderetur ustore.

Rufa from Bologna, wife of Menenius,
spends her time abed
draining the strength of Rufulus.
You must have seen the creature

at a funeral pyre, stealing food that's baking
with the bodies of the dead.
You remember how she seized a loaf of bread and
how a dirty slave drove her (O what a beating)
from his master's graveyard.

TR. HORACE GREGORY

What an extraordinary quick-sketch poem this is, in only five
lines in the Latin!

Edwin Arlington Robinson gives a quick-sketch portrait poem
in *"Richard Cory"*:

Whenever Richard Cory went down town,
We people on the pavement looked at him:
He was a gentleman from sole to crown,
Clean favored, and imperially slim,

And he was always quietly arrayed,
And he was always human when he talked;
But still he fluttered pulses when he said,
"Good morning," and he glittered when he walked.

And he was rich—yes, richer than a king—
And admirably schooled in every grace;
In fine, we thought that he was everything
To make us wish that we were in his place.

So on we worked, and waited for the light,
And went without the meat, and cursed the bread;
And Richard Cory, one calm summer night,
Went home and put a bullet through his head.

Edgar Lee Masters gives many quick-sketch portrait poems in
his *Spoon River Anthology,* including this first-person self-portrait:

Lucinda Matlock

I went to the dances at Chandlerville,
And played snap-out at Winchester,
One time we changed partners,

Driving home in the moonlight of middle June,
And then I found Davis.
We were married and lived together for seventy years,
Enjoying, working, raising the twelve children,
Eight of whom we lost
Ere I had reached the age of sixty.
I spun, I wove, I kept the house, I nursed the sick,
I made the garden, and for holiday
Rambled over the fields where sang the larks,
And by Spoon River gathering many a shell,
And many a flower and medicinal weed—
Shouting to the wooded hills, singing to the green valleys.
At ninety-six I had lived enough, that is all,
And passed to a sweet repose.
What is this I hear of sorrow and weariness,
Anger, discontent and drooping hopes?
Degenerate sons and daughters,
Life is too strong for you—
It takes life to love Life.

Ezra Pound gives two quick-sketch portrait poems that are scathing in their immediacy. The first one:

Clara

At sixteen she was a potential celebrity
With a distaste for caresses.
She now writes to me from a convent;
Her life is obscure and troubled;
Her second husband will not divorce her;
Her mind is, as ever, uncultivated,
And no issue presents itself.
She does not desire her children,
Or any more children.
Her ambition is vague and indefinite,
She will neither stay in, nor come out.

The second portrait poem by Ezra Pound:

Sketch 48 b, II

At the age of 27
Its homemail is still opened by its maternal parent
And its office mail may be opened by
  its parent of the opposite gender.
It is an officer
    and a gentleman,
        and an architect.

FROM *MOEURS CONTEMPORAINES*

13.   Credo poem. Write out a statement of what you believe,
as an artist and as a human being; try to include as many
areas of your belief as possible. Following are three examples of credos—the first by the Scottish poet Robert
Burns, in one stanza of the poem "Epistle to Davie, A
Brother Poet," where Burns summarizes what he feels
this life is all about:

It's no in titles nor in rank;
It's no in wealth like Lon'on Bank,
  To purchase peace and rest,
It's no in makin muckle, mair;
It's no in books, it's no in lear,
  To make us truly blest:
If happiness hae not her seat
  An centre in the breast,
We may be wise, or rich, or great,
  But never can be blest!
Nae treasures nor pleasures
    Could make us happy lang;
The heart ay's the part ay
    That makes us right or wrang.

The second credo is from George Bernard Shaw's play
The Doctor's Dilemma, where Louis Dubedat summarizes
everything he cares about in this life:

I believe in Michelangelo, Velásquez, and Rembrandt;
in the might of design, the mystery of color, the re-
demption of all things by Beauty everlasting, and the
message of Art that has made these hands blessed.
Amen. Amen.

The third credo is contained in the last stanza of Wallace Stevens's poem "Sunday Morning":

She hears, upon that water without sound,
A voice that cries, "The tomb in Palestine
Is not the porch of spirits lingering.
It is the grave of Jesus, where he lay."
We live in an old chaos of the sun,
Or old dependency of day and night,
Or island solitude, unsponsored, free,
Of that wide water, inescapable,
Deer walk upon our mountains, and the quail
Whistle about us their spontaneous cries;
Sweet berries ripen in the wilderness;
And, in the isolation of the sky,
At evening, casual flocks of pigeons make
Ambiguous undulations as they sink,
Downward to darkness, on extended wings.

Optimistic or pessimistic, religious or aesthetic or
atheistic—these credos present a summary of one's total
belief system. Try writing out a similar statement of be-
liefs without being too "intellectual" about it—simply
set down as many things you think you believe. But try
not to say you believe something because you think you
ought to believe it. Try to be honest about it.

14.   Oxymoron poem. *Oxymoron* is a technical term referring
to opposites; it is defined as "a radical paradox," a con-
junction of extreme opposites. For example: Dry ice is
so cold that it burns. In Racine's *Phèdre*, Phèdre reports
her deadly passion:

My body boiled and froze, then everything grew weak.

RACINE, *PHÈDRE*, I, II,
TR. WILLIAM PACKARD

Similarly, Chaucer's Troilus in *Troilus and Cressida* reports:

For hete of cold, for cold of hete, I dye . . .

TROILUS AND CRESSIDA, BOOK ONE

Write a poem of passion that embodies as many oxymorons, or extreme opposites, as you can think of.

15.   Synonyms and antonyms. Write out a list of synonyms, and another list of antonyms. Examples of synonyms:

love / like
hate / dislike
admiration / respect
contempt / scorn
fear / terror

Examples of antonyms:

love / hate
hate / like
admiration / dislike
contempt / respect
fear / calm

Some words in the English language are both homonyms and antonyms at the same time; for example:

raise / raze   (to lift up; to tear down)
let / let   (to allow; to prevent)

Write a poem as filled with homonyms and antonyms as you can make it.

16. Trauma poem. Write a poem that goes back to early childhood and some event that paralyzed you and rendered you motionless. It could be an emotional event, or a physical accident, or some sudden discovery that you made, or the death of someone close to you. Use as many specific image details as you can to recall the physical circumstances of the event. Don't try to convey the emotions themselves, or the thoughts you were thinking, as you'll probably get engulfed and overwhelmed by so much raw force. Just go for the facts, set down as many particulars of the memory as you can remember, and see where it takes you.

17. Catalogue poem. Try making lists of persons, places, or things that are important to you. For example, list the names of all the persons where you work; list the different place names where you have lived; make a list of all the persons you can remember who were in your senior class at high school. Catalogue listings can create a hypnotic effect through the sheer repetition of word after word after word. For example, in Book Two of Homer's *Iliad*, there is a catalogue listing of all the Achaian ships that sailed to Troy, beginning line 479:

> Of the Boiotians,
> Pênéleôs, Lêitos, Arkesílaös,
> Prothoênor, and Klónios were captains.
> Boiotians—men of Hyria and Aulis,
> the stony town, and those who lived at Skhoinos
> and Skôlos and the glens of Eteônos;
> Thespeia; Graia; round the dancing grounds
> of Mykalessos; round the walls of Harma,
> Eilésion; Erythrai, Eleôn;
> Hylê and Peteôn, and Okaléa,
> and Medeôn, that compact citadel,
> Kôpai, Eutrêsis, Thisbê of the doves;
> those, too, of Korôneia, and the grassland
> of Haliartos, and the men who held

Plataia town and Glisas, and the people
of Lower Thebes, the city ringed with walls,
and great Ongkhêstos where Poseidon's grove
glitters; and people too of Arnê, rich
in purple winegrapes, and the men of Mideia,
Nisa the blest; and coastal Anthêdôn.
All these had fifty ships. One hundred twenty
Boiotian fighters came in every ship.

ILIAD, BOOK TWO, LINES 479–500, TR. ROBERT FITZGERALD

Similarly, the first chapter of Matthew in the New
Testament begins with a genealogical catalogue that purports to trace Jesus all the way back to David and Abraham:

1. The book of the generation of Jesus Christ, the son of
    David, the son of Abraham.
2. Abraham begat Isaac; and Isaac begat Jacob; and Jacob
    begat Judas and his brethren;
3. And Judas begat Phares and Zara of Thamar; and Phares
    begat Esrom; and Esrom begat Aram;
4. And Aram begat Aminadab; and Aminadab begat
    Naasson; and Naasson begat Salmon;
5. And Salmon begat Booz of Rachab; and Booz begat
    Obed of Ruth; and Obed begat Jesse; . . .

MATTHEW 1:1–5

See if you can create a rhythmic repetition of proper
names based on your own family lineage. Then make a
list of all the names of students you remember from
seventh grade. Then make a list of all the towns and
cities that were close by where you grew up. Then make
a list of titles of all the books you have read over the
past three years. Then make a list of all the animals you
remember seeing in childhood.

Don't worry about whether any of these lists "make sense" or whether they are going anywhere, so far as poetry is concerned. Just get yourself into the rhythmic repetition of specific names, as if you were writing out a recitation or an incantation.

18. Persona poem. Write a poem using an assumed voice, some fictional dramatic mask that you can speak through instead of using your own voice.

In the following poem, the poet assumes the persona of a weary teacher who is packing his things after the end of a long class:

After the Class

after the class, after that last 11th hour asking
what did you mean by saying so & so
after the traffic of eyes into eyes has passed into air
i go to the windows and stare at the lighted windows outside.

then back to the desk to stack up my books
screw on the cup top of my steel thermos
pocket my pipe and rewrist my watch
pack everything together into my black leather shoulder bag

then exit into those tall empty halls
wait for the elevator to drop me down to the main floor
where i go out through the double doors to begin
the long walk home on concrete city sidewalks

it is raining words words words
the syllables go dribbling down my beard

WILLIAM PACKARD

And in the following poem, the poet assumes the voice of a seventh grade student who is being given a lesson in the reproductive process:

Science Class

In seventh grade, our class
got to see a special slide show.
A strange lady came in
to talk to us.
She showed us pictures of
hooks and scissors,
rubber gloves and tubes.
She passed around jars
of chemicals and salts.

Then came a picture of a baby
the size of a cricket.
It looked like it was sleeping
on a man's thumb,
but it was really dead.
She said it was alive once
but a doctor killed it.
He sucked it out with
some type of vacuum cleaner.

The next thing I knew
I was staring at pictures
of garbage cans filled with
beet red "candy-apple" babies
and shiny naked dolls
with see-through eyelids
and black eyes.
They all curled up in a ball
and looked like they were praying.

SERENA SIEGFRIED

And in the following poem, the poet assumes the voice
of a woman who is wrestling with her feelings of envy
and lust for another woman's man:

Bitch

I will not touch
her man

ever but
he is not
for her
his arms
   too strong
the jaw
  wide
he can swallow
souls
and pack them
in
his chest
so
   many
    scars
the hair on his leg
hands
that scare
eyes
so cold
I can swim
I swim
he is near
I
   want
his fingers
all
of him
inside
me

LISA PALMA

19. Ellipse poem. Try writing lines that have omissions or
     elisions of necessary words or parts of speech, to give the
     effect of speed or impetuosity. For example, William
     Blake in "The Tyger" creates an ellipse in the fourth
     line:

     And what shoulder, & what art,
     Could twist the sinews of thy heart?

And when thy heart began to beat,
What dread hand? & what dread feet?

Allen Ginsberg in the seventh strophe-line of "Howl" creates an ellipse by omitting the noun *behavior* from the modifier *crazy:*

who were expelled from the academies for crazy & publishing
obscene odes on the windows of the skull . . .

20.   Asposiopesis poem. Asposiopesis is a technical term referring to any sudden breaking off of a thought, or a self-interruption when a voice seems to catch itself in mid-thought. For example, Nina in Chekhov's *The Sea Gull* keeps interrupting and correcting herself:

I'm a sea gull. No, that's not it again . . . Do you remember you shot a sea gull? A man came along by
chance, saw it, and destroyed it, just to pass the
time . . . A subject for a short story . . . That's not it.
(rubs her forehead) What was I talking about? . . . Yes,
about the stage . . .

ANTON CHEKHOV, THE SEA GULL, ACT FOUR

Similarly, Yeats seems to catch himself in astonishment when he hears himself utter the phrase "the second
coming":

Surely some revelation is at hand;
Surely the Second Coming is at hand.
The Second Coming! Hardly are those words out
When a vast image out of *Spiritus Mundi*
Troubles my sight . . .

WILLIAM BUTLER YEATS, "THE SECOND COMING"

Try to write a poem in which your voice catches itself
in astonishment, or makes a self-correction.

21.   Caesura. A caesura is a breath pause between words, sometimes enforced, especially when one word ends with the same consonant that begins the following word. In this speech from *Hamlet*, Gertrude uses two crucial caesuras that force the actress to pause between the words *envious* and *sliver*, and again between *herself* and *fell*— which create a feeling of onomatopoeia about how Ophelia fell from the willow tree into the brook and drowned herself:

> There is a willow grows aslant a brook,
> That shows his hoar leaves in the glassy stream;
> There with fantastic garlands did she come,
> Of crow-flowers, nettles, daisies, and long purples,
> That liberal shepherds give a grosser name,
> But our cold maids do dead men's fingers call them;
> There, on the pendent boughs her coronet weeds
> Clambering to hang, an envious sliver broke,
> When down her weedy trophies and herself
> Fell in the weeping brook. . . .

> SHAKESPEARE. *HAMLET.* IV. VII. 166–175

Make a list of words that create caesuras when they are joined together, like *envious/sliver*, *herself/fell*, and then try to write a poem using this list.

22.   Enjambement. An enjambement is a spillover of poetry from the end of one line to the beginning of the next line. For example, in the opening of Cleopatra's death speech, there is an enjambement from the first line to the second line:

> Give me my robe, put on my crown, I have
> Immortal longings in me . . .

> SHAKESPEARE. *ANTONY AND CLEOPATRA.* V. II

Note that the enjambement creates a subtle momentary pause to create the illusion of energy being carried over from one line to the next. Write a poem using enjambements or spillovers on every line ending.

23. Syllabics. Some poetry is measured by syllable count instead of by count of accents, or meters. For example, if we rearrange the opening lines of Shakespeare's *Richard III* (which in the original are iambic pentameter) into a syllabic count of seven syllables to the line, we would have the following:

Now is the winter of our	(7)
discontent made glorious	(7)
summer by this son of York	(7)

Try writing a syllabic poem using the syllable count of seven syllables to a line, with no attention to accent or metrics.

24. Anaphora. The device of using repetition of key words at the beginning of successive lines of poetry is called anaphora. Martin Luther King, Jr., used this device in his 1963 speech during the March on Washington:

I have a dream today.
I have a dream that one day the state of Alabama, whose governor's lips are presently dripping with the words of interposition and nullification, will be transformed into a situation where little black boys and black girls will be able to join hands with little white boys and white girls and walk together as sisters and brothers.
I have a dream today.

Try writing a poem that uses a key repeating phrase at the beginning of each of its lines.

25. Cacophony. The use of extreme dissonance to create a sense of tension or conflict or disharmony is called ca-

cophony. Shakespeare uses cacophony in Sonnet 129 to show how ugly lust can be when it is kept bottled up inside:

> The expense of spirit in a waste of shame.
> Is lust in action; and till action, lust
> Is perjur'd, murderous, bloody, full of blame,
> Savage, extreme, rude, cruel, not to trust . . .

Try writing a poem that is so filled with awkward consonants brushing up against each other that they create a sense of cacophony.

26. Onomatopoeia. Any re-creation of a thing that tends to imitate the thing itself through rhythm or diction or syntax is called onomatopoeia. For example, Tennyson recreates the sound of doves and bees in these lines:

> The moan of doves in immemorial elms
> And murmuring of innumerable bees.
>
> SONG FROM "THE PRINCESS"

And Edgar Allan Poe uses onomatopoeia to recreate the sound of tolling bells:

> What a tale of terror now their turbulency tells!
>
> "THE BELLS"

Denise Levertov achieves onomatopoeia in the sounds of a lapping dog:

> Shlup, shlup, the dog
> as it laps up
> water
> makes intelligent
> music, resting

now and then to
take breath in irregular
measure.

FROM "SIX VARIATIONS"

Write onomatopoeia poems to recreate the following
things:

a fox   a grizzly bear
a subway   an air conditioner
a fireworks display   an automobile crash
a head of lettuce   a thunderstorm
a flushing toilet   a spring breeze

27.   Greek myths. Mythology has always been an inexhaus-
      tible source of poetry, using the stories and metaphors
      of the various gods and mortals in their adventures with
      one another.
      There are many guidebooks to the Greek myths, but prob-
ably the best is Ovid's *Metamorphoses* (A.D. 8), consisting of
fifteen books of hexameter lines, telling of all the miraculous
changes that took place among the gods and mortals of Greece
and Rome. There is a good translation by Horace Gregory in
paperback.
      Following are some of the principal gods and mortals who
figure in Greek and Roman mythology. Choose ten stories
from the lists, do some research on them, and then write poems
about each:

ZEUS: chief Olympian god, rules the heavens and causes
    rain and lightning and thunderstorms
POSEIDON: rules the seas, gave horses to mankind
ARES: the god of war, had an affair with Aphrodite
APHRODITE: the goddess of love and beauty, was born of
    the sea, was married to Hephaestos

ATHENA: goddess of wisdom, cities, and especially Athens; sprang full-blown out of the forehead of Zeus

APOLLO: the god of light, consciousness, truth, arrows, the lyre, the sun; had an affair with Daphne, who changed into a laurel tree

HERMES: god of speed and thieves

ARTEMIS: goddess of the hunt and chastity, the moon, and deer

HEPHAESTOS: god of fire, and armorers; married to Aphrodite, he catches Aphrodite and Ares together and traps them in a web

MENELAOS: husband of Helen and king of Sparta, he led the Achaian ships to Troy to reclaim Helen

AGAMEMNON: king of Argos and brother to Menelaos, chief Greek leader in Trojan War

ACHILLES: king of Myrmidons, quarrels with Agamemnon in ninth year of Trojan War, withdraws from combat

ODYSSEUS: one of the chief Greek warriors in the *Iliad*, his wanderings home from Troy to Ithaka form the subject of the *Odyssey*

PRIAM: king of Troy and father of Hector

HECTOR: chief Trojan warrior, married to Andromache

HECUBA: wife of Priam and mother of Hector and other Trojan warriors

PARIS: son of Priam, he abducted Helen to start Trojan War

CASSANDRA: daughter of Priam, she is cursed by Apollo with gift of prophesy which no one pays attention to

The numbers in the left margin indicate in which book of Ovid's *Metamorphoses* the following stories are found:

(1) PHAETHON: legendary son of the sun, asks to drive his father's chariot, horses bolt, he falls to earth

(2) JOVE AND EUROPA: in Ovid's version, Jove (the Greek Zeus) changes to a bull, takes Europa to Crete on his back, she gives birth to Minotaur

(3)　ECHO AND NARCISSUS: Echo is nymph who falls in love with Narcissus, he spurns her love, so his punishment is being enamored of his own image in a fountain; her punishment is to repeat the last words of anything that is said to her

(3)　PENTHEUS AND BACCHUS: Pentheus is king of Thebes, he spies on women revelers, they kill him, his mother Agave cuts off his head

(5)　PALLAS ATHENA AND THE NINE MUSES: CALLIOPE (epic poetry); CLIO (muse of history); EUTERPE (muse of flute music); MELPOMENE (muse of tragedy); TERPSICHORE (muse of dance); ERATO (muse of the lyre); POLYHYMNIA (muse of sacred song); URANIA (muse of astronomy); THALIA (muse of comedy).

(5)　DEMETER AND PERSEPHONE: Persephone is abducted by Hades and taken to the underworld, her mother Demeter pleads for her so Persephone is freed to come back to earth every six months

(8)　DAEDALUS AND ICARUS: Daedalus builds a maze in Crete for the Minotaur but then he himself is put inside the maze, so he makes wax wings to escape, his son Icarus ignores his warning and flies too near the sun, the wax melts and Icarus falls into the Aegean Sea

(9)　HERCULES: completes the twelve labors: conquers the Nemean lion; overcomes the hydra; slays the Erymanthian boar; catches the Ceryneian hind; kills the Stymphalian birds; cleans the Augean stables; conquers the Cretan bull; tames the horses of Diomedes; seizes the Amazon girdle; tames the Geryon oxen; gathers the apples of Hesperides; tames the dog Cerberus.

(10)　ORPHEUS AND EURYDICE: Orpheus' lyre tames the wild beasts, he goes to Hades to lead out Eurydice on condition that he not look back, but he does and Eurydice vanishes

    (10)   PYGMALION AND GALATEA: Pygmalion is king of Cyprus, makes a statue of Galatea and then falls in love with it

    (10)   VENUS AND ADONIS: Venus (the Greek Aphrodite) falls in love with the beautiful youth Adonis who is killed hunting

    (11)   MIDAS: king of Phrygia, he wishes that everything he touches be turned to gold

28.   Zodiac signs. Following are the various signs of the zodiac, with birth dates and astrological symbols and planets exerting influence over each sign. Locate your zodiac sign and write a poem using the information given in the chart below:

sign	dates	symbol	element	planets
Aries	3/21–4/20	the ram	fire	Mars
Taurus	4/21–5/21	the bull	earth	Venus
Gemini	5/22–6/21	the twins	air	Mercury
Cancer	6/22–7/23	the crab	water	Moon
Leo	7/24–8/23	the lion	fire	Sun
Virgo	8/24–9/23	the virgin	earth	Mercury
Libra	9/24–10/23	the scales	air	Venus
Scorpio	10/24–11/22	the scorpion	water	Mars/Pluto
Sagittarius	11/23–12/21	the archer	fire	Jupiter
Capricorn	12/22–1/20	the goat	earth	Saturn
Aquarius	1/21–2/19	the water jug	air	Uranus
Pisces	2/20–3/20	the fish	water	Neptune

29.   Birthstones and flowers. Following are birthstones and flowers for each month of the calendar year. Locate your own birth month and write a poem using the birthstone and flower indicated:

month	birthstone	flower
January	garnet	carnation
February	amethyst	violet
March	bloodstone	jonquil
April	diamond	sweet pea
May	emerald	lily of the valley
June	moonstone	rose
July	ruby	larkspur
August	peridot	gladiolus
September	sapphire	aster
October	opal	calendula
November	topaz	chrysanthemum
December	turquoise	narcissus

30. Open a notebook and begin to write stream of consciousness about what is going on inside your mind right
now. Don't stop to think about it, just begin writing and
keep writing—time yourself with a wristwatch and don't
stop writing continuously for ten minutes.

If you run into a block, then try writing about *that*:

> something is getting in the way of what I'm trying to
> write and I don't know what it is but it's beginning to
> make me angry just the way I got angry yesterday when
> I tripped on the sidewalk and almost fell down, the way
> it was when I was a kid and my mother always laughed
> at me when I couldn't do anything right . . .

So long as you're determined to keep the writing going, you'll
find a way of writing around any block or obstacle that comes
up. Stream of consciousness is exactly what it says it is: a stream,
a confluence of all sorts of currents intermingled with one another, with no set or predetermined form. Just a free flowing . . .

The thirty exercises in this chapter are meant to serve as
challenges, or triggers, or stimuli for one's own creative processes.
It may be that a poet will not be able to get any immediate direct
results from doing these exercises, but surely there will be indirect
responses that come from working on them. They're only meant

as guidelines to stimulate the practice of the art of poetry writing.

One should be able to keep coming back to these challenges again and again, to go at them from different angles and using different points of view. And of course one is always free to make up one's own writing challenges—all one has to do is come up with a premise that will guide one into some new area of poetry writing.

8

NUTS AND BOLTS

It's time to consider the practical side of poetry writing—what to think about poetry workshops, how to go about submitting work to poetry magazines, the problem of book publishing, the teaching of poetry in schools and universities, doing poetry readings, and finally, getting grants and awards.

Underlying all of these practical aspects is a deeper question, which is: How should one live one's life? Is there any special type of employment or enterprise that is peculiarly conducive to the art of poetry writing?

Speaking to these questions, the poet Richard Eberhart once commented:

> It's curious that people have preconceived ideas about poetry or about what a poet is or should be or has been in other times. I don't see why they should have any *a priori* notion about what a poet is. For instance, when I went into the Navy in World War II, everybody said that will be the end of you, you'll never write another poem, how could you write a poem if you're going into the war? Well, as it turned out, I wrote about 25 poems in the war, and at least one of them has been very well known ever since, "The Fury of Aerial Bombardment."

This poem couldn't possibly have been written if I hadn't gone to war.

Then I went into business, for seven years after World War II, and everybody said, oh, you will never write a poem if you go into business, that will kill you off, how can you be a poet if you're going into business? But I found business very conducive to poetry because in business one is on a one-to-one relationship with what I think is the reality of American life. I wrote some of my best poems during that period, "The Horse Chestnut Tree," for instance.

Then my poetry got well enough known around the country so that I was invited into the academy in 1952 at the University of Washington, in Seattle. And it's interesting, once I got into teaching, nobody asked those questions. The assumption was that somehow the poet and the teacher went hand in hand. And of course it is true that in the academy you have the continuous pleasure of talking about the thing that means the most to you, to people who want to hear about it—there is a profound give and take between professors and other professors, poets and other poets, and professor-poets and students, about the art of poetry.

THE NEW YORK TIMES BOOK REVIEW, JANUARY 1, 1978

As Eberhart implies, there is no special métier or vocation that is ready-made for the poet to pursue his craft, so each poet must find his or her own way that will enable them to keep practicing the art of poetry writing.

WORKSHOPS

Workshops are one such way to keep practicing the craft of poetry; there are thousands of poetry writing workshops that proliferate across the United States. University graduate writing programs, continuing education, poetry societies, and private workshop centers all offer classes where a poet can share his or her work with colleagues and get professional guidance.

Of course a poet must always beware of enrolling in any work-shop situation that may foster the very things the poet should be trying to wipe out of his own work: narcissism and careerism, those two deadly hydras that keep surfacing in so many different disguises and under so many different pretexts. For there are workshops out there that are every bit as meretricious and sy-cophantic as any poet himself could ever be. The problem is to spot these situations before one gets oneself too deeply enmeshed in their webbing. Many workshops merely encourage the writing of cliché poems out of cliché lives, and one can do very well without this sort of thing. It stands to reason: Put twenty-five amateur poets together in a workshop situation and give them an amateur teacher; the results will inevitably be the perpetuation of a kind of amateurism.

And no matter how professionally a poetry workshop may be conducted, there is always this comment by Galway Kinnell to consider:

> I never met a writer who thought he had learned much
> from a workshop.

And there is this poem by Norman Stock, which illustrates the kind of damage that can be done by the silly amateurism of a mediocre workshop situation:

> Thank You for
> the Helpful Comments
>
> I sit quietly listening
> as they tear my poem to shreds in the poetry workshop
> as each one says they have a "problem" with this line
>   and they have a "problem" with that line
> and I am not allowed to speak because that is the
>   eitquette of the workshop
> so I sit listening and writing while they tear the
>   guts out of my poem and leave it lying bleeding
>   and dead

and when they're finally finished having kicked the
   stuffing out of it
having trimmed it down from twenty lines to about four
   words that nobody objects to
then they turn to me politely and they say well Norman
   do you have any response
response I say picking myself up off the floor and
   brushing away the dirt while holding on for dear
   life to what I thought was my immortal poem now
   dwindled to nothing
and though what I really want to say is can I get my
   money back for this stupid workshop what I say
   instead is . . . uh . . . thank you for your helpful
   comments . . . while I mumble under my breath
   motherfuckers wait till I get to your poems

NEW YORK QUARTERLY, NUMBER 43

One must realize that the whole idea of going to poetry workshops is relatively recent, and indigenous to America. When
asked if he ever took a poetry workshop, W. H. Auden commented:

> Oh no, no that's only in America, Europe would never
> have such things.

The problem in America is how to locate a decent workshop
situation that is taught by a truly qualified writing teacher. One
can check around and audit classes until one locates a class where
the chemistry seems to be right and the instructor seems to know
what he or she is talking about. The only other touchstone we
can think of on this matter is the simple rubric offered by Ezra
Pound:

> Pay no attention to the criticism of men who have never
> themselves written a noteable work.

Patricia Farewell, one of the directors of The Sleepy Hollow
Poetry Series and currently residing in California, comments:

I think when I began taking poetry workshops I was looking for permission to be a poet. When I was growing up, all I ever heard was "Are you writing about death again?" and "When are you going to get out of your bedroom and go to a basketball game like the rest of the kids your age?" Poetry was an absurd choice, but taking a workshop was a way to feel legitimate. Here were folks doing the same god damn crazy thing! Here was a teacher telling you to write down whatever came into your head! It was great.

After I secured that permission to write, naturally the next thing I craved was constant approval . . . and many workshops provided me with that. I wanted to please that teacher. I listened hard. I did what he or she said. Much of my work was imitative and contrived, but I went home with a pat on the head.

Some teachers are ethereal angels and some are great bears. You feel attracted to them and you want to please them. They seem to live in a world deeper and better than your own. You make up all kinds of things about their lives. You hope that their dedication and produc-tivity will wear off on you. You want to make them smile and laugh now and then. They've memorized poems! They can scan all kinds of lines! You get this idea that they wake up and reach for a pencil, and this is what you want for yourself. It's rather harmless, isn't it?

NEW YORK QUARTERLY, NUMBER 45

Is it? We're not so sure. The one thing you can never teach in a writing workshop is the courage and character that it takes to keep on surviving over the long pull of a lifetime. Anyone can write a good poem or a good short story or even a good novel, but see if he or she can keep hacking it through the inferno for the next twenty-five years. Because that's what is really needed, and the only person who can ever give that is oneself.

Publishing in Magazines

The urge to send one's work out to journals and quarterlies and periodicals is the eternal desire to have one's work seen by others. It was even functioning in one of our most reclusive poets, Emily Dickinson, when she addressed the following letter to Thomas Higginson, a famous editor, in 1862:

> Mr. Higginson,
> Are you too deeply occupied to say if my Verse is alive?
> The mind is so near itself—it cannot see, distinctly—and I have none to ask—
> Should you think it breathed—and had you the leisure to tell me, I should feel quick gratitude—
> If I make the mistake—that you dare to tell me—would give me sincerer honor—toward you—
> I enclose my name—asking you, if you please—Sir—to tell me what is true?
> That you will not betray me—it is needless to ask—since Honor is it's own pawn—
>
> EMILY DICKINSON

It seems pitiful to us today to imagine Emily Dickinson submitting her work to someone like Higginson, who did not comprehend what the poet from Amherst was all about in her work. But that's how strong the eternal desire to have one's work seen by others can be. So the most we can say is that a poet should work out his or her own system of making submissions, based on the guidelines of sanity and one's own pace and method of composition.

Once a poet begins to submit work to magazines, he should realize always that any acceptance or rejection of his work can be a very arbitrary thing indeed, depending on the tastes and predilections of a particular editor. So a poet should always be more concerned with his own slow growth as an artist, than with what any editor happens to think of his work at any given time.

Because editors can do as much damage to a young poet by accepting an ineffective poem as they can by rejecting an effective poem. It's all a part of the breaks of the game.

With that said, following are a few guidelines on how to submit poetry manuscripts:

1. Always enclose a stamped self-addressed envelope with each submission.

2. Unless otherwise specified, enclose three to five poems per submission, never more unless asked.

3. Poems should be typed on 8½" × 11" paper. One should avoid tissuey-thin paper that will not stand up to passing through several hands. There is usually no objection to sending clear photocopies of one's poetry, as long as the copies are clean and legible.

4. Poems should be typed one per page, and one should number additional pages of the same poem with the title, for example:

    HIDDEN SUNRISE, page 2

5. Be sure to proofread poems for spelling and grammar errors, as misspelled words may bias a screener against the work.

6. Cover letters are optional, but it is a nice enough custom to send along a short note with one's manuscript submission saying who-am-I and what-am-I-sending, etc. Just be sure to keep the cover letter brief and courteous and sane, as any attempt to be clever or cute may backfire.

One can usually compile a list of literary magazines one wants to send one's work to by looking through the CCLM *Directory of Literary Magazines* (Coordinating Council for Literary Magazines). Or one can always go to the periodical section of one's local library, where the latest literary magazines will usually be available for perusal. The best gauge will be that those magazines one feels most interested in reading will probably be those that will be most hospitable to one's own work.

BOOK PUBLICATION

After one's work has appeared in the literary magazines, it's natural enough to want to get the first volume of poetry out—with the right publisher, in the right type style, and with all the right dust jacket statements on the cover.

But the sad fact is that there has been so much overpublication of poetry in the last few decades, most publishers look askance at the whole idea of doing poetry. The likelihood is that a poet's first poetry manuscript may very well fall into a publisher's slush pile along with the thousands of other first-volume manuscript submissions that are received by every publishing house in any given year.

In view of this, it may be a healthy thing for a poet to check his own impatience and concentrate instead on the ongoing mastery of his craft. Remembering his own early experience, Robert Frost once advised poets to "come to the market late" with their work. The poetry itself is always more important than the publication of it.

But when the right time does come to publish, the poet will usually know it. And when that happens, a poet may not care much about finding "the right publisher." In fact, some of our greatest poets have ignored the established publishers of their day and printed their work by themselves. William Blake designed his own volumes and offered them for sale himself, and so did Walt Whitman, who published the first edition of *Leaves of Grass* in 1855 and then wrote three "anonymous" book reviews in the same year:

An American bard at last! (*United States Review*)

Politeness this man has none, and regulation he has none. A rude child of the people!—No imitation—no foreigner—but a growth and idiom of America. (*Brooklyn Daily News*)

The most glorious of triumphs, in the known history of literature. (*American Phrenological Journal*)

We're not saying every poet should do what Blake and Whitman did; we're just saying there are other options than hitting one's head against the major publishing houses and waiting for some Big Break. The smaller presses produce chapbooks and first editions that are quite respectable; so do some university presses and local publishers across the country. And with desktop computers and word processors that have laser printouts using a wide range of type styles, it's easier to produce photo-ready copies of one's work to cut costs on book production.

Whatever one chooses to do with one's work, the most important thing is to stay close to one's ongoing work, which is the practice of the art of poetry writing.

TEACHING

There may be nothing more inimical to the metabolism of a creative artist than the experience of trying to teach his own art to others. He may feel it's impossible to impart the thing itself, and so he may choose to dwell instead on the techniques of craft, those principles of prosody that cut across any and all schools of poetry. And that's as it should be, since that's usually what's most needed by students.

One contemporary poet, Galway Kinnell, puts it this way:

> Teaching is exciting and interesting, and it is an honorable profession. But I don't think it nourishes a writer. Many of the people you are talking to are too much like yourself: it's too much like a conversation going on inside your own head. It would be much better if one could find a work by which you could enter a new world, a world different not only in its kinds of people, but also

in its materials and terminology. As yet I haven't found for myself such a work.

Be that as it may, the great majority of practicing poets in this country today support themselves by teaching in our leading schools and universities. And while they may try to maintain a strict objectivity about their teaching, even so, they usually develop some poignant anxieties over trying to develop their students into good poets. A poet-teacher may spend hours in written criticism of a student's work and still not see the student respond in any meaningful way to the critiques. And this may lead the teacher into profound doubts about his own adequacy as poet and teacher.

He may even find himself wondering: Can you teach the writing of poetry? And he might as well ask, Can you teach the search for truth, or the worship of beauty, or the experience of love? Because of course you can't teach any of these things, any more than you can teach the real reason for writing or the pain and labor and patience it takes to make a poem.

And he may not even be sure that he can teach the reading of poetry—at least not in the sense that Emily Dickinson meant when she said,

> If I read a book and it makes my whole body so cold no fire can warm me, I know that is poetry. If I feel physically as if the top of my head were taken off, I know that is poetry. These are the only ways I know it. Is there any other way?

And he knows he can't teach the excitement of sudden insight, such as A. E. Housman writes:

> Experience has taught me when I am shaving of a morning, to keep watch over my thoughts, because if a line of poetry strays into my memory, my skin bristles so that the razor ceases to act.

And he knows he certainly can't teach the process by which a poem becomes a part of you, as Robert Frost describes it:

> The right reader of a good poem can tell the moment
> it strikes him that he has taken an immortal wound—
> that he will never get over it.

In short, he knows there is a great deal about the essence of poetry that can never really be taught at all, although there are certain other very specific things about the structure and form of poetry that can always be taught.

For example, he can always teach the craft of poetry, and the techniques of style in writing; he can review the basic poetic devices, as we've done in chapter 2 of this book—metaphor, simile, imagery, rhyme, assonance, and alliteration; he can demonstrate the various metrical patterns and their usefulness in conveying different impulses of thought and emotion; and he can discuss the various levels of irony and connotation and texture in a poem. He can try to quicken a student's sense of the shape and weight of words, and he can stress the importance of expressing one's thought in clear and concrete images, and he can try to sharpen an appreciation for objective form, whether it be fixed form or organic form that is implied in the content of the poem. These things he knows he can do.

And beyond all this, he knows he can also try to teach a certain tolerance toward poetry itself. Because usually a student needs to be told that poetry is a very large country, and there is no reason for him to be provincial in his tastes and attitudes; instead, he should try to be open to poetry of all sorts—from the epigrammatic plain style of Ben Jonson and the very strict Alexandrines of Racine, to the long lines and broad cosmic scope of Walt Whitman. A student should try to encompass the sweetness and freedom of Keats, as well as the wry dialectical irony of Eliot.

And furthermore, the teacher can try to disabuse his students of the notion that there is any "fit subject matter" for poetry, and he can try to show them that the "message" of a poem is not the only thing that determines its objective merit. Just as one doesn't have to be a scholastic Catholic to enter into Dante's *Divine Comedy*, and just as one doesn't have to be Puritan to participate in Milton's *Paradise Lost*, so one doesn't have to be a beatnik to be deeply affected by Allen Ginsberg's *Kaddish*. The important thing is to approach the poetry as poetry.

For example, suppose one had two poems which made opposite statements about the world; one should not choose one poem over the other poem based on whether one agrees or disagrees with their respective "messages." One poem that comes to mind is Marianne Moore's moving "In Distrust of Merits," which is an impassioned plea for peace on earth. Here is the last stanza:

> Hate-hardened heart, O heart of iron,
>   iron is iron until it is rust.
> There never was a war that was
>   not inward; I must
> fight till I have conquered in myself what
> causes war, but I would not believe it.
>   I inwardly did nothing.
>   O Iscariot-like crime!
>   Beauty is everlasting
>   and dust is for a time.

Now this poem is in sharp contrast to Ezra Pound's ferocious, forceful rendering of the "Sestina: Altaforte," which is an outright appeal for war and bloodshed and conflict. Here is the first stanza of that poem:

> Damn it all! all this our South stinks peace.
> You whoreson dog, Papiols, come! Let's to music!
> I have no life save when the swords clash,
> But ah! when I see the standards gold, vair, purple, opposing
> And the broad fields beneath them turn crimson,
> Then howl I my heart nigh mad with rejoicing.

Surely these two poems are contradictory in spirit and message and meaning—and yet it is possible to admire the craft and skill of each poem objectively and for its own sake, regardless of whether one agrees or disagrees with what is being said.

Two further points about the teaching of poetry. When he is dealing with student poets, the teacher must realize he is confronting something quite unaccountable, since poets of any age are usually of a peculiar temperament; sometimes inspired by divine madness, sometimes on the side of the devil, poets are notoriously perverse, erratic, recalcitrant, obstreperous, and refractory. They need the greatest latitude for their eccentric sensibilities, and a good teacher has to give it to them. Yeats recognized the very special disposition of the creator when he wrote:

> We who are poets and artists . . . must go from desire
> to weariness, and so to desire again, and live but for the
> moment when vision comes to our weariness like terrible
> lightning in the humility of the brutes.

Heaven help any teacher of poetry who does not allow his student poets to pursue their own bent and discover their own tendencies in the writing of verse. The most that a good teacher can do is to try and create a climate of approval, a generous spirit of permission, so that his class can experiment and explore and engage in word play for its own sake. A student should be encouraged to feel that any impulse that comes to him is worth developing and elaborating and bringing to a skillful realization.

But that brings us to the second point, which is a very perplexing question indeed. What is the teacher of poetry to do about the great mass of mediocre work that is bound to come up in any workshop situation? How should he deal with the undistinguished verse, the terrible quantities of inconsequential poems which are not really poems in any true sense of the word? We're living in the midst of a great explosion of interest in poetry today, and we're being exposed to all sorts of pseudo-poems since verse has become a middle-class diversion and a leisure time activity. How is the teacher of poetry to cope with this sort of thing honestly?

Of course, he must say what he thinks, regardless. The housewife with her sentimental sonnets to the sunrise, the student crusader with his social protest poems, the pompous philosopher with his endless epigrams on existence—these must all be confronted and shown the triviality of their ways. After all, Shakespeare did not hesitate to lampoon the poetasters of his own time, when he spoke of

> the lover,
> Sighing like furnace, with a woful ballad
> Made to his mistress' eyebrow. . . .
>
> AS YOU LIKE IT. II. VII. 147–149

Yet while one must be merciless toward the work, a teacher must always bear in mind how damaging it can be to harass and bewilder a young poet who is unsure of his own direction. Because there are already so many hostile forces at work around us, there are so many self-appointed critics of creativity who are so adept at ridiculing the inept, there is no reason for a teacher of poetry to join in this chorus of scorn. We should remember the fate of *Endymion* with enormous shame, for we know how it affected John Keats—Byron sums up what happened in a single stanza:

> "Who killed John Keats?"
> "I", said the Quarterly,
> So savage and tartarly,
> "Twas one of my feats."

It's true that student poets can be dreadfully mediocre but then again, we should always bear in mind that even our greatest poets were capable of outlandish mediocrity—and not many students could rival the wordiness and sentimentality of Wordsworth at his worst.

But as we said at the outset, that's about all a good teacher of poetry can do. Art is hard, and the writing of poetry is a crucial experience consisting of crisis and sacrifice, and it must be pursued with pride and seriousness. After all, true poetry has to involve our entire being: it should be a risk of the will, a test of the intellect, and a heightening of the heart.

POETRY READINGS

Reading poetry in public is a radically different experience from writing poetry in private. Each time a poet stands in front of an audience, there is an unconscious theatrical element which comes into play. Because of this theatrical element, poetry readings tend to spotlight the poet, not the poetry. Therefore a poet may sometimes seek the esteem of his listeners, not his readership. He may even come to look at a poem not for what it is, but for how it will go over with an audience.

Ezra Pound says it better than anyone:

> The desire to stand on the stage, the desire of plaudits has nothing to do with serious art. The serious artist may like to stand on the stage, he may, apart from his art, be any kind of imbecile you like, but the two things are not connected, at least they are not concentric. Lots of people who don't even pretend to be artists have the same desire to be slobbered over, by people with less brains than they have.
>
> The serious artist is usually, or is often as far from the *aegrum vulgus* as the serious scientist.
>
> "THE SERIOUS ARTIST," *THE LITERARY ESSAYS OF EZRA POUND* (1954)

It's true that many contemporary poets have read their work in public with aplomb and delight. Dylan Thomas achieved a tragic grandeur through rich readings of his impassioned work; Robert Frost delighted audiences for generations with his urbane and witty performances of poetry; Allen Ginsberg mixed madcap antics with mystical incantations in his insistence on what was innately sacred.

Even so, the danger is still there, and the theatricalization of one's talents may be fatal to one's instincts as an artist. And the great majority of modern poets preferred the page to the stage; it would be difficult to imagine Emily Dickinson giving a poetry reading, or Charles Baudelaire, or Hart Crane. Rainer Maria Rilke used to get nosebleeds whenever he had to read his poetry in public.

And indeed, many contemporary poets are aware of the dangers of doing poetry readings. W. H. Auden comments:

> I like doing it if one gets into it; it is something quite different. The thing you have to be careful about is not to try and think of a style of writing that is too declamatory. There are 500 people out there in the audience, but they are thinking of you as speaking to one person.

> NEW YORK QUARTERLY CRAFT INTERVIEW, NUMBER 1

James Dickey feels there is a real menace in doing too many poetry readings:

> . . . it's fatally easy to fall into this business of doing nothing but going around giving readings, and I've been quite guilty of that—because after you've gotten up to a certain level, like Lowell and Berryman maybe and a few others, where you can get these enormous fees, you not only figure that you really don't have to write any poetry any more, you figure that it's better if you don't. Because the reputation that brings in this dough is already there, and if you write more stuff, you're just giving somebody a chance to bust you.

> The only thing that's going to save you is the basic love of *das Ding an sich*, the thing itself—poetry. That's the only thing that's going to save you. All this publicity, the dough, the women—especially them—are fatally easy to come by.

> NEW YORK QUARTERLY CRAFT INTERVIEW, NUMBER 10

Beyond one's personal attitudes about doing poetry readings, we can see the effect that all these readings have had on our contemporary poetry writing. They've certainly given rise to an entirely new way of writing, a more declamatory and public presentation of oneself in one's work. And they've also given rise to an entirely new kind of poem, something we could call the "voice stance poem." This kind of poem is easy enough to write; all you have to do is take a stance toward or against something, and then start talking—what comes out is "voice stance poetry."

For example, some of the stances one could take are the following:

> I'm lonely
> I'm horny
> I think all men are pigs
> I hate marriage
> I'm an Indian
> I'm gay
> I'm lesbian
> I'm black
> I'm Indonesian
> I'm from Missouri
> I'm a transvestite Eskimo

Then one talks and talks and talks about how it *feels* to be taking this stance. One can hardly go to a poetry reading without hearing at least one of these voice stance poems, for better or for worse. Voice stance poems are a little like modern television commercials: There's one central point that keeps getting plugged over and over and over again, until the viewer or listener or reader reaches a saturation point and succumbs to the product or the poem or the point of view, out of sheer weariness and fatigue.

Poetry readings, and recordings and tapes of poetry readings, can occasionally be enormously enlightening as to what rhythms and inflections are meant to be working in a particular poem. They can also help to create a spell that is enchanting and incantatory, something that echoes the early Orphic role of the poet as someone who mesmerized his hearers into a trance state.

A good poetry reader like Richard Burton or John Gielgud or Laurence Olivier can provide insight into a poet's intentions that few professors could ever hope to impart to their students.

One has to work out one's own relationship to poetry readings of one's own work, remembering always that the page and the stage are two very separate arenas for one's art.

GRANTS AND AWARDS

There is a wide range of support grants and fellowships and awards for the practicing poet, both from private and public sectors of our culture.

The best way to amass information on which grants and awards and fellowships one may be eligible for is to write to the individual private foundations (like the Guggenheim and the MacArthur foundations), or else go through the *Foundation Directory* available in any reference library to compile one's own master list of grant organizations to which one wants to apply. The directory will give details on eligibility requirements, application deadlines, and what sort of proposal is appropriate.

Then one can compile a similar listing of the federal and state arts grants by writing to the National Endowment for the Arts (NEA) and the National Endowment for the Humanities (NEH) in Washington, and to the various arts agencies that exist in one's own home state.

One will then have to decide which grants to apply for, and obtain the appropriate application forms and fill them out and get them sent off before the deadline dates. Usually the applications will require the writing out of some statement of purpose, and a proposal for work that one plans to do if one gets the grant. Usually too the applications will ask for the candidate to send along some printed copies of one's published work, along with letters of recommendation and/or background reference statements by artists and teachers in one's chosen field of work. These reference letters may or may not waive confidentiality, so the candidate may be able to see what has been said about him.

One should be aware that this grant-seeking and fellowship-hunting can become a vocation in and of itself, and in our time we have seen an enormous number of persons who go from one fellowship to another like some acrobat going from one trapeze to another in midair, and one wonders whether it might not be better for the person occasionally to touch down and walk among mortals from time to time. For example: V. S. Pritchett in his book *The Mythmakers* gives a stunning description of the sort of life Chekhov led:

> From the age of nineteen he supported his family—a bankrupt despotic shop-keeping father, his fretful mother, a string of bickering relatives and hangers-on—mainly by his writing, under knockabout domestic conditions which were farcically at variance with what a serious artist is supposed to need. He appointed himself—even at nineteen—head of this tribe . . . who he described as "people pasted together artificially."

No wonder Chekhov's great later plays are peopled by so many curious eccentrics, dawdlers and idlers and idealists who can never quite get their act together. Chekhov was probably venting his spleen against the households he was forced to support by his short stories in his earlier years. One artist, Shelly Estrin, comments on this:

> Quite an astounding energy that enabled Chekhov to work full-time as a physician, write stories, plays, serve as founder of clinics and hospitals, he also started schools and libraries, and then do his research on life among the convicts at Sakhalin Island.
>
> So ironic to think of the whiners today who need grants from the NEA and the arts councils, so they can write their poems or plays, or who have to go to writing workshops to "confirm themselves"—and then to remember the reality of Chekhov.

Well, of course it *is* sobering to think about, but then artists have always had odd tricks to turn a buck so they could keep on with their work. Phidias had Pericles in ancient Athens, and Leonardo had the Medici, and Michelangelo had the popes, and Mozart had the courts, and Beethoven had Prince Lichnowsky, and Rilke had all those rich duchesses he could borrow castles from. We shouldn't wax too moralistic about how artists hustle their bread, so long as the work itself remains paramount.

What we do feel is important to say is that there's nothing so hollow as the frantic scramble for literary grants—all those greedy egos mad for adulation. It may be that after writing out a few dozen proposals for what one intends to do with all that foundation money, one probably begins to believe that one really is all those phony things one says on the application form—and then one is in real trouble. It takes an extraordinary sanity to separate the honors from the honesty, as Robert Lowell implied when he introduced Marianne Moore in 1967 and said:

> Marianne Moore may be our most honored poet but in spite of that, she is still a good poet.

The final word on all these honors and awards was said by the great Spanish poet and playwright Federico Garcia Lorca:

> Some time in the past I made a firm promise to refuse every type of tribute, banquet or feast which might be dedicated to my simple person; first, because I know that each one adds more mortar to our literary tomb, and second, because I've seen nothing more desolate than a prepared speech in our honor, nor a sadder moment than that of organized applause, even if in good faith. . . .
>
> For poets and playwrights, I would organize attacks and challenges instead of tributes. . . .

Throughout this chapter, as we've looked at the practical side of poetry writing—what we call the "nuts and bolts" of being a poet—going to poetry workshops, submitting one's work to poetry magazines, trying to get one's work published in book form, teaching poetry in schools and universities, doing poetry readings, and getting grants and awards—we realize we've taken a somewhat acerbic view of allowing oneself to get caught up in the cynicism of self-seeking and the hustle of self-promotion.

In the early pages of this chapter, we even went so far as to say that narcissism and careerism are the two deadly hydras that keep surfacing in so many different disguises and under so many pretexts. They are deadly to one's art because nothing can stifle one's creativity faster than the wrong sort of egoism and self-love, and they are hydras because they are many-headed and proliferate—just when one thinks one has lopped off the head of one inner evil, a dozen new heads spring up to take its place.

The only thing one can do is go to the source of one's narcissism and careerism and rip it out by the roots—eradicate, deracinate it once and for all. That's what the great Russian actor and director Stanislavsky meant when he counseled young artists:

Love the art in yourselves, not yourselves in the art.

STANISLAVSKY. *My Life in Art*

Again and again we seem to be saying the same thing: Poetry is a solitary art, at least the writing of poetry is. It is an experience that takes place in the solitariness of an extraordinary individual. And unless one can accept that fact, one can't expect to do much with the art of poetry writing.

9

READING WHILE WRITING

No one writes in a vacuum. There's usually a direct relation between one's input and one's output—how much a writer can take from the various sources that are already all around him, and how much that same writer can carry over into his own writing.

That's not to say one has to read books in order to keep writing—nothing of the sort. One can always come up with original images and ideas out of one's own imagination without reference to anything one may or may not be reading at the time. That's what one's own writing should be all about. But it's more a matter of keeping one's psychic momentum going by taking advantage of what's already been written in the past.

We're talking here about reading really worthwhile books— not reading a lot of cheapo shlock paperback romances that are only one step ahead of the sick TV sitcoms that do nothing but rot the human imagination and take away one's desire to write. The books we're talking about are the primary sourcebooks of our civilization, what used to be called "classics" before our modern education system went to pot. It's shocking how many people have gone through four years of so-called liberal arts education and never once read Homer or Pascal or Dostoyevsky, or have any idea what Sir James Frazer's *The Golden Bough* is all about. Modern American universities have spawned the publication of a totally new kind of book—a book *about* a book—which is about on the same level as fast food for its synthetic, nonnutritive approach to literature.

We'll stay with Ezra Pound's definition of a "classic" as "news that stays news," and we'll insist that books are the greatest resource that's available to the practicing writer—as long as one bears in mind Emerson's gentle warning about books:

> Books are the best of things, well used; abused, among the worst. What is the right use? What is the one end which all means go to effect? They are for nothing but to inspire. I had better never see a book than to be warped by its attraction clean out of my own orbit, and made a satellite instead of a system. . . .
>
> Books are for the scholar's idle time. When he can read God directly, the hour is too precious to be wasted in other men's transcripts of their readings.
>
> RALPH WALDO EMERSON, "BOOKS"

We can cite some wonderful examples of the importance, and the nonimportance, of books in the lives of writers. For example, we know the very active life that Geoffrey Chaucer lived—serving with Edward III in the invasion of France, then serving in the court of Richard II and making at least three separate trips to Genoa and Florence in Italy, where he met Petrarch and most probably Boccaccio, and then bringing back some of Petrarch's sonnets to translate and use in his own writing of *Troilus and Cressida*, before he undertook his great masterwork the *Canterbury Tales*.

But on the other hand, we know that William Shakespeare never once set foot in either France or Italy, yet many of his greatest plays were set in Italy and France: *Romeo and Juliet*, *The Merchant of Venice*, *Othello*, and *Henry V*, to mention only a few. Although he was circumscribed by the relatively provincial roadways of Stratford and London during his entire life, Shakespeare was nontheless able to travel in his imagination to Scotland,

France, Italy, Austria, Egypt, Greece, and ancient Rome through the books he had in his possession—Ovid's *Metamorphoses*, Holinshed's *Chronicles*, Plutarch's *Lives*, Montaigne's *Essays*, and of course the great Geneva Bible.

And in more modern times, we know the poet and translator Dante Gabriel Rossetti did one of the most exquisite translations that has ever been accomplished of Dante's early *La Vita Nuova*, as well as works of other early Italian writers—St. Francis of Assisi, Guido Guinicello, and Guido Cavalcanti, to mention only a few. Yet Rossetti himself never set foot in his beloved Italy, and did most of his great translation while sitting in the library of the British Museum. As John Wain comments,

> Italy, for Rossetti, was a place of the mind; he never went there. . . .
>
> ROSSETTI, *THE EARLY ITALIAN POETS*

It's astonishing to think of what the human imagination can achieve on its own, without any direct or empirical contact with a body of knowledge. Blaise Pascal is said to have memorized the entire Bible, both Old Testament and New Testament, before his death at the relatively young age of thirty-nine. And Scottish natives have a hard time understanding how Shakespeare could have written the play *Macbeth* without once having visited Scotland, so authentic is the imagery and atmosphere of the play.

In this chapter we're going to list some of the great major works of Eastern and Western civilization, books that have become indispensable texts of our common heritage, books that any writer would do well to read and reread and keep reading in for the rest of his or her lifetime. But we should say at the outset that this chapter is meant more as a reference tool and a checklist to be used in one's reading than as any authoritative or comprehensive listing of books that someone *should* read, the way it was done in high school with compulsory book reports and dopey questions to be answered by the student. No, these are just some books that may be of value to anyone who is seriously interested in keeping on with the art of poetry writing.

First, here is a brief listing of some of the sacred texts of the East and Mideast:

1. Vedas. Sacred Hindu scripture as early as 2000 B.C., explain the creation of the world and the division of mankind into separate castes. The Upanishads are Vedas that expound the doctrine of "karma," how the human soul travels through many bodies and how one soul reaps in one lifetime what had been sown in previous lifetimes. The Bhagavad-Gita are Vedas that depict armies that are arrayed for battle, and how the hero Arjuna lays down his arms and does not want to slay his fellow man; the god Krishna, disguised as Arjuna's charioteer, discourses with Arjuna and urges him to do his caste duty by joining the battle.

2. Mahayana. Lotus Sutra, compiled before A.D. 250, teaches that salvation is open to all who seek it.

3. Confucius: *Analects*. Kung, the Master, teaches *Li*, or perfect virtue, and what one's civic responsibilities are. *The Book of Mencius* (372–289 B.C.) expounds the teachings of Confucius and shows how human nature is innately good, and all evil is a perversion of this good.

4. Laotse: *Tao Te Ching*. The great sixth-century B.C. contemporary of Confucius, Laotse taught the Tao or Way, and how man was to follow *wu-wei* or nonaction, what Westerners would call quietism.

5. The Koran. Revelations from Mohammed (A.D. 570–632), who declared himself a prophet in A.D. 611 and sought to restore the monotheism of Adam, Noah, and Abraham. The Koran worships Allah as the one Supreme Being, and teaches a fourfold life of devotion: prayer, fasting, alms, and pilgrimage to Mecca.

And here is a brief listing of some of the sacred texts of the West:

1. The Old Testament. Commonly divided into the Law, the Prophets, and the Writings:
   a. The Law—The Torah, from verses of the Pentateuch: Genesis, Exodus, Leviticus, Numbers, Deuteronomy
   b. The Prophets—Isaiah, Jeremiah, Ezekiel, Daniel, Hosea, Joel, Amos, Obadiah, Jonah, Micah, Nahum, Habakkuk, Zephaniah, Haggai, Zechariah, Malachi
   c. The Writings—history and poetry and theology: Samuel, Kings, Chronicles, Job, Psalms, Proverbs, Ecclesiastes, Song of Solomon

2. The New Testament. Commonly divided into the Gospels, the Acts, the Letters, and Revelations:
   a. The Gospels—Matthew, Mark, Luke, and John
   b. The Acts of the Apostles, written by Luke
   c. Letters of Paul, Peter, James, John, and Jude
   d. The Book of Revelations, by John

Following are some of the outstanding works of Greek literature:

1. Homer: The *Iliad*. Composed in ninth century B.C. about the Trojan War that raged 1194–1184 B.C., concerns the anger of Achilles in ninth year of that war and how this one man's withdrawal from the war caused devastation to both Greeks and Trojans. Keats praised an early English translation in "On First Looking into Chapman's Homer," but both Chapman and Pope translations tend to be jingly; the following opening lines of Pope's translation tend to awkward diction and are filled with pointless inversions:

   > The wrath of Peleus' son, the direful spring
   > Of all the Grecian wars, O goddess sing!

   Richmond Lattimore led the revolution of modern translation in our time, and rendered Homer into a more placid diction. Robert Fitzgerald is more textured, retains the Greek spelling of names (Akhilleus for Achilles) and uses gut language when he has to (thus Akhilleus calls Agamemnon "dog face").

2. Homer: The *Odyssey*. Concerns the wanderings of Odysseus on his way back home to Ithaka from Troy, after the ending of the Trojan War. Odysseus has adventures with Kalypso, Circe, the Sirens, the Cyclops, the Lotos-Eaters, Scylla and Charybdis, and finally with the suitors in his own home who are courting his wife Penelope during his absence. The *Odyssey* has been used as an allegory for the trials of modern man by such authors as Tennyson, James Joyce, and Ezra Pound. The translation by Robert Fitzgerald is excellent.

3. The poems of Sappho, seventh-century B.C. lyric poet who lived on the island of Lesbos in Mytelene, are exquisitely translated by Willis Barnstone. We know Sappho was married, had a daughter named Cleis, and gathered together a group of women around her to teach music and poetry and to share in the worship of Aphrodite. Sappho wrote some nine books of odes and elegies and hymns, although only a few fragments have come down to us; even so, these brief poems are among the most incandescent lyric poetry ever written. For example:

> To me that man equals a god
> as he sits before you and listens
> closely to your sweet voice
>
> and lovely daughter—which troubles
> the heart in my ribs. For now
> as I look at you my voice fails,
>
> my tongue is broken and thin fire
> runs like a thief through my body.
> My eyes are dead to light, my ears

pound, and sweat pours down over me,
I shudder, I am paler than grass,
and am intimate with dying—but

I must suffer everything, being poor.

TR. WILLIS BARNSTONE

4. Greek plays. Following is a complete listing of the major tragedies and comedies of the classical Greek theater:

   a. Aeschylus (525–456 B.C.; wrote 90 plays, 7 are extant): *Agamemnon*, *Libation Bearers* (*Choephori*), *Eumenides*, *The Persians*, *The Suppliant Maidens*, *The Seven Against Thebes*, *Prometheus Bound*

   b. Sophocles (ca. 496–406 B.C.; wrote 120 plays, 7 are extant): *Oedipus Rex* (*Tyrannos*), *Antigone*, *Oedipus at Colonos*, *Electra*, *Ajax*, *Women of Trachis*, *Philoctetes*

   c. Euripides (ca. 484–406 B.C.; wrote 80–90 plays, 18 are extant): *Medea*, *The Trojan Women*, *The Bacchae*, *Ion*, *Hippolytus*, *Heracleidae*, *The Cyclops*, *Rhesus*, *Alcestis*, *Heracles*, *Hecuba*, *Iphigenia in Tauris*, *Iphigenia in Aulis*, *Helen*, *Electra*, *Orestes*, *Andromache*, *The Suppliant Women*, *The Phoenician Women*

   d. Aristophanes (ca. 450–388 B.C.; plays, 11 are extant): *Lysistrata*, *The Clouds*, *The Birds*, *The Frogs*, *The Wasps*, *The Knights*, *Peace*, *Acharnians*, *Thesmophoriazusae*, *Ecclesiazusae*, *Plutus*

   e. Menander (342–292 B.C.; wrote 100 plays, 3–4 are extant): *The Girl from Samos*, *Arbitration*, *Shearing of Glycera*

   Early Gilbert Murray translations of the Greek plays are stilted and archaic; Yeats gave an excellent example of how the great plays might be translated with his verse version of *Oedipus at Colonos*, which has these lines:

Never to have lived is best, ancient writers say;
Never to have drawn the breath of life, never to have
   looked into the eye of day;
The second best's a gay goodnight and quickly turn away.

   In contemporary translation, David Grene and Richmond Lattimore divide the plays between them in excellent modern versions; also, William Arrowsmith, Dudley
Fitts, Robinson Jeffers, Ezra Pound, Rex Warner, Witter
Bynner, Emily Townsend Vermeule, and Elizabeth Wyck-
off are recommended. Robert Fitzgerald translations are
probably the best.

5. Greek history. Following are the two major historians of
   the Greek era:
   a. Herodotus: *The Persian Wars.* Chronicles the Greek
      war against the Persian invaders 490–470 B.C. under
      Darius and Xerxes, with special attention to the out-
      standing battles of Marathon and Salamis.
   b. Thucydides: *The Peloponnesian Wars.* Chronicles the
      Greek wars between city-states of Sparta and Athens,
      431–404 B.C. Sparta with her land army eventually
      overcame Athens with her strong navy, and the out-
      come was the demise of Greece as a world power.

6. Greek philosophy. Following are the principal Greek phi-
   losophers:
   a. Pre-Socratics: Anaxagoras, Anaximander, Democritus,
      Parmenides, Zeno, Protagoras, Heraclitus
   b. Plato (ca. 428–348 B.C.). In translations by Benjamin
      Jowett, the great Platonic dialogues by this early disciple
      of Socrates record the trial and execution of Socrates
      in *Apology, Crito,* and *Phaedo,* then go on to develop
      Plato's own philosophy in the *Republic, Phaedrus, Ti-
      maeus,* and the *Symposium,* using Socrates as the
      central figure in the question-and-answer dialectic met-
      hod of Plato.
   c. Aristotle (384–322 B.C.). In translations by Richard
      McKeon, Plato's student Aristotle developed a more
      empirical scientific approach that was often at variance
      with Plato's doctrine of Ideas. In the *Physics, Meta-
      physics, Posterior Analytics* and *Anterior Analytics,* Ar-
      istotle developed a theory of logic and four causes be-

hind every event (material, final, efficient, and formal); *Poetics, Rhetoric,* and *Ethics* he developed application of these views to art and life.

Following are some of the outstanding works of Roman literature:

1. Catullus (ca. 84–54 B.C.). Catullus went to Rome about 62 B.C., where he met a woman he calls "Lesbia" (probably Clodia, wife of Metellus Celer who was proconsul of Cisalpine Gaul). Catullus wrote poem after poem for Lesbia, exploring the immediate passion and misery of Eros; he also wrote scathing poems excoriating his contemporaries. Following are some of his finest verses, in excellent translation by Horace Gregory:

V

Come, Lesbia, let us live and love,
nor give a damn what sour old men say.
The sun that sets may rise again
but when our light has sunk into the earth,
        it is gone forever.
    Give me a thousand kisses,
then a hundred, another thousand,
another hundred
    and in one breath
still kiss another thousand,
another hundred.
    O then with lips and bodies joined
many deep thousands;
    confuse
their number,
    so that poor fools and cuckolds (envious
even now) shall never
learn our wealth and curse us
with their
evil eyes.

LXXXV

Odi et amo, Quare id faciam, fortasse requiris
Nescio, sed fieri sentio et excrucior.
I love and I hate, You may ask how this is so,
and I answer, I don't know, but I feel and suffer it,

CI

Atque in perpetuum, frater, ave atque vale,
And always, dear friend, hale and farewell!

2. Virgil (70–19 B.C.). Written in Latin hexameters, Virgil's *Aeneid* is an epic poem about Aeneas's escape from Troy and his travels to found the city of Rome. Robert Fitzgerald's translation is splendid.

3. Horace (65–8 B.C.). In various translations, Horace's *Odes* and *Satires* and *Epistles* offer an *ars poetica* and what Petronius terms a "studied felicity."

4. Ovid (43 B.C.–A.D. 17). Ovid's *Amores* and *Metamorphoses* have been the delight of poets through the ages. The *Metamorphoses* contains fifteen books of hexameters, written just before Ovid's exile by Augustus in A.D. 8, and tell the principal myths of Greece and Rome. Stories include Apollo and Daphne, Pan, Pentheus and Bacchus, Echo and Narcissus, Tiresias, Jove and Europa, Mars and Venus, the nine Muses, Persephone and Demeter, Jason and Medea, Daedalus and Icarus, the twelve Labors of Hercules, Orpheus and Eurydice, Pygmalion, Adonis, Midas, the Trojan War, Hecuba, and Hippolytus.

5. Seneca, Plautus, and Terence, the principal Roman playwrights

6. Plutarch: *Lives of the Eminent Grecians and Romans*

7. *Discourses of Epictetus* (A.D. 55–135) and *Meditations* of Marcus Aurelius (A.D. 121–180). Principal texts of the philosophy of stoicism

Following is the principal text of the so-called Dark Ages and early medieval period:

> St. Augustine (A.D. 354–430). Augustine's *Confessions* is one of the first autobiographies, tracing his birth in North Africa, his childhood and early awareness of sexuality, his sojourn in Carthage where he was immersed in carnal pleasures; then his education in rhetoric, his journey to Italy to meet with Ambrose in Milan, and finally his conversion to Christianity. The *Confessions* ends with a meditation on time and memory and the creation of the world. One of the milestone books on self-awareness.

Following are three principal texts of the so-called Middle Ages:

1. Dante Alighieri (1265–1321). His early work *La Vita Nuova*, translated as *The New Life* by Dante Gabriel Rossetti, remains one of the most sublime examples of "the sweet new style," including poems on how Dante first met Beatrice, his adoration of her from a distance, and poems on her death ("Beatrice is gone up into high heaven"). Dante's major life work, the *Commedia* (translated as *The Divine Comedy*), moves through *Inferno* and *Purgatorio* to *Paradise*. In Dante's scholastic Catholic worldview, punishments of the damned fit the sins; thus the carnal lovers in Canto V of the *Inferno* will be blown about on restless winds, as they themselves had chosen the restless winds of their own desires during their lifetimes. As one translator, John Ciardi, comments: "Hell is not where the damned are; it is what they are." For overall performance probably the best extant translation of the *Commedia* is by Laurence Binyon, using terza rima throughout.

2. Giovanni Boccaccio (1313–1375). The *Decameron*. During the years 1346–1348, the Black Death or bubonic plague swept through Europe, decimating populations and forcing people to abandon their homes in the cities

and flee to the less densely populated countryside. The *Decameron* tells how two men and seven women fled to an abandoned estate and passed the time by telling stories of love to each other, most of them raucous and bawdy.

3. Geoffrey Chaucer (ca. 1342–1400). Chaucer's *Troilus and Cressida* was written during the period 1372–1386. The later *Canterbury Tales* (1387) may have borrowed something of Boccaccio's *Decameron* in the tale-telling motif of having each character tell two tales on the pilgrimage to Canterbury, each tale embodying some folk wit about love and life.

Two figures dominate the early Renaissance for the influence their French thought had on English literature:

1. Michel de Montaigne (1533–1592). Montaigne's *Essays* express a skepticism that is refreshing after centuries of medieval orthodoxy. Countering the dogmatic certainty of Thomas Aquinas's *Summa Theologica*, which had answers for every conceivable question, Montaigne's skepticism is encapsulated in his expression *"Que sais-je?"* which proclaims the fallibility of human reason and the relativity of human science. "The pro and con are both possible" anticipates the free thought of the Renaissance and the later Age of Enlightenment of Voltaire and Rousseau.

2. Blaise Pascal (1623–1662). Known to us as a brilliant mathematical theorist and physicist, Pascal gathered together his *Pensées*, or *Thoughts*, which are his notations toward a massive *apologia* for religious faith in general and for Christianity in particular. His appeal is to intuition as the highest human faculty, far transcending the reaches of reason; for example:

Le silence éternel de ces espaces infinis m'effraie. (no. 206)
The eternal silence of these infinite spaces terrifies me.

Le coeur a ses raisons que la raison ne connaît point. (no. 277)
The heart has its reasons that Reason knows nothing about.

We've already discussed the English Renaissance in chapter 1, with special emphasis on the life and work of William Shakespeare. All that leaves for us to do here is provide a list of approximate dates for the various plays, in hopes that one will want to use it as a checklist for one's own reading, to circle play titles one has not read and make a point of reading them. Here is the list:

1592/93	Henry VI (3 parts)
	Richard III
	Comedy of Errors
1593/94	Titus Andronicus
	Taming of the Shrew
1594/95	Two Gentlemen of Verona
	Love's Labour's Lost
	Romeo and Juliet
1595/96	Richard II
	A Midsummer Night's Dream
1596/97	King John
	The Merchant of Venice
1597/98	Henry IV (2 parts)
1598/99	Much Ado About Nothing
1600	As You Like it
	Twelfth Night
	Julius Caesar
	Henry V
1600/01	Hamlet
	Merry Wives of Windsor
1602/03	All's Well that Ends Well
	Troilus and Cressida
1604/05	Measure for Measure
	Othello

1605/06	King Lear
	Macbeth
1606/07	Antony and Cleopatra
1607/08	Coriolanus
	Timon of Athens
1608/09	Pericles
1609/10	Cymbeline
1610/11	Winter's Tale
1611/12	The Tempest
1613	Henry VIII

Following these great plays of Shakespeare, the English Restoration theater (1660–1776) of Congreve and Goldsmith and Sheridan may seem too prosy and obsessed with middle-class surface satire. We would have to go to the French theater of Molière and Racine to feel the intensity of the mantle of Shakespeare passed on in both comedy and tragedy:

1. Molière (1622–1673). Plays of ridicule and satire of the hypocrisy in French society, Molière's great masterworks are *Tartuffe* (1664), about an inveterate liar and social climber and poseur who exploits the credulity and pretensions of other people; and *Le Misanthrope* (1666), about a character (Alceste) who detests the hypocrisies and white lies of a society he is not able to flee from because of his deep love for Celimene, a woman who is deeply entrenched in all the roles and poses of her social life. Tartuffe and Alceste are satirical prototypes of our modern civilization, which requires a talent of feigning one's way through the lives of others. The translations of Molière by Richard Wilbur are skillful and witty and faithful, retaining the rhymed couplets of the original.

2. Jean Racine (1639–1699). Behind the surface *politesse* of the most pure poetry in strict Alexandrines and absolute caesuras, the plays of Racine embody subtexts of violent incest and alienation and murderous repression. Racine

achieves his greatest intensity in *Phèdre* (1677), based on the Euripides play *Hippolytus*, about a woman who is hopelessly in love with her stepson Hippolyte. Yet Hippolyte has his own passion for the young Aricie, which he declares in these lines:

> *Moi, vous haïr, Madame?*
> *Avec quelques couleurs qu'on ait peint ma fierté,*
> *Croit-on que dans ses flancs un monstre m'ait porté?*
> *Quelles sauvages moeurs, quelle haine endurcie*
> *Pourrait, en vous voyant, n'être point adoucie?*
> *Ai-je pu résister au charme décevant . . .*

> Madame, could I hate you?
> No matter what they say or how they paint my pride,
> Do they suppose some beast once carried me inside?
> What mind that is unkind, what heart that may be hard,
> In viewing you, would not grow soft in its regard?
> Could any man resist the charm of what you are?

> PHÈDRE. II. II. TR. WILLIAM PACKARD

The Puritan Revolution in England (1642–1660) closed the theaters, so the native genius had to express itself in lyric and Cavalier poetry—Herrick, Lovelace, Waller, Carew, Suckling, Marvell, Crashaw, Vaughan, and Traherne. And there was also the epic work of John Milton (1608–1674), who had served as Latin Secretary to Cromwell and then after his blindness devoted himself to *Paradise Lost* and *Paradise Regained*, using unrhymed blank verse and a curious Latinate syntax that evoked sonority and a sense of grand rhetoric. Only when Milton assumes the voice of Satan in Book Four does the poetry come alive with deepest passion:

> Me miserable! which way shall I fly
> Infinite wrath, and infinite despair?
> Which way I fly is Hell; myself am Hell;

And in the lowest deep a lower deep
Still threatening to devour me opens wide,
To which the Hell I suffer seems a Heaven.
O then at last relent: is there no place
Left for repentance, none for pardon left?
None left but by submission; and that word
Disdain forbids me, and my dread of shame
Among the Spirits beneath, whom I seduc'd
With other promises and other vaunts
Than to submit, boasting I could subdue
The Omnipotent. Ay me! they little know
How dearly I abide that boast so vain,
Under what torments inwardly I groan,
While they adore me on the throne of Hell.

We've already discussed the poets of the Romantic era—Wordsworth, Coleridge, Shelley, Byron, Keats, Blake, and Burns—in chapter one of this book. Because this present chapter is devoted to making suggestions of reading that may be of value to the practicing poet, we'll mention some prose works that are indispensable to an understanding of the era we are living in presently. Following are two novelists who have a peculiar resonance for our own world:

1. Herman Melville (1819–1891). Melville's *Moby-Dick* (1851) presents us with the spectacle of a monomania that is so godless it seems to herald our modern predicament. Ishmael, the narrator, tells us he has decided to go to sea and so travels to Nantucket, Massachusetts, where he meets Queequeg the cannibal, and together they sign onto the *Pequod*. Not until after the ship has left port do they discover that the captain, Ahab, is on no ordinary whaling venture; Ahab appears and reveals he is out to revenge himself against the white sperm whale Moby-Dick, who took Ahab's leg on the last voyage out. Starbuck, the first mate, senses immediately how maniacal Ahab is, but also realizes he is powerless to do anything about it. The book is an awful metaphor of the blind

power of evil, not unlike some twentieth-century experiences with fascism and madness.

2. Fyodor Dostoyevsky (1821–1881). Dostoyevsky's mother died when he was six, his father was murdered when he was nine, and it's as if Dostoyevsky's entire life were hounded by the specter of lovelessness and parricide. Sentenced to Siberia in 1849, he lived there in convict prison until 1854, and when he was released he traveled through Europe, came back to Russia where he wrote *Crime and Punishment* (1866), *The Idiot* (1869), and his epic novel masterpiece *The Brothers Karamazov* (1880). Sigmund Freud wrote of him:

> As a creative writer, Dostoyevsky has his place not far behind Shakespeare. *The Brothers Karamazov* is the greatest novel that has ever been written, and the episode of the Grand Inquisitor one of the highest achievements of the world's literature, one scarcely to be overestimated.

SIGMUND FREUD, DOSTOYEVSKY AND PARRICIDE (1927)

Our modern era is profoundly affected by the publication of four prose works, and we strongly recommend the practicing poet look at good translations of each of these books. They are:

1. Charles Darwin: *On the Origin of Species by Means of Natural Selection* (1859); Darwin's theory of evolution.

2. Sigmund Freud: *The Interpretation of Dreams* (1900); Freud's theory of the Unconscious, with dreams as the vessels of our secret wishes. This is the book in which Freud also sets forth his theory of the Oedipal Complex.

3. Albert Einstein: *General Theory of Relativity* (1917); once high-speed transportation came in with the Industrial Revolution, physics was ready to speculate that the same

thing seen from a racing train was different from what was seen by a standing observer.

4. Karl Marx: *Das Kapital* (1867); Marx's critique of capitalism made it necessary to rethink the whole basis of economy and how to set value on human labor.

We could add to these four great shaping works of our modern era a fifth book: Sir James Frazer's *The Golden Bough*, one of the most enlightening studies that gave birth to modern anthropology. *The Oxford Companion to English Literature* gives a good summary of the book's scope:

> *The Golden Bough* begins with a treatise on the ancient rule of the priesthood or sacred kingship of the grove of Nemi or Aricia near Rome, by which a candidate for the priesthood could obtain the office only by slaying the priest, and held it until he was himself slain. The grove was devoted to the worship of Diana Nemorensis. In it grew, according to legend, a tree of which no bough might be broken, save by a runaway slave. If he succeeded, he might first fight the priest, and if he slew him, take over his office. The golden bough which Aeneas broke off at the bidding of the Sybil before venturing to the nether world (Virgil: *Aeneid*, vi, 136) was believed to be a branch of this tree. The explanation of Frazer of the priest of Aricia as an embodiment of the tree-spirit, slain in his character of incarnate deity, led to the discussion of a vast number of other primitive customs and superstitions, contained in the successive volumes of this monumental work.

T. S. Eliot, in his notes to *The Waste Land*, pays tribute to Frazer's monumental work:

> To another work I am indebted in general, one which has influenced our generation profoundly. I mean *The Golden Bough*; I have used especially the two volumes *Adonis, Attis, Osiris*. Anyone who is acquainted with

> these works will immediately recognize in the poem cer-
> tain references to vegetation ceremonies . . .

We're now ready to look at some of the themes of modern and contemporary poetry. In addition to the great shaping forces of our modern era which we've just looked at—and especially the work of Darwin, Freud, Einstein, Karl Marx, and James Frazer—there are a number of revolutions that have taken place over recent years (say, since 1945) which have been of extraordinary importance in molding contemporary thought. Following is a list of some of the major revolutions in the second half of the twentieth century:

nuclear energy
the cold war
psychoanalysis
the sexual revolution / birth control pill / AIDS
the educational revolution
"God is dead" theology
the generation gap / nuclear families
race awareness and ethnic origins
the urban revolution
affluence-poverty gap
cybernetics and the silicone chip / computers
paperback publishing
the population explosion
ecology and the vanishing wilderness
communications / media image / TV and satellites
transportation
outer space exploration
the drug culture
literacy-illiteracy gap
the neutron bomb

Because most of the above revolutions have been going on concurrent with each other, there is a sense of acceleration and change that is compounded by so many things happening simultaneously. It would be an interesting challenge for the reader to go back over the above list and number in circles from one to five which revolutions the reader thinks are most important to a shaping of modern awareness. It wouldn't be an easy task, as so many of these changes are going on all around us right now and it would be difficult to gauge which ones are more significant culturally than which other ones.

We can see certain consequences of so many things happening at the same time. For one thing, it creates a sense of "contingency" in our lives, that things are happening by chance or at random, and it feels like a breakdown of traditional grammar and logic as well. For another thing, it leads to a distrust of universal principles and more of a reliance on individual "thisness," the particular thing in front of us—what William Carlos Williams meant by the phrase, "No ideas but in things."

Surely this list has profound meaning for our understanding of what is happening in contemporary poetry. The bewildering range and diversity of styles in contemporary poetry may be a reflection of the breakdown of almost all our traditional assumptions and assurances. This may lead inexorably to the contemporary poet's seeking to reclaim his own threatened sense of individuation, by searching for his own inimitable way of saying something. It may also lead to the poet's experimenting with chance and randomness in arbitrary line arrangements, in order to explore entirely new energy principles in our universe.

And behind all these possibilities there may be a more compelling one, which is that the contemporary poet may be trying to define his role as Orphic priest in an agnostic world that has lost faith in itself, as a bewildered and godforsaken people feel themselves accelerating headlong to apocalypse.

In this chapter we've offered some reading suggestions as one keeps on with one's writing. And we mean this in a very personal and organic way, not as any academic exercise done for its own sake. Ideally, reading and writing should go together in a dynamic interaction of energies, each feeding the other in a mysterious flow of awakening spirit forces.

We should add one word about reading—something the Russian novelist Vladimir Nabokov once noted:

> Curiously enough, one cannot read a book: one can only reread it. A good reader, a major reader, an active and creative reader is a rereader.

So we wish the practicing poet much good reading and rereading of some of the books listed in this chapter.

10

THE POET'S LIFE

In this final chapter we'll consider some of the key features of the poet's life: where and how he gets the inspiration for his work; his crucial relationship to solitude; the problem of aesthetic distancing in his life and work; the challenge of doing translations; and finally, his choice of an appropriate life-style that will help to enable his ongoing poetry writing.

INSPIRATION

Where and how does a poet get the inspiration for his or her best work?

It's not an easy question to answer, but then none of the essential mysteries of life and love and art is ever easy to designate and talk about, even though one feels the temptation to jump in and get chatty and glib about things that are so continuously elusive and incomprehensible.

But then our great literary tradition doesn't offer us that much more of an answer. Plato in the great *Dialogues* tends to sidestep the question of inspiration, and instead waxes rapturous over the fact that madness must be seen as a precondition for creating poetry:

> But he who, having no touch of the Muses' madness in his soul, comes to the door and thinks that he will get into the temple of art—he, I say, and his poetry are not admitted: the sane man disappears and is nowhere when he enters into rivalry with the madman.
>
> PLATO, *PHAEDRUS*

And in his characteristically terse manner, Aristotle similarly sidesteps the question of inspiration, although he does offer a second alternative to Plato's "madness":

> Hence poetry implies either a happy gift of nature or a strain of madness.
>
> ARISTOTLE, *POETICS*

The Old Testament claims that all poetry is divinely inspired as a revelation from God to mankind; even the highly erotic lyric love poetry of the Song of Solomon is presented to us as a metaphor of religious ecstasy. David refers to himself as "the sweet psalmist of Israel," and in 2 Samuel 23:1 he says:

> The spirit of the LORD spake by me, and his word was in my tongue.

In other words, David claims that the Psalms were divinely inspired and he himself could never have written them if he had not had a special revelation from God.

In the New Testament, Jesus also makes an extraordinary assertion, that truth and freedom are somehow mysteriously interrelated; as he says in John 8:32:

> And ye shall know the truth, and the truth shall make you free.

This is like saying the more one sees things as they are, the more one is able to free oneself from delusion and unreality—which is a kind of inspiration that is akin to modern psychoanalytic insight and healing.

In the English Renaissance, Shakespeare in A *Midsummer-Night's Dream* echoes the Platonic idea that poets are madmen:

> The lunatic, the lover and the poet
> Are of imagination all compact . . .

Madness and eros and poetry may indeed be seen as interchangeable trance states, but that doesn't answer our question about where one gets one's inspiration.

During the Romantic era, William Blake proclaimed himself a radical visionary:

> I am not ashamed, afraid, or averse to tell you what Ought to be Told: That I am under the direction of Messengers from Heaven, Daily & Nightly: but the Nature of such things is not, as some suppose, without trouble or care. Temptations are on the right hand & left; behind, the sea of time & space roars & follows swiftly; he who keeps not right onward is lost, & if our footsteps slide in clay, how can we do otherwise than fear & tremble?

With the advent of modern psychology, the sources of inspiration are more identified with an inner quest. The philosopher Henri Bergson predicted that this pilgrimage within would become the chief feature of the modern experience:

> The major task of the twentieth century will be to explore the unconscious, to investigate the subsoil of the mind.

The psychologist Carl Jung describes what it feels like to begin on the long descent inside:

> At first we cannot see beyond the path that leads down-
> wards to "dark and hateful things"—but no light or
> beauty will ever come from the man who cannot bear
> this sight.

The American playwright Eugene O'Neill extended this psychoanalytic insight into the realms of art, and he defined drama
as "an exercise in unmasking" based on the following statement
of faith:

> If a person is to get at the meaning of life, he must learn
> to like the facts about himself—ugly as they may seem
> to his sentimental vanity—before he can lay hold on
> the truth behind the facts; and the truth is never ugly.

And the Irish poet William Butler Yeats gives a graphic image
to describe this descent into the forbidden zones inside oneself.
In "The Circus Animals' Desertion" he writes:

> Now that my ladder's gone,
> I must lie down where all the ladders start,
> In the foul rag-and-bone shop of the heart.

This modern psychoanalytic insight locates "inspiration" in
what Yeats called "the foul rag-and-bone-shop of the heart,"
what Jung calls the "dark and hateful things" of the unconscious,
and what O'Neill calls the ugly facts about oneself. This is quite
a reversal from the deist approach to divine inspiration that
comes to one from the heavens. In fact one modern scientist,
J.B.S. Haldane, extends the psychoanalytic insight to the heavens themselves, seeing them as hopelessly askew and incomprehensible:

> My own suspicion is that the universe is not only queerer
> than we suppose, but queerer than we can suppose.

Actually this modern psychoanalytic insight is nothing more
than an elaboration of Wordsworth's formula that all poetry arises

from the "spontaneous overflow of powerful feeling" which derives from "emotion recollected in tranquillity." And the best
description of how one can induce this "recollection" of one's
deepest emotion is contained in the opening pages of Sigmund
Freud's *The Interpretation of Dreams,* which shows how one can
go about achieving a trancelike "tranquillity":

> For this a certain preparation on the part of the patient
> is necessary. A twofold effort is made, to stimulate his
> attentiveness in respect of his psychic perceptions, and
> to eliminate the critical spirit in which he is ordinarily
> in the habit of viewing such thoughts as come to the
> surface. For the purpose of self-observation with con-
> centrated attention it is advantageous that the patient
> should take up a restful position and close his eyes; he
> must be explicitly instructed to renounce all criticism of
> the thought-formations which he may perceive. He must
> also be told that the success of the psychoanalysis de-
> pends upon his noting and communicating everything
> that passes through his mind, and that he must not allow
> himself to suppress one idea because it seems to him
> unimportant or irrelevant to the subject, or another be-
> cause it seems nonsensical. He must perceive an absolute
> impartiality in respect to his ideas; for if he is unsuccessful
> in finding the desired solution of the dream, the obses-
> sional idea, or the like, it will be because he permits
> himself to be critical of them.

Through endless practice of this trancelike "tranquility," one
notices that so-called forbidden or undesired ideas are changed
to "poetic" and "desired" ideas, a curious transformation that
may appear to be the Muses' "madness" that was described by
Plato and Aristotle. One will also notice that during this curious
transformation, extraordinary quantities of psychic energies will
be released, energies which had been used to repress the forbidden
and undesired ideas, and this release of psychic energy will simulate the sense of "divine inspiration" that was reported by King
David and Blake.

It may all be the same thing, masquerading under different terminologies: "the Muses' madness"—"divine inspiration"—"modern psychoanalytic insight"—it may all add up to a belief in the same essential "inspiration" that is working through all these different approaches.

There is one further dimension to inspiration we should mention, and that's when one's own work seems to be inextricably linked to the search for values in one's life. The Chinese poet Lu-Yiu (1125–1210) once wrote to his son:

> Poetry is not child's play,
> but one of the noble arts.
> If you would be a poet, know
> that the real work is done outside poetry.

In other words, total "inspiration" may be a combination of "recollection" through "tranquillity," which one undertakes inside oneself, and one's confrontation with external reality to achieve one's own values as an individual human being.

One's entire life, then, becomes metaphorical of both the inner and the outer quest. John Keats indicated something of the sort, in his 1819 letter to George and Georgiana Keats:

> A Man's Life of any worth is a continual allegory—and very few eyes can see the Mystery of his life—a life like the scriptures, figurative—which such people can no more make out than they can the hebrew Bible. Lord Byron cuts a figure—but he is not figurative—Shakespeare led a life of Allegory: his works are the comments on it.
>
> JOHN KEATS, LETTER 123

This becomes especially so if one enters into some strong moral struggle in the political arena, as Gandhi indicated when he wrote:

> What message can I send through the pen if I am not sending one through the life I am living?

One feels this eloquence of moral struggle working powerfully in the public utterances of Martin Luther King, Jr., as he comes up against the obstacles of intolerance and interposition in his own life.

E. E. Cummings summarizes everything we've been trying to say about inspiration in the second of his six "non-lectures":

> But if poetry is your goal, you've got to forget all about punishments and all about rewards and all about self-styled obligations and duties and responsibilities etcetera ad infinitum and remember one thing only: that it's you—nobody else—who determine your destiny and decide your fate. Nobody else can be alive for you; nor can you be alive for anybody else. Toms can be Dicks and Dicks can be Harrys, but none of them can ever be you. There's the artist's responsibility; and the most awful responsibility on earth.

SOLITUDE

Every poet must work out his or her relationship with solitude. It may take the form of creating a place where the poet can go to be completely alone; or it may mean severing certain relationships that may get in the way of one's ongoing work; it may even go so far as to force the poet to relocate in some new part of the country, or even to leave one's country completely and go abroad in search of some isolation that will make it easier to create the solitude one needs.

Rainer Maria Rilke, in his *Letters to a Young Poet,* insists again and again on the importance of solitude for the artist, not only for the creation of his own work but also for the ability to comprehend the work of others:

> Works of art are of an infinite loneliness and with nothing to be so little reached as with criticism. Only love can grasp and hold and fairly judge them.

Another artist, Ernest Hemingway, who always appeared to be living a life of strenuous challenge and action, insisted on the same importance of solitude that Rilke did. In his 1954 Nobel acceptance speech, Hemingway said:

> Writing at its best is a lonely life. Organizations for writers palliate the writer's loneliness, but I doubt if they improve his writing. He grows in public stature as he sheds his loneliness, and often his work deteriorates. For he does his work alone, and if he is a good enough writer, he must face eternity, or the lack of it, each day. For a true writer, each book should be a new beginning where he tries again for something that is beyond attainment. He should always try for something that has never been done or that others have done and failed. Then sometimes, with great luck, he will succeed.

The solitude that Rilke and Hemingway are both advocating is a crucial condition for doing one's work, and it must take precedence over writing workshops and graduate writing programs and writing out proposals for grants-in-aid so one can continue on with one's writing.

Of course if one has a strong ambivalence toward one's own solitude, and if one sees it as an inhibition on one's natural energies, then one is going to have additional complications to work out. The contemporary American poet Diane Wakoski comments on this:

> I grew up extremely timid and shy and it was very, very hard for me to even be interested in making friends with strangers. And consequently I always had a lot of enforced solitude in my life. And I grew up hating being alone, being terrified of being alone. And yet I spent a lot of time alone and it took me many years to learn to be alone and not freak out, to begin to appreciate that I really liked being alone and I didn't have enough privacy for being alone, and I got equally disturbed.

NEW YORK QUARTERLY CRAFT INTERVIEW, NUMBER 17

Surely our own experience of early grade school when one was never alone, and summer vacations when one was forced into group activities and made to feel dysfunctional if one had a deep need to be alone—these are conditioning factors that will remain with us for the rest of our lives. And it seems as if these strong collectivizing group instincts became more vivid as we grew older, so we felt we always had to be with others—at bars or at baseball games or on beaches or at barbecues—and at odd times when we found ourselves unaccountably alone, we instinctively reached out to turn on talk radio or the incessant clatter of commercial television. Indeed, the entire civilizing process in our lives seemed to be aimed at creating a mindless group amalgam, and even our American behavioral psychiatrists kept telling us about "group dynamics" and "personality interaction" and "transactional analysis."

Well, we can take a rain check on all that. Because we know that to be an artist is first and foremost to care about our own work, and that may mean our being able to separate ourselves radically from all the compulsory family and other social and cultural activities that are going on around us always. Let them say that we're selfish and antisocial and uncivil; that's okay with us because we have to keep exploring our solitude so we can continue on with our work. And this is a decision that we have to make for ourselves, as it's rare that anyone else will ever be able to advise us in such matters.

But at least we have the models of great poets and artists in the past who lived in their own solitude, and one can always take courage and solace from their example. And there are also these simple lines from the Psalms which tell one to trust one's own solitude:

> Stand in awe, and sin not: commune with
> your own heart upon your bed, and be still.
>
> PSALM 4

AESTHETIC DISTANCE

The deeper one goes into one's own work, the more it may change one's perception of reality—and this may be an extremely disconcerting experience.

For example, the more one works and the deeper one delves, one may begin to lose certain romantic attitudes about things, as one comes closer to seeing things for what they really are. And one may even feel a strong nostalgia to reclaim one's earlier state of innocence, when one was awash with general emotions instead of the hard, sharp edges of the particular.

No one expresses this curious aesthetic distancing better than Mark Twain in *Life on the Mississippi,* when he describes how his becoming a steamboat captain seemed to rob him of his romantic illusions about the Mississippi River, forever. Because he was no longer able to indulge his boyhood dreams about the great river, Mark Twain now had to see deep into what was really there. Even the surface texture of the river changed forever because of his new awareness of what was underlying the contours and channels of the moving waters. It's a remarkable passage and worth quoting in full:

> Now when I had mastered the language of this water and had come to know every trifling feature that bordered the great river as familiarly as I knew the letters of the alphabet, I had made a valuable acquisition. But I had lost something, too. I had lost something which could never be restored to me while I lived. All the grace, the beauty, the poetry had gone out of the majestic river! I still keep in mind a certain wonderful sunset which I witnessed when steamboating was new to me. A broad expanse of the river was turned to blood; in the middle distance the red hue brightened into gold, through which a solitary log came floating, black and conspicuous; in one place a long, slanting mark lay sparkling upon the water; in another the surface was broken by boiling, tumbling rings, that were as many-tinted as an opal;

where the ruddy flush was faintest, was a smooth spot that was covered with graceful circles and radiating lines, ever so delicately traced; the shore on our left was densely wooded, and the sombre shadow that fell from this forest was broken in one place by a long, ruffled trail that shone like silver; and high above the forest wall a clean-stemmed dead tree waved a single leafy bough that glowed like a flame in the unobstructed splendor that was flowing from the sun. There were graceful curves, reflected images, woody heights, soft distances; and over the whole scene, far and near, the dissolving lights drifted steadily, enriching it, every passing moment, with new marvels of coloring.

I stood like one bewitched. I drank it in, in a speech-less rapture. The world was new to me, and I had never seen anything like this at home. But as I have said, a day came when I began to cease from noting the glories and the charms which the moon and the sun and the twilight wrought upon the river's face; another day came when I ceased altogether to note them. Then, if that sunset scene had been repeated, I should have looked upon it without rapture, and should have commented upon it, inwardly, after this fashion: This sun means that we are going to have wind tomorrow; that floating log means that the river is rising, small thanks to it; that slanting mark on the water refers to a bluff reef which is going to kill somebody's steamboat one of these nights, if it keeps on stretching out like that; those tumbling "boils" show a dissolving bar and a changing channel there; the lines and circles in the slick water over yonder are a warning that that troublesome place is shoaling up dangerously; that silver streak in the shadow of the forest is the "break" from a new snag, and he has located himself in the very best place he could have found to fish for steamboats; that tall dead tree, with a single living branch, is not going to last long, and then how is a body ever going to get through this blind place at night without the friendly old landmark?

No, the romance and the beauty were all gone from

the river. All the value any feature of it had for me now was the amount of usefulness it could furnish toward compassing the safe piloting of a steamboat. Since those days, I have pitied doctors from my heart. What does the lovely flush in a beauty's cheek mean to a doctor but a "break" that ripples above some deadly disease? Are not all her visible charms sown thick with what are to him the signs and symbols of hidden decay? Does he ever see her beauty at all, or doesn't he simply view her professionally, and comment upon her unwholesome condition all to himself? And doesn't he sometimes wonder whether he has gained most or lost most by learning his trade?

MARK TWAIN, *LIFE ON THE MISSISSIPPI,* CHAPTER 9

There is a curious irony about this passage by Mark Twain. He claims that "all the grace, the beauty, the poetry had gone out of the majestic river" when he had to learn his craft as steamboat captain; and he claims that he could never get back "the romance and the beauty" of the river, not ever again. It is a poignant and overwhelming indictment of the role of knowledge on the aesthetic sensibility. Or so it seems, at least, to Mark Twain, in the writing of this passage.

But then we recall that these perceptions of poignance and loss came to Mark Twain long before he began to write his two great masterworks that were set on the Mississippi River—*Tom Sawyer* and *Huckleberry Finn.* Surely by painfully dispelling his early romantic notions about the river, Mark Twain had prepared himself to see a new grace, a new beauty, and a new poetry to the river: deeper and more meaningful than his earlier romantic view, more mature and incisive and reality-oriented.

What this must mean is that one may have to be prepared to yield up all one's cherished naive romantic views, in order to be given a more rich and real and meaningful view of things. Although at the time this painful aesthetic distancing is going on, one can feel only the loss and distress that Mark Twain expresses so eloquently when he says "the romance and the beauty were all gone," yet the fact remains that without this critical distancing, one will never be able to do any really worthwhile work.

Patients in therapy often experience the same stubborn resistance to giving up their romantic delusions about themselves, as well as their naive distortions of memory and perception— yet unless these patients are successful in giving up these errors of judgment, there can be no real healing that will ever be able to take place.

William Faulkner summed up this phenomenon of aesthetic distancing in a single phrase—

> You must kill all your darlings.

—by which he meant, one has to be ruthless toward one's first drafts, and get rid of all those easy and facile phrasings that one thought (at the time) were so sacred and right. Only by clearing them away from the surface of one's worksheets will one be able to write more deeply, more clearly, more truly.

Ralph Waldo Emerson says the same thing at the end of his poem "Give All to Love":

> Though her parting dims the day,
> Stealing grace from all alive;
> Heartily know,
> When half-gods go,
> The gods arrive.

The ideal of aesthetic distancing is to overcome one's subjective impressions so one can come as close as possible to *das Ding an sich*, to the thing itself. Aristotle implies that the mind has to be able to participate in this act of intellection, in any true perception:

> The form of the mind becomes one with the form of the thing perceived.

Even so, one hears young artists insist on their own subjectivity instead of working toward an authentic perception of the thing itself. And sometimes only the long practice of a craft, the endless vision and revision that is required in extensive rewriting, and an understanding of the form of the mind and the form of the thing to be perceived, can ever achieve the aesthetic distancing that is needed to attain one's very best work.

TRANSLATING

The whole notion of translation has always been considered slightly suspect and alien to the instincts of a creative artist. This ambivalence is revealed in the vocabulary of the various languages: in German, *übersetzen* means "translate" but it also means "interpret"; in French the verb *traduire* means "to betray"; and in Italian, *traduttori* means to be a translator but it also means to be a traitor.

On the other hand, Pushkin called translators "the post-horses of enlightenment," and we remember the exaltation that John Keats felt when he came on Chapman's translation of Homer:

> Much have I travelled in the realms of gold,
> And many goodly states and kingdoms seen;
> Round many western islands have I been
> Which bards in fealty to Apollo hold.
> Oft of one wide expanse had I been told
> That deep-browed Homer ruled as his demesne:
> Yet did I never breathe its pure serene
> Till I heard Chapman speak out loud and bold:
> Then felt I like some watcher of the skies
> When a new planet swims into his ken;
> Or like stout Cortez, when with eagle eyes
> He stared at the Pacific—and all his men
> Looked at each other with a wild surmise—
> Silent, upon a peak in Darien.

"ON FIRST LOOKING INTO CHAPMAN'S HOMER"

In this sense translation can be seen as an authentic act of discovery, a very real extension of one's own poetry writing. So it is no wonder so many of our contemporary poets will do translation from time to time, as a way of honing their instrument and coming on a kind of poetry they could never experience using only their own apparatus.

And indeed we've been living for some time now in a golden age of translating. If one wants anything good to say about American schools and universities over this past century, one can say that they served as excellent hospitable havens for translators to keep practicing their craft. In the past hundred years virtually every major work of world literature has been retranslated into eminently readable, accurate, and contemporary versions. The University of Chicago and Bryn Mawr College fostered the superb translation of Greek plays by David Grene and Richmond Lattimore; and the University of Iowa encouraged translating of poetry from lesser-known languages such as Yugoslavian and Korean and Romanian and modern Chinese; and other universities have been similarly supportive of translations from the classical and modern romance languages.

The German poet Rilke tried to imagine what goes on inside the mind of the serious translator:

> . . . the translation does not give back the full meaning and he wants to show to young people the beautiful and real fragments of this massive and glorious language which has been fused and made pliable in such intense flame . . . he warms himself again to his work. Now come evenings, fine, almost youthful evenings, like those of autumn, for instance, which bring with them such long calm nights. In his study the lamp burns late. He does not always bend over the pages, he often leans back, closing within his eyes a line he has read over and over, until its meaning flows into his very blood. . . .

And the Irish poet and playwright Synge sets a simple high standard for what has to be achieved in the translation of poetry:

A translation is no translation unless it will give you the music of the poem along with the words of it.

Ezra Pound, in many ways the great pioneer of modern translation, stated his ambition for translating:

> I resolved that at 30 I would know more about poetry than any man living, that I would know what was accounted poetry everywhere, what part of poetry was 'indestructible,' what part could NOT BE LOST by translation and scarcely less important—what effects were obtainable in ONE language only and were utterly incapable of being translated.

The contemporary American poet Paul Blackburn describes the psychology of translating:

> You see, it's not just a matter of reading the language and understanding it and putting it into English. It's understanding something that makes the man do it, where he's going. And it's not an entirely objective process. It must be partially subjective; there has to be some kind of projection. How do you know which word to choose when a word may have four or five possible meanings in English? It's not just understanding the text. In a way you live it each time, I mean, *you're there.* Otherwise, you're not holding the poem.
>
> NEW YORK QUARTERLY CRAFT INTERVIEW. NUMBER 2

Following is an example of a translation of a poem in French, rendered into four different English versions. The reader can examine the rhythms and rhyme choices and the diction of each version, to see what critical choices were made by each translator. One can see the enormous range of word choice and metrical texture that is possible in translating such a terse lyric form. The reader is challenged to choose the one version he feels is the best translation of the original, and defend it against the others.

The identity of the individual translators will be revealed at the end of this section.

Here is the original poem in French:

Il Pleure dans Mon Coeur

Il pleure doucement sur la ville.
ARTHUR RIMBAUD

Il pleure dans mon coeur
Comme il pleut sur la ville;
Quelle est cette langueur
Qui pénètre mon coeur?

Ô bruit doux de la pluie
Par terre et sur les toits!
Pour un coeur qui s'ennuie
Ô le chant de la pluie!

Il pleure sans raison
Dans ce coeur qui s'écoeure.
Quoi! nulle trahison? . . .
Ce deuil est sans raison.

C'est bien la pire peine
De ne savoir pourquoi,
Sans amour et sans haine,
Mon coeur a tant de peine!

PAUL VERLAINE

Here is the first English translation of the poem:

Tears flow in my heart
As rain falls on the town;
What languour is this
That creeps into my heart?

Gentle sound of the rain
On earth and roofs!
For an aching heart
Is the song of the rain!

Tears flow senseless
In this breaking heart,
With no betrayal?
This grief is senseless.

This is the worst sorrow
Not to know why,
Without love or hate,
My heart has all this sorrow.

Here is the second English translation of the poem:

Rain falls in my heart
As rain falls on the town,
What is this languor
That penetrates my heart?

O soft sound of rain
On the earth, on the roofs!
For a listless heart
O the song of the rain!

It rains without reasons
In this disheartened heart.
What! No betrayal?
This grief's without reason.

The worst of this sorrow
Is not to know why—
Without love, without hate—
My heart brims with sorrow.

Here is the third English translation of the poem:

It rains in my heart
as it rains on the town:
where did it all start,
this longing in my heart?

O sound of the rain,
on earth, on the roof tops;

for a heart in pain,
O the song of the rain.

Rain has no reason,
this heart that has lost heart
is out of season,
to hell with all reason!

God knows the worst pain
is never to know why
one man must maintain
a heart so full of pain.

Here is the fourth English translation of the poem:

Tears fall in my heart
As rain falls on the town.
What languor is here
Which transpierces my heart?

O rare sound of the rain
On ground and on the roofs!
For a heart filled with pain,
O the hum of the rain!

For no reason tears fall
In this disheartened heart.
What! No sign of guile?
This grieving has no cause.

The most piercing pain
Is in not knowing why,
Without love, without bane,
My heart has so much pain!

The first English translation of the Verlaine poem is by Muriel Kittel; the second English translation is by Stephen Stepanchev; the third English translation is by William Packard; the fourth English translation is by Daisy Aldan.

LIFE-STYLE

What is the appropriate life-style that will enable a poet to keep on with his poetry writing?

The following poem by Karl Shapiro states the case for one life-style that can end in an impasse of narcissism and careerism:

Creative Writing

English was in its autumn when this weed
Sprang up on every quad.
The Humanities had long since gone to seed,
Grammar and prosody were as dead as Aztec.
Everyone was antsy except the Deans
Who smelled innovation, Creativity!
Even athletes could take Creative Writing:
No books, no tests, best grades guaranteed,
A built-in therapy for all and sundry,
Taking in each other's laundry.
No schedule, no syllabus, no curriculum,
No more reading; knowledge has gone elsewhere.
Pry yourself open with a speculum
And put a tangle in your hair.

It spread from graduate school to kindergarten,
It moved to prisons, to aircraft carriers,
Competing with movies, blackjack, and craps.
Civil war flared up from time to time
When pure professors decided to weed the Grove,
Insecticide the pest, but the creative seed,
Stronger than gonorrhea or the med-fly,
Bounced down the highways like a tumbleweed,
Took to the air and the ocean seas,
Mated in Paris with the fleur-de-lys.

NEW YORK QUARTERLY. NUMBER 40

If indeed our schools and universities are to blame for allowing the classics to erode and permitting prosody and grammar to go dead as Aztec, churning up a kind of pseudo-creativity potash in the name of "self-expression"—then it's a little too late for anyone to do anything about it. What we have to discover is what kind of alternative life-style or commitment is appropriate for the individual poet to pursue his or her poetry writing with the least amount of pretension or obfuscation.

One contemporary American poet, Gary Snyder, spent a good part of his life away from academia, hiking and camping out and learning to live in wilderness conditions. Snyder offers an interesting comment on the survival of the psyche:

> Creativity and maintenance go hand in hand. And in a mature ego system, as much energy goes to maintenance as goes to creativity. Maturity, sanity and diversity go together, and with that goes stability.
>
> NEW YORK QUARTERLY CRAFT INTERVIEW. NUMBER 22

Another contemporary poet, Leo Connellan, has balanced a good deal of his life between teaching and working in commercial sales, writing insurance policies and selling carbon ribbons. Connellan offers the following comment on motivation of the human animal:

> I don't know where personal motivation is going to come from in America. I think I mean we're getting awfully good at heart transplants and computers; we're putting computers in front of children to talk to them and tell them how to multiply, how to do geometry, how to do everything for them. And I don't know, you know, a hungry man fights to get a meal, and I think that a good writer is hungry to write. I don't know what will motivate anyone in the future to try to write or to act or to put themselves into something.
>
> NEW YORK QUARTERLY CRAFT INTERVIEW. NUMBER 27

One has to be clear about what one wants to do in one's writing. So many poets talk about making statements in their work, or having some kind of vision; and that's all right although God knows we've suffered through enough eras that were so hell-bent on "statement" and "vision" that the poetry itself got lost in the wash. Too much emphasis on "statement" and "vision" leads to impotence and academatization of Poesy, the obfuscation of intuitive truth that exists on more subliminal levels.

To say nothing of the fact that contemporary American poetry has been in desperate quest of radically new coordinates since 1945, has hardly had time or talent for "statement" or "vision." Consider modern developments in nuclear energy, ballistic mis-sile foreign policy, urban dehumanization on gargantuan scale, worldwide nonstop population explosion, rape of planet ecology, media exploitation imagery, rampant random crime and drug culture proliferation, the AIDS epidemic making us afraid to touch one another for fear of virus annihilation. With acceler-ation of all these phenomena going on around us simultaneously, we need "statement" and "vision" like a hole in the head—our job as poets is to maintain our inner pipeline to the music of the Muse under these worst of circumstances.

At least our contemporary poetry has accepted its karma of evolving new forms out of all this godforsakenness. What more could one ask?

AFTERWORD: WHAT IS POETRY?

We've come full circle to the question we raised at the beginning of this book: What is poetry? And what is its importance in our world?

In one of the great sacred texts of the East, the Vedas, Hindu scriptures that date back as early as 2000 B.C., this sacred hymn describes Creation:

> from it were born the verses and the sacred chants,
> from it were born the meters, from it the sacred formulas,
> from it horses were born, and those animals with double
> rows of teeth, cows were born from it, also goats and sheep

This is astonishing—verse and rhythms and meters were created at the same time as cows and goats and sheep! This is to say there is some mysterious interstitial relationship between all living things and with poetry and rhythms that inspire and embody them.

It leads us to speculate that if, indeed, this is a spiritual universe after all—that is to say, a universe made up of the power of living spirits—then poetry can surely be seen as one way of entering into that universe of spirits. All the great major religions have always taught that this was so.

For the individual poet, then, this means that his best poetry will be written at the highest moments of his own solitariness, when he is most in touch with the living spirits that are all around him always. And in between such high moments, the individual poet has to sensitize himself to the various resources that are at work in the poetry of his own language, because that language will contain the alphabet and grammar and secret code of our deepest feelings.

Craft and prosody, then, will be the artist in action. Marcus Aurelius, writing almost two thousand years ago, urged the individual poet to realize this was the true way of inner freedom:

> Love the art, poor as it may be, which thou hast learned,
> and be content with it, making thyself neither the master
> nor the servant of any man.

Appendix: Selective Bibliography

Following are books that are generally useful for the art of poetry writing:

1. Plato: *Ion*

2. Aristotle: *Poetics*

3. *Oxford Companion to Classical Literature*

4. *Oxford Companion to English Literature*

5. Sir James Frazer: *The Golden Bough*

6. Robert Graves: *The White Goddess*

7. Samuel Taylor Coleridge: *Biographia Literaria*

8. C. S. Lewis: *The Allegory of Love*

9. Edgar Allan Poe: *The Rationale of Verse*

10. Percy Shelley: *A Defense of Poetry*

11. *Princeton Encyclopedia of Poetry and Poetics*

12. William Wordsworth: Preface to *Lyrical Ballads* (1800)

Following are books that are useful for contemporary poetry writing:

1. Karl Shapiro and Robert Beum: *A Prosody Handbook*

2. Ezra Pound: *The ABC of Reading*

3. Rainer Maria Rilke: *Letters to a Young Poet*

4. William Packard: *The Poet's Dictionary*

5. Barbara Smith: *Poetic Closure: How Poems End*

6. Lewis Turco: *The Book of Forms: Handbook of Poetics*

7. Miller Williams: *Patterns of Poetry*

8. James Dickey: *Babel to Byzantium*

9. Clement Wood: *Complete Rhyming Dictionary*

10. Babette Deutsch: *Poetry Handbook*

11. Paul Fussell: *Poetic Meter and Poetic Form*

12. Francis Stillman: *Poet's Manual and Rhyming Dictionary*

ACKNOWLEDGMENTS

Grateful acknowledgment is made for permission to reprint se-
lections from the following:

"The Instruction Manual" by John Ashbery from *Some Trees*,
© 1970 by John Ashbery, reprinted by permission of Georges
Borchardt, Inc.

"The New Spirit" by John Ashbery from *Three Poems*, © 1970,
1971, 1972 by John Ashbery. Reprinted by permission of Viking.

"Paysage Moralisé," "Canzone," "Diaspora," by W. H. Auden
from *Collected Poems*, edited by Edward Mendelson, © 1976 by
Edward Mendelson, William Meredith, Monroe K. Spears, Ex-
ecutors of the estate of W. H. Auden. Reprinted by permission
of Random House, Inc.

"Dream Song #36," "Dream Song #352," by John Berryman
from *The Dream Songs*, © 1959, 1962, 1963, 1964, 1965, 1966,
1967, 1968, 1969 by John Berryman. Reprinted by permission
of Farrar, Straus & Giroux, Inc.

Catullus #61, #33, #59, #5, from *Catullus*, translated by
Horace Gregory, © 1956 Grove Press. Reprinted by permission
of Grove Press.

"A Question" from *The Poetry of Robert Frost*, © 1969 by Holt,
Rinehart and Winston. Copyright © 1962 by Robert Frost. Copy-

right © 1970 by Lesley Frost Ballantine. Reprinted by permission of Henry Holt and Company, Inc.

"Ku Klux" from *The Panther and the Lash* by Langston Hughes, © 1967 by Arna Bontemps and George Houstonbass. Reprinted by permission of Alfred A. Knopf & Company.

"16-A Chorus Mexico City Blues" by Jack Kerouac from *Mexico City Blues* © 1959 by Jack Kerouac. Reprinted by permission of Grove Press.

"Benediction" from *Selected Poems, 1928–1958* by Stanley Kunitz. Copyright © 1958 by Stanley Kunitz. Reprinted by permission of Little, Brown and Company.

"Dolphin" from *The Selected Poems of Robert Lowell* by Robert Lowell, © 1972, 1974, 1975. Reprinted with permission of Farrar, Straus & Giroux, Inc.

"When the War is Over" from *The Lice* by William S. Merwin, © 1963, 1964, 1965, 1966, 1967. Reprinted by permission of Alfred A. Knopf & Company.

"What Lips my Lips have Kissed" from *Sonnets and Lyrics* by Edna St. Vincent Millay, © 1941. Reprinted by permission of HarperCollins, Inc.

"In Distrust of Merits" from *The Collected Poems of Marianne Moore* by Marianne Moore, © 1935, 1941, 1944, 1951. Reprinted by permission of Macmillan Publishing Company.

"The Ballad of the Lonely Masturbator" from *Love Poems* by Anne Sexton, © 1967, 1968, 1969 by Anne Sexton. Reprinted by permission of Houghton Mifflin Company.

"Do Not Go Gentle into That Good Night" by Dylan Thomas. Copyright © 1952 by Dylan Thomas. Reprinted by permission of New Directions Publishing Corporation.

"The Red Wheelbarrow" from *Collected Poems Volume I, 1909–1939* by William Carlos Williams. Copyright © 1938 by New Directions Publishing Corporation. Reprinted by permission of New Directions Publishing Corporation.

"Crazy Jane Talks with the Bishop" from *Selected Poems of William Butler Yeats* by W. B. Yeats. Copyright © 1935 by W. B. Yeats. Reprinted by permission of Macmillan Publishing Company.

"Bitch" by Lisa Palma, reprinted by permission of *The New York Quarterly*.

"Science Class" by Serena Siegfried, reprinted by permission of *The New York Quarterly*.

"Thank You for the Helpful Suggestions" by Norman Stock, reprinted by permission of *The New York Quarterly*.

INDEX

ABOUT THE AUTHOR

Since 1965, when he assumed the poetry writing classes that Louise Bogan had been teaching at the Washington Square Writing Center of New York University, William Packard has taught poetry and literature at NYU, as well as poetry, acting, and playwriting at the H.B. Studio in Manhattan. His translation of Racine's *Phèdre* was produced in New York with Beatrice Straight and Mildred Dunnock, and won the Outer Circle Critics Award.

Packard is the author of *The Poet's Dictionary*, published in 1989 by Harper/Collins, and he earlier edited *The Poet's Craft: Interviews from* The New York Quarterly, published by Doubleday and Paragon House. Since 1969, William Packard has been founder and editor of *The New York Quarterly*, a national poetry magazine devoted to publishing the best cross-section of contemporary American poetry.